Hebe Uhart

The Scent of Buenos Aires
STORIES

Translated from the Spanish by
Maureen Shaughnessy

archipelago books

Archipelago Books
232 3rd Street #A111
Brooklyn, NY 11215

www.archipelagobooks.org

Library of Congress Cataloguing-in-Publication Data
Uhart, Hebe, author. | Shaughnessy, Maureen, 1979- translator.
The scent of Buenos Aires / stories by Hebe Uhart
translated from the Spanish by Maureen Shaughnessy.
First Archipelago Books edition. | Brooklyn, NY : Archipelago Books, 2019.
LCCN 2019003571 (print) | LCCN 2019013125 (ebook)
ISBN 9781939810359 (ebook) | ISBN 9781939810342 (paperback)
LCSH: Buenos Aires (Argentina)--Fiction.
Short stories, Argentine--21st century--Translations into English.
LCC PQ7798.31.H3 (ebook) | LCC PQ7798.31.H3 A2 2019 (print) DDC 863/.64--dc23
LC record available at https://lccn.loc.gov/2019003571

Distributed by Penguin Random House
www.penguinrandomhouse.com

Cover Art: *Vuel Villa*, Xul Solar, 1936

This book was made possible by the New York State Council on the Arts
with the support of Governor Andrew M. Cuomo and the New York State Legislature.

Archipelago Books also gratefully acknowledges the generous support of
Programa SUR – Ministry of Foreign Affairs and Worship of Argentina,
Nimick Forbesway Foundation, the Carl Lesnor Family Foundation,
Lannan Foundation, the National Endowment for the Arts,
and the New York City Department of Cultural Affairs.

PRINTED IN THE USA

The Scent of Buenos Aires

CONTENTS

Guiding the Ivy 7

It Was the Cat's Fault 15

The Cake 39

The Stories Told by Cecilia's Friends 44

The Scent of Buenos Aires 49

Tourists and Travelers 58

Christmas Eve in the Park 75

At the Hair Salon 84

Leonor 89

Possibly An Old Husband 113

Angelina & Pipotto 121

Human Beings Are Radically Alone 131

Sunday Afternoon Visit 153

Miss Irma 161

The Boy Who Couldn't Fall Asleep 176

The Wandering Dutchman 179

Quitting Smoking 207

Impressions of a School Principal 212

New Times 226

Luisa's Friend 249

Bees Are Industrious 260

I Don't Have Wings 271

Coordination 281

Paso del Rey 286

Gina 314

Hello Kids 331

The Old Man 336

My New Love 352

Events Organization 354

Boy in a Boarding House 364

Mister Ludo 387

The Light of a New Day 396

Homeowners Association Meeting 414

The Uncle and the Niece 427

The Piano Recital 438

Just Another Day 445

Nothing but Shadows 461

Dear Mama 473

Guiding the Ivy

HERE I am arranging the plants so they don't overcrowd one another, pulling off dead leaves, and getting rid of ants. I enjoy watching how they grow with so little. They're sensible, they adapt to their pots. If the pots are small the plants seem to shrink. If they have more space, they grow bigger. They're different from people: some people—small-minded people—acquire a stature that masks their true nature, while others—generous and open-hearted—can be trampled and confused by the weight of life. This is what I think about as I water and transplant, this and the different personalities of each plant: I have one that can withstand the sun. It's tough, like a desert plant, it's secured only the green it needs to survive. Then there's a big ivy, pretty and inconsequential, it doesn't have the slightest claim to originality because it looks like any old ivy you could buy anywhere, with its iridescent green. But I have another plain green ivy that has gotten smaller. It seems to say: *Iridescence is not for me*. It grows so slowly, shaded and assured by its own restraint. This is the plant I love most. Every now and then I guide it. I sense where it wants to go and it senses where I want to guide it. Sometimes I call the iridescent ivy "stupid" because it forms into pointless arabesques. And the desert plant I respect for its hardiness, but sometimes I think it's ugly. It seems ugly when I see it through the eyes of others, when someone comes over for a visit. In general I like them all. For example, there's a species of small wild daisy known as the red bug flower. I don't know what makes it any different from a regular daisy. Sometimes I look at my garden as if it were someone else's and I discover two flaws: one, that few plants hang gracefully, with the right verdure and sinuous movements. My plants are motionless, stumpy, lodged in their pots. The second flaw is that I have a lot of small flower-pots, in different sizes, instead of large solid pots that are well made, well designed. It's because I keep putting off the task of lightening my load. And there's something dreadful about the idea of "lightening my load" or tidying up—at least when it comes to my plants. For as long as I can remember I've put off using the hatred one needs to survive, ignoring it in myself and in others. I associate hatred with the mundane, with the ability to discern in an instant whether a plant is a red bug flower or a daisy, whether a stone is precious or worthless. I associate (or I used to associate) hatred with choosing to be disrespectful, according to some intentions that no longer surprise me: the way I treat people (lots of people), grudges, the way people and situations seem to repeat themselves. In the end, replacing wonder with an inquisitive temperament has tainted me with hatred, too. But some things still amaze me. About four or five years ago

I prayed to God (or to the gods) not to let me become drastic, scornful. I would say: Dear Lord, don't let me become like the mother in that play *Las de Barranco*—that woman's life was in a perpetual state of disaster. She poked her nose into everyone's business. She lived her life through them vicariously, to the extent that her real wishes were unclear; shrewdness was her only pleasure. Before I started turning into the Barranco mother I was horrified by that archetype, but once it was part of me I felt more comfortable: the comfort of letting go and forgetting when there's so much to remember that you don't want to look back. Nowadays, I think one thing in the morning and something else in the afternoon. My decisions last no longer than an hour and they're missing the sense of euphoria they used to have. Now I make decisions out of necessity, when there's no other option. That's why I rarely even value my thoughts and decisions. I used to love my thoughts; whatever I was thinking about was something I wanted to happen. Now I think about what I want first—but that gets mixed up with my obligations and I can't cry anymore. I have to forget all about what I want and what I have to do, otherwise I just end up in a state of limbo, feeling distressed: setbacks (it's easy to foresee how they'll pan out), or minor frustrations (prone to being analyzed and compensated for). I've discovered the hint of fabrication that goes into needs and obligations, but I respect them—period, without much commitment, because they organize life. If I do cry, it's most likely against my will. I have to distract myself from what I want and from my obligations. I allow only a few tears to well up. My feelings toward people have changed, too. What used to be hatred—sometimes for very elaborate ideological reasons—is now only a bellyache. Boredom now translates into a headache. I've lost the immediacy that makes it easy to interact with children and even though I know I could get it back with some quick games and a couple of funny faces, I don't want to because I envy everything they do: run, swim, play; they want so many things and ask for them endlessly. Lately, I've spent a great deal of time criticizing the manners of young people in Buenos Aires—with whomever, especially with taxi drivers. In general we agree: the kids here are unquestionably rude. But it's such a sad consensus that no conversations can develop from there.

I've now decided that the reason for the witch hunts was not because they flew through the air on broomsticks, or because of their covens. No, it was because they chopped up bones, they ground up brains. They also soaked pigs' ears and then used the brew to polish the floors. You never know, someone might slip and fall—which is an extremely ulterior motive the witches didn't give much importance to. That's how witches would kill three birds with one stone, and *that* was their power. Thoughts they reconstructed by mulling them over, boiling them up. And they manipulated time, too, to get the same product in different forms. For example, the cat: a witch has no ancestors, or husband, or children. The cat represents all of these for her, she uses the cat to invalidate death. A witch works like the Jivaros to reconstruct an order of the half-alive. That's why she soaks, boils, and mixes perfumes with vile substances: it's to rescue them from oblivion. She reminds those people who want to forget about vile substances in the name of charm, aesthetics, and the living. No, those women weren't punished because they could cover great distances; they were punished because they schemed to alter the immediacy of the feelings, decisions, and creatures upheld by life according to its own rules. And a witch does not recoil before the cross, as the legend goes, because the cross is an inanimate object. She recoils from the Easter lamb.

Now that I am a bit of a witch I can see my rude streak. I eat directly from the pot, I gobble up my food. Or I do the opposite: I go to a restaurant where everyone painstakingly chews each bite six times in the name of health and I get a kick out of chewing, as if we were horses. I've taken a fancy to old slippers. I toss too much water on the plants after mopping the balcony, so that mud splatters from the pots onto the clean tiles—I invalidate time, since I have to clean up again. I cook a lot, because I delight in the raw becoming cooked. And I entirely dismiss ecological arguments, if the planet self-destructs in two hundred years I'd like to rise from the grave to watch the show. I swap stories with my witchy friends and our conversations are limited to fleeting words, tales of our various obsessions. We keep an eye on each others' witchcraft, to perfect it. For example, learning to kill three birds with one stone—not necessarily to do bad things, but to beat time at least, to pick our battles wisely. Who would go around flogging a dead horse when a dead horse can't even take you for a ride?

But it wasn't always like this, it wasn't like this. Before I thought about letting go and killing two birds with one stone, I spent two years suffering like never before. One morning I sobbed in equal measure for two entirely different reasons.

I realized what happens to people who die and people who leave. They come back in our dreams and say: "I'm here, but I'm not here. I'm here but I'm leaving," and I say back: "Stay a little while longer," but they don't explain themselves. If they do stay, it's as if they were withdrawn, somewhere else, and they look at me like distant visitors. In that realm of oblivion where they've gone they have other professions and they've become someone else. And all the times we argued, all our conversations, all the meals and laughter we've shared—they all become part of that oblivion and I don't want to meet new people or see my friends.

Whenever I start talking with someone it's me who sends them to the realm of oblivion, before it's even their time to leave or die.

I wake up and sense that I'm alive. Morning breaks. My mind is blank; nothing to do, nothing to think about. I'm not about to stay in bed smoking with no ideas in my head. Suddenly, I'm overcome with extremely good intentions unrelated to anything in particular: I shower, comb my hair, put the kettle on. As I perk up for the day my good intentions surge. It's a day in March and the sunlight shines evenly; the little birds toil, they flit from here to there. I am going to work, too. I know what I'll do: I'm going to guide the ivy—but not with ordinary string. I'll use tomato twine. There she is, clinging to the wall. I remove dead leaves from the ivy and from everything else in sight. You could call it a dead-leaf-removing fit, but that expression isn't quite right because I'm so calm; still, I wouldn't dare stop until I've removed the very last ant, the very last sickly leaf. I pile all those small flowerpots to one side; they'll go to other homes, maybe with other plants. An airplane flies by high above and suddenly I'm filled with such immense joy and peace from performing this task that I work even more slowly, so as not to finish. I'd like someone to come find me like this, in the morning. But everyone else is absorbed in their own worlds—maybe they're suffering or complaining or coming down with the flu—it doesn't matter, it'll pass and at some point they'll experience their own moment of happiness like I'm feeling now. I'm so humbled and so satisfied at the same time that I could thank someone, although I don't know who it would be. I inspect my garden and I'm hungry, I deserve a peach. I turn on the radio and hear them talking about the troy ounce. I don't know what it is, nor do I care. Time to get a move on, beautiful life.

It Was the Cat's Fault

ON a block full of apartment buildings with glass doors, shiny mirrors, and foyers with red rugs and orange walls, there was an old house with the door painted purple and green. Of course, these weren't bright shades of purple and green, they were muted and well matched. To be sure, the red rugs and orange walls of the other buildings were lovely, but their appeal came from the price tag, the kind of beauty that anyone with money can buy. But the people who lived in that old house—with a paint job that was so bizarre and yet so pretty at the same time, and a sign over the door that said "Dance School"—those people were, well... let's just say there was *something* about them. The "Dance School" sign showed a dancer who was all hair, as if her tresses had tumbled loose from so much dancing. Studied in detail she caught your eye, but way up high she'd been drowned out by all the neon lights and business signs, and nobody noticed her.

It was seven o'clock in the morning. In wide exercise pants, Doris, the director of the dance school, was sweeping the hallway herself. She'd had to fire the cleaning lady because she'd come to realize the lady had been a real idiot. That said, she'd once been pleasantly surprised by her: the students were practicing the lotus flower position when the cleaning lady, from the hallway, had contorted her body into the position better than anyone else. They'd all admired her. Doris had used the cleaning lady as an example for her students, pointing out how well she bent her knees.

She'd asked her to assume the position several times, praising her briefly. But overall, she decided that the cleaning lady was a real idiot—or, more specifically, she was self-serving.

Until Doris found a replacement, she'd just have to sweep the place herself. So there she was, sweeping, when her ex-husband walked in. The only reason her ex-husband would show up at that time of day was because he was drunk, drunk as a skunk. Her face and movements reflected how she felt about his presence. Her loud sweeping was not a good sign. Neither was the look on her face. She said to him curtly:

"I've got class at eight o'clock."

In a conciliatory tone of voice, stemming from fear, he said:

"Alright Doris, but can I stay? I'll go sleep in the room upstairs."

"You can stay in the kitchen," she said without looking at him.

She didn't have to meet his gaze to know what his eyes looked like. She knew he'd been out all night, wandering around aimlessly.

He headed to the kitchen, trying to walk a straight line, which lent a certain ease to his step. Doris was extremely annoyed. The practice barre still hadn't been mounted to the wall and that meant she would have to play the drum during the rhythm exercises. Playing the drum wore her out. It was a big heavy drum with a thick heavy stick, and today was the day the women with no sense of rhythm had class. But she vowed to get them dancing in time with the drum. They would start slow and then pick up the pace.

When they arrived, the drum beat faster and faster, louder and louder. From the kitchen, her ex-husband Agustín, who was drinking wine straight from the bottle, shouted:

"Tambour! Tambour!"

The students didn't notice because they didn't know he was there. But Doris, feeling mortified and infuriated, said:

"Just a moment, please."

She was as dignified as a queen. She walked to the kitchen and asked him:

"Why didn't you go to sleep, you fool?

"But Doris, you told me…"

"Get the hell out of here."

But as he got up to leave, she realized just how inebriated he was: the students were bound to notice when he staggered by the studio. So instead she said:

"Go on, go sleep upstairs if you want."

"No, no," he said. "If you're kicking me out, then I'll leave."

He'd been struck by an attack of pride and she couldn't persuade him otherwise. She changed her tone.

"Alright, I'm sorry. I'd like you to stay and get some sleep, okay?"

"I can't. I'd love to stay but I have important responsibilities to take care of."

Doris was on the verge of losing it, but she told him:

"I know. I know you have important responsibilities, but you'll just have to take care of them later."

Agustín hesitated as he walked up to her room, saying:

"I should go get some things done."

But he was exhausted. She walked him upstairs and he laid down. Once she was back with her students she shut the studio doors tightly; then she played the drum louder than ever.

Her current husband was going to mount the practice barre for her students to use. He didn't live with her because the daily grind deteriorates marital relations. He came and went as he pleased. Now, as she anxiously waited for him to mount the barre, she strived to ensure the circumstances would be conducive to him working with tenacity and perseverance. What would be better—to kick Agustín out when he finished sleeping off his bender, or invite him to join the…What to call it? The "work team." Even if he could barely hold on to a nail. Her husband and ex-husband were good friends, having similar aesthetics. In Sweden, for example, everyone works together. No one is self-serving. In fact, anyone who doesn't pitch in is reported to the police. It wasn't that her husband had an uncooperative spirit, he just had aesthetic reservations. He thought modern dance was incomprehensible, on a par with coin collecting.

When he arrived, he realized now wasn't the time to get into any of his theories. Almost without greeting, Doris asked him:

"Did you bring the hammer?"

"Unbelievable! Of course I brought the hammer. Who would try to nail something into the wall without a hammer?"

From one coat pocket he removed a hammer, and from the other, a bottle of wine.

"So," he said, "How do you want me to mount it? With nails, bolts…?"

"What are bolts?" asked Doris with profound contempt and suspicion.

"You surprise me, teacher," said Miguel. And from his upper pocket he took out a bolt and showed it to her.

"No, not with that," she replied. "It's thick and ugly. They'll show, and I want the barre to be smooth."

"Now, c'mon. Who would be crazy enough to think they're going to show?" he said, pouring himself a glass of wine.

Just then, Agustín came down and brightened when he saw the wine and the company.

"Let's see here, Maestro. What do you think? What should I use: nails or bolts?"

"In my opinion, they both involve a dishonorable task," replied Agustín, who still hadn't gotten enough sleep.

"There's no doubt about that. No debate whatsoever. Right now we're debating something else entirely."

"Does anyone ever really debate anything?" asked Agustín.

Doris set to doing the dishes left from lunch and didn't say a word. The two men went into the dance studio. Agustín was tempted to play the drum, but he knew it might cost him dearly. With an irritated, skeptical expression on his face, Miguel began to scatter nails all over the place, as if he'd been a carpenter his whole life and the trade had given him nothing but minimal satisfaction. He strewed them about as if they were miserable and sordid, as if they were the very nails that had been used to kill Christ himself. While Miguel nailed a piece of the barre, Agustín sat on a little wicker chair and kept him company. Miguel hammered with all his might as an image of Doris' overweight student popped into his head. He thoroughly calculated the bulk of the overweight student's leg. Doris said:

"She's remarkably flexible. And more than a few envy her ability."

"Could be, teacher," said Miguel. "But flesh is flesh."

From flesh, they moved onto the concept of mass and the relationship between mass and energy. While they talked, Doris walked back and forth from the kitchen to the studio. She would have preferred for the work group to be more preoccupied with finishing the barre. Less talk, more action. If by some chance the Pope had showed up at her house that day, she would have invited him to nail down the barre as well.

But, as it turns out, there was a technical problem: they ran out of nails. Miguel invited Agustín to accompany him back to his house, where he had some crooked nails. It was just a matter of going there, bringing them back, and straightening them out. Agustín replied:

"I am a Spanish gentleman."

Miguel burst into a peal of laughter. He knew the theory about Spanish gentlemen. Spanish gentlemen rescue princesses trapped in terribly high towers, they fight in duels and go to war, but they do not fetch crooked nails at two o'clock in the morning. After hearing that, Doris, who also knew Agustín's theory about Spanish gentlemen, said:

"Get out of here!" and she kicked both of them out.

The following day her husband came to work alone. The distant and serious look on his face assured her that he had actually come with the intention of working. He greeted her and they exchanged a few words, acting as if he had been hired for the job. Then he went into the dance studio. His cold entrance and bad mood made Doris think that perhaps he had been offended by something, but now was not the time to ask. Everyone knows that's the type of thing one brings up on the weekend, when there's time to sleep and recover from all the hard work.

He got right down to business; at first he was still in a bad mood. Meanwhile, Doris walked back and forth from the kitchen to the studio, back and forth to see if he needed anything, to spy on him, and to check how the barre looked. As he hammered, however, he became more invested in the project and he even started to whistle.

What a delight it is to have a man doing wood work in the house! It's like having one's own personal male saint, it's a beautiful sight. Only, to complete the picture she would have to be spinning thread. But Doris didn't want to spin thread; she walked back and forth from the kitchen to the studio, but Miguel didn't acknowledge her. Her excitement from watching his carpentry skills started to dwindle. It wasn't long before she started to eye the barre critically and said:

"Don't you think that part is higher?"

He stepped back to get a better look and said: "Which part looks higher, woman?"

"Is it going to stay like that?" she asked pointing to another section.

"Well, just how do *you* think it should look?"

"I don't know. I just thought the nails wouldn't show."

"They're not going to show."

Then, wagering a guess, she said, "What if, instead of mounting it like that, you turned it around to the other side...Like this, I mean."

And she showed him how she thought it would look better. He said icily:

"What are you suggesting, that I take the whole thing down and start over?"

"I didn't say the whole thing," she replied sensibly. "Just that part where the nails are showing."

"You don't like how it turned out?"

"I didn't say that," she replied somewhat unconvincingly.

He concentrated on the barre and continued hammering intently as if it were the love of his life. She went to the kitchen and didn't go back to watch him or make any more suggestions. In the kitchen she decided to meditate.

In Sweden it's different, she thought as she fed one of the seven cats in the house. Everything follows a logical sequence according to the weather: in summer they have sex on the islands, the beaches, under the sun. During the long winters they meditate in their houses sitting by the stove. Winter in Sweden is as long as their meditations are deep. The people there choose to work together out of their own free will, because they're not a country of idiots. Sure, they've all got their own problems, like anywhere else, but their problems are...different. Not to mention that European aloofness, that refinement. She looked at the cat with profound compassion and affection, because she had no choice but to live out her life right where she was. Then Doris described to her cat what their life would be like in Sweden, but the cat didn't say anything. Suddenly, from the studio, there came a terrible yowl and Doris rushed out in alarm. Miguel had finished and was on his way to the kitchen.

"What happened?" she asked.

"Nothing, I stepped on him by accident," he said.

"Of course," she replied in a strange voice with unprecedented European aloofness.

"I didn't mean to, I swear," he said.

"Of course not," Doris answered. "What would ever lead me to think that you would do such a thing on purpose?"

The dignity and European aloofness in Doris were growing.

She didn't go to see how the barre had turned out, and she didn't invite him into the kitchen, so he left.

All that fuss over mounting the barre meant she had been neglecting the cats. Ana Poteraika, the most beautiful cat, was anorexic. She didn't want to eat liver so Doris bought tenderloin steak, chopped it up, and fed it to her. But since she didn't really want the tenderloin either, she ate only two or three small pieces apathetically. Then Dagoberto came along to gobble up the rest. Doris said to Dagoberto:

"Do you think I'm going to continue to deprive myself of eating meat, as I've been doing so far for poor Ana Poteraika's sake, just so that you can come along and steal it out from under her nose?"

That cat was a good-for-nothing, she'd had it with him. Plus, she had to buy antibiotics for Jorgelina, who had conjunctivitis. And another cat, who was also a lazybones and went out on the rooftops at night, was pregnant again. She needed to get that cat fixed to stop her from having any more litters of kittens. The operation cost forty million pesos and Doris needed a new pair of shoes; but it wasn't the expense that concerned her. The real reason she hadn't taken the cat in for the operation was because she wasn't convinced it was a humane practice—or rather, a "feline" practice. By the time she'd bought all the medicines and given them to the cats, she felt so tired and sad that she wanted someone to come over and comfort her. Who would be home tonight, Saturday night, when everyone else was out? Maybe her ex-husband—he went out during the week. She had kicked him out for good a few days before. He was a fool and an idiot... But... She was deeply unsettled by the fact that the cat didn't want to eat. So she gave him a call and said:

"Ana Poteraika is anorexic. Come over."

"Um, okay," he said. He was sober and contemplative. "What could I do to..."

"I'm telling you to get over here."

"Okay," he replied.

While she waited for him to arrive, Doris got more and more anxious and desperate. She felt a strange uneasiness like she'd never felt before. When he got there she told him, her eyes wide and scared:

"She hasn't had anything to eat for three days. I called the veterinarian and he told me it was just temporary, that animals go through stages like this. What kind of idiot says such a thing? What does he mean by 'just temporary'? Three days for her tiny little body is like twenty days for us."

"And around two months for King Kong," said Agustín. "Well Doris, don't get so worked up," he said, thinking about a tooth that was bothering him. It was a molar that had come in on top of another tooth; it needed more space and he felt like his whole mouth was going to burst. But now was not the time. He poured himself a glass of wine and so did she.

After she drank her wine—maybe because she hadn't eaten—she started to cry and went to the bedroom. Agustín wavered. Perhaps he should follow her and comfort her? Then again, it was also possible that she wanted to cry alone. Besides, if he went in to comfort her she might kick him out.

So he drank a little more wine in the kitchen, and she didn't come back. What was this? Had he been invited over just to be left there all alone? So he started singing really loudly—loud enough for her hear him.

"If dancing doesn't cheer you up, screw it all, just let her die!"

But Doris didn't come out to bad mouth him or to kick him out like she usually did. That worried him, so he decided to go in to the bedroom. There she was, quietly crying in bed. He asked her:

"Do you want me to call Miguel?"

"No, don't call him. I don't want that."

He grabbed the telephone. She tried to wrestle it away from him, but he pushed her away saying:

"Miguel? There's an emergency. Come over. Ana Poteraika is anorexic. No, seriously, it's an emergency."

Doris reproached him.

"You idiot! I'm going to call him right back and tell him not to come." Doris couldn't contain her anger, but once her husband arrived she threw herself back on the bed and started to sob again.

"Teacher!" Miguel cried. "What's going on?"

"Nothing," she said, looking at him accusingly. So he chatted with Agustín about Ana Poteraika's health, on purely lighthearted terms. Doris kept her eyes on Miguel as he spoke. Then he turned to her and said: "C'mon, teacher. Get up. We're going to dance a ranchera."

"No, no," she replied weakly.

But he succeeded in getting her up, and without so much as a record playing they danced a ranchera, humming the tune. Miguel was persevering and joyful; Doris, despondent, practically clung to him like a convalescent.

The following day was a splendid spring day, albeit a little cold. The blue sky beckoned one to go outside.

As she watered her pretty sweet potato plant, Doris decided to meditate. She couldn't possibly stay cooped up in that house, listening to nonsense all day. The world was filled with people who went waterskiing or bought new coats; some of her colleagues had staged their dance performances, exhibiting their work and demonstrating the progress of their students. Doris was not about to put on a performance like she had the year before, at one of those pitiful neighborhood auditoriums offered out of courtesy, where everyone in the neighborhood comes with their kids in their arms. Then the kids start to run around; they run back and forth from the stage to the exit.

To top it off, right at the end of the show, which was the culmination of the entire dance and the moment the kids would begin to run around, Agustín showed up and walked down the aisle. Everyone stared at him as he found an empty seat. He didn't do anything out of the ordinary, but Doris trembled until the end. What if he had blurted something out? No, this time she was going to put on a show at a real theater. So, she called some friends who knew a businessman with a theater—good friends. It was all about knowing the right people, going to visit them. Their house was a haven of peace and quiet where everyone drank fruit juice, which is a healthy habit. They talked about air pollution and neither of them littered on the street because they believed in protecting the environment.

Yes, yes, it was so great to see her. Of course they would put her in touch with the businessman who owned the Argentina Theater of La Plata—they were just about to see him in a few days. When she got home, as she fed birdseed to the canary, she thought cheerfully, *it's all about networking: who you know, getting out and about.* She would invite the businessman over for a delicious meal.

The day before the meal, they started getting ready. Doris bought a massive fish, a beautiful fish. She prepared a tomato cream sauce that was reminiscent of sunrise near a beach in northern Brazil, and she decorated the dish with arabesques of mayonnaise. She made deviled eggs and placed them around the fish in a circle. Little green sprigs to garnish here and there. That afternoon, Agustín came over while Doris prepared everything. He kept her company, politely watching all the unusual ingredients she used. Meanwhile, she lectured him on the rules he had to follow if he wanted to be invited to the meal the next day.

He would be invited, as long as he followed these rules:

1) He was not to mention that he was a Spanish gentleman.
2) He was not even to *think* about saying that any type of business was dishonorable.
3) Any reference to race, religion, clothing, people's stature, or the eating habits of different countries was prohibited.
4) Ideally, he should brush his teeth, which were extremely nicotine-stained. To this end she promised to provide him with a piece of steel wool which would leave them immaculate—bearing in mind that steel wool should be used with caution because it strips away enamel.

Miguel was going to pitch in by bringing some bottles of wine from the 1908 vintage, which he'd been stockpiling at his house for quite some time. Doris hoped to give Miguel some advice about his behavior. She wanted to tell him that after a certain time of night he tended to soliloquize, or sometimes he shut down into a sort of silence followed by long solitary musings, but she didn't mention it.

The businessman arrived. He wore a jacket so beautiful they had never seen anything like it out on the street. People with jackets like that probably hide away in their houses. The businessman was tall and he bumped into an adornment Doris had hung in the doorway, an oriental trinket that jingled when the door opened. If he hadn't been warned he would have tripped over a wooden plank being used to block off the dance studio from the hallway, meant to keep the cats from getting in.

Seeing that plank of wood propped up, out of place, it made him realize that the house must not receive many visitors. They went to the sitting room with Doris leading the way; she was grandiose, cordial, and decked out in a long skirt. There was a table set up in the sitting room to display the magnificent fish. The little table was too small for all those glasses and all that food, plus it wobbled. The businessman glanced around, and quickly found a piece of cardboard that he wedged under the table leg. When Doris noticed the cardboard, she asked him in a disproportionately incredulous voice:

"Did you do that?"

"Yes," he said, like someone who wants to change the subject of conversation.

"Thank you," Doris snapped haughtily.

Throughout all this, Miguel and Agustín sat expectantly. Miguel asked if he should bring anything in from the kitchen. Doris, in an impersonal and respectful tone, answered:

"Napkins, if you would."

Agustín remained silent. He didn't normally converse with strangers unless spoken to first. He felt as if an inspector had come over—a gracious inspector, but an inspector nonetheless. On the one hand, having an inspector in the house pleased and relieved him; on the other, just being in his own body was painful. He would have liked to be invisible, to watch it all unfold. The businessman, noticing there were no cushions on the wicker chair he'd been offered, asked permission to remove a little round cushion from another chair to place on his own. He put a round cushion on a square chair. If he had been paying attention, he would have noticed how that cushion had never been removed from the little armchair, it had been there for many years and was destined to stay there, sweetly, alongside the matching armchair, until its dying day.

From the kitchen Miguel brought cheese, olives, and an aperitif, for starters. He said to the businessman, "Maestro…" and served him some olives.

Miguel figured the man must be a master in his field, he was sure of it. He was fond of and respected the talents of different people, as long as they were specific and didn't overlap: there are master poets, schoolmasters, master gardeners and—why not—master custodians.

The businessman said:

"Yesterday I saw a very interesting show at the SHA."

"Oh, I've heard," said Doris

Although she hadn't gone, she was in the know.

"More than the play itself, the staging was interesting."

"Which play is that?" asked Agustín in a polite voice, demonstrating unusually good manners.

"*The Fir Tree Forest*," said the businessman.

"Based on a story by Gogol," said Miguel.

"Yes," replied the businessman relaxing now and popping a piece of cheese in his mouth. He relaxed because he realized these were his kind of men, clearly. One never knows the company they'll end up with in these situations.

Agustín said: "I know that story, but it's not one of his best." And he started to name other stories by Gogol that were much better, all the while sipping on his wine.

The businessman sized him up: skinny arms, missing tooth. From all the time he spent observing and listening to the people he hired, he had gotten used to paying attention to two things at once. At moments he paid attention to the conversation, perking up an ear if there was something that truly struck him, like when you're picking out sounds from a backdrop of silence. At the same time as he listened he also thought: *What scrawny little arms. Surely this man didn't do his military service. He wouldn't even be able to cultivate a crop of potatoes if it came down to it.*

Doris was tense; she was worried that Miguel and Agustín would start to argue about Gogol's stories, which was clearly a respectable topic but nevertheless felt like old news to her. To keep them from talking about Gogol, she said:

"I saw the staging of *The Straw Hat* at the SHA. I found it pathetic."

"Yet I do think there were some redeemable moments," said the businessman.

"For example?" replied Doris in a tone that seemed to say: *All right, name one.*

"The second act had some successful moments," he answered somewhat reluctantly, which didn't seem characteristic of him.

Doris said:

"Well, in the second act there were a few good moments, that's true. They've got to get *something* right..."

Agustín was relaxed. Luckily Doris had gone back to her normal self. Wisely, Miguel remained silent, like someone intent on keeping himself company, although he did look a bit tired and somewhat misplaced. Doris began to object:

"But when he gives those long, useless soliloquies, which are a complete waste of time; and when that…that half-idiot comes on stage, the one whose name makes no sense…"

"Oh, sure," said the businessman.

Having downed some more wine, Agustín now joined in the conversation. He hadn't seen the play, but felt as if he had; he could imagine what the soliloquies were like. So he said:

"Yeah, it must have been a total waste of time. What a drag," and poured himself another glass of wine.

Just then Miguel burst into a fit of laughter: healthy, cheerful, and carefree laughter—only it wasn't clear what he was laughing about.

While Doris chattered away, the businessman found himself looking at her to his heart's content: What a beautiful woman. Which of the two men was she with? Her eyes made her look Spanish with some Arab features; her hands were dry and her ears were small.

"As for me," Agustín was saying, "it's been seven years since I've been to the theater. Let's see, the last time I went—"

"He's a poet," Doris said quickly, "a very good poet."

"Have you published anything?"

"No," he replied. He was about to say that "publishing is dishonorable" but then he remembered the rules he'd agreed to, so he kept his mouth shut.

"What do you mean you haven't published anything, Maestro?" said Miguel. "What about the magazine?"

Doris got tense again. Anything to do with the magazine generated conflict; they'd spent entire evenings arguing about whether or not it was a "publication," which depended on whether or not the "magazine" was really a magazine.

Doris said: "Shall we eat?"

"Whenever you like," replied the businessman casually.

The food looked appetizing to him. They walked back to the kitchen to get something they'd left behind. Only Agustín stayed, waiting for them to come back. He walked around the room a few times amusing himself by looking at some pictures on the wall. Suddenly everyone was startled by a noise and they all ran over to the table: the cat had jumped up on the table, tipped over the entire contents of the platter, and eaten the fish. There was nothing else to say. A hush fell over the group and then Doris, in a detached voice, asked Agustín:

"How did the cat get in?"

"I don't know Doris, I didn't see her come in."

She couldn't say "stupid cat" in front of the businessman—

she'd have to defend the cat with him there because, after all, it was her cat. They all pitched in to clean up the floor. Agustín was really helpful; he moved quickly and nobly; he took initiative, cleaning everywhere that needed it. He felt happy and calm because he kept thinking: *This time it wasn't all my fault; it was the cat's fault.*

There wasn't anything else to eat except cheese with jam, but that couldn't be served right after a vermouth. Doris offered the businessman another glass of wine, who said:

"No thank you. Actually, I shouldn't have promised to stay for dinner because I haven't got a lot of time," he glanced at his watch. "I have to be downtown in an hour. Do you think I'll have problems hailing a cab at this time of night?"

"A cab at this time of night? That'll be hard," said Miguel.

The businessman looked at him slightly alarmed. Then, getting up with a sense of determination, he said:

"I'll find one, no problem."

Miguel told him where to find a taxi and walked him to the door. Agustín circled the room a few times and Doris went to the kitchen without saying a word. When he came back, Miguel said:

"He found a cab."

Then a silence fell; it was tense. Agustín momentarily forgot to be happy it hadn't been his fault; the businessman had left.

That savior with the silk thread jacket—harmonious, modest, and worldly—that savior of theirs was gone. Where to, who knows? All because the cat had eaten the fish. Who knew whether he'd come back? After a moment of silence, Doris grabbed a stick and chased the cat out to the terrace; she slammed the door violently, barred it, and went back inside. Then they started drinking wine.

The Cake

I WANTED to make a cake that was light and fluffy. I didn't want to make cookies because they don't have that third dimension. You eat cookies and it's as if they're missing something—that's why you can't stop eating them. With cookies it's like they're made out of reconstituted bread or breadcrumbs. Only dogs know how to eat cookies the right way: they snatch them in midair, bite into them with a loud crunch, and devour them in one gulp, bobbing their head a bit.

I didn't want to make flan either because it's a proto-food and it looks like a jellyfish. I did *not* want to make a tipsy cake, that's a sneaky cake. You pour wine into the batter. Then someone bites into it with confidence, expecting it to taste like cake but instead it tastes like something else, something strong and rancid.

The fluffy cake I wanted to make was just like this instant cake mix from a beautiful little box I had eaten once. It was called "Paradise Cake." On the box there was a picture of a woman wearing a long dress. (I can't remember if it was a woman *and* a man or just a woman, but if it was just a woman she was no doubt waiting for a man.)

The Paradise Cake was so fluffy—I've never eaten anything else quite like it. It's not that it melted in your mouth. Instead you'd take a bite, chewing ever so slightly, and all the steps that followed—chewing, swallowing, and so forth—were perfect. Plus, it wasn't like cookies. Cookies are for eating when you're bored. When it came to Paradise Cake you'd envision eating it some afternoon, some afternoon filled with lovely thoughts. When I saw the recipe for a "fluffy cake" I said to myself, "This will be just like the Paradise Cake." I asked my mama if she'd let me use the cook stove to make it.

"Not in your dreams," she said.

We never lit the cook stove; it was a cumbersome black contraption with a blackened door. I had never seen inside it, nor did I know how it worked. We didn't use it because apparently it was a pain in the neck. There it stood in the kitchen, everyday, like an uninvited guest. It was like the bread oven out back—I never saw anyone baking or roasting anything in there. That oven was considered to be another pain in the neck at my house, only outdoors. To me they were different; I barely registered the cook stove because it was more like a piece of furniture. But the bread oven I knew my way around because every time I went out to play I would climb up to peer inside, its dark pit filled with ancient gray ash, and then leap to the ground. The bread oven looked like a pigeon coop and if anyone had ever baked bread there, it was long forgotten now, and no one wanted to remember either. It was as if the oven brought back unpleasant memories. I couldn't make my fluffy cake in the cook stove or in the regular oven. So I asked:

"Can I make it in the shed?"

"Yes," said my mother. I could make it in the shed using the brazier.

Not in the kitchen, because children make a mess in the kitchen. My mama was going to light a fire in the brazier, out in the shed. (Lighting fires is too dangerous for children.)

I mixed up the batter in a little pan that wasn't the right size for soup or anything else. I'd never seen that little green pan before; it must have come from some set my parents used before I was born.

If braziers are as dangerous as they say, I don't know why my mama decided to use a bellows. The more she pumped, the closer she came to being scorched; maybe death didn't faze her.

Glowing embers had to be placed over the top of the little green pan so the cake would turn golden on top. I wanted my friend who lived across the street to give me a hand. The day before I had told her that I'd been given permission to make a fluffy cake and she said she'd come over. I knew by the look on her face when she arrived that she'd come only because she had nothing better to do. She played the part of the reluctant onlooker, but she wasn't afraid of death-by-exploding-brazier, and when the flames died down she pumped it gladly one last time using all her strength, as if to say *this crap is cooked*. I knew she wasn't tending to the fire because she cared about the cake, rather to partake in the act itself, to do *something*, because she knew how to keep a fire going and the idea of letting it go out seemed wrong to her.

By now the little pan with the fluffy cake was heating up, but I couldn't wait any longer to see if it was done. More specifically, I wanted to watch the fluffy cake rise; like a Japanese gardener who wakes up in the middle of the night to watch how his plants grow.

But I couldn't lift the lid by myself either, because there were glowing embers piled on top. I asked my friend but she just shrugged.

"Oh, I know," I said. "We'll use a long pole."

I grabbed a long broomstick and tried to loop it through the handle of the lid. Reluctantly, my friend helped me. Right when we were about to lift it off my mama came back in. My friend made like she had nothing to do with my bright idea or the broomstick—which was true, after all. Mama knew right away it had been my idea.

"What's gotten into you!" she said. "Checking the batter before it's done? Why, you've just put it in!"

Once she left, I was able to lift the lid with a thinner pole and I saw the cake for a split second. I got a vague idea of what it looked like, but it was still a pancake: no third dimension.

"Maybe it will still rise," my friend said and she suggested doing something else while we waited. But I wasn't going anywhere until I saw how it turned out.

After a while I took it out for good, because you can't be removing the embers and putting them back on, over and over. The cake had turned dark brown, it had shrunk into itself in every direction. It was nothing more than a little brown pastry, like a stubby croissant.

Mama said:

"That makes sense. I figured as much."

So, in the mind of an adult, baking turds was something logical and inevitable.

I didn't eat the cake, nor did anyone else. You wouldn't have been able to eat it either.

The Stories Told
by Cecilia's Friends

THE friends arrived, they removed their overcoats and hung them on a large coat stand. Then they sat down to chat with Cecilia, who had asked them over. Cecilia had invited them all together—that way they would talk among themselves and she could just sit back and listen: she was tired. Now they were all sitting around the table telling stories.

The first guest told a story about monkeys. One monkey climbed on top of a box and, using a stick, it grabbed a banana and then peeled and ate it. Cecilia listened to him attentively and brought out small cups of coffee on little saucers. Everyone stirred his or her coffee until one guest said:

"Let's tell stories about thieves."

"No, not stories about thieves," said one lady with a bun in her hair.

So they all drank their coffee without a word, glad to be warm because outside it was freezing. Every time the door opened, someone would quickly shut it, and they would all content to be warm again. Then they started to tell stories in smaller groups, each chatting with the person beside them. Cecilia listened to the person next to her, whose story happened to be the one about thieves.

They frittered away the evening chatting, until the door opened again and another friend came in. This friend didn't take off his overcoat and he never stopped smiling. He sat down keeping his hands in his pockets. Cecilia went off to bring him a cup of coffee, without saying a word, and everyone told him what they'd been up to:

"We were telling stories, but your stories are the best of all. We've never met anyone else with so many stories."

The friend smiled, as if to excuse himself, and he started to tell a story just as Cecilia brought in his coffee and sat down.

"I'm going to tell a story about something that happened a long time ago," he said sticking his hands in his pockets again. "Once upon a time, there was woman washing her hair. She looked in the mirror to see if her neck was clean. When she looked in the mirror she noticed that she had a red round spot next to her ear and said to herself, *It must be a spot of ink.*

"She tried to rub out that spot she'd never seen before, and ended up using all the soap. When she realized it wouldn't come off she thought she might be sick, so she went to see the doctor. The doctor said:

'It's just a spot. It's not an ink spot and you, madam, are not sick.'

"The woman went home but she couldn't stop thinking about the red spot on her face. Whenever she could, she covered it up. When she was with other people, she thought they might notice the spot and it embarrassed her.

"Consequetly, she ended up alone for a long time. Everyone who knew her wondered why she had undergone such a change, but no one could explain it. The fact that she had changed meant they'd changed too—they were polite to her yet distrusting. She sensed their misgivings and suffered a great deal.

"One afternoon she was looking at herself in the mirror absentmindedly, thinking about nothing in particular, when suddenly she realized something: the spot wasn't there! She checked again and her heart skipped a beat. The spot was gone. She braced herself and sat down because her knees felt weak and she was about to cry. The spot was gone. The woman piled her hair on top of her head as high as she could and went to bask in the sun in her yard. She wanted to feel the sun on her neck. When she came back inside she felt good and went to bed. When she got up the next morning, the spot was back in the same place as before—a red round spot. She still has it to this very day."

The storyteller chuckled and removed his hands from his

pockets to drink his coffee. One of the friends said, looking at Cecilia:

"What a strange story."

"Sometimes spots are really birthmarks," said the lady with the bun in her hair.

Another friend yawned, looking at his watch. "It's midnight. We should get some sleep."

They all got their overcoats and left; the last to leave was the man who had never taken off his coat. He smiled at Cecilia and said goodnight.

Once everyone was outside someone said: "Cecilia never talks, she just listens to everyone else."

"I've never even heard her speak," said one bald man.

"It's as if she weren't even there—but she does make delicious coffee," said the lady with her hair in a bun.

Then they all went their different ways, each to his or her own home.

The lady next door was always knitting and Cecilia wound hanks of yarn into balls for her. That's how she kept herself busy while the next-door neighbor carried on, but Cecilia herself didn't knit. She bought catalogs about dogs of all shapes and sizes, at every price imaginable—but she never actually bought any dogs.

Cecilia invited these friends over regularly. She always made them coffee, and when there was a new arrival she went to the kitchen in silence, added some water to the kettle, and then brought them a cup of coffee. On their way out she held up their overcoats and brushed them off, and everyone said thank you very much.

Cecilia often went to the cinema. She was frightened when one tall man wanted to kill another, and she laughed when there were children playing or when people fell in love.

She worked too: it was her job to take papers from one place to another. She checked these papers meticulously, erasing any spots of ink and organizing them in piles according to color, all day long.

Once, on her way home from work, the wind disheveled her hair and when she got home she carefully combed it back into place. On one side, under her right ear, she had a red round spot. She stared at it. She scrubbed it with soap, but the spot did not come out. Cecilia changed into her nightgown and got into bed. Sitting there in bed she said her prayers, like she did every night, and then she took out a little mirror. She glanced at herself once more, smiling ever so slightly, and said to herself:

Why not me?

And then she went to sleep.

The Scent of Buenos Aires

I HAD just learned about how people break up from reading
romance novels by Rafael Pérez y Pérez. I was fed up with
stories about love because it was always the same old formula:
the girlfriend was good, pure, and even went to Mass. The "other
girl"—the one who temporarily stole the boyfriend away—was a
bitch. She was entirely disagreeable and unable to love anyone:
she stole him away *just for the hell of it*, but when all that he had
lost dawned on him, he always went back to the good girl.

But the books about couples who were separated had an interesting twist: even though they only split up for a time and then
always got back together, when they first broke it off the woman
slept in one room and the man in another—sometimes on the
sofa. The book never specified whether the door between them
was open or closed. In real life, however, I didn't know anyone
who had separated, but now we were going to Buenos Aires to
visit a friend of my youngest aunt. This friend had recently given
birth to a baby boy and she had separated, too. Now, this couple
had separated because they were from Buenos Aires—not from
Moreno. Although they were only a mere twenty miles apart,
people in Buenos Aires were different from people in Moreno.
For example, when my Uncle José's niece Chiche came to visit

us in Moreno for the day, she chased the chickens until they went nuts. It was as if she'd never seen a chicken before. Some of my other cousins from Buenos Aires had a giant teddy bear and a piano in their house. Even the scent of Buenos Aires was different—it smelled almost as if the walls were impregnated with sulfur.

Already, on the train, I couldn't wait to get to that house where my aunt's separated friend lived. How exciting! I was going to meet a separated person. My aunt scored extra points in my book because of this trip—you could almost say that I loved her more dearly as a result: first, for giving me such an opportunity; secondly, because she knew such exotic people from Buenos Aires. She told me: "Her father is a great pianist. He composed famous tangoes. Now he's practically blind and ailing." So when they say on the radio "tango composed by so-and-so"—those are real people? And I'm going to meet one of them? Then she told me: "Don't even think of mentioning any of this to them." I hoped with all my heart that I would be up to the challenge. We didn't speak for a while.

It was a two-story house, nicely painted with ogive windows. We were greeted by a maid—she wasn't anything like the people who worked at my house. There had been Ramona, who had a big butt and was almost always furious; Aida, who was as sweet as an angel but whose lipstick was crooked—she cried at the drop of a hat and then her make-up smudged; and Petrona, who came from a family of gypsies. The maid at this house was straight out of a book; she was sweet and kind without being pretty. Her clothes were immaculate—not one strand of hair out of place. With a neutral politeness, she showed us in to see my aunt's friend, who was with her baby. I was certain the baby wouldn't cry—and, if he did, it would be a faint, civilized mew. His cries would match the furniture and the light, which was muted—not too bright—while much of the furniture was covered with dust sheets.

Carmen, the woman, was a little chubby, but the palette of the room matched so well. She made it look like being plump were something desirable. She didn't act like a separated woman, at least not according to my book. In Rafael Pérez y Pérez's novels they cried buckets of tears. I wanted to ask her if I could hold the baby—something I wholeheartedly enjoyed at the time—but I didn't dare. Besides, even though I was dying to hold the baby, I was scared I might drop him. How commendable of my aunt to have a friend with such a lovely house!

The baby was going to get a bath and I didn't want to miss it. The maid was going to bathe him in the bathroom (that way I got to see the bathroom, too)—but I didn't want to miss out on any of the conversation between my aunt and Carmencita, either. I never got the chance to listen in on entire adult conversations, but I had a strategy to pick up little bits and pieces. I would interrupt them with some surprising news—and the baby was a perfect excuse. I went back to where they were and said: "He clapped his hands!" They smiled at me, annoyed, and I returned to the bathroom, but I overheard: "He's an air-head." It wasn't the first time I'd heard someone use this term, although in Rafael Pérez y Pérez's novels it was always used in reference to women, to the "other women." They weren't just capricious—they were hussies, which is basically the same thing as being an airhead. The men in those novels—the boyfriends— were really good fellows at heart who had just experienced a moment of weakness, tempted by the airhead. So just how was it that Carmen could call her husband an airhead, as if it were nothing, as if she were calling him a lawyer, or saying he was from Rosario? I went right back to the bathroom to look at the baby. Not only was he not crying, he already looked like a pre-mature citizen. I wanted to pick him up and the maid let me, cupping her hands around mine. I was going to tell them how I'd held the baby, but something stopped me. Anyway, since I was going back and forth, Carmencita gestured to the maid on her way out of the bathroom: Bring the baby to the living room. With no more than a gesture, he was in his carriage asleep. No orders, no disagreements. Could that house have something special to make things happen differently? Just when my aunt was making all those silly faces at the baby, the ones that look like crazy miniature gnomes, the doorbell rang. It was the ex. He was a little fat, just like Carmen, but his features were drabber. It reminded me of when my Uncle José described someone as "lacking in character." And then he would add: "And common sense." Since I didn't understand what he meant by common sense, I didn't apply that part, but I did feel like the ex was lacking in character. We all greeted each other on friendly terms and I paid close attention to see how the two of them treated each other. They were really nice to one another, as if they were still together. At one point, Carmen said to him:

"Pick him up."

And he hesitated, but finally he picked up the baby. I understood his hesitation entirely.

I was watching for one of them to shoot a look of profound hatred, and although I kept my post for a long time, the three of them were just chatting away so I ended up going down to the kitchen to see what the maid was up to. Their conversations filled me with the same perplexity as my Aunt María's plants. My aunt was absolutely crazy, "insane," people said. She bathed the chickens, signaled from her house that the train was leaving by blowing a carnival whistle, and she chased people off the sidewalk, saying it belonged to her. But she had a big garden filled with plants—some of them were dried up but others bloomed in abundance. She had rosehips, a privet hedge, and a jasmine plant. And I wondered how she could grow normal plants, just like everyone else. Her plants should have looked like they belonged to someone insane—that is, when the plants sprouted they should have looked deranged. Furthermore, I never saw her go anywhere near them—she never touched the plants or even looked at them. And here it felt the same: these two people were separated and yet they spoke as if they were still together. There was nothing in their faces or their tone of voice to imply they were separated. Besides, neither of them even acted like they were separated. And, as if that weren't enough, Carmen— who had just finished calling him an airhead—was talking to him in a tone of voice that suggested his head was filled with useful thoughts.

I don't remember at what point he left, but not long thereafter the composer father appeared. He came downstairs with one of those dogs that has long hair like a blanket. That blanket of a dog smelled like velvet. The composer, aside from being blind and ailing, seemed quite content. Carmencita told him in a weary tone:

"The dog, Enrique..."

What problem could she possibly have with the dog? He was the most beautiful part of the afternoon. And she called that famous composer—who was none other than her own father—"Enrique"? And he let himself be criticized? And if he was almost blind or ailing, just how did he compose songs? And why was he in such a good mood? I'd seen sick people around before, in Moreno. They stayed in bed, or sat down. They didn't want to do anything. Sometimes they were taken out to the patio and every once in a while, they were offered something. Carmencita told him, in a weary voice:

"You've been smoking, Enrique."

"No," he said. "I've been fumigating. This house needs to be fumigated, it smells too much like health."

I was not familiar with the scent of health. In my opinion, that house had some sort of very faint perfume that came from the walls. And my aunt spoke to that famous man so naturally, as if she'd known him forever.

In real life I didn't know any geniuses, but I did have a book with drawings that told the story of Beethoven's life when he was young. There was a picture of him drawing water from a well, because he was so poor. The pictures in my book were black and white and Beethoven had a big head full of curls. Just to think—his deafness was already looming. How did he compose if he was deaf, anyway? Now, Enrique, Carmen's father, was different because he was almost blind. Which would be better? Being blind from birth or losing one's sight later in life? But there was something else: those snappy quips Carmen's father had—who did they remind me of? Of Yayo. Yayo was Olga's son. Olga was my father's cousin who actually lived in Buenos Aires. Six months earlier they'd come to visit one of my other aunts, and I just happened to be there. They'd sent the two of us off to play. Olga said dreamily:

"What a coincidence, Yayo and Yayi!" (People called me Yayi.)

That aunt invited everyone over, but there was something about Olga that made her different from my aunt and her sisters: while they wore little blue jackets and gray skirts, Olga had dyed her hair blond and wore sunglasses. I'd heard them calling her a little scatterbrained (they always toned everything down using the qualifier "a little"). And with my aunts it was impossible to ask about scatterbrainedness.

Yayo had blond hair—it was a beautiful copper color, and his face was a soft copper. I figured that Olga must take him out in the sun, but my mother told me the color of his hair was a result of the water in Buenos Aires. And that copper color gave him a slightly sickly appearance, which was very interesting in my opinion. But he didn't play with me, instead he tried to pester me. I had a dress with a bow in the back; he came running and untied it, I retied it. I wasn't annoyed: I felt flustered, out of place. I was almost a head taller than him, ten pounds heavier, and there I was, like a pole smack in the middle of the garden. And he said to me:

"I could run rings around you."

It's not that Enrique looked like Yayo physically—he was an old man, somewhat fat and certainly much nicer than Yayo. But there was something similar about their brisk gestures, the way they both left things unsaid.

We left. In the train on the way home we didn't speak much. I asked my aunt:

"So do you think the two of them will get back together?"

"I don't think so," said my aunt with that certainty adults had. I never knew just where they got it from.

"And is her father going to get better?"

"Nobody knows."

"But just how sick is he?"

"Oh…" said my aunt. The way she said that "oh" meant that I should stop asking questions.

When I got home, I told my mother everything, like I always did—with sound effects, stressing certain parts, etcetera. But I kept a few details to myself.

Tourists and Travelers

YOU'RE right, we did go to Miami. But that was different. Miami is all about "shop till you drop," that's what a tourist does. But on that program "Around the World" I heard Pepe Ibáñez explain the difference between tourists and travelers. A tourist is when you let yourself be led around like a sheep, and you don't notice anything around you. Like a horse in blinders. But seriously, did I even bother to tell you about my trip to Miami? All I saw was a couple of shopping malls and some palm trees. But I've got ever so much to say now! Besides, when I saw the pictures of Naples and Capri in the Sunday supplement I said to Aldo: "That's where we're going." Because you can never tell with him, you can never get a clear answer. You have to get him to sign a piece of paper just to find out what he wants. Why is that, anyway? I read it in an article called "Personality." Oh well, I forget. We scraped together all we could because I wasn't about to leave Leo behind. Besides, Leo studies Italian. I always wanted him to study English, which is so much more useful, and I thought: *Now is the time to cash in on that Italian.* But it was as if they didn't understand what it meant to have a project—I don't know which planet men live on. When I started pinching pennies—serving rice, eggs, and sausages—Leo kept saying,

"But Mama, but Mama!" with that scratchy voice of his (poor angel, his voice is changing). And Aldo just stirred his rice around in circles, as if he could magically whip it into cream, something that drives me up the wall. You can bet they got on my nerves once we were in Naples, too. You should have seen the hotel room, filled with antique furniture. (All three of us slept in the same room because that's how they do it there.) Aldo peeled back the bedspread as if it were a ghost's cape to see what was underneath—he's always poking around as if he were in search of some sort of dark secret. And Leo looked at the round chest of drawers with warped legs and said: "What a piece of shit!" The words that come out of that kid's mouth! And to make matters worse, he does it in front of other people. Aldo took out a guidebook but I said:

"We aren't going to go where everyone else goes. We are going to explore those little streets that wind around in circles. And if we get lost, even better."

They didn't like the idea of getting lost because they have no imagination. I've spent my whole life dreaming that I could just walk along until I end up somewhere new. It was as if I'd been given the chance to become someone else. So to convince them, I said:

"We'll walk straight down one street then turn around and walk back on the next street over."

We went out and realized that you can't walk straight: the streets just dead-end all the time: at an angle, in a circle. And the first thing we saw were three men arguing. They were gesturing vigorously, and I would have given my life to know what they were saying. I asked Leo and he told me:

"Just what do you think, Mama? They didn't teach me insults. What could they possibly be saying? 'I'll break your face, you bastard.'"

And I can't set him straight. He's got some reputation to live up to. Aldo stopped in front of a shop window to look at some food, all garnished. His mouth hung open like he'd never eaten in his life. I got all worked up and I said to him in a rage:

"Nobody looks at food! You look at clothes, magazines—but people don't get all worked up about food displays!"

He seems to understand me when I tell him stuff like that, but then he's back to his old tricks. He can't help looking at that kind of stuff. Another time he grabbed me by the arm and said:

"Look, a Neapolitan fag just walked by."

"A gay man, you mean."

"Same thing," he said. "You missed it."

And well, like I was telling you, we were walking down those little streets and we didn't even know where we were anymore, when some kids who must have been around eleven years old started throwing eggs at us. And they had pretty good aim from far away: eggs in my freshly washed hair, eggs on my ICARO jacket. There were two groups, one from the front and one from behind, because I turned around to see where the eggs were coming from and—*wham!* Right in the back of my head. And that boy of mine must have a screw loose. He was laughing! And just a hair away from teaming up with the others to go throw eggs at all of Naples. I'd had it with him. I asked him:

"Whose side are you on, anyway? Ours or theirs?"

"Uff! Mama!"

And since I noticed some policemen, I shouted for them to come over. They looked at me, scared. Clearly they thought there had been a crime or something like that, and I told them, using gestures, about how we had been pelted with eggs. The idiots just laughed and one said:

"Well, it's Carnival."

I would have given him a piece of my mind but I didn't know the language. And it took us a while to get back to the hotel, all covered in muck, because we ended up about ten blocks away. Why am I calling them blocks? More like ten spirals, because if the streets of Naples were all in a grid, we would have made it back just fine.

And I thought: *I didn't come all the way to Italy to do laundry.* Plus the water in Naples, which is really more like drool, got all mixed up with the disgusting egg. I wanted to cry. Those two dopes of mine turned on the TV and started watching soccer, which the Italians call *calcio*. It made me want to get on the first airplane home. I couldn't stop thinking about my show. You have to tell me what happened while I was gone. Did she marry the blond guy or the delinquent? Well, it turned out alright. Thank heavens. An afternoon frittered away, but the next day we went to buy some secondhand coats at the Naples flea market, just like a lady told me, and she also told me to keep an eye on my purse because you can get robbed there.

We set out for the market and the fight was on to keep our belongings safe; we weren't about to have another stroke of bad luck. And we walked to the bus stop, that way we could see everything. You wouldn't believe it—the windows of the houses look directly out on the street and you can see everything people are doing inside, as if you were right there with them. You can see if they're in bed, or if they open the refrigerator. Through one window I saw a piano, and on top of the piano there was a fruit bowl. I guess they like a real mishmash of styles. They like a real mixed bag when it comes to anything, because next to the church there's a fishmonger and the fishmonger picks up the fish as if he were picking up a cat by the ears and says: "*Mirate, mirate!*" And there goes Aldo again all dumbstruck as if he's never seen a fish before. And some of the people I saw through the window, they're so fat! It's really bad for their health. And they put huge death notices up on the walls. Leo noticed them (he *did* know how to read those). He came over and told me:

"Look, Ma, what a creepy sign!"

And I'm always trying to teach him about how we have to respect people's differences—although honestly the size of those things... But right by the bus stop there was something I just fell in love with. I just swooned. A giant charming manger where someone had sculpted the fishmonger, the baker, a bicycle—all crafted so beautifully. There were also sculptures of two women who were completely plastered in make-up, they looked like whores to me, but what do I know? Maybe they shouldn't have been included, I don't know. Say, did Teresa's apartment sell? Fat chance. Anyway, their buses are really nice. On the bus there were quite a few Africans, or *extracomunitarios*, which is used to describe anyone who lives in Italy but isn't from the EU. They're really well-behaved, really well-mannered. There was one man all dressed up in African garb and Aldo was just gaping at him. I had to pinch him because it's rude to stare at people like that. When you go on a trip you have to act like everything is perfectly natural. Besides, what if someone decides to beat the living daylights out of you? And the flea market has anything you could

ever want: beautiful shoes, boots, jackets, dresses. Dirt cheap!
In every stall there's a man up on a little stepstool who starts to
yell: "*Comprate, comprate!*" Beats me. They must climb up there
to get a better look at what's happening below because everything happens so fast that somebody comes along and snatches
something right out of your hand. I went to grab the same thing
as another lady and she could have just said: "I saw it first." You
have to pounce on everything you like and then take it over to a
little corner, which I did. But the guys are no help at all. If you
tell Aldo: "Grab that," he says: "Where?" And by then somebody
else has already taken it. Now, the vendors couldn't be sweeter
until they've sold you something, at which point they turn their
backs on you. They don't even look at you anymore. Afterwards
we sat down at a café and Leo wanted to open up all the packages
right away, wrapped in second-rate paper with flimsy strings.
We would've had to carry everything back to the hotel, slipping
out all over the place. I felt so good in that café! I started day-
dreaming: *To think I'm here in Naples! Who would have thought? If
only my great aunt could see me now, she was from somewhere around
here. Where was she from? I can't remember, and anyway, that woman
never did say a word about anything. Let me tell you: next time I'm
going alone, without those two.* Then I gave my order:

"*Un cortato. Cúanto costi?*"

And Leo goes:

"Aww, jeez Mama!"

The waiter just looked at me, he didn't understand (or he acted like he didn't understand) so Leo ordered for me. Since everything there ends with a "t" and an "i," so I honestly thought I was saying it right. At least that boy is good for something. I swear to you, I'm going to go back there one day and walk up and down all those streets that go in a circle.

The day we walked down Via Toledo (which is like their version of Calle Florida) we got into an argument. Leo wanted to go to a cybercafé and Aldo wouldn't get dressed to go out: he was watching television. I always have to be the one to lay down the law. He never says anything to that boy. He ends up being the absent father, like Dr. Socinsky says, and I flew off the handle—I'm telling you I just lost it. I told him that if he didn't speak up sometime soon he was going to get an ulcer, an anxiety attack, or something worse. And that boy of mine must have a screw loose because he grinned at me and said: "You want him to get an ulcer." I nearly slapped him across the face. He might know some Italian—that I won't deny—but he is not playing with a full deck. I thought: *I am all alone*, and again it made me want to get on the first plane home. Which is just a figure of speech because I was actually dying to go out to Via Toledo and just forget about the argument. Tell me: Did Adriana's mother get better? What a relief. Via Toledo is bustling with movement under a blue sky, which is not like the sky here, it's a vibrant light blue that fills you with life. How can I explain it? For starters, the street is filled with *extracomunitarios*, Africans. They pretty much all sell the same thing: Band-Aids and stuff, watches. Leo spoke with one man who said in Africa he had been a prince. Could that really be true? A prince, even an African prince, who sells Band-Aids? Who knows? And there was a Romanian sitting on the ground, selling kittens. He wanted to sell us one that was just darling, but you can't take a kitten into a hotel room. He said his brothers had immigrated to Argentina and he was there alone, with his cats. And he told us the name of one brother who's in Rosario, to see if we knew him. Just what does he think Argentina is? A speck on the map? I took the opportunity to tell him that Argentina is a huge country, that he's got it all wrong. That made me remember just how big it is, I'd like to explore the whole country, top to bottom. And right next to the Romanian there was a storefront with dolls. Heavens! No comparison to the dolls here. Have you ever noticed there are no nice dolls here? In Naples each doll was dressed for something different: a model walking down a catwalk, a skier on her ski slope, a little cook in her kitchen. It was a dream. When I stopped to look, Leo ducked into a cybercafé without telling us. Later that day we went back to look for him at the cybercafé and he wasn't there. And then Aldo made me even more nervous, he kept saying: "He'll show up." When that man gets an idea in his head there's no telling him otherwise. I went back to the hotel at my wit's end, ready to call the police or the consulate, and I realized just how much I love that boy. When we got to the hotel he was just sitting on the bed clipping his toenails. I could have killed him. That's when I decided that each of us should go out on our own and do whatever we wanted. Because Aldo wanted to see some catacombs with volcano lava—and I'm not about to go underground, it makes me claustrophobic. And if Leo wants to spend his life inside a cybercafé, he can go right ahead. Besides, with so much to see above ground, why would you bother with what's underground? At night Aldo would look at the guidebook over and over again, which makes my blood boil. You have to forget about the guidebook. You're in Naples and you're going waste your time looking at the guidebook? Go ahead, do whatever you want. I went out walking, to explore everything around me. I took a cable car—I didn't even know where it was headed, what a thrill! And I ended up in a rich neighborhood, right by the sea, all new houses. And there was a travel agency with a sign: "Weekend getaway to London, two hundred dollars." Just think, they go to London like we go to Mar del Plata. Two hundred dollars! I couldn't believe it. If I'd been by myself, I would have gone to London.

Later I reassured myself with the thought of how much more I still had left to see.

I've always been quite sensitive, things always really affect me deeply, you know? While I was out walking and walking I started to think: *Why did I ever get married to Aldo?* If you ask him whether he likes his food he says: "It's edible." He's like that with everything. And that boy of mine isn't interested in anything, only the cybercafé. He made a friend there who looked like a bona fide angel: blue eyes, curly hair, innocent little face. Then what do I find? The two of them in a plaza down the street firing rocks at the dogs with a little slingshot they'd made. That—and the fact that it took us forever to find each other when we went out on our own—led me to make a new rule: we were going to go out as a group again. Like Antonio Kalina says: family first, family has to be cultivated, if something's not growing, it's dying. And we were not growing as a family. Certainly I was growing, I was maturing, but family is like an animal: if one paw is wounded, the whole beast takes a turn for the worst. Plus my feet were covered in blisters from so much walking. No exaggeration. So at night, when Aldo took out the guidebook, I told him to pick somewhere we could all go together. Right away Leo says:

"Aww, Mama, I thought you said the guidebook was a pain in the neck!"

"Sometimes it is. Sometimes it isn't," I told him firmly.

"Uff!"

Leo wanted to hang out with Pier Paolo, angel face. So we had to drag him along on the excursion to Saint Francis of Assisi. The journey was unbelievable, filled with castles from long ago. The guide went along telling us which era they were from—although I'll bet he didn't even know them all himself. There were more castles than you could count. We went by a striking black castle, which I imagined to be inhabited by ancient ghosts, and Leo blurted out:

"What a piece of shit castle!"

I didn't say anything because I didn't want to make a scene on the bus, but also because he was actually paying attention to the guide—not that you could call the man anything remotely close to a real guide. He spoke Spanish—in a manner of speaking. And he said he had lived in Quilmes. I didn't believe a word of it because he looked like a rehabilitated prisoner. You know the type? Like rehabilitated alcoholics who look like they've just stepped out of confinement. This guy said:

"When Saint Francis got hot flashes he jumped in the river because the fires burned everything up."

Would you believe it! Just how is Saint Francis going to get hot flashes! It's him, the guide, who probably gets hot flashes and jumps in the river. With that no-good face of his. He was not a proper guide. A real guide should know more than the people he's guiding; but I had to keep my mouth shut because it was my idea to take the excursion. Somebody must have taken pity on that man and given him the job so he could earn a few bucks. What other job could he possibly get?

I always count my money because I think I don't have enough and when I find out I've got more than I thought, it makes me so happy. I wasn't about to do the laundry. I set off for the flea market to buy some things and the second time I was such a pro that I snagged the best of the bargains. I went on my own—the guys are a drag when it comes to shopping. How different it all is from the first day you get somewhere and your eyes take it all in—but now everything had become so natural! I'd already gotten used to seeing everyone through their open windows. A fat lady watching TV? Why not? The guy selling bootlegged CDs on the street? Might as well—I even said hello. I felt like I'd been born there. I loved the fact that they took me for a local, not a tourist. And I went back to Via Toledo, which by now I knew my way around like the back of my hand. It made me remember how impressed I'd been the first time I saw those Russians: two girls and an older man, two blonde girls playing the violin as if it were a real concert, and the man directing them as if he were the conductor of the Teatro Colón. They followed his every move.

Back in Russia they must play at a real theater. The girls were all dressed up. At first I would stop to watch them, they were there every day no matter what time and they passed around a little plate to collect coins. Then I stopped watching them, but I kept thinking about how they couldn't make any progress in life or get off the streets because the man playing the part of the conductor must have been their pimp. I walked by a bookstore and the bookseller was at the door. He spoke to me in Spanish:

"Argentina?"

How did he know that? What, do we all have it written across our forehead? At first I didn't like it one bit. I figured, of course, he'd noticed all my purchases. Besides, I didn't like him seeing all those flimsy packages because he was an elegant man. He spoke good Spanish because he'd lived in Argentina for a few years. He told me he had a house in Siena where everything was peaceful and quiet, but he'd moved to Naples because he missed the noise and the hubbub. What a conversation! A real Renaissance man. But that part about noise and silence didn't quite add up, because I heard on that program "Our Country from Top to Bottom" how everyone crowds together in Mar del Plata. It becomes a city brimming with noise, while there are so many havens for solitude out in nature where the silence is deafening. No, that wasn't it, it was "silence roars." And I also heard on "Our Country from Top to Bottom" that silence is superior to noise, it's more supreme. And that Italian gentleman, who was so cultured, surrounded by books, says he prefers noise over silence? What do I know? I had washed my hair the day before and my eyes looked good—because right after I wash my hair my eyes get all small and dark. And I have this problem: either my hair is clean and my eyes are flat, or my eyes are gleaming and my hair is *comsi-comsa*. My eyes were gleaming because I had been out walking. And since the bookseller kept talking and talking to me, and he told me about such-and-such festival of the Virgin where the men jump into the sea fully dressed, I thought: *Could he just be trying to pick me up? Could this all just be a pack of lies?* Who knows, maybe in Naples that's how they do it, just make up a bunch of nonsense. And then he told me how famous people, famous writers, walked up and down Via Toledo all the time. And they'd written almost everything there is to write about that street. Sure, they'd poked around town a bit. But one writer—I can't remember which—he'd spent the whole time in his room and he wrote about the city anyway. What? Could that bookseller surrounded by books have been lying to me? I wanted to leave because it was time to go eat and I couldn't figure out how to get away from him; but also because I wanted him to stop filling my head with all that nonsense. Those writers he named weren't who they claimed to be. Writers study, they research, and now it turns out that I had walked around town more than they had? Me, who only finished my freshman year? It didn't make any sense. Finally I made my exit like a real lady. I made a little gesture, gave him a little smile to stop him short, and he understood. Too bad I had to pick up all those damn packages from the ground because ladies do not carry packages. One of the strings started to unravel on my way out, but he didn't notice.

On our last day the guys really started to get under my skin. Aldo waited until the last minute to pack his suitcase. He packed it all wrong so I had to unpack everything and repack it for him. I arranged everything just so. He didn't even bat an eye—he doesn't give a damn. Leo didn't want to wear his jacket. We were like the Three Stooges as we walked down the street arguing. On the plane I said to Leo:

"Don't put that bag up top because it's going to fall."

But he put it up there anyway. I don't know what he had in there, and I don't care. I was annoyed and I don't know why: it wasn't because of them. Was it because I was leaving Naples? On the way to the airport there was a beggar waving a hat around as if he were bidding farewell to someone leaving on a train, and I felt like he was waving goodbye to me. I got a little bit emotional because I thought: *Who knows if I'll ever come back?* I'm always talking about going everywhere, walking around, exploring—once I even wanted to go to Antarctica but you just can't go wherever on a whim. I gave them a look that said *Don't even talk to me*, and I was so annoyed that I forgot how scared I was to get on airplanes. Then I tried to calm myself down because it can't be good for the flight, that doesn't help. I closed my eyes and the beggar waving his hat on the street came to me, fanning himself with the hat. Then I remembered about how everyone jumps into the sea, fully dressed. One by one they jump in, and I also remembered how they pour milk into the coffee. They pour it from a distance, in circles, as if they were gently tucking in a baby. And then I fell asleep.

Christmas Eve in the Park

I T'S nine o'clock in the evening and there's a strange mix of people in the park. One guy is out for a run, but not like someone who consciously prepares to go jogging. He looks disheveled, like someone who's just about to wrap up his day after a million comings and goings. Finally, after that last little lap, he'll go home to shower and change. There's a boy riding around on his new bike. The lights from the Christmas tree reflect off the bike, making it shine. A beautiful woman is out walking a handsome healthy dog, his tongue hangs out affectionately. The dog has a white coat and his body is an enormous mass that glides along, his fur grazing the ground. On the sidewalk, two old neighbors weighed down with bundles greet each other as if they haven't crossed paths in a long time; they get caught up in gossip as they say their farewells.

Across from the park is the San Gabriel Veterinary Clinic: they treat dogs, cats, parrots, and also one sheep. Most of the animals are members and pay a monthly fee. In the waiting room, an employee sits at the computer admitting clients. She gives them each a slip of paper, constantly picking up the phone to say: "San Gabriel, good evening." The computer keeps the animals' names on file. They strut on by: Felipe, Celeste,

Duquesa, Pituco, Beethoven. Her tone is flat and neutral as she pronounces their names. To her, they're just clients. The walls are lined in white tile up to the ceiling; the light is even and yellow. Where it comes from is a mystery—not one light fixture, not one lamp. In the park, the Christmas tree, all decked out, shines its light onto the people passing by, who then cross through a patch of darkness. Inside the veterinary waiting room the light softens people's idiosyncrasies, as if they were all the same patient. One lady has a kitten in her arms. The two are motionless, waiting for a dose of medicine. It seems as if she's been waiting a long time in the same position. She looks like a sad and somewhat poor mother, as if she were embarrassed by her child's disease. In the far corner, a much younger woman sits scowling with a mutt passively next to her. She's done its hair up with a little red ribbon, forming a lopsided plume, which the dog wears with complete disregard, as if the hairdo were not part of its body. She speaks to it in a hushed voice—a voice that must be much louder and more energetic at home. She talks to the dog so everyone knows that she is a tough and progressive woman:

"Pamela, sit up straight."

And farther down, alone, an elderly couple and a dog that's lived with them for a long time: you name it, he's got it; and it's clear they will patiently cure him of all his ills. He looks pleadingly at his owners, as if to ask, *What does fate have in store for me today?* The only voice calling the shots is the employee's: the telephone calls continue. Name? Farolero. Problem? Ear infection. Name? Jasmine. Problem? Mumps.

Perhaps the people in the waiting room feel somewhat overwhelmed by the realization that there are so many critters with problems in this world. It's not just them. The world is filled with problems; they feel like a needle in a haystack. And perhaps that feeling is heightened when a sleek, skinny young woman comes in with a greyhound, her canine doppelganger. They walk in with the flippancy of frequent visitors, just dropping by on their way to a more pleasant place: this dog is the picture of health. The employee says to the dog:

"Hello baby…"

Inside, beyond the waiting room, the atmosphere changes entirely. There are three nurse's stations where the dogs and cats get their IV lines. Here the light is different; there are bright spotlights above the stretchers and areas of shadows. At one station sits a couple with a kitten: the woman is blond and the man has dark hair. They are smiling and calm, as if they were sitting under a tree chatting. In another room there are more people monitoring their pets' IV lines; the mood is cordial, everyone talks to one another, and a handsome young veterinarian named Roman strides around as if he were walking down the street. A couple who look like they come from a modest neighborhood sit watching over their dog hooked to an IV. They're both dressed in shabby clothes, her hair is somewhat mussed. They both exhibit exuberance; they come off as a couple with four dogs, five cats, and one sheep. The woman says to the veterinarian, teasingly:

"Roman, be careful that Popi doesn't bite you."

The chances of this happening seem slim because Popi is in a lethargic state. Roman doesn't answer, he just walks back and forth. She presses him further:

"Roman, should I feed him that special dog food? Last time it didn't go down so well."

"Mhh-mmh," says Roman, as if echoing the first suggestion.

And at a much larger table, alone, there's an older man of an indeterminate age. His hair is dyed a chestnut brown, but there's nothing charming about him: it's as if he started to dye his hair a long time ago and now he does it out of habit. His clothes are reminiscent of something an athlete might wear, throwing on whatever they can find to cover up; and his brown coat is like an old habit. His haggard appearance contrasts with his energy; when Roman walks by he says loudly:

"The care today pales compared to yesterday. Yesterday they gave him a real massage so he would poop. This is ridiculous."

Roman paces back and forth; he doesn't seem to take the hint. The man is holding on to a cat's paw, with an

IV line in it. He's an alley cat who showed up at his mechanic's garage, he says. Luckily, a nice lady started to feed this cat and some others, too. The cat is splendid, filthy and—with what's left of his health—ornery. The man says to him, over and over:

"C'mon little guy, lie down a bit. That's it, that's right."

And he carefully holds onto the cat's paw so the IV line doesn't fall out.

"Lie down, lie down. The care yesterday was much better. I've been here since eight o'clock."

It's ten o'clock at night and this man will keep holding onto the cat's paw as long as he has to. Suddenly his mobile phone rings and he says:

"No, I won't make it to dinner. I'm still here."

The cat is bored, but he puts up with the immobility as if it were a necessary evil. At times he tries to get up, but his owner lays him back down so that the sacred IV line doesn't fall out. The cat looks at him every once in a while as if to say: *Alright, if you say so.* And he lies down to humor the man, curling his backside up against the man, as if to take a nap.

The man says to the couple with the dog:

"He's so smart. As soon as he sees me, he comes running. Yesterday they gave him a massage, like this."

And he pats the cat's behind with one hand, without letting

go of the paw. The cat's rump seems to say, *I'll poop when I'm good and ready.*

Roman walks by, like someone making the rounds at a dance hall.

"Is he getting enough saline?"

No answer. Then he says:

"Maybe it's the water he drank. When he was out on the street he didn't have access to good water. Why don't you give him some more saline?"

Roman answers these questions by gracefully tossing his lab coat onto a chair. As if by magic, he's wearing a jacket and he's at the door; his replacement has arrived. The replacement is an old man with a pained, canine expression. His face is that of one who has seen it all and who every so often takes pity on someone. He says:

"That's enough saline for today. We'll keep him ticking as long as we can."

And then, as if he were suffering on behalf of the cat, as if it were his own, the replacement vet says:

"He's very sick, but spry at the same time."

"Should I come back tomorrow?"

"Come on back tomorrow, we'll be here. Good night and good luck."

"Thank you, doctor."

The man grabs a cardboard box printed with the words: SMALL ANIMAL CARRIER. It's decorated with dogs, little cats, and flowers: a clear, happy box fit for a picnic. The glass door of the veterinary clinic is printed with the same design: little cats and dogs, flowers. The proximity of the green park affords a glimmer of hope. The man hesitates at the door and then walks to the only open bar, on the corner. Some fireworks go off and the cat stirs inside the box.

"C'mon little guy, we'll be home soon."

He enters the bar with his box.

There's only one customer inside, a harmless drunk, the kind who has the same temperament whether it's one drink, two drinks, or five. The drunk clears his throat and the waiter brings him another glass of wine. The waiter blithely watches the television, switching between a European league soccer game and a Venezuelan soap opera. The drunk clears his throat again, and the waiter brings him another wine. The man places the little box with the cat on the ground next to him. He sits down and orders:

"Boss, I'll have a glass of cider and some olives."

Some kids, far from the bar, are setting off fireworks in the park. The sound is muted and the cat is still in his box, as if it were his little house. The man runs his hand over the box and thinks: *Who knows if he's going to live? No, the care was no good today…If only the tall man from yesterday had been there…What if he doesn't make it? What if he doesn't live? Then I'll donate his organs to science. They study all sorts of things.*

He gets distracted thinking about science: What a wonder! All that progress that nobody could even imagine fifty years ago! And how they study and learn all about those tiny little bodies! But then he thinks about the little guy, dead, and he says to himself: *No, not his whole body; just a couple of organs.*

"Waiter, I'll have another glass of cider and some more olives."

He's not going to have more than two glasses. After the second he decides that he'll bury what's left of the little guy in his backyard, his name written on a slab of wood. Maybe he'll make it, maybe he won't. His enthusiasm for science peters out because it dawns on him: *They die without knowing any words. They die as if it were nothing.* He always reads the back page of the newspaper, the section with quotes by famous people who leave some sort of advice when they die, something they wanted people to know, anything at all. But in this case…No, that wouldn't work out.

"Waiter, a cup of coffee, please."

He'll stay a bit longer. He'll go back to the clinic, maybe there will be someone new on duty. He's going to suggest another round of saline and a good pat on the rump.

"Merry Christmas, waiter."

"The same to you," says the waiter, smiling, and he walks back behind the bar to change the channel.

At the Hair Salon

THE hair salon feels entirely separate from the outside world, as far removed as the cinema. It's so isolated that when I'm bored at the hair salon I can't help but think about my favorite bar on the corner, and with my hair covered in that tar they use to dye it, I say to myself: "I want to go get some coffee right now, wearing this black smock, with my hair all plastered down." Luckily, for the sake of my reputation, I then conclude that getting coffee is as far away and impossible as a trip to Chascomús. With my dyed hair I look at myself in the mirror. It's not like my mirror at home—at home I look better. In the mirror at the hair salon I notice all my imperfections, like the tired eyes that make me look groggy. I wore an old sweater so I wouldn't have to worry about getting it stained, and in the light of the mirror I can tell how old it really is—it doesn't look like this at home. Since I look so shabby I have to be nice to compensate; I have to demonstrate that I'm a reasonable person, that I would never say out loud what I'm thinking: *I want to go to the bar on the corner, or to the ATM, or to buy some pears.* So I chat with the hairdresser—he says his name is Gustavo—and I ask him if he works long hours and what time of day business gets slow and whether they cut children's hair. I know all the answers, and even if I didn't, I couldn't care less. My conversation with the hairdresser leads me to reflect on all the time and effort we spend on small talk, which in turn makes me feel tired and resentful. I figure if I were more attractive he would treat me better. If I were pretty I could be pushy and I'd be able to put up with them using toner on my hair. I wish I could be one of those ladies who drives her hairdresser crazy saying, "Higher up... shorter... No, the other side... No, more down the middle." But even if I were attractive, I would never have the patience to make all those demands. I'm more like this taxi driver I met once. We chatted about teeth and dentists, and he told me what he said to his dentist:

"Look, I don't have time to get my teeth pulled one by one. Just take 'em all out."

Six teeth.

With my hair covered in dye—my head is freezing—I'm going to get my feet done, and I feel better there. They show me to a cubicle in the back because heads can be displayed in public, but feet cannot. There are two pedicurists, Violeta and María. (The hairdressers are always changing.) Violeta is Ukrainian and I want to know all about her country but I can never get her to say anything more than, "Oh, it's a little different, but mostly the same as here." I don't know if she's hiding something or if she just doesn't give a damn—she's really pretty and no one seems to have noticed. She walks around like a shadow, gliding along as if she didn't even have a body. No, she couldn't care less about being pretty. That's why, when she's there, I prefer María, who comes from Corrientes. She reminisces about all the animals her father kept in the countryside: the armadillo, the little mare fed on a bottle, and the woodpecker. And suddenly that cold, stark white cubicle is bursting with little animals from the countryside and the forest. Now I couldn't care less about the bar on the corner. I've forgotten about the ATM and the pears: I want to go to Corrientes to see the woodpecker. I'm starting to relax somewhat because the goop on my head is drying out while they do my feet. I can't bear to sit still—doing nothing or having nothing done to me—because I feel like the world around us never stops. It's like when I'm boiling vegetables and at the same time keeping tabs on a soccer game or a tennis match on TV if Argentina's playing: I do everything all at once. So, on my epitaph, they'll put what they did for Roman matrons: *Fecit lanam*. (She spun her wool).

Then the girl who washes our hair calls me over. These girls are always changing too, but for different reasons than the hairdressers: the stylists walk out slamming the door behind them, or they find work at another salon. When the girls who wash our hair realize they'll never be given a job as a stylist (except the occasional girl who's really bright and pursues a career), they start staying home to watch the afternoon soaps. There are different social classes at the salon. The guy who runs the register, sitting in a tall swivel chair, is upper-class. Everyone has to take their paperwork over to him. The pedicurists are like their own parallel group: hard to classify because they don't interact with each other as much as the hairdressers. Besides, the hairdressers move around in a central area, with mirrors and posters of gorgeous women with shiny hair. There are no photos of hands or feet, it seems that limbs are merely accessories. The girl who sweeps up the hair from the floor is part of the lower class; she doesn't make coffee for the clients or blow-dry their layers. There's nothing special about her hair, she just wears it up in a regular ponytail. When the girl washes my hair I'm relieved, I'm one step closer to that coffee on the corner. She scrubs my head with her pointy fingernails. If she really went to town, my scalp would bleed. Instead, she rations out the assault like a cat.

It was Natasha the pedicurist who really went the extra mile; she was the opposite of Violeta. Natasha was like a tractor plowing away in that white cubicle. She used some sort of gadget that runs along the soles of the feet, as if she were tilling the soil or a vast field of wheat, for example. She was destined for heroic deeds, like driving a tank in the steppe—not for minor remedies of the hands and feet. She couldn't handle the clients' complaints (they said everything hurt) and she went back to the Ukraine.

Once my hair has been washed I go back to find the hairdresser. Was it Gerardo or Gustavo? I forget that I'm supposed to come off as a sensible, courteous lady and I tell him gruffly:

"Trim all along the top and down the back, but on top I want it to look like a carancho's nest."

He doesn't ask what this hairstyle involves. I don't know whether even he knows what a carancho is, or what its nest looks like (I sure don't). He looks at me like he's heard it all before and readies his scissors. I leave upbeat.

Leonor

WHEN Leonor was a girl her mother made cassava flour balls, which are hard as lead, dry as sand, and viciously compact. If you eat them when you're feeling sad it's like ingesting a wasteland. But if you're happy, those brown balls, without a trace of oil, are a well-deserved, nutritious food.

When Leonor grew up and turned eighteen her mother told her, "It's time you get married, dear. You get a certificate when you get married. The man brings white bread and high-heeled shoes. After you marry the Pole, he'll bring your mama some earrings."

Leonor said, "Alright Mama, but the Pole is so tall."

The Pole was over six feet tall; he pulled up weeds all day and never went dancing on Sundays. He worked.

"What does that matter?" her mother asked.

"Alright Mama," said Leonor. "I'll get married, but I'm embarrassed to speak in his presence."

Her mother said, "You won't be embarrassed forever. Besides, he never talks. Just ask him, 'Would you like a bowl of beans?' And one day you'll eat beans; another day, you'll make bread with white flour, and he'll be happy because you're such a good girl. Always make sure there's a smile on your face, never talk back to him, and he'll soften up and speak. One thing for sure: never provoke him. He knows how to use a hoe and a shovel."

The wedding party was beautiful. He gave Leonor a pair of high-heeled shoes and a red dress. She couldn't walk very well in those shoes, and he sensed she wasn't comfortable so he walked her over to a chair. They watched the whole spectacle seated right there and people came over to greet them. But the real champions of that lively party were the musicians. Someone had invited musicians from another village; they weren't from around there. At times, Leonor thought, *This whole party is because I got married, because it's an important day.* Then she forgot, she listened to the music and watched people dancing as if it were all for someone else.

Her mother was calm and quiet at the party, she relaxed. Afterwards, Leonor went to visit her mama. She took the earrings with her and a bit of white bread. As she was leaving she hesitated and said:

"Mama…"

"What is it, dear?"

"The Pole treats me right, but I'm scared of him."

"Have you wanted for anything? Has he hit you, m'dear?"

"No Mama, but he speaks in strange tongues when he's out among the fields and if I ask him a question when he's talking like that, he shoots me a furious look. So sometimes I don't even know when to speak up."

Her mother thought and thought and then she said:

"Perhaps he's been bewitched by a bad spirit. Let's go see Isolina."

When they went to see Isolina, she asked, "Which type of plant is he standing next to when he speaks in tongues?"

Leonor, troubled by the imperious tone of the question, didn't quite know how to answer.

Isolina said the spirit wasn't bad or dangerous, just reluctant. Leonor would have to be patient until it went away. Isolina could send for another spirit to confront the reluctant one—but then they ran the risk of the reluctant spirit getting jumpy, which could be serious. Isolina advised prudence and patience to see what came of it.

Leonor was unhappy when she left Isolina's because she hadn't been able to say what she had really wanted: she hadn't been able to express herself properly. The words just didn't come to her. There were so many things that she couldn't tell her mother, like how every Saturday from her house she could hear the sound of music coming from a dance hall, and she felt like her feet were going to walk right out from under her and take her over there. After she'd done all her chores and cleaned the house she would walk a little closer to listen to the music and watch the people from afar.

Once she had children she forgot about her husband, and even about her mama. She loved her children dearly. She liked to watch how they walked—how tiny their feet were—and she never hit them.

If a few days went by without Leonor going to see her mother, her mother would say:

"M'dear, don't be spoiling the children so."

"Alright, Mama," Leonor would say.

But she thought, *I think maybe Mama's jealous.*

By the time Hugo turned five Leonor took him with her to collect firewood and he said:

"Careful where you step, Mama."

He wanted to carry a big bundle of firewood all by himself. Once the younger ones fell asleep, she'd say to Hugo:

"Want to come with me down by the road, Hugo?"

And Hugo would go along with her. Down by the road a car passed every now and then and sometimes they saw someone they knew. They stayed awhile and then Hugo said:

"Let's go back, Mama, it's cold."

"Yes, dear," she answered.

When Hugo was eight and Maria was six, Leonor wanted to send them to school. Until then she hadn't been able to, because sending Hugo alone would have been unproductive: Hugo worked with his father while Maria didn't do anything. But if Hugo and Maria went together it would kill two birds with one stone: Hugo would learn something *and* accompany his sister. The father was of another mind: wait a bit longer, until the third child was old enough too. When he expressed his opinion Leonor raised her voice, she looked at him scornfully and said:

"School means an education!"

Hugo said, "I want to go to school."

The father became nervous, his eyes flashed and he went out to get the hoe, jabbering nonsense. Outside he struck the ground with the hoe several times and when he came back in he started drinking wine. From then on, at night, after work, he drank a few glasses of wine. Hugo drew a cow in his notebook taking great pains to make it look like a real cow. Leonor watched him and said:

"Good work, son."

But what she really enjoyed were the verses Maria learned. At night, after dinner, Maria recited:

La casita del hornero
tiene sala y tiene alcoba,
limpia está con todo esmero
aunque en ella no hay escoba.

The ovenbird's little nest
Has a lounge and a room,
It always looks its best
But inside you'll find no broom.

Soon enough, Leonor sent the third child to school because she loved education.

Their father became more and more distant, as if he didn't care about anything. He showed up only for meals.

When Hugo was fifteen years old he said to Leonor, "Mama, I want to go work in Buenos Aires. There's no work here."

"Alright m'dear, if it's to make a better life for yourself and your family, go ahead."

Father didn't say anything about Hugo's idea. Grandmother was a little worried about him leaving and said to Leonor, "What a spoiled little boy you've raised!"

Leonor lost her patience and said, "He's not spoiled, Mama! Hugo is going to work. He's a serious boy."

Before he left, Leonor washed and ironed all his clothes. He borrowed a suitcase and was given a little red kerchief as a gift, to keep his neck warm. She told him:

"Son, you're going to make a better life for yourself and for your family. Don't keep bad company, work your tail off, and behave yourself. You have to find your way without stepping on anyone else's toes. Understand, son?"

"I know, Mama. I know," Hugo said.

He held onto his suitcase like a man and he didn't want anybody to go to the station with him. Nobody cried on account of his leaving—he would be back, or they would go visit him. Hugo was glad no one went to see him off. What if he ended up crying himself?

The first few days after he got to the city he constantly felt dizzy, but he told himself, "I've got to give it six months, then I'll get used to it." Someone from work taught him how to use the door phone; a lady helped him with the elevator. One Saturday night he went out with another fellow and they took the subway for the first time. Being in the dark tunnel was frightening yet thrilling.

A few days after Hugo had left, a Turk holding a suitcase stopped outside Leonor's house. He was selling handkerchiefs, combs, little boxes, and miniature statues. This Turk didn't travel by foot, he had a car and he brought out things to show her: teacups, glasses, vases, napkins. There were some beautiful little floral teacups.

"Those are from Japan," said the Turk.

"From where?" asked Leonor.

"From Japan," said the Turk matter-of-factly. "Brought over."

"Of course, from Japan, Mama," said Maria, irritated because her mother didn't know where they were from.

And Leonor went crazy buying little teacups and handkerchiefs and everything she liked.

"Don't buy so much, Mama. Papa will get angry."

"Then we won't tell him," said Leonor, who was happy.

Maria felt annoyed with her mother just then; the reason (or reasons) were unclear to her. The Turk was worldlier than Leonor, as if he were wiser and more respectable. Leonor made her purchases rashly, without stopping to think about all the things the Turk wanted to sell her. In the end, a large part of Maria's annoyance came from seeing her mother so happy, beaming in a way that Maria couldn't handle. So she told her father what Leonor had done; his face darkened. Leonor, who barely noticed, looked at him and thought, *Bah!*

The father drank quite a few glasses of wine and went to bed.

That week there were developments. First there was the Turk, and then there was a letter from Hugo. He had always been a good writer. The letter read:

Dear Mother, Sisters, and Brother,
I hope everyone is well. I'm doing fine here in Buenos Aires. Mama, please give Grandmother the brown blanket because I'm

sending another one for you. I'm also sending a dress for Pili, for her to use when she goes to town. As for Maria, I don't know her size so I'll have to wait. Tell Maria to write if my little brother goes to school and to keep him on a short leash. I'll visit in December, but meanwhile keep me abreast of any news. Send my love to Papa.

Hugo Bilik

Grandmother didn't understand anything anymore. Nobody asked her opinion about anything. There were actions and events occurring at that house that bewildered her. Something just wasn't right at that house. You shouldn't give your children more education than you received yourself—then your children get ahead of you in life. For example, Isolina's son buys the newspaper and reads it in front of his own mother. When it comes to girls, things have gotten even worse. Girls, with all that education, start looking at men eye-to-eye; they get used to talking to men as if it were nothing, and then they start saying things a girl shouldn't say. The words that come out of a girl's mouth these days!

Leonor started to raise chickens to sell them down by the road, and her youngest son went along with her. There were more people and more cars on the road now and she learned how to do business with all those people in their cars. Sometimes they paid well.

Once she had saved up some money she told her husband, "I'm going to Buenos Aires for a few days to see Hugo. I'll be back soon."

He said, "Go on, I'm staying here."

He seemed so bitter, so sad, and so withdrawn that she said, "But I'll only be a few days."

"Go on," he said.

And that was the end of it.

The little one stayed with Grandmother; Maria and Pili got brand-new shoes for the trip. They took some plates, some clothes, and a lot of food to eat on the train.

Leonor loved education, but she enjoyed the trip even more: the entire train was one big celebration. One man played the accordion; a group of people drank yerba mate and told jokes in another row. Further down some men played cards on a suitcase.

When nighttime came the temperature dropped, and it was very cold on the train. The lady sitting in front of them, who had given them some mate, said:

"You didn't bring any blankets?"

"No ma'am, what for?" Leonor asked.

"Because it gets cold on the train and you have to bundle up."

"Oh…" said Leonor, confused.

"Just a moment, ma'am," she said. She opened her suitcase and gave each girl a sweater, and she gave Leonor some sort of knit blanket that was purple and very warm. Pili went right to sleep while Maria gave a grumpy look to Leonor and the lady. Finally, the two girls were both fast asleep, leaning against one another. After that first deep sleep they woke up halfway. Then a man passed by; he walked up and down the aisle all night while the others slept or spoke in low voices. He brushed up against Pili, which startled her. She wasn't sure whether it had been a man, or if maybe she'd been dreaming—maybe it had been a cat or she'd just brushed up against the seat. At first she was scared, but then she fell back asleep on Leonor's lap.

By daybreak, lots of people were awake, preparing mate. It felt like a regular house inside the train, but outside daybreak wasn't the same as in Chaco. In Chaco when the sun rose, its rays immediately lit up everything. Here, from the window, there was a big sun on the horizon delicately casting light over the plains.

As it dawned, even though there was nothing but fields in every direction, signs of something else started to emerge: there were bridges all around, big iron equipment, cars crossing here and there, indifferent to one another, and huge signs advertising cigarettes and beer.

By the time the sun had risen completely, almost everyone was busy. They rearranged their suitcases, brought down bags: everyone set into motion. Leonor didn't know who to ask about getting to Hugo's place: "El Zorzal and Jorge Newberry, Paso del Rey." The only person walking up and down the train was the man who had brushed up against Pili; he didn't seem to have a suitcase to fuss with so Leonor asked him. He wasn't sure, but he walked up and down the train asking everyone until he found out. She eventually found the place even though she ended up asking directions at least ten times.

When Hugo saw Leonor and his two sisters approaching—two overgrown girls in their canvas sneakers—he wasn't surprised. He felt embarrassed and ashamed. What were his neighbors going to say? Not only that, he was ashamed of his own embarrassment. He found them on the street, half lost, and Leonor pounced on him as if she had unearthed heaven itself. He said somewhat standoffishly:

"Hello Mama, did you just get in?"

"Yes, son," replied Leonor, perplexed, because she thought Hugo was acting strange. He asked another question:

"Is that your only suitcase?"

"We only came to visit you." She took a look around and smiled, "And to see Buenos Aires, which is so lovely."

Hugo didn't exactly live in Buenos Aires proper. Paso del Rey was a place with low-rise housing and empty lots, a little garden here, a horse and cart over there, and a road filled with cars and big trucks that read: "Goya Freight," "Goya–Buenos Aires Express Coach," "Freight Products."

Once they were inside Hugo changed. He became more affectionate, more pleasant, the Hugo they knew and loved. The girls seemed awkward; they stood motionless in their sneakers, too self-conscious to sit down. And then there was his mother, with nothing more than a suitcase—no doubt penniless—and the girls like two sparrows waiting for a meal. He didn't speak. He didn't know whether to reproach his mother, ask her why she had turned up like that, or cover her in hugs and kisses. Looking out the window at a plot of land with beams and pipes lying in a pile on the ground, Leonor promptly asked:

"Is that land part of this property?"

"No, Mama. I only rent this room."

Leonor wanted to cook right away. She'd brought a kerosene stove with her, but Hugo said:

"No, Mama. There's already a stove here."

All you had to do was light a match and the stove lit up. Hugo's house was a marvel! There was a sponge, powdered soap, bunk beds with a little ladder to climb up top, a lamp, and a bicycle.

"Oh, Hugo, it's all so lovely!" said Leonor.

"Yes Mama," said Hugo, somewhat guarded.

For the girls, it felt like being at a pasha's house. Hugo went out; he seemed worried again. When he returned he'd brought another fellow with him, who he introduced as Antonio. He said:

"Pleased to meetcha, lady…My pleasure, miss."

He drew out the words at the end of each phrase, as if he were waiting for something. Hugo asked Antonio, in what seemed like a calm voice, his anger bottled up inside, "Could you lend me a mattress?"

"Aw, really kid?" said Antonio. "Of course!" Teasing him melodramatically in that raspy voice.

"Thanks," said Hugo. He smiled, perking up a bit, and cracked some jokes with Antonio while they brought in the mattress.

Leonor was impressed by Antonio. What a fine accent that boy from Buenos Aires had! Wait, was he from Buenos Aires?

"Hugo, is your friend from Buenos Aires?"

"No," said Hugo, "But he came here when he was really young."

"No wonder, he sounds just like someone from Buenos Aires!" Leonor said. Buenos Aires was a fascinating place.

One day while Leonor and the two girls were together she told them, "Girls, it's time you get married."

"But Mama," protested Pili, "the boys here aren't like the ones from Chaco. Here they say one thing but they're thinking something else. Back home I always knew exactly what they were thinking. All it took was a look."

Leonor just laughed and pulled Pili down on her lap. The girls had grown so big.

Maria said, "They're the same here and there and everywhere. It's just…" she added with disgust, "you're just thinking of Roque…"

Pili didn't say anything. Leonor asked Pili, who was still on her lap, "What about Antonio? You don't like him?"

Pili said, "Sure Mama, but…"

Leonor ran her fingers through Pili's hair, pinning it back, and said, "Antonio's a good fellow. I'm telling you he's good."

Pili was quiet and contemplative for a while, then she left feeling relaxed and calm

Maria repeated to herself, "They're the same no matter where you go."

Maria found a boyfriend, but it was strange how it happened. The boy started to court her by saying:

"You're fat. That coat doesn't fit you."

To which she retorted, "What about your hair? It looks like a wire brush!"

To anything he said, Maria remarked, "Sure, sure, just because *you* say so."

Sometimes he said, "Don't be such a pain! The day you least expect it I'm out the door and..."

To which Maria responded, "Go ahead and flap your gums, but it'll cost you!"

At first, seeing them fight like that, everyone thought they'd gone mad; then people started to see the humor and finally everyone got used to them, it all became perfectly natural. They were an indestructible couple.

Leonor went out to buy herself a dress one day when the stars were favorable for buying clothes. On such days, you could look at the storefront and say:

"That's the one for me."

And you knew it would fit like a glove; in fact, you knew it had been made just for you and you adored that dress. When the stars send us indecision we scrutinize every color, shape, and texture. We study everything with a critical eye.

Leonor wore the new dress home from the shop. Next to the new dress, her old one, limp and sad, seemed to say, *You'll never love me again.*

It was Saturday night. Maria had gone to Chaco for a few days. Hugo combed his hair, changed his clothes, and shaved.

"I'm going out dancing for a while, Mama," he said in a serious voice.

"Oh…" said Leonor.

She was alone. Pili had gone dancing with Antonio somewhere else. They were going to get married.

"Of course, Hugo," said Leonor. "Go on, go out dancing."

But the thought of staying home in that new dress was unbearable. Then, out of the blue, Hugo proposed, "Alright, let's both go dancing. C'mon, c'mon."

Pleased as pie, Leonor went to the dance. First she danced a cumbia with Hugo. Then she thought, *Now I'll just watch.* As she watched on, enchanted by everything, a blond fellow with blue eyes came over to her. He was younger than Leonor, around thirty-four years old. Why did he ask her to dance? It had been a long time since she had danced.

He asked her, "Do you dance with younger men?"

"No," Leonor said smiling proudly, "that's my son."

He seemed to be from Buenos Aires, but his voice was so smooth—not like Antonio's scratchy voice. He told her his parents were French. Leonor thought of how the French have lots of money.

He wasn't from Buenos Aires, he was from Neuquén, but he spoke like a Porteño. It was clear he was a sensible fellow, he wasn't trying to step on anyone's toes; he was a gourmet. When he'd asked her whether she liked dancing with younger men there was a certain degree of mockery in his voice, as if he found it mildly humorous, but feasible nonetheless. He wasn't shocked, but he'd asked her coyly, as if he had some sort of right to know.

He told her that his family was rich and powerful. *Of course,* thought Leonor, *could you expect anything less from the French?* He'd quarreled with them, but some day he would go back south to reclaim his part of the inheritance. Meanwhile, he was a gourmet. Leonor asked:

"What's a gourmet?"

"Restaurant guild, pizzerias, stuff like that."

He was really important. And she danced with him all night. She couldn't say "no" to that voice of his—a voice that was domineering yet somehow soft-spoken. It wasn't like Hugo's voice, which sounded like her own; this voice was different, foreign. At first she wondered why he had chosen her, but when they danced it was all so natural.

Hugo came over to the table with a girl that wasn't from the neighborhood and said, "Mama, tonight I'm not going home because we're going to another dance after this. Do you want me to walk you home?"

"Go on son, don't worry about me."

After all, Hugo always did the right thing.

Only afterwards did it dawn on her that he was with a girl she'd never seen and the two of them were rushing out the door, but she could only remotely register any of this, so in a strange stern voice that she hardly ever used she said:

"Bundle up!"

Hugo turned around, puzzled at first, as if she'd been talking to someone else, but when he understood her message, he left smiling. Calmly, the blond man watched all this unfold. When the dance ended Leonor took him home with her. And that's how things evolved; sometimes he stayed at Leonor's house and sometimes he went home.

On Sundays, he came over while she was sleeping, calling out, "Loli!" because that's what he called her. Then he would cook and prepare cocktails because he was a gourmet.

One day, referring to Maria, he said, "Your older daughter is so mean!"

Leonor didn't know what to say. Why would he say that?

He drank wine sometimes, but it didn't hurt anyone. Once Maria told Leonor, "He drinks wine and he's too young for you."

He got along with Hugo. Hugo had gotten married. The two told jokes together, and Leonor pretended like she had another child in the house. Maria approached the blond fellow one day and said to him:

"Get out! Leave my mother alone!"

He didn't respond. He just told Leonor again, "Your older daughter is so mean!"

Absent-mindedly, Leonor thought, *I wonder why he thinks Maria is so mean.*

She didn't listen to what he said. She was happy, everything felt normal. They had a little girl together, who turned out blonde Creole, with skin the color of sawdust. All the older children had gotten married and they pampered the little girl.

When Leonor's boyfriend was around it was all fair weather. He made delicious food and cocktails, and when everyone got together on Sundays it was a downright celebration. But when the children left, it was just the two of them. Leonor stayed in bed and he went out to do the shopping. She slept with confidence, and by the time she woke up he had purchased everything and started to cook. He spoke to her from the kitchen while she lounged in bed awhile longer.

One Saturday he told her:

"Tomorrow I'm not coming over. I'm going to a soccer game."

Surprised, Leonor said, "You didn't use to go to games."

"Well," he said, "but now I do. I'm going to watch Perfumo. See? This is him," he said, showing her. "Perfumo takes the penalty kicks. He always scores."

"Oh," said Leonor.

Then he started going to soccer games every Saturday and she said, joking and laughing:

"You always go to soccer games now. You never come see me anymore!"

He opened the newspaper and showed her, "Look at all the people who go to soccer games."

It was true. The number of people who went to soccer games was impressive. If so many other people went, why shouldn't he go, too? The following week he said, "This weekend I'm going to Rosario because Perfumo's playing."

She heard the game broadcast from Rosario on the radio and thought to herself, *He's there.*

When he came back from Rosario, he spent an entire afternoon talking with Hugo about penalty kicks, the left wing, and shots on goal.

One day, they were joking around like always but suddenly he said, "In case I leave."

And Leonor said, "Just where would you go!" following his lead, as if it were a joke.

She felt jumpy, on edge; but she ignored it. The next day he didn't come around, nor the following day. She went over to his house but he wasn't there. When Maria stopped by Leonor eyed her to see whether she knew something, but Maria's face was a blank slate; she didn't know a thing. Leonor argued with her anyway, for no particular reason. Maria didn't lose her cool. She held her own, calmly and patiently.

Leonor kept thinking, *Tonight he's going to come.* And she waited for him. She didn't cry because he had left, instead she found herself looking for him around the house all day; she searched the bathroom and sought him out in bed at night. Sometimes she thought she heard him coming, but it wasn't him. She said to herself:

He has to come back at some point.

She figured if she thought about him enough, he would come back, but he didn't. When it had been three years since he left, she said:

"I have to forget him, even if it takes everything I've got."

So she got a job as a cleaning lady at lots of different houses. She scrubbed from eight in the morning until eight at night, without stopping. And it worked because the job was exhausting and at night she would fall right asleep, without having to think. She was so tired that she couldn't think about anything. She told the whole story to one of the ladies whose house she cleaned and the lady said:

"But if your daughter didn't like him you never should have let him move in."

"Oh..." said Leonor.

But she didn't quite understand how that would have worked out. Then the lady said:

"Don't you have his address?"

"No," said Leonor. "He must have gone to Neuquén, to claim his part of the inheritance. Who knows where he is now."

He wasn't going to come back anymore, she knew that now, but it felt better to work than do nothing all day. By now she had five grandchildren plus the little girl, who she spoiled rotten. A traveling photographer took ten color photographs of her by the new brick house Leonor was having built. Sandra—that's her name—is crazy about dancing; she wants to become a famous dancer, like Raffaella Carrà. One day, Sandra asked her mother if there was a school where she could study to be an artist, to be like Raffaella Carrà. Leonor asked the lady whose house she cleans, the one she trusts, and the lady said:

"Even a starlet has to have an education. She must finish high school and study languages."

So Leonor bought Sandra a new textbook, but she also bought her boots to dance like Raffaella Carrà, an Italian singer who dances in boots and sings, "*Fiesta, qué fantástica, fantástica la fiesta,*" with an energy verging on fury.

Sandra knows perfectly well how to imitate all of Raffaella Carrà's moves, but she doesn't have the same energy—Sandra's movements look strange and slow. Her entire dance routine is nothing more than a silly fad, there's no real audience. She sings, too. When Sandra sings "*Fiesta, qué fantástica es la fiesta*," her voice is pleasant enough, but it's not dynamic. She's too occupied by matching the lyrics with the steps. Besides, she has a frail little voice that sounds as if she hasn't quite grasped the importance of exclamation points or whole phrases, which contain a beginning, middle, and ending.

Leonor watches her tenderly; she looks at the girl's beautiful boots which—praise the Lord—she was able to afford, the pretty sweater, and that blonde hair that Sandra has learned how to tame.

She's already eleven years old and before long Leonor's tender gaze won't be enough; Sandra will want to dance for others. Will she have enough conviction to pursue her dreams? Because dreams, like the saying goes, need someone to pursue them, to take care of them. And, with a bit of luck, Sandra will find someone to help her in that pursuit.

Possibly an Old Husband

NOT long ago, I had this idea that I should marry an old man. It only lasted a few days. I imagined a strong, stout old man over the age of sixty—not a middle-aged man. The old man would have what's known as "life experience" and I'd do whatever I pleased. He would love me, protect me, stay by my side when I needed it, and give me some space when he realized he was bothering me.

And when I didn't know what else to do, I would fall back on the old man's experience for amusement, let him come up with ideas on how to pass the time, that sort of thing. I mean, I've never much believed in life experience. What I expected from the old man was competence and a lack of anxiety. It never even occurred to me that I could end up being mean to him, or resentful—so mean that he could get sick or die, or that the old man could be a complete maniac and I would always have to tell him what time it was or what the weather was like.

I had almost forgotten about all this when one afternoon, at a café, I met up with a group of acquaintances. We'd been there a long time already without saying much, but there was this vague sense of hope lingering around the table and that's when an old man showed up. He was around sixty years old. I didn't know him, but some of the other people at the table did.

I rallied and gained interest. He wasn't really the old man I had imagined; this guy was an old painter with a black bow tie and a poet's long wavy hair. Realizing the old man was lucid— which was ideal—I told him:

"Sit down."

The painter sat down next to me and in a competent voice without a hint of anxiety he asked me:

"What's your name?"

"Catalina," I told him, which was a lie.

A younger man would have asked my name with reservation, irony, or shyness; but the painter asked like an old teacher who's seen so many students come and go, and yet wearily, with renewed interest, learns the name of one last student. He spoke like a gaucho recalling some saintly or mythological reference to Catalina. I can't remember which because I was too amused by the fact that I'd lied about my name.

I was intrigued by that mix between Martín Fierro and Joan of Arc. Since I was smiling, he stopped his digressions and asked me:

"But seriously now, is your name really Catalina?"

"Yes," I said. And it was a lie.

"Then that's that: Catalina it is," replied the old man and he latched onto that reality, willing to play along. Everyone else at the table looked on—half curious, half worn out. The old man kept talking and I got a little bored. I was starting to get infected by everyone else's fatigue when he began writing things on a piece of paper and showing them to me; then I wrote other things and passed them back to him. It was all a bunch of nonsense and I couldn't figure out whether the old man was trying to inject some hidden meaning in the notes beyond the words themselves.

His handwriting was neat and clear so I could read everything perfectly.

After passing back and forth three or four nonsensical notes our friends had to leave and he told me:

"C'mon, let's go get coffee somewhere else."

We went nearby for some coffee, but it was nothing like that old café where we'd just been. This was some sort of American café with bright tables and colorful cups.

He obviously knew the waiters there, calling them by name. *It's alright*, I told myself, *it's just because he's so competent.*

But I was surprised that he would drink coffee in one of those colorful plastic cups. *Well*, I thought, *it must be normal.* Otherwise old people would never learn to say words like "melamine" or "nylon," (which I would have preferred). We started talking about the world and about life in general. I spoke mostly about the Bible. I like talking about the Bible, especially about the Book of Job, but perhaps I was casting pearls before swine because the old man had an amazing ability to roll with the punches, while my principles were set in stone. When I told him he was wrong about something, he said:

"I don't mean it's exactly like that, I mean it's vaguely like that—which is entirely *different*," emphasizing the word "different" and sidestepping any further confrontation by quickly turning to the waiter to request another melamine cup of coffee.

That's when I realized that discussing the Bible with him was my way of demonstrating my ability to be melodramatic. I wanted to see how far I could take things when I noticed that my voice was getting stubborn and childlike, but the old man just smiled. *There's that lack of anxiety*, I thought. And then I looked deep into his eyes, but immediately I turned away.

Talking about the Bible segued into the old man telling me about the death of his father, which I imagined had occurred some forty years earlier, but in fact it had only been two years, and he told me:

"You can't imagine how broken up I was."

I thought to myself, *his father must have been ninety-eight years old*. And he told me how he'd wanted to keep him alive as long as possible, no matter what. He told me that his father had wanted to die because he was suffering so much, but he'd kept his father alive with shots and advice and the like. But his father would say to him:

"Let me die, please."

Plus, his father wanted to receive the sacraments before dying, but to keep him alive, one of the words to the wise he'd spouted off to his father—this very old, bedridden man—was that receiving the sacraments was cowardly at that point, in addition to a series of other similar suggestions. When it came to his father, the painter's behavior seemed incompetent and fraught with anxiety, which concerned me and made me think twice.

I'd assumed the old man had been around the block a few times since he was sitting there with me drinking coffee, but I didn't mention it. Now he wanted to invite me out to dinner. He said:

"Let's get dinner, Catalina."

"I'm not in the mood for dinner," I told him.

He insisted several times but I didn't want to. By then it was late and all the cafés were deserted or closed. I told him:

"Alright, I'm heading off."

"I'll walk with you," said the old man. "Where are you going?"

"Home," I told him.

But we ended up walking by the cafés, in silence, and I told him:

"I'm going to check out the cafés, to see if there's anybody I know."

"Like who?" asked the old man, and I could tell by his tone that he felt left out, but the possibility of being excluded didn't surprise or offend him. It was natural for him to be excluded, because we had only just met. There I was, walking down the street with the old man looking for my friends, who by this time of night had surely left. There we were, the two of us, for different reasons, as forlorn and anxious as two children.

Me, because I was looking for people who weren't there—and I really did search them out at several empty cafés—and him, because he was keeping me company, looking for people he didn't even know with his bow tie and his poet's hair.

"Stop looking for them," he said, rolling with the punches. "Can't you see there's no one here?"

"There's no one here," I said, and I felt sad and could hardly say anything else.

The old man looked at me and said:

"You're sad, Catalina. You're sad about something." And then, in a more matter-of-fact and gaucho-like tone:

"What about Cupid? How does Cupid treat you, *che*?"

Just what I needed, I thought. That's all I needed, for the old man to ask me about Cupid. With a sad smile, I surprised myself by responding without a hint of irony:

"So-so."

Then he said to me hesitantly:

"One of these days you can come see my paintings. My studio's at such-and-such street."

I realized this was his way of competently trying to gloss over a defeat. He wanted me to stop by and hoped I would, but he also knew deep down that I wouldn't. Still, his nature led him to think, *you never know*. Whether I did or didn't go, his plans would be the same.

But one afternoon, when he was thinking about what a good idea it had been not to let his father take the sacraments, he would remember someone named Catalina—ever so vaguely —and then he would paint a picture, which would surely be expressionist and abstract.

I knew for sure that I wouldn't go, which is why I told him:

"Yes, one of these afternoons I'll stop by."

We gave each other a very hard squeeze of the hands. I didn't want him to be upset when I left because it was so late and cold outside. I didn't want him to go to sleep with a hot water bottle.

I wanted him to keep walking around the streets of Buenos Aires, and when people saw him they would say:

"He must be a famous painter."

And for him to feel their gaze upon him and then walk into some party where there was good jazz music playing, for example, where he would call his friends or his enemies by name.

I also think I didn't want him to be sad because, selfishly, I wanted to keep all the sadness for myself. I left him without looking back and set out on a desperate search for everyone I knew at all the cafés in Buenos Aires.

I didn't find anyone.

Angelina & Pipotto

ONCE upon a time there was a woman named Angelina, but the people from the village called her an old lady and the children called her a crazy old lady because once, at the market, she hit a merchant with a stick. And the children said that's why she used a cane, but she didn't use a cane. She walked nice and tall. Her husband's name was Pipotto. He was fat and red and spent the whole day drinking wine, which he kept in a barrel in the basement. Every day, while Angelina slept, he went to the basement and drank from the same barrel. Then she woke up and said:

"It smells like wine."

Angelina went to the basement to chase him down. Pipotto left the barrel uncovered, and since no one put the cover back on, the goat came and lapped it all up. Then Pipotto ran around yelling:

"My wine! My dear sweet wine!"

When the goat got drunk Angelina would beat it, to teach it a lesson. And if her husband Pipotto was drunk she would hit him too—but if he wasn't drunk he would lose his temper and the two of them would beat the goat together and then put it in the stable.

When it came time for the harvest, Angelina cleaned the pitchfork and got it ready with plenty of time, and sometimes she harvested from sunrise to sunset. Once she had to burn all the grass because she'd found a red lizard. Red lizards bring on fevers and toothaches. Pipotto was crying and said:

"It's too much grass. It's the best grass I've ever had in my life."

And he sobbed.

Meanwhile, Angelina lit torches and laid them in the grass. She looked at him with a torch in her hand and Pipotto said:

"Fevers *are* really bad."

And he started to burn the field too, but he didn't want to burn the lizard. He didn't want to let it live either, so he watched as his wife threw it into the river and said:

"In the water it looks different."

He lay down on the bank to get a good look and then got up and ran back to the house.

On Sundays, the church bells rang loud and clear and Angelina put on a purple dress. She was very thin and the dress was too big on her. Pipotto wore his new watch and they went to church in the buggy, to hear the preacher. Pipotto had been drinking wine since the cock's crow, but that was alright because it was

Sunday. He drove the buggy and sometimes he sang softly and Angelina looked at a prayer book that said:

con flores a porfía
que madre nuestra es

And she told her husband:

"You should sing 'Porfía'—not those sinful tunes. We're just two blocks from church."

And she gestured with two fingers, but Pipotto didn't remember the tune to *Porfía* so he stopped singing all together.

When they got to church the preacher said:

"No one should burn the fields or drink too much wine, because he who drinks too much wine later burns the fields. This is just a general reminder—I'm not talking about anyone in particular. And now, let us sing together."

And everyone sang:

con flores a porfía
que madre nuestra es

Once a stranger came to town saying he knew some of their relatives who lived in Aquitaine. And this stranger wanted to buy a plot of land. Pipotto remembered Aquitaine so he said:

"There were so many cows there!"

And the other man said:

"So many cows!"

"There was a deep blue river—it wasn't dirty at all."

"That's true."

"And it wasn't just a river, it was a river with a bridge. And it wasn't a wooden bridge, it was an iron bridge."

"Yes," said the other man modestly, "it was an iron bridge."

Meanwhile, Angelina watched them and put on her glasses. She arched her eyebrows and noticed that the stranger had red hair and, just in case, she made the sign of the cross.

Then Pipotto said:

"That's where Mule's Tail lived."

"Mule's Tail died."

And Pipotto stared at him and said:

"Then it's not the same."

But the other man laughed and quickly said:

"Ah, but there are so many other things. There are lanterns for Carnival and the Feast of Saint John. There's a store that sells walnuts and lottery tickets."

Then Pipotto stamped the ground with his foot and said:

"Without Mule's Tail it's not the same."

And he started to get drunk.

The other man said:

"True, it's not the same."

But the stranger didn't get drunk and he said:

"You have a lot of land. It's too much land for just one house."

Angelina again noticed his red hair and then she said:

"It's 887 pesos."

But the stranger didn't want to discuss it with her. He wanted to talk with Pipotto because Pipotto said:

"What use is the land? The land isn't worth anything."

Then Angelina tossed a bucket of water on her husband and the redhead grabbed his umbrella and gloves and said:

"Goodnight. Enjoy your evening. It's gotten so late, I must be going."

And he disappeared.

Once Pipotto was very sick but he didn't want to get prepared for the good death. Angelina looked for the prayer book that had belonged to her grandmother. She found it in a trunk in the corner under some dried olive branches.

Angelina sat on the edge of the bed and said:

"Repeat after me: 'I take back what I've said, I disregard what I've heard, and I undo what I've done.'"

Pipotto kept his head under the pillow, checking every so often to see if dawn was coming. If it was still nighttime, he would repeat the lines from the prayer book, but when he heard the rooster crow he sat right up in bed and said:

"It's light outside. Daytime has come."

It was the same every night. Then Angelina would say:

"He's been possessed by the devil and I have to cast him away."

And she walked around with a bucket of water, sprinkling water everywhere—even on Pipotto, who didn't notice and said:

"I take back what I've said." All of a sudden he looked out the window and saw light and said, "Daylight has come. The rooster crowed."

One morning the collector came. He was wearing a white straw hat and although they didn't recognize him, they let him in. They didn't vote because they were very old, and didn't know which government was in power anyway. They thought the collector worked for King Victor Emmanuel. Then the collector said:

"After Victor Emmanuel there were eight first kings and three second kings and one third king who only lasted two days before the revolution took him out. Now King Evaristo is in power."

The two old folks looked at each other and shrugged and then Angelina asked:

"So what does the King want? Pigs, goats, or cheese? I haven't got any cheese, but I do have a goat and three pigs."

The collector went to the stable to look at the animals. He kept touching his white hat and furrowing his eyebrows. Then he made note of the pigs and Angelina caught a glimpse of what he was writing. She looked again at his white hat and then walked him to the door. When he left, the collector cupped his hands and called out graciously:

"Remember, it's King Evaristo."

And they went to fry up a piece of bacon.

One day Pipotto took the money out of the mattress, because they had to cut it open to change the wool. Afterwards, he couldn't remember where he'd hidden it. Pipotto didn't tell his wife that he couldn't remember because he was scared, but one day he started to look in all sorts of boxes and Angelina, who was doing the laundry, asked him:

"What exactly are you looking for?"

"Nothing," said Pipotto.

"It's the money," said Angelina. "It's been missing for a while. If you spent it I want it all back, every single cent."

And so the two of them started looking together. It was nighttime, and they didn't have a lantern or anything. But just then Angelina saw a patch of loose dirt and she started to dig there with a shovel and said:

"Here it is. You hid it right here."

And they took out the coins and started to clean them very slowly, until they were shiny, and then put them back into the mattress that had recently been discarded.

Angelina had fried up some bacon and she called Pipotto to eat. She called him several times and she also banged on a can. She looked for him inside the house but he wasn't there. She went outside but he wasn't in the stables either. She went where they kept the unthreshed grain and there he was, sitting behind a pile of it. He looked like he was asleep but she knew he was dead. So she went to tell the undertakers and asked:

"What's the best burial? I want three carriages, all filled with flowers."

She had taken with her all the coins they had cleaned. The coachman looked at her. He looked at her shoes and said:

"One carriage will do."

And she said:

"No, I don't want 'whatever will do.' I want three carriages filled with flowers—and not just any flowers. I want white carnations."

The man wrote it down. Angelina told the preacher and all the neighbors found out and they went to her house. Pipotto was laid out in bed and they said:

"He was a good man."

"He was a good neighbor."

"Yep, one of the best neighbors there was."

Angelina was talking softly to herself saying:

"I told him: Don't drink that wine. Your belly's already too full of wine and it makes your veins swell up."

She looked up at them and said out loud:

"He drank too much wine."

Then they were all quiet and one lady with a handkerchief on her head said:

"Yes, but he was so happy. He was always singing. Poor thing!"

"He was a founder. He was a founding neighbor."

Suddenly they heard the goat bleating, and another two neighbors went to look. The goat was drunk because the barrel had been left uncovered. Angelina threw the goat outside and covered the barrel, and everyone went over to Pipotto. Then they recited some prayers and the preacher blessed them all with holy water and spoke of eternal life. At five o'clock in the afternoon they all walked to the cemetery. The men carrying the casket were sweating because it was a very heavy casket. They buried him in a remote spot and one lady said:

"That's not a spot for a founder."

Then they all went back to town, and they kissed Angelina on both cheeks and said goodbye.

She went home and saw that the bacon was all cold—nobody could eat that. Now the sun was going down and she searched for the goat to feed it the bacon. The goat was very drunk. She watched him for a while and grabbed the pitchfork to beat him, but then she slowly let it drop. And since the sun was setting, she sat down in the last rays of light. She just sat there staring as the goat bit into the bacon and tugged on it. Once the sun had set, she said:

"The goat isn't feeling well and it's cold outside."

So she made him a bed of grass in the kitchen. She slept in the bedroom and during the night she got up twice to give the goat some water.

Human Beings Are
Radically Alone

EVERYONE at Franco's house was focused on some task, except him. He walked around offering to help, but was rejected. If a plank needed to be held up in one spot, he would get bored and lean it up against the wall. So, they told him to go outside and play.

And off he went, somewhat bewildered, wondering who he could play with. The kids playing seemed to be busy with something, too: putting a toy boat in the water, pushing a little train along. He didn't know how to break their concentration. So he went back home, and if his parents had finished what they were working on, if they were relaxed, they would say to him, "What a fine boy we have!"

He really was quite handsome. His mother and father were ugly, a bit hunchbacked. Franco was tall. He had a nice body, nice hair, and nice legs.

At school he gained a short-lived reputation because he learned the word *dash* before anyone else. They would ask him, "What's a 'dash'?"

And Franco, his voice a bit deeper than his schoolmates, would say, "A dash is a short line used in an interjection or to separate a clause."

Their eyes shone with a mixture of suspicion and fascination. They were all happy with their discovery of the dash. Then he asked the teacher:

"Shall I make a line or a dash?"

The teacher was busy with some papers. She looked up annoyed, saying:

"Whichever one you want!"

He walked back to his bench, mortified, thinking how unfair it was. Better put, now he knew what injustice felt like: it was a mix between humiliation, wounded pride, and embarrassment. He experienced injustice as something physical, although he wouldn't go so far as to try and change or rectify it. But he did have to speak up. When something wasn't right, Franco would say: "This is an injustice."

Nobody listened. They didn't care about defining dashes or injustices.

By the time he turned eighteen he had become extremely handsome. He was so attractive that people looked at him on the street. He started to pick out clothes that flattered him and he usually chose to wear black, a color that made him appear to be a very interesting young man.

He spent practically that whole year walking up and down the streets, and honestly, he got looks from everyone. Knowing that he was being watched gave him an air of haughtiness and triumph that suited him well. He had once read a poem that started like this:

"Human anthills that pass on by..."

And as he made his afternoon rounds he remembered the part about those human anthills, while carefully studying each and every ant that passed him by. By sunset he was tired and a little bored. Sometimes he bumped into people, like once when an old lady ran right into him.

Franco, in his most cordial voice, said to her, "Excuse me, ma'am."

But she made a fuss. "Don't you look where you're going? People these days are so inconsiderate, so rude—they don't even pay attention!"

And off she went yelling and mumbling. Now, this type of encounter made Franco feel so disillusioned and perplexed that it could end up ruining his walk. That was unfair. His face changed; for the next hour or so nobody even looked at him. His eyes became troubled, his expression humbled, and even if he tried to put on a face that was beyond good and evil—which was the one that suited him best—the expression didn't come out right because he was preoccupied by tedious yet pressing thoughts. *How had they ended up running into each other?* Let's see, he was walking on the right-hand side, as always, and suddenly the lady—who was fidgeting with her her purse...But it was worthless, that's as far as he could get, so he walked into a café, splashed some water on his face, and looked in the mirror.

The mirror told him, "Yes, you are handsome." And then he went out to walk awhile longer. After he'd gone inside to cool off he walked by a different café. Some people were studying, others were engaged in a heated debate, an old man was sipping a drink in peace. Everyone at that café was doing their own thing, and yet it seemed like they were all connected by something. What was it? He didn't know so he sat down to figure it out and because he liked the place. He felt comfortable there. Across from him there was a blond man, more or less the same age as Franco, dressed all in brown. He was studying something that seemed mesmerizing. He asked Franco what time it was and Franco responded, "I don't know what time it is. I can't be bothered by the time."

The other guy smiled and asked him, "What do you do?"

Franco said, "I think, I read, I wander."

Using short answers made his voice sound provocative. It was a deep voice—somewhat condescending, but still interesting.

"What are you reading?" asked the blond man.

Franco told him that he was reading a book of poetry about the anthill of humanity. The blond guy agreed with Franco: the anthill's incomprehension—how it lacked any clarity, any sense of freedom or passion—was impressive. They each continued to add more details about the anthill's incomprehension, agreeing about everything.

Incomprehension is a fascinating subject, but after there is utter agreement about every type of incomprehension, a silence ensues, like an embarrassing interlude after which no new conversations can be started. There's nowhere to pick up from. Finally, the blond guy said, "Would you like to study with me? I'm reading *Essence and Existence*."

"Yes," Franco said.

He didn't know whether he wanted to study. Maybe it would be nice.

He started to read *Essence and Existence* with the blond guy every afternoon, for around two hours. Franco always got there first, after a bit of a stroll. Before his new friend arrived he would think, *Who will walk through the door now?* Perhaps a King and a Queen. The King and Queen would walk up to Franco's table. The King would say:

"Son, take care of the Queen while I'm away."

Franco would take care of the Queen until the King came back. He would go wherever they led him. Every time he went to the café his greatest joy was imagining that someone attractive, powerful, and charming would walk in. This person would approach him and regale him with splendid clothes and a home with wall-to-wall carpeting. When the blond guy arrived, he started reading from *Essence and Existence* and Franco listened. When the blond guy understood something he'd say, "Of course, of course," as if to himself. If Franco didn't understand something he didn't mention it, and that's how foggy areas began to accumulate in his philosophical understanding, which led to his complete indifference. But he couldn't say anything to the blond guy, who was so excited because he'd discovered the underlying connection between essence and existence, which Franco had somehow missed. And while they studied, Franco secretly wanted to go out to the street to see if people would look at him.

The blond guy eventually realized that Franco was distracted and told him, "Franco, I can't study with you. You can't concentrate."

That let Franco off the hook, filling him with relief. The philosopher added, hesitantly, "We could still meet up to chat…"

"Of course," said Franco.

By now he greeted people at the neighboring tables. At the next table over, there was a theater director whose play was about lack of communication; each character said their lines, but they had nothing to do with what the next person said. It was about lack of communication and retrogression; all the furniture was in ruins, but there were still remnants of former grandeur. There was petrified food and a big cobweb to symbolize the general sense of entrapment caused by lack of communication and retrogression. When one of the female characters said, "Charles has arrived," the entire audience already knew that Charles wasn't a person who came to visit; he was a ghost, or in any case it was a visit so private that only she could see him.

Now the director had a problem. He was about to put on the show for the first time, but all the actors had gotten into a fight. One fellow, who had a small part, had lost his temper and sworn never to lay eyes on any of them ever again. The director had become disillusioned by the actors; he thought they were twisted people with problems. Lately, he didn't care much about talent. What he really wanted was to direct people with principles, people who say they're coming at five o'clock and follow through—not people who show up an hour later. People who know how to get along with each other, who have a sense of justice. He was hopelessly thinking about how to replace the man who had walked off the set when he noticed Franco: lovely face, attractive body, pleasant appearance. So he called him over.

"Franco."

"Yes," Franco said courteously.

"I need an actor. I'd like to audition you for a small part. Are you up for it?"

Franco was flattered. He said yes, he thought so.

"Let's see," said the director. "Say: 'These early autumn evenings make me daydream.'"

Franco said the line, albeit a bit rushed.

"Alright," said the director, "that wasn't bad. We've got to take your nerves into account, because you're new. But you've got a nice voice. And a hint of nerves in a new actor is natural. It's natural. I'd almost take it as a good sign."

That was how, day after day, Franco ended up going to rehearsal after his walk. He had to wait an hour to say, "These early autumn evenings make me daydream." And although he only had one line, he spent the whole rehearsal thinking about the moment he'd walk in and say it. With the director's help, he had learned how to control himself, how to say it in a particular way. Still, he was curious to know how it would turn out, as if he were spying on himself. He thought about which tone to use, how fast he would speak, etcetera, when he said: "These early autumn evenings make me daydream."

By now word had gotten out all around the café: Franco was an actor. He didn't think about the King and Queen anymore. Now that he had become an actor he was more dynamic, he visited several tables. He felt like he had wings on his feet. You could almost say he wasn't afraid of interrupting anyone.

One day, a guy from the café asked him, "Franco, are you an actor?"

"Yes," said Franco cautiously.

"So why don't you invite us to see the play?"

He didn't know why, but he didn't want to invite this guy to see the play. "It's almost over." Franco said.

"Exactly, that's why you should invite us, because it's almost over," said the guy.

"Well, I don't know if there are any tickets left…"

"But we want to go," said the guy, acting as the group's spokesperson.

Franco didn't invite them, but they still showed up. When he saw them he became more nervous than usual. Instead of walking meditatively across the stage, he moved quickly as he said, "These early autumn evenings make me daydream," and since his voice was monotonous and deep, it sounded bad.

The next day, Franco sat down at the same table as that guy who had made him nervous. His name was Guillermo. Franco waited for some sort of comment—good or bad. He'd come in expecting a change in the table and the faces, as if the faces, table, and coffee cups should look different because he'd performed and they'd seen him, but that didn't happen.

Guillermo, with a blank face—the same expression as always—said to him:

"Hey, Franco, these early autumn evenings make me daydream."

Franco didn't know how to take it so he smiled, confused. Guillermo was drinking wine and lately Franco had been drinking a bit, although he tried not to because it affected his voice. But this time he drank two glasses and plucked up the courage to ask Guillermo what he thought of the play. Imitating Franco's deep voice in a mocking tone, Guillermo said, "These early autumn evenings make me daydream."

Franco took offense to what Guillermo had said. It was an injustice, but there was something new about it. In addition to his perception of spitefulness, his embarrassment, and the violent sense of discomfort in his body, there was something new: immense grief and uneasiness. And using his embarrassment, grief, and uneasiness, Franco—who wouldn't harm a fly—grabbed a chair and broke it over Guillermo's head. This fight was discussed at length in the café. Someone said, "There's nothing worse than getting hit by a first-timer. When a first-timer punches, they give it everything they've got. They're capable of anything." As if by magic, everyone at the café agreed with this, except for the old man, who just sat there drinking his wine alone because he hadn't even noticed. That fight earned Franco an ambiguous reputation. On the one hand, they laughed at his outburst, on the other, they were somewhat afraid.

When Franco left the café, he felt better. So good that for a while he didn't look at anyone on the street like he usually did.

He felt solid, heavy, and calm all at the same time. He started to think, *Nope, I'm not going back to that place. Never again.* The play had ended and he said to himself, *I should work.* After brooding over the idea of working he looked around and saw a woman around the age of thirty. She looked back at him, and her expression wasn't one of utter awe. Her look seemed to say, *Yes you should*, and this reaffirmed his intention to work.

He got a job at an office. A woman explained the job to him and helped him at the beginning. Sometimes she looked at him, at his haggard, troubled face that was beyond good and evil, and she said to him sweetly:

"What's wrong?"

"Nothing. I'm thinking."

"What are you thinking about?"

"Nothing. It's nothing. Let's leave it at that."

She started to grow curious about him, wondering what he thought about. What does he think about? And she told her friends at the office there was a man with a mysterious face who looked like he had complex and profound thoughts.

She also suspected him of great sadness, or maybe he had a secret weighing him down. She began to worry about him, to take care of him. He got used to that tenderness. Once in a while he'd say, "Oh!" like he was disillusioned. That mystery tortured her; they got closer and he thought that maybe they could even move in together or get married. But when she started up about the house they'd live in, the furniture they'd have, it made him feel strange. He thought, *A house? Furniture?* as if it were all surreal, impossible. He thought, *Isn't having a house and furniture for mediocre people?* Besides, they'd undoubtedly end up with a small house.

He no longer referred to "the anthill," now he spoke about "mediocre people." But he couldn't tell her he didn't want to get married, because he couldn't bear to shatter her fixation with furniture, pots, and pans. Something strange was happening to her. In the afternoon, when she saw his indifferent face she'd become disappointed; but by the next morning she'd forget about that look on his face and jump right back into talking about what to buy, what to choose, which she found quite pleasant. Finally, when she could no longer ignore how disconnected he was from the entire project, she said to him, "Just tell me. What's wrong?"

And Franco responded, "Human beings are radically alone."

The girl, remembering all the pots and pans she'd purchased, said to Franco, "You're a real asshole."

And he left, so as not to become involved in mediocre arguments.

Human beings are radically alone, Franco repeated to himself. This thought—which could seem to be so harrowing—comforted and encouraged him: "Ah, solitude amidst the masses, among those who don't understand." And since he was radically alone, why not go to the café for a while? Who would he find? Would anyone still be there a year later?

All the mutual accusations and the breakup meant he hadn't bathed in two days. When he took a bath he thought, *Baths are so refreshing!* Back out on the street he was still in awe: *A bath makes all the difference!* But that thought didn't do him any favors; nobody stole even the slightest glimpse at him. He tried to concentrate. Let's see, "Human beings are radically alone... Humans are more than just humans, they're also a result of their circumstances... Man and his circumstances... Man and his habitat..."

The "habitat" of the café was exactly the same; only the old man with his glass of wine was no longer there.

Guillermo, the guy he'd gotten into a fight with, saw him come in.

"Franco!" he called out. "How's it going? Where have you been hiding?"

"I wasn't hiding," Franco said, somewhat irritated, and added, "I'm up to my same old tricks."

"Ah!" said Guillermo. "Well, I was on my way out but I hope to see you again soon."

"Of course, of course," Franco said.

"I'd like you to meet a friend, Gustavo."

Gustavo was dressed entirely in gray. He was fat, and on top of all that gray, as if to add a hint of color, he was wearing a small tartan scarf.

"Alright man, I'm leaving," Guillermo said to Gustavo. "We'll continue another day."

Franco asked, "Am I interrupting a conversation?"

"No, not at all," said Gustavo.

Referencing something from before, Gustavo said to a short little man, "I think it's simple alienation."

"I think it's second-degree alienation," said the short little man with a briefcase. He wasn't drinking anything and he kept his hands on the briefcase. *What they're saying is so interesting*, thought Franco. *It really is*. But who else was at the café? Over there was Rolando, acting like a real gentleman. He'd gotten older, but he was still as pretentious as ever.

As Franco prepared to greet Rolando, a young woman came over and stood next to the guy with the briefcase. He introduced her as "my partner."

The partner gave Franco a merciless look. Franco took the opportunity to head over to Rolando's table. Rolando asked him politely, as if there were no past, present, or future in this life, or rather as if they were meeting in another, different life, or as if they'd seen each other two days ago, "How are you Franco? What's new?"

"Good. I'm good," Franco said, somewhat disconcerted, without knowing what had perplexed him. He couldn't help but admire Rolando just like before. His nonchalance, his tact, the way he never minced his words...

"How are things going?" Franco asked.

He couldn't remember exactly what Rolando did.

"They're going," Rolando said with charming indifference. "Weren't you in the theater at some point, or am I mistaken?"

"I was, for a spell." Franco said reluctantly.

"A play called *Only a Few Concomitances*, wasn't it?"

"No, it was *Only a Few Consequences*."

"Oh, right, *Only a Few Consequences*."

Two tables over a woman around the age of thirty-five sat down. She seemed proud and arrogant. Franco looked at her, then looked at her coat. He didn't know which was more incredible: the girl or the coat. Franco started to think, "She'd take me home with her. Then I'd have a splendid overcoat, too. We'd have tea in the garden." He looked at her, but she didn't take the hint. Rolando asked him, "Would you like to meet her?"

Rolando knew her! Of course, how could Rolando *not* know her. He was a King and she was a Queen. With a roguish wave of his hand Rolando called her over. "Monica!"

Monica got up, pleasantly startled. She came over and said to Rolando, "How are you, darling?

Rolando said, "Hey there, sweetheart."

They used Sweetheart and Darling like proper nouns, like Florencio and Susana. She looked at Franco out of the corner of her eye. Rolando, in that same great tone, with the tact he used to ask about other people's affairs, said to her, "How are things going?"

"They're going," she said.

It was as if things could walk on their own, on a slippery course.

"Alright, dear," she said, "I'm off. I'm actually in a real hurry."

She said *dear* like she might say Antonio.

"Go on, go ahead," Rolando said.

What a prudent man. So respectful of other people's affairs.

"What does she do?" Franco asked.

"I think it's something to do with sales, although I couldn't be sure."

Franco looked over at the table where he'd been sitting before. The guy still had his hands on the briefcase. Gustavo was talking endlessly. His partner wasn't talking, but her eyes were engaged and her whole body was leaning forward in anticipation. Franco wanted to go back over there for a while. He didn't want to interrupt or anything, but they looked so lively!

He didn't have to explain himself. Rolando knew how it worked: today we sit at one table, tomorrow another. Today we're here, tomorrow we're gone, and so it goes. Rolando realized that Franco was about to get up, so just when Franco was about to say goodbye, Rolando pretended to be momentarily distracted, as if suddenly wrapped up in his own affairs. Franco said, "See you soon, Rolando."

Rolando, apparently startled, responded warmly, but obviously without losing his usual tact: "Farewell, until eternity."

And Franco went back over to Gustavo's table. The Queen hadn't looked at him once. Franco didn't even know if she was still there or not. Some people were blocking his view of the table where she'd been sitting. What fun, not knowing whether she was still there. Bah, she was missing a tooth. That girl was missing a tooth. Gustavo's table was like a non-stop cinema: you could take a seat anytime, and the sacred fire of conversation never went out.

The subject was alienation, with all its implications. Alienation was like one of those sea creatures with lots of tentacles; its interrelated tentacles formed a living organism. For example, if you touched the consumerist society tentacle and were momentarily able to express yourself clearly and eloquently on the subject, the tentacle would retract. A brief sensation of triumph would settle over those present, having made a stand against consumerist society. A silence ensued and then another of the monster's tentacles emerged: the mass media and their pernicious influence on the education of children.

Yes: Gustavo, the short guy with the briefcase, and his partner were right. When everyone worked together to defeat the thousand-headed monster, human beings would be free from a series of absurd impositions; together they would commence a more humane, natural life. Why drink Coca-Cola and Orange Crush when water is better and more natural? Why do we need powdered detergent when we can make our own soap at home? So, can't people have anything at home? They can have books, CDs, recordings of concerts. The guy with the briefcase had a friend who had visited the Puna region. He had decided to stay in a small village of illiterate goat herders. Right there, in the middle of that incredibly silent desert, while chatting with an old local man, he took out his portable recorder and played Beethoven's second symphony. The old man was spellbound because he was pure, his ears were pure. The desert stretching out before him was pure and the river running through it was pure, too. If we don't take urgent measures we'll all drown in a sea of trash. Which one is Beethoven's second symphony? Is it the one that starts, "dundundun-dun"? No, you animal, that's the fourth.

Excited by the conversation, Franco wanted to be part of it and he said, "I read in *People* magazine that..."

The partner looked at him with utter disdain. "You read *People* magazine?"

"At the barbershop," Franco said timidly. "I certainly wouldn't buy it. You thought I would buy it? C'mon..."

"Not even in the bathroom," said the partner.

People magazine was for shallow types. Therefore, he was shallow. The partner began to think less and less of him. Eventually, she stopped listening to him altogether, so he ended up not saying anything at all. Since he never said anything, they didn't even notice he was there. One day he was tired and he said, "Well, I'm going to go..."

Nobody asked him if he had something else to do, or why he was leaving. As he left he said to himself, *Perhaps I shouldn't go back.* He didn't bother to say, *I'm never going back* because he knew that sometimes he said that and then went back anyway. These thoughts flooded him with grief. He wanted to cry—not burst out sobbing, but his eyes welled up all the same. It wasn't an intense feeling, it was a light mist that had risen to the surface without his consent, persistent and underlying. If his thoughts drifted to something else, the mist would suddenly return. It was so persistent that it began to annoy him. He looked at himself in the mirror to see what the crying fellow looked like. His face was gloomy. He had a few gray hairs, but they weren't distinguished or emphatic. His face was lifeless.

"Well," said Franco, "pompadour hairstyles are out, so I can't wear my pompadour shoes anymore. Sleek hair is in, so I should use sleek shoes to match."

He bought a pair of simple loafers. And a pullover with a high collar looks good when you're tan, but when you're pale, a bit haggard if you will, that high collar seems to swallow you up, as if you'd just as well hide your face behind the collar. What about a plain, simple white collar that's inconspicuous, paired with a pullover in a discreet color; not gray—you don't want to look like a priest. Yes, that's nice. The truth is, it suited him. He wasn't going to stay at home dressed in such nice clothes. He hadn't been to the café in a long time. Would Guillermo be there? Nobody had ever seen Guillermo again. Rolando? Rolando was hanging out at a different café now, he ran with a new crowd. Franco sat down and remembered how Rolando would call the waiter over. "*Waaiiter,*" he would say, emphasizing the first syllable, sing-songing at the end, with neither humility nor arrogance. Now that Franco was a gentleman, the waiter came running. Being a gentleman, he could have his shoes shined, and while the man polished them, Franco put on his expression that was beyond good and evil. But he was thinking, *Guillermo isn't here, Rolando isn't here and there's nobody I know. If only Corrales would drop by…* Corrales always used to pop in, in and out, in and out, sticking his head through the door. Sometimes he would be invited to sit at a table. He was considered to be a mediocre person…Although he did know all about coin collecting, so who knows…

But Corrales didn't stop by either, he must have had something better to do than go to the café. Was it possible that Franco didn't know anyone at any of the tables, not even someone he recognized from the street? It was as if the world had entered a different orbit, spinning on another axis, following other plans. He ordered a whisky. As soon as he started to drink, he realized both his thoughts and everything around him would be exactly the same once he had finished. It wouldn't matter if he had ordered roast kangaroo. Suddenly, someone broke the spell. He saw a familiar face, someone he knew from a long time ago. It was the Bible salesman. Nobody knew his name, and no one asked him either. Back in the day he had been an old man, but he hadn't aged much since. He wore the same clothes in winter and summer, and in winter he didn't wear socks. He was still enthusiastic—socks or no socks—going from table to table. Only one out of every ten tables he approached would engage with him, briefly, but he was undeterred. He didn't care whether they accepted or rejected him because he was on a mission to spread the word of God. As soon as Franco made eye contact, the man approached, taking purposeful strides, and Franco, who had always considered him to be mediocre, said, "Sit down. Would you like some coffee, or something else?"

"Thank you," said the Bible salesman.

He never drank anything. He took out the Bible, opened it to the book of prophecies and started to read about all the calamities predicted by the prophet Ezekiel, because of all the sinners. It was impossible to interrupt the Bible salesman; neither Franco nor anyone much more seasoned could have done it. But why should he send him away? He ordered another whisky and felt reassured; he was alive, he had some money to spare, the weather was nice. He had completely disengaged from what the Bible salesman was saying. Once in a while he heard something like, "but then Jonas…" or "Thou shall never say." At some point the salesman lifted his finger and said, "The path is narrow." Franco stared at him as if he were listening. Once in a while he heard something random. It didn't matter. He was filled with a new, joyous sensation. He was alive and he had some sort of hope. He didn't know what for, but it didn't matter.

Sunday Afternoon Visit

MRS. Emma found lots of little ways to pass the hours, and although she was mostly content with them, she didn't know what to do when there was too much time to complete a simple task, but not enough to take care of something more involved. It was idle time and lately she felt like there was both too much time and not enough. When she wanted to start on some task—for example, organizing the shelves—she would say to herself: "But I won't have enough time." That's how she felt on Sunday afternoons when she thought about cleaning out the drawers or pulling dead leaves off the plants. It filled her with a sense of sadness, too, because the city was absolutely silent. She wondered where everyone had gone—not one noise, not one sign of life. Besides, she'd realized that plants can survive a long time without someone fussing with them, and as for the drawers and the shelves—let them fill up with whatever they wanted. There were so many exhibitions, concerts, and conferences to attend. She read about them diligently in the newspaper—but how to know which one was the best? They all seemed equally interesting; she found herself saying, "Yes, I could go." She'd tried going to some exhibitions, book launches, forums, and debates, but once she'd arrived she felt like she could have stayed there forever and never gone home. On Sunday afternoons her house became even more monotonous than it was on other days. Sometimes she felt like doing something extraordinary, but she didn't know what that could be. As a result, she'd come up with a new way to kill time that wasn't too demanding. Every two weeks, on Sunday afternoon—never any other day—she invited over Paula, the girl from the apartment next door. Paula came over with her puppy dog, which was going to grow to be the size of a small horse and was already enormous. The sheer size of the animal seemed inconsistent with its leaps and twirls; you'd think a beast of such stature would have reached the age of moderation. Mrs. Emma poured him water in a red bowl and gave him an old piece of string from a roller curtain to play with; the dog had learned to expect both these items when he arrived. Paula often would tie an elegant bandana around his neck, knotted stylishly at the nape. As soon as they'd walk in, the dog would tug at it until it came off and play with it, sprawled on his back, paws up in the air as if he were doing the air bike.

"It's because he's so excited to come over here," Paula explained.

Paula had already gone through her fashion phase last year, when she wanted to be a catechist and a model. She arranged her scarf just so—tucked in, in an attempt at both practicality and functionality. Indeed, the dog got all riled up when he came over—like an overwrought actor effusively thanking his audience. Paula was the dog's trainer: there was a sharp contrast between the animal's merriment and the little lady's sense of restraint. Paula's stern tone of voice, with menacing undertones, foreshadowed a personality that has what it takes.

"Enough! I've said it once and I won't say it again."

Mrs. Emma felt sorry for the dog—getting scolded so harshly. She brought over his bowl of water. The dog took a few laps to show his appreciation and then trotted right back over to the sofa, so as not to miss a thing. He seemed to be pulled in every direction, he went from exploring to licking their faces, and then right back out to explore.

Mrs. Emma gave Paula a book about astronomy (now she wanted to be an astronomer). It explained the hole in the ozone layer and the possibility of life on Mars. She'd rationalized it to the bookseller by telling him it was for a 12-year-old girl— she didn't want him to think the book was for her. She couldn't stand the idea of people imagining she were even stranger than they already thought. Since she spent all her time alone she figured some people in her neighborhood must think of her as a harmless lunatic.

And there they were, reading questions and answers posed by the book. While Paula read about Ganymede, the dog ripped a piece of paper into tiny bits and ate it: his trainer was distracted. Other strange planets followed and the reader became entirely absorbed.

"Does he eat paper?"

"He eats everything," she said without looking up.

Mrs. Emma gave the dog some old crackers which he crunched up loudly, in celebration.

"Look up something about Mars."

Mars had always intrigued her when she was a girl, and even much later in life. Now, after so many years, she was still drawn to it: there may have been life, there still could be, but no one knows. The dog was lying at his owner's feet, undoing her shoe-laces. What did the book say? Was there or was there not life on Mars? But of course there was! It was a *nebula*. Paula blurted out enthusiastically:

"There's a probe that's going to reach Mars in the year 2004!"

"Wow!" replied Mrs. Emma hypocritically. In truth, she was thinking about several things, other things, all at once. She was remembering how passionately, at the age of fifteen or six-teen, she'd wished there were life on Mars. As if it would have changed her destiny. She was also thinking about how her blouse needed to be washed; how she couldn't forget to buy mandarin oranges when she went out; and how the dog had fallen asleep at his owner's feet. Why did she enjoy their visit so much? If they'd come over separately—just the girl or just the dog—she wouldn't have liked it as much. But the subject of astronomy was getting tedious now: they'd come to a part about planets from another galaxy, which were something like 10,000 light years away, so Mrs. Emma asked her:

"Tell me about the little gypsy girl."

Paula had a classmate at school who was a gypsy, and whose mother was even more of a gypsy. If the little gypsy girl was somewhat unorthodox, the mother was even more so—at least according to Paula's aesthetic criteria. It seems the little gypsy girl had some learning problems and she hardly ever spoke to anyone.

"Don't be cruel to her," Mrs. Emma said, adding some explanations about why gypsies were the way they were.

"No," replied Paula.

This *no* was meant to say they were hardly cruel to her; in fact, they'd never even spoken to her.

"I mean, her mother wears high heels that look like this," she drew them painstakingly, remembering exactly what they looked like, as if it were a scientific drawing. In her depiction the back was rounded and the high heel was sectioned off from the rest of the shoe, which had little strings hanging from it. The shoe looked like a bizarre animal, as if it were alive. "And her hair combs look like this," she said drawing them. "Like she's wearing a birdcage with exotic birds on her head: greens, blues, and reds."

She wanted her drawing to be an exact replica of real life. Suddenly she realized she'd forgotten one detail and said:

"Wait. Do you have any markers or glitter?"

"No... The little gypsy girl wears high-heels to school?"

"Nooo—her mother."

The sleeping dog let out a sigh.

"All that patchwork of colors mixed together is unbelievable; they mix purple with red—I mean, when it's a muted red, that's one thing, but..."

Those words seem to expound upon Paula's aesthetic criteria—criteria that were also ethical, like the Greeks: the qualities of restraint, moderation, and harmony are equally good and beautiful. Then, as if driven by an impulse, she abandoned her reflection and began to pull at her dog's jowls.

"What are you doing? Leave him alone," said Mrs. Emma.

Paula replied apologetically: "It's just that while he's sleeping is the only time I can check to see how his teeth are growing."

The dog let his teeth be prodded and stayed asleep. The teeth were perfect: huge and white.

By now nighttime had come; that unpleasant hour between seven and eight o'clock had come and gone. When Mrs. Emma was alone she always kept her eyes glued on the clock at that time of day. First came a thin layer of gray, as if the sky itself were growing faint. The sun set slowly, which made everything glow. Night had fallen without her even realizing it. Lately, not only had she felt like there was both too much and not enough time, she'd also felt, now and again, that time was frozen. And when time was frozen, Mrs. Emma took pleasure in its passing—although she knew it was a guilty pleasure. But today, time had been good to her, it had sped by, and the dog was awake again. She asked Paula somewhat apathetically:

"What have you taught him to do?"

"Lie down, sit, and shake. Shake, boy."

The dog looked at Paula as if to say: *What could she possibly want with me now?* Coolly, he held out a tepid paw.

"Don't force him, let him be."

When the dog heard this, he walked over and started to lick Mrs. Emma.

He always sensed when the visit was over, even before the humans themselves. When there was a lull in the conversation he went to find his leash and headed to the door.

"Alright," said Mrs. Emma. "I *am* going to buy him that ball—this time I'll remember."

In a flash they were at the door and she started to make a list in her head: she needed to buy a very heavy-duty ball, some markers to draw gypsies and little gypsy girls, and some glitter. Perhaps she should learn something new about Mars or Venus? Who knows.

Miss Irma

MISS Irma was the youngest of three sisters. The elder two, who married young and produced several children, had somewhat horse-like features. The prettiest of them all was Irma, and she was both lucky and unlucky to have those sisters. Lucky because when it came to comparing their features and figures she carried the day; unlucky because there was still a family resemblance between the three. They lived in a small town and Irma read poems as a girl, but not just love poems. She read poems about landscapes and frames of mind, too. She studied to be a teacher and admired important historical figures, scientists, and self-sacrificing people. Her favorite poem was one that described how the whole world was just one big prison. Deep down she wanted to be an actress, but she also thought contemptuously that every stage was like a big prison. She made grandiose gestures with her hands. for example, if she made a movement to express "Let sleeping dogs lie" she could conjure up spite flawlessly, together with her haughty expression and squinty eyes. If there was something she truly treasured—namely a landscape from a book she had read—she clasped her hands together as if she were praying and her eyes lit up.

Then she had a boyfriend who she never introduced to anyone, and no one ever knew why she stopped seeing him. Afterwards, it wasn't clear whether she'd suffered or cried, but she did become more of a loner and cared less about petty things. By this time, she no longer thought the world was a stupid prison; she'd simply resigned herself to her own toxic prison to be braved without trusting anyone. If someone at work started a conversation with her by saying, for example: "What crazy weather we're having! One minute it's raining, then the sun comes out..." Miss Irma would answer: "It's true, what crazy weather."

But there was something in her voice that was strained, as if any sort of weather could be crazy. A mixture between reservation, sadness, and distraction. She also used some slang words from *lunfardo* that had become common among the teachers, for example *despelote*. But when she said *despelote* it didn't evoke an image of what the word meant: chaos, a three-ringed circus, a riot. It was as if she were caressing the word with that sweet, flat little voice of hers.

Miss Irma was the type of person who truly abhorred ignorance. At school, the other teachers and the principal were indifferent to ignorance. But nobody hated the rural schoolteachers. Everyone admired them from a distance—how could you not? But they occupied about as much space in her coworkers' brains as nuclear fission. In contrast, Miss Irma was capable of quoting Ms. Ermelinda de Suárez, the teacher from Faimallá who had invented a reading method based on color-coded index cards. Miss Irma was in favor of working with minimal resources, for example old matchboxes, rolling papers, etcetera. The children used the matchboxes as a place to keep little bugs. She decorated the classroom with dolls that all looked alike, wearing dresses trimmed with garlands. These dolls were made of cardboard: the top half was flat, but to make their dresses round and get them to stand up, she put carrots under their skirts. To celebrate Independence Day, on May 25th or July 9th, the dolls (which she crafted all year round to play with) wore lace mantillas on their heads and held cardboard fans in their hands. For the May 25th celebrations it was Miss Nélida's turn to decorate the school staircase. The Cabildo tower had been constructed from an empty toothpaste tube—but it seems she hadn't had time to cover it with paper. It was plain to see how it had been a toothpaste tube, brand name and all. And in front of the Cabildo tower there were two big potatoes, which must have been meant to represent the cannons. When another teacher saw it—Miss Amanda, who wore a gold watch and beautiful shoes—she said:

"How tacky! We'd be better off just decorating the stage with a big bouquet of red roses, or some other sort of flowers."

Two different styles, what can you do?

But what Miss Irma really loved was the students, and she bent over backwards for them. When she taught her seven-year-olds about the word "air," she used the same voice one might use when talking to baby chicks:

"Let's see, let's see, who will bring me a little bit of air?"

And the word "air" sounded imploring, as if she were begging them for a bit of air.

They all formed their hands into little bowls to gather some air and she called on one student who, taking himself very seriously, brought some air up to the front of the class in the hollow of his hand. With Miss Irma the children smelled the perfume of imaginary roses, and when she turned around to write on the blackboard they imitated the sound of the wind and swayed like trees in the forest. Another of her exercises involved pretending to be asleep, but all the while thinking about things. Then she would say:

"Dreaming…"

And everyone crossed their arms on their desks and laid down their heads; sometimes they stayed like that for ten minutes. Miss Irma had always been slim, but at that time she was so skinny she seemed to quiver every now and then. When someone proposed an idea to her she said: "Of course, of course," in a seemingly understanding tone of voice, but she was clearly distracted. She didn't quiver at the wrong time, nothing that spectacular, but when she said: "Yes, yes," the last "yes" ended with a short hissing sound.

Since she loved her students so dearly, she followed them to second grade. But there were two new girls: Alejandra and Silvia. Alejandra had really big light-blue eyes; they were disproportionately large. She was pretty but her mouth turned down slightly. She barely knew how to read and at any given time in class she seemed to be yelling. Straight away both girls started to fight with the boys, although each in a different way: Silvia argued about what was or wasn't fair. Alejandra imagined she had been hit, robbed, or insulted. She stood up to the oldest teachers at school and if they scolded her she just stood there staring at them, her rage contained within those big light-blue eyes. Miss Irma couldn't stop saying:

"What a creative child!"

Alejandra learned how to accurately draw those dolls in long dresses. She drew them all day long, on any given sheet of paper instead of using it to write. When the children learned about the different school authorities, Alejandra drew a doll in a long dress and wrote underneath (with some help):

"The principal is a queen."

Then she drew another doll in mourning, and underneath—also with some help—she wrote:

"The secretary is a dead widow."

One day Alejandra dressed up using a piece of tulle she found just laying around and she didn't take it off all day. It made Miss Irma think to herself: "There's so much to learn from these children! They have so much to teach us! We're going to put on a play in this class. I'll get more costumes."

She gathered all the rags she could find and asked them to bring as many items from home as they could. Alejandra always played the blonde fairy, and Silvia—who was a brunette—always wanted to be a witch. As for the boys, only one of them liked to dress up. He pretended to be a policeman directing traffic. The traffic director would let the blonde fairy pass, but he would stop the witch. The witch told him off, she pretended to scratch him, and concluded by doing somersaults on the floor. Another important character was a thin blonde girl with translucent skin; she was mild-mannered, but also incredibly bossy. She always played the princess who was about to get married. At first no one noticed her, but then she suddenly emerged on stage with great conviction, leaving the witch, the good fairy, and the traffic director speechless. The entire class fell silent, as if it were some sort of scandal.

The boys didn't act, but they were absorbed by the show. The most aloof of them all was Marcelo Riquelme. He sat in the last row with a buzz cut, apparently entirely unaware of his buzz cut. Marcelo's face was as dirty as his school smock and his notebook was even dirtier than his face and smock put together. He used a thick tracing pencil and you could barely tell the difference between real words and scribbles. As soon as he could, Marcelo hurried outside to the schoolyard to spy on the other students, or to the kitchen to ask the custodian for a bread roll. Miss Irma never noticed he was gone.

One fine day, Alejandra started out to the schoolyard dressed up like the good fairy, with red dress-up shoes, a swim cap on her head, and a piece of tulle that framed the swim cap dragging a few feet behind her. When recess was over, instead of going back to the classroom, she was just about to walk up the staircase that led to the rooftop terrace when Ms. Bianchi saw her. Ms. Bianchi immediately sensed an infraction of school rules. She could be thinking about anything at all, distracted as all get out, but if something were amiss she noticed immediately.

"Where are you going?" she shrieked.

"My teacher gave me permission," said Alejandra in her costume.

"Get down from there," Ms. Bianchi yelled vehemently.

Alejandra didn't budge so Ms. Bianchi went over and pulled

the girl down by the arm. Bursting with rage, Alejandra tried to resist and then went to tell her teacher.

The next day, wearing the same getup, Alejandra was put in charge of taking some paperwork to the principal's office and to some of the other classrooms. The secretary, who had the voice of a telephone operator (and also spent the whole day on the telephone), said to her:

"Child, why on earth are you dressed like that?" But then she got distracted because the phone rang and Alejandra went back out on the schoolyard and ran all around.

"You think you're so special?" One boy called out from a classroom.

But she just kept running in circles, the tulle dragging behind her, her eyes fixed dead ahead as if she were on a mission.

The next day, Luisa the custodian was furtively tanning behind the flagpole, her legs exposed to get some sun on her varicose veins. She'd wrapped a towel around her head and put her legs up on a little stool. Marcelo Riquelme went to make a deal with her.

"Gimme a bread roll."

"Pick up the papers," Luisa said.

"Alright, but make it two rolls," said Marcelo.

"Deal," said Luisa, dozing off.

He went out to the schoolyard because it was really dark in

the classroom. Miss Irma hadn't opened the blinds and they were putting on another play. This time it was about some false gossip. There were rumors that the witch had given birth to a child. The scene went like this:

"Who says so?"

Two girls accused each other.

The good fairy came and gave the witch a good push, who then fainted and fell down. The two girls spreading the rumor spun in circles from their desks all the way to the door. The circles were meant to be purifying.

Mitropoulos, a clever boy who sat in the front row, watched it all thoughtfully, as if intrigued. Miss Irma was beaming. The principal watched the scene—she didn't exactly think it was normal, but since it was improv she let it go. She was surprised by the musty smell in the classroom, and by how hot it was in there. She was tempted to ask Miss Irma to open the windows, but there was such a grin plastered across her face that asking Miss Irma to open the windows would have been like offering her a photograph to eat. The principal left the room with a slight sensation of disgust, which she forgot almost immediately. More pressing matters required her attention.

That same week the inspector came, wearing big tinted glasses. She didn't want to inspect anything and she would have given her life for a Coca-Cola, but everything was closed. When the custodian heard that the inspector was there she rolled her eyes as if to say, *what do I care?*

"She wants some coffee," they told her.

"Oh, let her wait," replied the custodian.

It was sweltering and the custodian wasn't thinking straight.

The inspector said, "I want to see a nice class."

She wanted to sit down inside a cool, peaceful classroom and listen to the teacher discuss cattle and take out lots of little cows from all over. What she wanted more than anything was to see something green, lots of grass. She was also willing to listen to a mellow song—as long as the children didn't sing too out of tune—or sit in on a geography class to see the sea painted on a map.

The principal said, "A nice class? Let's go to Irma's room then."

"Alright," said the inspector.

Miss Irma's class was dramatizing Queen Isabel bestowing her jewels upon Columbus. Queen Isabel was played by Alejandra, who wore the swim cap on her head and the long piece of tulle that had been dragged around the schoolyard all afternoon. Columbus wore tennis shoes, red socks, and a colorful visor hat, looking more like an Apache.

When the inspector arrived, the windows were shut airtight.

Miss Irma was unfazed by the inspector's arrival, greeting her as if the woman's presence were entirely natural, as if she had always been a fixture in the classroom. Miss Irma continued to focus on the dramatization.

The children who were acting spoke in low voices, and Miss Irma—practically bent over—cued them anxiously about what to do. The Queen's crown was an elastic band on Alejandra's head. There were delays because Alejandra couldn't remove the band and Columbus couldn't figure it out either. Columbus said:

"What should I do with the rubber band?"

"With the Queen's crown!" corrected Miss Irma, thereby converting it into an extremely valuable object. Timidly, Columbus stood there with the elastic band in his hand, and then Miss Irma said:

"Now, the Queen's silver tureen."

The silver tureen was actually an enormous tin kettle used to serve an infusion of *mate cocido* to the whole class.

"Here's the kettle," said one girl readily.

"Look how the Queen's silver tureen shines!" said Miss Irma enthusiastically.

Columbus held onto the kettle as if it were a watering can. Miss Irma readjusted his hands, placing them underneath it as she said: "It's such a beautiful gift!"

But the kettle was too big and Columbus couldn't manage

to hold on to it. It fell to the floor and Miss Irma said, in a lively voice:

"Alright, alright, let's start over."

When Miss Irma said "Let's start over," the smell of pee wafted into the inspector's nose. She was sitting next to Marcelo Riquelme and she asked to see his notebook. She looked at the first page and that was enough: she could tell exactly what the rest of them would be like. She didn't want to look at the same old notebook again. She said to Miss Irma:

"I'd like to see how your students read."

Miss Irma said: "No, they can't read right now because we're in the middle of our play. If they start reading it will confuse them."

"They could read the play out loud. How about that?"

Grudgingly, Miss Irma handed out their books and the children read in low voices. Columbus was especially hard to hear.

"I can't hear," the inspector called out from the back.

"These are seven-year-old children reading," said Miss Irma. "Not television hosts."

The children became even more confused as they read. Miss Irma whispered from behind, but she whispered so loudly that her voice was the only one to be heard, saying emphatically— voluptuously—as if it involved something that could be eaten:

"The Queen's necklace."

The inspector left without a word and she told the principal in a dull voice, as if mildly disgusted:

"She's crazy."

Her tone also conveyed that this wasn't so out-of-the-ordinary; it was a fairly common circumstance, just another ingredient in the inspector's discomfort, added to the heat, the lack of Coca-Cola, and the coffee that had never arrived.

"I'd like to speak with her later," she said. "She encourages the confusion of roles. The children are going to mix up queens with beggars."

Miss Irma came in to speak with the inspector, her eyes were on fire. The inspector lit a cigarette and said:

"Upon observing your class, Miss (stressing the word 'Miss,' as if she were naming the servant who worked in her house), what is your last name?"

"Irma Santini," came the heated reply.

"Upon observing your class, Miss Santini, I noticed that you create confusion with regard to roles; the children are going to have a distorted view of history. The entire play would lead one to believe that Queen Isabel was a beggar."

"If you'll excuse me," said Miss Irma curtly.

"Just a moment," said the inspector. "I'd like to add that the cleanliness of those costumes could be improved upon because…"

"I won't hear it," said Miss Irma and she walked out in a rage.

"Where is she going?" the inspector asked the principal.

"I don't know," was the answer.

The two of them waited for her to come back.

Miss Irma returned carrying a cardboard box filled with costume skirts. She started to pull them out one by one, her eyes flashing. There were at least twenty skirts, all of them long and faded.

"Is this dirty?" she said, her eyes looked as if they could take a bite out of the inspector. Finally, she threw the contents of the box on the desk and disappeared.

"She should be removed from the classroom," the inspector said. "She can't teach."

"She's extremely dedicated to teaching," said the principal. "She doesn't have any friends, she lives alone. She puts everything she's got into her students... Besides, you should see some of the other things she does..."

"No," said the inspector, "Please, don't ever take me back to her classroom again."

It was stifling hot and the inspector was tired.

She sent for someone to buy her a Coca-Cola.

The principal insisted, "She's so dedicated to teaching."

"Since the moment I stepped inside this school," said the inspector, "that blonde girl has been just standing there on the staircase all dressed up. That's something I don't care for one bit."

"I'm going to tell her to stop with all that. Her service record…"

"How was she rated the last time?"

The inspector checked and all the reports on Miss Irma were filled with praise: nothing less than a sublime teacher.

She decided to write a moderate report. Just then she remembered that she'd parked her car in a bad spot and by now it would be blazing hot inside.

"Well, just tell her to stop all that nonsense," she said.

And she left.

The next day the principal saw Miss Irma arrive, her eyes smoldering. The principal tried to calm her down.

"Irma," she said, "look what a nice report the inspector gave you."

Miss Irma didn't want to read it. She said:

"What do I care? If she left a good report then she's crazy. Why would she say one thing and write something else entirely? I don't care about reports anyway, that's not why I do this job."

And she thought to herself, with profound anger and contempt, that the world was just one big prison.

The Boy Who Couldn't Fall Asleep

ONCE upon a time, there was a boy who couldn't fall asleep. Every night his mother left a table lamp on, a very beautiful lamp with a light bulb as small as a chickpea.

First, he called his mother, saying:

"Mommy, I'm thirsty!"

His mother got up and brought him a glass of water. Then he closed one eye and left the other one open. He called her again:

"Mommy! Do you remember when we went to that place? That place! What was it like?"

"Go to sleep, now," said his mother, who wanted to go to sleep because mothers need rest too.

He looked at the chair and it didn't look like the chair he saw everyday. Now it looked like the chair was wearing a long dress with a little head on top. It kept getting easier and easier to see through the darkness.

"Mommy!" he called.

But his mother had gone to sleep. So he closed his eyes. When he closed his eyes he saw hundreds of little circles float by like grains of rice, they passed by and by. There were so many it was as if the whole world were covered in grains of rice. When he opened his eyes, the rice disappeared.

His mother had told him:

"To fall asleep you must count sheep. Sheep that jump over a fence, one after another they jump on over. Sheep—not bees—because bees buzz from flower to flower so you can't count them."

What if I count dogs? the boy said to himself. He closed his eyes and started counting dogs. But the dogs made a horrible ruckus, they ran in a pack and they didn't jump over the fence one after another. One got tangled up in the wire fence, another barked with his ears perked up.

I'm going to count sheep, he thought.

He closed his eyes and one little sheep appeared all alone, his coat a little mucky. The sheep reluctantly nibbled a bit of grass. He seemed somewhat sad and certainly didn't want to cross the fence. No way.

The boy couldn't sleep because the next day his class at school was going on a field trip to Buenos Aires, on a bus, and he had never been on a field trip. That morning at school the kids had all jumped up and down shouting:

"Field trip! Field trip!"

He had to take a lunchbox with him on the field trip, with

sandwiches and apples. Then he thought, *Is the lunchbox packed? I'd better go check.*

He got up and went to the kitchen and confirmed that the sandwiches and apples had been packed. Then his mother noticed that he was up and about and she said:

"What are you doing?"

"Nothing, nothing."

His mother took him back to bed and said:

"Alright now, go to sleep." She gave him a kiss and tucked him back into bed because he'd taken off all the covers.

Then he started to see sheep, one after another. They were fat sheep, with soft curly wool. Up went their little hooves and *one*...Up went their little hooves and *two*...And they continued prancing on by. It was as if they were floating. The sheep kept getting bigger; now everything was pale, soft, wispy, a white mass drifting slowly, and he fell asleep.

The Wandering Dutchman

ONCE upon a time there was a Dutchman who traveled so, so much that he barely had enough clothes to stay put in one place. He always wore his shorts, his indestructible thick sandals (the Dutch used to wear clogs, but then they caught up with the times and starting wearing sandals, which make the same clunky noise as they walk), and sunglasses. He carried a flashlight so he could always shine a light on anything he saw— bugs, storefronts, or tile floors. He carried all this and much more in his heavy pack, which he wore on his back throughout the countryside and cities of the world. And he traveled the world so much that he'd already seen the kangaroos of Australia, the bottlenose whales of Alaska, the customs of the people of Bali, and the tombs of the pharaohs. And when he met up with his traveler friends to exchange tips they all relied on him, because he was the one who kept his guidebooks in alphabetical order by country. He would never say it out loud, but sometimes when they named a place he would think, "I've been there" or "I've been there three times." He didn't speak up because he didn't want to come off as someone who's better than everyone else. But now, for the first time in his life, he was stumped: he didn't know where to go. He unfolded a huge map in his room, as big as the room itself, and after studying it he felt as if he'd already been on a trip. Where to go? To the North Pole? But it was winter now. To Africa again, to see new animals? But it was summer in Africa. To Fiji? Yes, but not quite yet. Farther north, farther south, not quite yet, I've already been there. He had yet to discover himself among all those maps that are supposedly meant to orient oneself. Finally, feeling flustered—and when he was flustered he always said "*Hans, tribauss, mackassen*"—he tossed a coin: heads for north, tails for south. It came up south and he almost cheated at his own game and tossed the coin again. But since he was so honest and respectful of his own fate, even though he thought going south sounded absurd, he traveled to Argentina. He'd never been there and he loved the idea of discovering somewhere new.

When he got to Calle Florida, a steady stream of people walked in one direction and another mass walked in the other— it was a pedestrian highway, without any cars. At times he got lost, or tripped over. The street was filled with banks showing the exchange rate in dollars and he wanted to change money, but the bank employee didn't understand his English. The Dutchman's name was Goran Shikendanz and Goran didn't understand the banker's English either. At least three or four more employees came over to try and figure out what he was saying, each of whom understood something entirely different:

one of them thought he needed to use the bathroom, another that he was looking for a hotel with a private bathroom, and the third just played dumb. And poor Goran really put his foot in it, because one thing led to another and they asked him his name. He answered "Juan Pérez," which figured in his guidebook as a very common name in Buenos Aires, and he'd already noticed how puzzled people looked when he told them his real name. But when he replied "Juan Pérez" in his thick Dutch accent, they all burst out laughing. Then he overheard one banker saying to another:

"There's no sense in beating a dead horse."

The employees turned their backs on him, so he got out his dictionary: *What did horses have to do with anything? Why were they talking about horses when he was just trying to exchange money? Besides, why would anyone beat a poor horse?* Bewildered by these thoughts, he asked a girl walking along Calle Florida for the name of a street that wasn't in his guidebook. The girl was sophisticated, very tanned, and she looked like an expert in all trades. She glanced at him coldly out of the corner of her eye and said:

"No clue."

He became even more perplexed when he got to the corner of Bartolomé Mitre and Florida: there were some Peruvians playing music from the Altiplano. They were pretty good. Next to them a sign read: AWAY WITH THE CLOSED-LIST SYSTEM. Across the street—not listening to the music and clearly indifferent to the closed lists—a bunch of people were pounding on the door of a bank with little hammers, saying: "Thieves! Low lives!" Each group had their own set of onlookers, like at some sort of fair. Next to the Peruvians there was a lady dancing a little waltz all on her own. Referring to the Peruvians, a man standing next to her said:

"Who would stop to watch such a thing!"

To be on the safe side Goran didn't say anything, but another man who'd overheard the first one said:

"What a moron."

He had to look up the meaning of "moron" and "closed list" in his dictionary. And then, with only an inkling of understanding, he headed off to his hotel.

When he walked into his hotel room the windows were closed, boarded up. If there was one thing Goran couldn't stand it was boarded-up windows. So he said "*Hans, tribauss, mackassen,*" and was about to burst into a fit of rage, but then he suddenly lost heart. He said to himself, *What am I doing here? Who told me to come here?* Whenever he was out traveling around the world, far from home, he remembered his dog Guga: with his dog everything would have been different. But since he'd experienced these same emotions so many times, he was reassured knowing that the first day one arrives in a new place isn't like the rest: on the first day everything seems disconnected, rough around the edges, but then, hour by hour, day by day, those rough edges start to smooth over. That was what he most enjoyed about traveling. By the third day, even the sky, which at first seems strange and unknown, becomes friendly, as if to say: *I am the same sky covering the whole planet.* If only he could have a dog in Buenos Aires. In India they'd let him keep a dog, a parrot, and a monkey. But now, when he got a good look at the hotel concierge, he realized how preposterous this wish was: the concierge's hair and moustache were dyed black, and the dye-job made him look angry. So Goran set back out into the street with his small backpack (he kept three bags inside the big backpack), and went to eat at a café that served coffee, food, and drinks. While he ate he listened in on the conversation at the table next to him, in an attempt to learn some Spanish. One fellow said:

"Uff, today sure is *jorobado*..."

Jorobado? He looked the word up in his dictionary and read: *Joroba: the camel's hump.* How could the day be humpbacked? And then he asked the waiter how to get somewhere:

"Uff, getting there will be *jorobado*."

Goran asked:

"Why? Are there many hills?"

"No," replied the waiter. "In other words, getting there is complicated."

And then he understood that, in Spanish, saying "The camel *es* jorobado" means the camel has a hump, but "The camel *está* jorobado" means there's something wrong with the camel. He was further confused when someone at the table next to him said:

"That guy? He's top dog."

But there weren't any dogs in sight. It was a mystery, they were alluding to something else. And since they were taking about people, someone else spoke up:

"That guy? Nah, he's a *pichi*."

What could *pichi* mean? He looked it up in his dictionary and it said: *Big hairy armadillo*. By the man's derogatory tone, there couldn't be anything nice or pleasant about running into one of those creatures; he'd have to ask around. But now they'd moved on to talking about money and checks, and one was saying to the other:

"You'll get your money—when pigs fly."

Just when was that? The national holidays were listed in his guidebook: National Flower Day, Mother's Day, Animal's Day— but since when did pigs have their own special day? And just how would they get up in the air? In hot air balloons? Or maybe there was a special day for flying kites with pigs on them. He couldn't find the answer in his guidebook and he really wanted to go over and ask them, but he'd already been ridiculed at the bank and he couldn't handle another ordeal. He started his meal and drank a beer. Then he heard one guy say to the other:

"Under the weather? Drink some yerba mate and you'll feel better."

That's what he should do—drinking mate would help him get back on his feet.

He was upset, angry, and confused: they spoke of armadillos, horses, and cats—he'd heard someone say, "Don't let the cat out of the bag," and also, "What a cash cow." But where are all the armadillos? What about the cows and the horses? They're nowhere in sight. He wasn't furious—he was defeated, so defeated that he did something out of character: that night at the hotel he plopped himself down to watch television next to a deaf lady with a little cat. At first the lady smiled at him, which made him happy. At least someone acknowledged him, but then he realized the smile was plastered on her face permanently, hard to tell why. Turning back to the television he regained a sense of hope: the program was called "Rural Tourism." It followed the lives of people who were preparing to host tourists: some women were cooking, another milked a cow, and one man— this was what made him want to go—was pumping a railroad handcar. The program host said, "You can ride on a handcar if you'd like." And then there was a clip of the handcar gliding along the tracks. That's when Goran yelled enthusiastically: "*Piriviridam!*" (which is the word for handcar in Dutch). The deaf lady heard and Goran felt she approved. The cat seemed to agree, too. The program host said, "You can ride a horse, milk a cow, and watch otters groom themselves." Goran thought, *That's where all the animals are! I want to go there. Everything will make sense once I get there.* Then, without realizing the irony, he blurted out: "The heart of Argentina—once I get there, I'll make sure they let every single one of those poor cats out of the bag."

When he got to Iramain—that's what the town was called—it was even better than he'd imagined. The train station was straight out of a children's book, there was a red sign stamped with the town's name. On one side of the station there were houses, and on the other, green pastures as far as the eye could see. It was as if the houses were lined up on the shore of a vast sea. And in the fields, clustered into groups as if gathering for a country festival, there were little cows under a bright blue sky and wispy clouds of cotton. But the cows weren't just out in the fields. Back across the tracks, there were cows in the yards too, since there was so much space between the houses. He stopped to look at some cows in front of one house, and a villager told him:

"That's Gabriela over there, and this is Estela. Gabriela's a good girl, but Estela can be pig-headed."

"Pig-headed? Pig-headed? What do you mean?" Goran said in alarm. Again, he was missing something. How could a cow have a pig's head?

"You're not from around here, I can tell by your accent."

"No, I'm from the Netherlands."

"From where?"

He had a map in his pack, but he wasn't about to take it out now, before he'd gotten settled. So, pointing beyond the field, he said:

"It's that way."

"Ah," said the villager. "I never met anyone from present-day Uropa. We've got some of your kinsfolk here, but from way back."

"Oh. What do you mean?"

"I mean people who came over a long time ago, too long ago to count. My wife's grandmother came from Uropa as did her mother, my late mother-in-law. She knew the whole story, but my wife doesn't remember any of the details."

And Goran understood almost everything the villager said!

"What does *mañera* mean?" asked Goran.

A skittish animal. They're just like Christians: some you can count on, while others are *mañeros*."

After that conversation, Goran went to look at two sheep in another yard. They were eating grass and the lawn was as trim as if it had just been mown. On the dirt road there were three southern lapwing chicks, as big as pigeons. A woman walked up to him and asked:

"Would you like a mate?"

"Yes," said Goran, "because in bad weather a little mate helps you feel better."

"Don't you know it," said the woman and handed him a yerba mate gourd that was as big as a pumpkin. Goran made a strange face because it was the first time he'd tried yerba mate, and the woman said:

"You have to get used to it—it's bitter, but it always does the trick."

"So it's not pig-headed?" said Goran.

The woman laughed, they laughed together. She said:

"Will you be staying at Susana's place?"

He didn't know where Susana's place was, he thought it might be far, but it was right down the street. There was a row of houses that were sturdy but old, and across the street was the station with its toy sign. The woman who walked him to Susana's wanted him to take off his backpack so she could help him, but he refused. He guessed women in Iramain were used to carrying large bundles. Susana herself was standing in the doorway and she waved him in. He asked her:

"Madam, may I have the key to my room?"

"No," said Susana. "We don't use keys here. Just make yourself at home."

"Madam, would you like to see my passport?"

"No, m'dear. No need for that."

Susana already knew that he came from Uropa and carried around a bag that weighed something close to a hundred pounds.

He set down his pack in the middle of the room. It looked out of place. The room looked like it belonged to a family member who'd gone on a trip but might move back any time. On the nightstand there was a Bible, although luckily for him the print was too small, thus releasing him from the obligation to read it. Still, there it was, just in case . . . And the window, which looked out onto a garden, was plastered in stickers. One of them said: "Udder cream for cows." Another depicted a field of wheat. The lowing of a young cow rang so clearly from outside, it felt like the cow was calling to him in particular. Next to another bed there was a homemade cradle where they kept sheets and tablecloths. Why was the window so low? A person—or a sheep—

could walk right up at any time to converse with him as he lay in bed. On the wall there was a cupboard made with the shell of an old television set and next to it a dark wardrobe that looked like it had been brought over by the Uropeans from back in the day. But why was he getting sidetracked by the room's décor? He wanted to explore every nook and cranny of the town, through and through. He removed a smaller bag from the big pack and set off. The town was three blocks long and three blocks wide. It was surrounded by fields on all sides. As soon as he stepped outside, as if sensing his intentions, Miss Betty from next door asked him:

"I can go with you if you'd like, so you don't get lost."

"Oh, no thanks," he said.

As if Goran Shikendanz, of all people, was going to get lost in that speck of a town—he who'd been to London, India, and Timbuktu. *Which way should I go?* he wondered. First he imagined exploring the town systematically, walking up and down each block, but then he decided: *I'm just going to go wherever my feet take me.* His feet led him straight to the square. It wouldn't have mattered which path he'd taken because they all led straight to the square. The square recalled some not-so-distant time when the cattle would have congregated right there. In fact, there was a sheep grazing next to the statue of San Martín. The statue was somewhat obscured behind the bulky mass of the sheep and two dogs lying there absolutely still, in such contrast to urban dogs, who want to get their paws on everything they see and smell. It was as if these dogs had seen and smelled everything they needed. There was also a monument to the fallen soldiers of the Malvinas War, with a collective mask to represent them all; it looked like a Mycenaean mask. At the other end of the square a man was teaching a boy around the age of four to ride a horse; from the park bench where Goran sat he could hear the lesson perfectly. No one would ever make a point of visiting this square—get dressed, take some money along, elect to move from inside to outside. In fact, he discovered there wasn't much difference between inside and outside. It was more about shade and sunlight. For example, the house where he was staying and the houses along his street—all at least a hundred years old—didn't have front windows. It was to keep the sunlight from pouring in. Once you stepped inside, darkness ruled. The rooms were like trees lending their shade. When he stood up and started walking around town he noticed there was an Iramain style for decorating gardens: each rosebush had been planted in a tire, like a whitewashed pot. In one garden there were so many roses that it looked like a lifesaving contest. And farther out, on the edge of the countryside, they'd laid down stones around the base of a large tree, and next to it was a huge tire with firewood inside. Indeed, Iramain had its own unique style. As he listened to a bird that sounded as if it had the hiccups, he noticed a small windmill decoration and he brightened: a windmill, like the ones in Holland, and all those automobile tires (he liked circular things). As the day carried on he saw people coming to town from the countryside—only a few, but their silhouettes came into view so clearly that he could watch them approach from afar. Where were their houses? Everything was in plain sight; and when he went back to his room and looked at his big pack, squat in the middle of the floor, he thought, *It looks like an animal*. And for the first time he didn't open the pack to check that everything was there, or to make sure the things he'd need next were on top, or to look up the time zones. He knew everything was in the right place. And as he drifted off to sleep he thought, *After all, what's so great about bags? They're just filled with stuff*. Then he took a long nap.

On the street—if you could even call it a street—Goran saw an equal number of light-skinned and dark-skinned folks. This made him want to learn more about the history of the town. He asked Alicia, who sold school supplies, candy, and cigarettes, and served coffee in a big, grim room. What did she know about the history of Iramain? He was the only customer drinking coffee, and she drank a cup along with him. Goran didn't know whether he was a customer, a friend, or whether he should buy one of the objects for sale hanging on the wall. She told him:

"There aren't any thieves in Iramain because we've only got a population of three hundred. But do be careful with the dogs, because you never know how they'll act around someone from out of town. Now, if you want, you can go to Don Monticl's place—he can explain better than me. But come back whenever you'd like, that way I can ask you all about the Netherlands. I'd love to go on a trip, but when someone comes to visit from abroad, or from Buenos Aires—not long ago they came from Buenos Aires to film the giant pumpkins—it's like traveling without even having to pack a suitcase."

He went to see Don Montiel, who was sitting on the sidewalk in a pair of traditional gaucho pants with a belt to match. His wife walked up soon after. She didn't seem too convinced by their conversation. She looked faded and withered, as if the dust from the streets had penetrated her skin. Goran asked Don Montiel:

"Are you *criollo*?"

"*Criollo* and headstrong."

"Pig-headed?"

"No, never. Pig-headed, what for?"

"Ma'am, what's your last name?"

"Decker," she said austerely.

"So you're German."

"I'm Russian."

"With a German last name."

"How should I know?"

She wasn't the least bit interested in her roots. Don Montiel said, his eyes twinkling:

"Now, *she's* pig-headed."

At first Goran was shocked, then he realized it was a joke. He asked:

"How old is your house?"

"Uff, at least a hundred years old. These houses used to belong to the foremen, really rich folks. My mama lived out in the country, and grandfather used to lash us with a whip. My mama had a thousand hens and she made her own butter."

Don Montiel's wife interrupted and said:

"Used to be all Russian carts."

Goran didn't inquire about grandfather's whip, but he did ask about the Russian carts.

Don Montiel said:

"They're gonna make a museum inside the station: put the carts on display, the ones that used to be called *troikas* back in the day."

There was a certain reluctance in his voice, as if to say, *What will they think of next!*

"Gonna display all types of old-fashioned things, even spittoons. Who keeps somethin' like that? If you got one, you use it. Otherwise, who's keepin' a spittoon around the house? Now people even use 'em as flowerpots."

From the museum they moved on to animals, and that's when Goran really learned a thing or two: how an animal knows when it's going to die, how a horse recognizes its master by their tone of voice, how people become fond of the animals they raise. "Especially the ones fed on a bottle," said Don Montiel. "Once I had a pig used to follow me around for three miles at a time." He also said they named the cows—there was a calf named Maruca, and another with curved horns called Bugle; there was even one called The Girl of Seventeen. And when Goran didn't understand the Spanish word for "curvy" Don Montiel made gestures until he did. Suddenly, taking him by surprise, Don Montiel asked:

"Tell me now, how come everyone hates the Jews so much?"

Goran had studied at the university in Leuven; he thought back to all the things he'd read in the past and tried to explain the best he could. He didn't feel like he'd given a good enough explanation, and Don Montiel seemed to agree because he said:

"But that's all water under the bridge. What about now?"

So Goran painstakingly tried to explain again, but Don Montiel just said:

"Aha."

Then he added:

"The Germans appear to be more easily seduced by evangelists, and the Christians too, I guess. I'm not a hundred percent Christian myself, but I suppose I'm more drawn to the priest. Although deep down, not really. Once we had a real good priest, he'd show up no matter the weather—rain, hail, or shine. Truth is, one day I got tired of him comin' around so much, always ridin' his bicycle down the same street, so I laid out a dead snake right where he got off his bike, just to see what he'd do."

"What for?"

"Whatcha mean, what for? Just so he'd go somewhere else to ride his bike, so he'd stay home when it rained. When it rains everybody wants to stay in the houses. The pastor we got now ain't worth a cent, just like the choir leader. We used to have one who could get even the stones a-singin'; the one we got now can barely hold a tune. Tell me now, how come there's people you can't understand when they talk? Some evangelists come down here from North America, white and black folk, built a church right next to the old bridge. You seen it? Brought a translator with 'em to sign the deed for the land, because the deed's gotta be in Argentinean, and then they disappeared. Never came back. Makes sense, anyway. How they gonna give a sermon? Who's gonna understand 'em?"

"Do you understand me?"

"Everything, son. Every word you say."

Goran felt a bit shook up when he left: they'd spoken of guinea pigs, Protestants, Jews, Russian carts. What had the conversation amounted to? Clearly people in this town didn't worry about exhausting every subject—in fact, when they said "certainly" it was almost as if they were distracted, as if "certainly" were an answer for anything. He noticed when they responded with an "aha" they actually *were* interested, as if reflecting on something new. But the occasional reply was enough, they didn't inquire further, perhaps they were processing all the information in their heads. And then he noticed some people had approached them to listen in—around five or so—but they weren't actually interested in the discussion itself. They just walked off without saying goodbye, as if the conversation had been part of a movie or on the television, and once you lose interest you can just change the channel. No greeting. But Goran was so thrilled that people really understood him when he spoke, he promised to come back and visit Don Montiel the next day.

On the third day Goran went out for a walk—which is just a figure of speech because in that town all you could do was glide gracefully from inside to outside. There were no doorsteps, you were just suddenly on the sidewalk without even thinking about it. Across from the station the vast countryside unfolded in every direction. Everything was so uncluttered, so indistinguishable, there was no room for secret thoughts. He looked down at the ground, at some dried manure, at a sheep in one yard standing by a lawnmower, a red plant in the next yard over, the kind you'd expect to find in a suburban garden. From another house came the murmur of the radio, there were chickens out back and a car out front. That's when he understood why they interweaved topics of conversation: because everything was a mixture. Two southern lapwings hopped down the street in front of a couple (he was dark-skinned and she was blonde) with some sort of outdoor furniture workshop across the street under a parakeet cage. Goran asked the man whether he knew of anyone whose grandparents had been immigrants, to hear their story. He said:

"Of course, there's Don Herman. He doesn't live far, although he's a little messed up, poor guy."

"Messed up?" Goran asked in alarm. But he understood that the man was sick because "messed up" meant twisted, pig-headed, and sick, too.

"I'll walk you over," the man offered.

Don Herman's house was only twenty feet away, but it must be tradition to accompany everyone in town where they're going. The house was white with a garden in front, and Don Herman was standing at the door as if he knew they were coming to see him. He was a very tall, thin old man who looked fragile, as if his body were uncomfortable with its surroundings. After Goran had bid farewell to the carpenter he explained to Don Herman that he'd come from the Netherlands and asked him:

"Where was your family from?"

The man started to speak in the weary voice of a convalescent. When he realized that Goran could barely understand him, he yelled back into the house:

"Eva!"

Out came Eva, her face bearing the expression of someone who'd done this all before; "same old story," it seemed to say. She was carrying a tattered sheet of yellowish paper with the family history. The paper stated that in 1470 they'd been Czechoslovakians emigrating to Germany. The year 1470 seemed so long ago, especially because a ton of grandchildren were running around the table, that Goran asked him:

"And your grandfather?"

So Don Herman told a long story: from Germany to France, from France to Paraguay, and while his aunt was in Paraguay his brother was in Olavarria—but then they returned to breed sheep. He said:

"We were the first settlers in Iramain."

Wow, thought Goran, *what a fascinating story*. But between the man's wavering voice, the exasperated look on Eva's face as she did the dishes, and the ten children running circles around the table, it was hard to sort out. Besides, it seemed like Don

Herman wasn't far from joining that long list of ancestors from Essen, Alsace-Lorraine, and Paraguay. So he said:

"I don't want to tire you out."

Eva concurred—silence gives consent—and Goran asked her:

"Do you like living here?"

"What do you think? I'm going to move to Buenos Aires."

Her tone of voice made it obvious she thought no one could possibly enjoy living there. Don Herman looked even more shriveled and yellow, like the edges of the tattered paper about his ancestors.

When Goran left—the house was directly across from the square, he couldn't get away from that square: the Mycenaean mask and the dog laying beside it, the same old tree with the "artistic" structure around its base made from leaves and a tire, the same tiny church—he said, "*Hans, tribauss, mackassen.*" What am I doing here? Don Herman was about to croak any day now, and what do I care if his sister's aunt was from Alsace-Lorraine? Who could care less? I could die, too—I'll be damned if it's while I'm in this godforsaken town. And the Mycenaean mask and Don Herman's aunt who went off to Paraguay, everything began to meld into part of the same era, all forming part of an irrelevant yet grueling past.

He saw a market called "The Redhead." His first thought was, *I should find out what that name's all about.* But then, like Don Montiel's wife, he said to himself: *What do I care?* The Redhead could be a woman, a cow, anything—whatever had occurred to the shopkeeper. The town was coming to an end, abruptly; he could hardly believe a place could have such perfectly defined limits, that everything could be so still and so out in the open. Then he decided to try something new: to reach the countryside (which was his goal) he decided to make himself smaller, to move more slowly, so that the town would last longer. He looked down at the ground. Sure enough, the ground was filled with things to look at; sure enough, there was cow manure, both fresh and dry, but what do I care? On the edge of town he saw a magnificent vegetable garden at least half a block long with giant pumpkins and cornstalks. It was next to a tin house and right by the door there was a sleek car. A young man who looked like he belonged in the city was washing the car. He seemed out of place next to that house; his face didn't look like the face of someone who tends a vegetable garden. Goran walked closer to look at the garden with feigned interest; he was still feeling the negative effects his last encounter, but he was curious to know what the relationship was between that man and the shack. He called out, hypocritically:

"What beautiful pumpkins!"

The young man stopped washing his car and said:

"Come closer, come get a good look."

But Goran didn't want to go look at the pumpkins or the cornstalks or any other vegetables cultivated by humans since the beginning of mankind. The young man graciously welcomed him into the shack and back out to some sort of shelter with a dirt floor, an unsightly shelter. And in a cosmopolitan voice, with flawless manners, the young man called inside:

"Mama, could you please bring out the chairs?"

From inside emerged an old lady with bright eyes and the face of someone who has hardly any friends. The son said:

"This man is Dutch."

The old lady seemed unfazed by this news, so to flatter her Goran said:

"What beautiful pumpkins!"

She replied:

"Yep, 'cept when they came from the television to film 'em there was only about seven. I always keep a club behind the door because there's a lotta bad folks out there."

She wasn't a grouchy lady, just someone who seemed like she'd been born a sourpuss, and he couldn't imagine her looking different or younger. She started to list all the bad things in the world: a woman who'd twisted her arm while rescuing a calf from a well, corrupt politicians, immoral behavior, and evil ways. Since she was a little *jorobada* and complained of pain in her legs, Goran imagined that each and every wrongdoing had somehow become embedded in her bones. Plus, she looked like the type of person that fought with her husband, who was walking up to them now with an egg in his open palm. He was an extremely tall man, and to change the subject Goran wanted to ask him what his heritage was, but the man obviously didn't care because he looked at Goran flatly as if he'd always been there, without a trace of curiosity. He practically lived in the garden and every once in a while, he would walk over to the shack to say something, like now, with his palm stretched wide open:

"The hen laid an egg outside the coop."

Without waiting for anyone to answer, or take the egg from his hand, or acknowledge him in any way, he turned back to the garden. When Goran got up to leave, the queen of wrongdoings told him:

"Careful with that dog, he's a scrounger."

"What do you mean?"

"He'll bite you in the butt."

Trying his best to make sure not to upset the scrounging dog, Goran said goodbye to the son who was still washing his car with gusto.

Curiously, his visit to the sourpuss-witch had been stimulating. The sun was setting and everything seemed more beautiful: the sounds, the colors. The decorative plant seemed even redder and the white mark on the white-faced calf looked like a cloud; the birdie with hiccups sang with zeal. The whole world was a concert of cows, doves, and frogs; there were no soloists. And recently, he'd been feeling thankful and happy that time was passing inadvertently, as if he couldn't handle the passing of time from one hour to the next, and he was grateful to nature for taking care of it for him. He knew there was something wrong about that, about killing time, but the satisfaction of feeling another time of day arrive, of everything changing, was worth it. He made his way back to the houses (now, like Don Montiel, he said "the houses" and understood the expression: in the city it's my house or your house because there are so many of them; here the houses are human shelters, they belong to everyone and no one, like shady groves). On the sidewalk he saw Don Montiel drinking yerba mate, who said:

"Come on over and cool off. Would you like a mate?"

He drank some mate to get back on his feet. Don Montiel was with one of his sons, one who looked like life had got the better of him. Don Montiel spoke and the son looked standoffish. Goran told them:

"I went out on the edge of town, to a shack."

"Aha."

"And I spoke with a woman there," he described her using gestures. "And met her husband. Is she pig-headed?"

Don Montiel laughed and told his son:

"Did you hear that? He went out to…"

He said this half laughing, half in awe, as if Goran had stuck his foot into an anthole. The son didn't share his father's amusement; he seemed wary. Don Montiel said:

"She came to town with a circus and ended up staying. She married that poor soul later on."

Don Montiel's son kept quiet, as if he didn't feel comfortable sharing these details with a foreigner. Talking about other people's private lives disturbed him, gave him a bad feeling, yet he stayed. And since it was just the three of them there, and Don Montiel and his son were but two, as if there was a void, as if the world only takes shape when there's a group, a group as varied as the sounds of the cows lowing, the frogs croaking, and the southern lapwing calling. They were choral people.

That same day he put the small bags into his pack, said goodbye to Susana, and called at the door of Don Montiel, who said:

"Are you leaving, friend?"

"That's right."

He looked Goran straight in the eye as he said "friend," not like when he said "certainly" and then looked all around.

"You really found your tongue in this town," said Don Montiel. And then, in the tone they used amongst themselves—which wasn't the same one they used with visitors, it was more assertive—he said:

"You're gonna have to come on back."

"Ah, yes, yes," said Goran, but then he thought, *It's just a figure of speech, like Don Montiel says*. But not a minute later he was surprised when he found himself thinking, *How will I ever return to a place I've never left?*

Quitting Smoking

I T'S no secret there are support groups to quit smoking, drinking, and gambling. But there are no groups to quit gossiping, stealing, or bribing, which could also be considered addictions since they're associated with bad habits and misconduct. It would seem these groups arise when the misconduct is self-destructive, although in North America they've instilled the belief that smoking is bad for others, so if they see a mother smoking while holding her baby they want to slap the death penalty on her in the name of healthy living.

Whether the purpose is to quit smoking, drinking, or gambling, the group methodology is similar. Let's imagine a group of gossipers who want to redeem themselves. The coordinator would say:

"So, tell us: when was your last relapse?"

And then the gossiper would start to tell a story, which would be highly instructive for everyone. Then each person would tell their own story (as it always goes in these groups), with the purpose of overall improvement.

I went to a group to quit smoking. The coordinator's name was Leonardo and he was a mix between a recovering smoker, a preacher, and an activist. He also reminded me of an older brother—not a father figure, because Leonardo always found a way to understand the most incomprehensible things and didn't make any judgments like God the Father does. He had the body of a tenacious bear and the head of a lion. He wore a shirt from which all color had faded, as if its purpose were merely to cover his skin, not actually resemble clothes. He was an inspiration to those on the right path and to those who were struggling. He didn't discriminate, although in my opinion some sort of self-inflicting ritual, like coating oneself with cigarette ash for two weeks, would have been an effective tool to remind us what we had given up. Truthfully, all these group techniques are profoundly Christian: there's the fall of man, the redemption, and finally, the conversion. Evil is temptation—even if our savior Leonardo (who also happens to be a shrink) refuses to acknowledge it. At Group, we spoke of "the fatal moment" (which we'd conjure up by drinking a glass of water) or having a "good group connection," and Leonardo would do what he called "awareness raising," so that people would become conscious of why they smoke. He also drew connections between the how, the when, and the where of smoking cigarettes.

At Group, there was a dentist in the purification stage (he'd come from two days of abstinence). To keep himself from smoking he had showered six times a day and hand-washed all the clothes in his house—he'd become a launderer-dentist. There was another man who'd retired and bought a lovely country home outside the city. He showed us a picture of the house—splendid in contrast to his destitute appearance—while saying:

"All the hard work I put in on this house is useless. It's not worth a thing if I can't sit down in the afternoon with a smoke and a glass of water: nothing else matters."

His words filled me with sheer terror. How could that beautiful house—which took him twenty years to build—be of no use to him? In my mind, he was the spitting image of vice. Compared to him, I felt much better adjusted. Recalling a Hindu saying about Westerners, I felt even more renewed by my path: they say Westerners don't know what happiness is until someone comes along and hands them a cigarette and a glass of water.

Leonardo asked:

"Which is the most important cigarette of the day for you?"

One by one they replied:

"For me, it's the one after lunch," and then someone else said:

"For me, it's the one at six o'clock in the evening." I wondered just how they'd come to realize this. It felt like they'd been privy to some wisdom I'd missed out on, and that was discouraging, because it felt like I'd gotten off track. I started thinking about Spinoza, who said: *Man thinks smoking makes him free—but free he is not, because he knows not why he smokes.* I had to sit back and learn humility from everyone else. Humility, another Christian virtue at play: confessing deprivation exactly as one experiences it; asking the group for help in times of temptation; not becoming bigheaded over little triumphs or losing heart with failures. But that type of humility makes me nervous. I've seen it in recovering alcoholics—they don't drink anymore but they've become misplaced, grizzled, as if they were toting around something embarrassing.

The most striking case was a young man who'd gone through an extended withdrawal, undertaking huge sacrifices: he'd buried his cigarettes in the backyard, steered clear from bars and public places, and even taken up craft projects to keep his hands busy. This is exactly what the eremitic monks of the fifth century did. They didn't work to make money, but rather to keep their hands busy because evil feeds on idle bodies, leading them to use their hands for wicked deeds. I've always been disturbed by the work of those monks, especially the ones who spent more transporting palm leaves to keep their hands busy than they earned from the work itself. But they were happy that way.

As I was saying about the young man who'd gone through withdrawal, he asked Leonardo:

"So, now what?"

Leonardo said:

"What do you mean, 'now what'?"

"I mean, what's next?"

"I don't understand."

But I did. He was hinting at the reward theory: he felt all his effort should result in something extraordinary in return. Leonardo said to him, smiling:

"Now you continue down your path."

The kid's face dropped, as if he'd been genuinely deceived. And I understood him, because even God rested on the seventh day to delight in his own work. (Which is the perfect moment for lighting up a smoke.)

To conclude, the funniest thing I've read about cigarettes, which really hits the nail on the head, was by the Peruvian writer Julio Ramón Ribeyro, a close friend of Bryce Echenique:

"I don't know if I smoke so I can write, or if I write so I can smoke."

Impressions of a School Principal

I'M the principal of a school in an outlying part of town. The produce man passes through the neighborhood announcing his produce with a bullhorn. Since it's practically the countryside, his voice can be heard from afar announcing something that sounds exciting: A party? A dance? It gets closer and you hear, "Potatoes, 4000 pesos; squash, 5000 pesos," proclaimed in an enthusiastic tone of voice. Once, we put on a festival at school and he was the announcer. Some lady gave us the idea because, like she said, the produce man had all the PA equipment. The Japanese flower-growers live way back near the fields. They always drive by in their cars but I've never seen any of them come by the school.

On the far side of the school there's a little field to go romp around in; it has a lagoon where we study something modern called "the ecosystem." The ecosystem is how living creatures relate to one another, how some eat others, why spiders are useful even though they seem useless, stuff like that.

The teachers say, "We're going to the lagoon to study the little animals that live there."

I know they're really going to romp around in the little nearby field, but they're so happy on their way out. Besides, they know the creatures in the lagoon like the backs of their hands: frogs, worms, and—when the rain comes—tiny fish. When the children come back, rosy-cheeked from having run around, I ask them:

"Did you study the ecosystem?"

"Yes," they say enthusiastically. "We brought back an earth-wern."

"An earth*worm*," says the teacher. "Where did you learn to call it a 'wern'!"

I've noticed when the teacher corrects the children, none of them want to repeat the word; they keep quiet. And if the teacher says:

"Repeat after me: earth*worm*."

They say "earthworm" in a somber, sad voice. Like the children, I prefer "earthwern" to "earthworm." It's more humble, shadier, more intimate. Earthworm is a little dry.

The children in first, second, and third grade say, "Should I draw the stripe, madam?"

The teacher corrects them, "Shall I trace the line, teacher?"

The truth is that either way you can understand what they're trying to say. The expression "draw the stripe" does seem suitable for that age group. Eventually they learn to say "line" on their own, when they know what "line" means in a greater context: like learning how to stay in line, learning how to adapt to school. Before a certain age, a line is the same as a stripe for kids. Now where they came up with "madam," I couldn't say…

They read the book *Platero* and then write sentences about it.

One kid wrote: "Platero sniffered the flowers."

They're always throwing rocks at the dogs because any one of them could have rabies and nobody wants them getting too close and, besides, it's like a game. There aren't any sports fields.

I've also seen them use sentences with the words "build" and "destroy."

One child wrote: "My aunt built an apartment. My godfather destroyed an apartment."

Naturally, the teacher gave him a good grade. There's one teacher who cares for them deeply, she looks like Snow White. She studies architecture and when she's absent I ask the children:

"Did the teacher tell you she wasn't coming today?"

They say, "Today she's not here because she has to take an exam."

And they pronounce "exam" correctly. For them, the word "exam" is associated with Snow White, whom they love very much. They don't plan on taking many school exams in life, but Snow White has surely told them how much she studies, about all the exams at college, and I'm sure many of them hope she does well on the exam.

Mrs. Betty lives across the street from the school and has one glass eye. Her dog is called Mole and he used to come into the principal's office and sniff the wastebasket to see if there were any bits of food. It didn't bother me: if he didn't find anything he would just lay down and keep quiet and I didn't even notice him. Mrs. Betty liked me a lot, she was so gracious that even with my terribly obsessive gaze I had entirely forgotten she had one glass eye. But once Mole ate twenty salami sandwiches; he ate the ones with salami and left the cheese sandwiches intact. Perhaps if he had eaten the ones with cheese the teacher would have forgiven him, but she threw him out violently, pushing him out the door.

When that happened I appealed to logic, to my common sense and my adult feelings. I said, "That's awful!" Part of me thought it was funny.

The teacher said to me angrily, "He can't just come in here everyday like he owns the place and take something!"

A little voice inside me was saying, "I don't really care." But the voice of reason prevailed and I told her:

"You're right, he can't. We aren't going to let him in anymore."

Ever since, Mrs. Betty doesn't send him over anymore. It's like when children go to play at someone else's house and do something disrespectful, and then their parents don't send them back over again.

Betty is still friendly, but more restrained. There's been a change. Before, when she talked to me, she was always beaming and the healthy eye smiled, too. Now, sometimes there's a flash of anger in the healthy eye when she talks to me. She says, "Sure, sure," in a reluctant tone of voice. Now, whenever I see her, I notice her glass eye. I don't know how to fix things. I can't tell her, "Send Mole over, we miss him so…" That would be lying and besides, lots of teachers don't want the dog at school.

THE STUDENT NAMED MONSOON

"A pencil fer my brother?"

"No, I don't have any pencils today."

But he doesn't leave. It's Monsoon.

"Go back to class."

"But she sent me here."

The teacher sent him to the office because she couldn't stand him anymore. He's in the afternoon group that starts at one o'clock, but sometimes by ten o'clock in the morning he's already spying through the window at the morning kids. When the morning teacher sees him, she sends him on an easy errand. After that, he goes to his classroom but it's still the morning group and says to the teacher:

"Should I stay?"

"Alright," she says, "but be quiet."

He stays a while in the morning group until the teacher gets tired and throws him out. At one o'clock, when his classmates are in school, he spies at them through the window. The teacher pretends not to see him.

The children say:

"Teacher, Monsoon is at the window and he didn't come to class!"

The teacher opens the window and asks him:

"Why didn't you come today?"

"Because I don't got shoes."

"And the ones you're wearing, what about those?"

"They're my brother's. You don't got no shoes?"

"No I don't and you have to come inside."

The teacher says it feebly, because she has to. He's always coming and going.

"Okay," Monsoon says, "I'm going home and I'll be right back."

Half an hour later he's in the principal's office because the teacher can't handle him a minute longer. He doesn't seem to mind. I can't scold him because he isn't angry or scared, nor is he resentful.

I write something down and pretend he's not there. He insists:

"Do you have a pencil fer my brother?"

"I already told you I don't. What did you do with the pencil I gave you yesterday?"

"That was fer my brother."

I can't scold him. He just needs a few kind words.

"Alright, write the vowels."

"Which one, the 'a'?"

He makes the 'a' contently, triumphantly.

"Now the 'e'."

He mixes it up with the "i." The he asks:

"The curly one?"

"Yes, the curly one."

He makes a curl.

"Now the 'o'."

He doesn't remember and he asks me:

"You have sheet fer writin'?"

"Yes." I get him some sheets of paper.

"Tell me," I say to him, "what were you selling the other day, when I saw you outside?"

"I sell combs. I got one right here. Will you buy one? Fer my brother. Fer the little one."

"But he doesn't have any hair."

"Yes he does, he does. He got lots of hair."

"No, thank you. You should sell something else, no one's going to buy those."

"Can I go to my house? I'll be right back."

"Alright," I tell him.

I figured he wouldn't come back. Ten minutes later he was back selling chewing gum. He sold it all and made 5,000 pesos.

"Will you hold on to the money fer me?"

"Okay."

Ten minutes later:

"Can I have the money to buy an ice cream?"

"Okay."

He ate the ice cream, walked a few laps around the playground, and since the teacher didn't want him in class anymore, he went back home on his own. Later he came back to the front door to watch the kids getting out of school. I called his mother, who's a bright and intelligent lady, and I asked whether she had thought about sending him to another school so he could learn at a slower pace. I could feel her rolling her eyes, as if to say *This lady's got no clue*, and she explained:

"No, ma'am. The thing is, it's in his genes. My brother's a

company manager now. He's got a house, a car, and he's pretty well-off. When he was a kid he fell behind in school—and my brother the pianist, too. He was a really slow learner at school."

I don't know why I believed her. She had such conviction in her words, she seemed to understand the situation so clearly. *Besides*, I thought, *what if she's right?* Once she had explained it all, I felt better.

The teachers are gathered on the playground and I tell them what Monsoon's mother told me about the boy. I tell them in a neutral voice, neither approvingly or disapprovingly, to see what they say.

Alicia, the chubby one, is somewhat annoyed and says:

"No, they gave him an IQ test and he got a ridiculously low score."

Another teacher gives me a dubious look, unconvinced.

"What do I know?" I say and walk off.

Sometimes I find it difficult to appeal to logic and common sense; sometimes they escape me. And a principal should never give up on logic or common sense. That's the worst sin for a principal. I have to demonstrate that I know lots of things, at all times, and especially that I use logic. Sometimes I'm eager to work and I'm quick to delegate when a problem arises. Sometimes I don't want to, and if they tell me:

"The cesspit's backed up."

I don't have an answer. I want to say, Why are you telling me! What do I care? I'm not going to be the one to unclog it.

Or perhaps:

"I think Lima has scabies. What should I do? Should I send him home?"

I don't know what to do. Besides, I don't think that scabies are contagious. I don't think a cesspit can get clogged unless you can actually see the shit, and then it's already outside. I can't imagine the scabies bug being passed from hand to hand.

But since there's a lot of pressure for me to send him home I say:

"Yes, send him home."

And Lima, sadly, full of scabies, goes home.

Sometimes I have to take charge of the classes and they can really catch me off guard. For example, the last time I went to first grade a boy told me:

"I lost my pencil."

It seemed like a loss that was beyond repair.

Or perhaps:

"Somebody stole my eraser."

I never can figure out who steals these things.

But I ask:

"Alright, who stole his eraser?"

"It was him," says the victim, pointing at another child.

"But he took my colored pencils," the other one says.

This narrative can go on for half an hour and I still come up with nothing. Or take, for example, when there's a fight. I ask:

"Who started it?"

"He did," says the one who got hit.

"But he was making fun of me and yesterday he hit my brother."

Very rarely have I ever discovered a true culprit. Perhaps because I absurdly think that a culprit should have a guilty face, or a certain expression. It's the same story when they walk on the benches, sometimes I let them and sometimes I think it's wrong. Then I use my indifferent, somewhat commanding voice:

"Don't walk on the benches."

A teacher who takes her job seriously should know how to feign anger and astonishment. She should say:

"What? Walking on the benches!"

But somehow, the anger has to come off as genuine because children can always see right through their teachers and if the anger isn't real, they'll walk on the benches anyway.

Or when a teacher tells me:

"Yesterday I didn't come because, well, the truth is, I slept in."

After all, isn't sincerity important? How do you teach someone who's very sleepy not to sleep in?

THE MOTHER'S DAY GIFT

For Mother's Day the children make gifts. It's my job to go see
what they've made. In one grade they've taken the paper off tin
cans (the same cans the children use to store their "werns"), and
then they've wound yarn around the can. "Nice and even so you
can't see the tin," the teacher tells me. "It's like a little jar to keep
something in."

"What do you keep in there?" I ask.

"What do I know?" she tells me, "Whatever you want."

The best part is a bow in the middle of the can. The can looks
like a fat, crazy old lady in a wool dress who's put a girl's bow
around her waist.

"Looks good," I say.

In another grade they've done a craft project with matchboxes. It consists of four empty matchboxes (matches are expen
sive) stuck together with glue. Each little box has a thumbtack
in the middle, imitating a small drawer with a tiny handle. I try
to think of it as a miniature chest of drawers. I tell myself, "how
pretty!" But it's a thumbtack.

"Very good," I say.

Suddenly I'm overwhelmed by despair and sadness. The

children were content making those little gifts, as were the teachers. One teacher said patiently:

"Now, children, we place the thumbtack here…"

They were all excited, making things. Their excitement didn't rub off on me. It was a rainy day and everything was flooded. I had the feeling that life was sad, but I didn't have the right to bring anyone else down with me.

During recess the children got in trouble for getting wet. I had been forgetting about recess for some time, I hadn't made my rounds on the playground. I had been neglecting everything for a while. All I noticed was how much the teachers yelled at the children, and it felt like they were yelling at me, but I couldn't put a stop to it—that would have meant putting myself in the role of the yeller. Lately, lots of teachers had gotten into the habit of yelling at the children, embarrassing them for their clothes or their hair. When that happens I hole up in the office and don't come out. It's as if they are yelling at me, I don't move and I can't start working on anything until the yelling stops.

The other day, Alicia, the chubby teacher who yells the most, just wouldn't let up. I wanted to think about something else but I couldn't. Suddenly I realized that the only thing I wanted was to eat a cookie. If I didn't eat that cookie I was going to die.

I started to eat—better said, to nibble on—the cookie. Outside, the yelling got louder and louder. I closed the door to the office but I could still hear everything. The noise of my own nibbling frightened me, so I chewed even more slowly, trying not to make any noise at all.

I was completely alone in that place.

New Times

TIMES were changing. By 1960 the Church was becoming more modern and change even found its way to the town of Moreno. It all started when they got a new priest. The old priest, Father Sotelo, had been a Spaniard with a heavy accent who was always in a bad mood. Once, instead of giving a mattress to the poor—which had been donated by the congregation specifically for that purpose—Father Sotelo decided to put it in the guest room of the clergy house instead. The only guest who came to town once a year for two days was the bishop—and he rarely quartered at the church. Even though the congregation was somewhat miffed at Father Sotelo after the mattress incident, they were quick to acknowledge that some of his sermons touched the bottom of their hearts. And the most brutal references, such as Saint Lawrence the Martyr who was roasted alive over hot coals, gave them all goosebumps.

But now, on account of Father Sotelo, there had been an estrangement between the young and old members of the congregation: the young announced they could no longer stand to look at him. Furthermore, when he saw them sitting with their legs crossed he would say:

"Wastrels! Who sits like that? A wastrel, that's who."

That's exactly why they thought the whole mattress incident had been so appalling, it was like making fun of the poor—all he really wanted was to be under the bishop's wing; he was subservient, etcetera.

The old people had their arguments too: the guest room was a cold damp place with an iron bedframe and a straw mattress. And the bishop, judging by what they had seen of him, was a refined man with graceful manners, a lean face, and long thin fingers that looked like doves when he blessed the worshipers. He wore his miter and purple zucchetto elegantly. So, how was such a fine man—who never said one word too many and never made the slightest spare gesture—just how was someone like him going to lay down on that straw mattress?

In any case, there was so much pressure from the young members of the congregation that Father Sotelo felt rejected and misunderstood. He started to lose weight and asked to be transferred to another parish. Sent to replace him was a young priest, around thirty years old, who acted even younger. He always wore a leather jacket and almost always wore pants, a custom that was beginning to take hold in the Church in those days.

The young folks were thrilled. They took their guitars to church with them, had barbeques, ate empanadas, went out on dates—and nobody got on their case. Quite the opposite: Father

Roberto even joked around with them. Many of the Church's customs were changing. The bells, for example, no longer chimed on Palm Sunday, Good Friday, or Christmas Eve. Those bells, which used to cheerfully fill the air for ten whole minutes, had been abolished. A strict ordinance had been imposed for all noise disturbances, and since some of the townspeople were bothered by the toll of the bells they'd submitted a complaint to the local government. Father Roberto had stopped ringing the bells. Now he just gave them a few sharp clangs on Easter and Christmas Day. As for the funeral toll, it was entirely done away with because many citizens felt it was a bit of a downer. Father Roberto thought it over and decided that, indeed, it could be somewhat depressing. Now, instead of those long spaced-out, melancholy gongs every time someone died, the rule had changed: one normal stroke of the bell.

Other things began to change, too—things we'll see farther along in the story—and as a result of these changes the old people started to distance themselves from the Church—not from the actual place of worship, because they still felt a connection to the building: they'd baptized their children there and attended church with their parents. But, for example, instead of following along at mass, they walked over to the side altars and prayed to the saints. Or they didn't join the confraternity societies; in fact, the confraternity societies they'd been familiar with no longer existed. There were no more Daughters of Mary. The new priest said:

"Potentially or virtually, all females are daughters of Mary."

They didn't know what potentially or virtually meant; they only knew that they used to be Daughters of Mary because they were given a light blue ribbon with an image of Mary on it, and it was their job to arrange the altar. And don't forget to be on your best behavior—you wouldn't want to be unworthy of the image you wore.

That's why, when that new Father Roberto came to town, of the twelve ladies who had been members of Catholic Action (all of whom were over the age of fifty-five), only four remained. One of them was the president, Forti's wife. She was a big-boned Italian and wore a dark beret over her coal-black hair à la Christopher Columbus. She was said to have been frivolous as a young woman; she'd flitted from party to party in Europe; she'd been one of the first women to wear a bathing suit while all the other girls still wore long swimming trunks. She still preserved vestiges of coquetry: she took great care of her hands and wore colorful garments that were a certain color of purple, a specific tone of red; she had become something of a female bishop, majestic as an adult. She also wore lipstick more often than not.

It was said that she had gone from being vain and flighty to the sanctimonious woman she was now all on account of the war. She had suffered many hardships during the war: her siblings had died, she went hungry, and from one day to the next she had started to pray and pray and had never stopped since. She still prayed loudly at church—in Italian—and she didn't care what anyone else, except God our Lord, thought. On the first day that Father Roberto attended a meeting she said:

"*Oggi ricordiamo a Santo Giaccomo de Compostela, che e preciso non confondere con Santo Giovane Bautista, discípulo di Nostro Signore e evangelista.*"

Father Roberto immediately responded with:

"The veneration of saints currently occupies its proper place. The saints are not inaccessible beings who are beyond our reach or holier than us. In fact, they are like us—with their weaknesses and their misfortunes...That's why we say the saints are no longer on the altars, that they've descended from the altars to be closer to us, to blend in with us, the inhabitants of this very town."

Mrs. Forti couldn't hide the look of irritation on her face and she thought, *If the altars are there, there must be a good reason for it.*

She was enraged by the priest's intrusion, which prevented her from talking about Saint James the Greater, which reminded her of her own childhood in Europe, now so far away. When her mother was alive she would say, "Put some flowers on Saint James the Greater's altar."

The silence was immediately broken by Manuelita Catella. She said, "Father, Father" (she always said "Father, Father"), "isn't it true that the Protestants don't have any saints, and instead of the host they eat bread, and they drink wine in a glass but not at communion?"

"We must be tolerant with our Protestant brothers, Manuelita."

"I don't like their saints, Father. They haven't got any grace, have they? But if they're our brothers, Father, we must accept them anyway, right?"

Father smiled.

In Manuelita's mind, although Father was young enough to be her son, the fact that he was a priest made her feel as if he could have been her own father. She'd been raised at a nearby orphanage and her voice had the solemn, stealthy tone of people who'd spent their childhood at such a place. But since she was a happy, curious, childlike soul, her voice came out dissonant, shrill. Manuelita liked Father Roberto. When she asked the old priest a question (she always started by saying, "Father, Father, I have a question"), he would tell her: "Be quiet now."

Then they remembered they hadn't said the prayer to the Holy Spirit, which they always recited at the beginning of every meeting. They stood up and said:

"Come Holy Spirit, fill the hearts of your faithful and enkindle in them the fire of your love…"

Father Roberto took this prayer very seriously, and he said it with complete concentration.

Mrs. Forti, who was an exuberant spirit at heart, imagined the Holy Spirit as mighty tongues of fire approaching and burning everything in sight. The one who had a pretty reliable version of the Holy Spirit was María Pérez. She was a widow; her children had grown up and moved far away, and she tended to get depressed. Sometimes she got so depressed that she sat still for hours, unable to move. Then, without knowing from where she found the strength, she'd stir and say:

"It's the Holy Spirit."

It was something rare and mysterious for her—like the evil eye, but sunny-side up. María Pérez was unobtrusive; she hardly spoke and everyone adored her.

The last member of the group was also the oldest: she was around seventy. She dressed completely in black, stockings and all, and at this particular meeting she hadn't taken off the black tulle she wore at church. She had something of a hooknose and never spoke, although she did pray along with everyone else, but in a hushed voice. She no longer helped out with the parish activities, or when they handed out clothes to the poor, or anything else—and no one knew why. It was as if she had been born with the tulle on her head and the black stockings, and nobody would have ever expected anything else from her. If it hadn't been that she was so old, they might have mistrusted her: her eyes were small and beady, her jaw stuck out, and her nose was big. But, admittedly, she was harmless. They didn't know her last name, just that she went by Botznia. She was Croatian. The truth is everyone figured she had a few screws loose, but at her age they weren't about to kick her out of the group for that reason. One afternoon Botznia started coughing loudly and Father Roberto told her:

"As I've said before, if you're not feeling well you shouldn't come. Now that it's gotten cold we all need to take care of ourselves."

But she came, unfailingly—and the colder it got, the earlier she showed up.

Father Roberto continued his "Christianizing" crusade, as he called it. The young folks were right there with him: they were soldiers, apostles, martyrs, while remaining kind, modern in appearance, but profoundly religious at heart. It was up to Father Roberto, intelligent and philosophical, to discern case-by-case who was just there to put on appearances and who was religious at heart. The gentlemen of the parish were middle-aged, balding, and had a sense of good judgment; and the women of Catholic Action had made some real progress. For example, Manuelita would come and say:

"Father, Father, isn't it true that we have to accept the Protestants? The lady next door ripped up a Bible right in front of them when they came around selling Bibles and I told her it was wrong to do that. Isn't it? Because the Protestants are our brothers."

"Very good, Manuelita."

Although Mrs. Forti still prayed to the saints (she said novenas for herself), she no longer imposed saint veneration and devotion on everyone else, which they were all relieved about because she used to endlessly name saints that no one had ever heard of—some of whom were no doubt only well-known back in their own day, some thousand years ago, and were still awaiting canonization by the Holy Office, which nobody knew about (except for Mrs. Forti). Now she spoke only of general principles, such as charity and grace, and when she went off on a tangent, when she explained how Saint Cajetan Christ had appeared to her in the form of a tree, Father Roberto gently steered the subject back to more general and operational concepts.

María Pérez had always been modest and straightforward, so she liked the new spirit of the Church, especially because it had been simplified. She said:

"All those altars with embroidered linens! People used to wear out their eyes—they spent their entire lives embroidering altar cloths. And all those high altars made of gold—keeping the dust off them was an uphill battle! Now everything is so much quicker, the prayers are shorter."

Botznia was the real mystery: nobody knew whether she agreed with the new spirit of the Church or had preferred the old one, because she didn't speak her mind. She continued to attend assiduously. Now, according to the new customs, each of them had to explain the gospel; when it was Botznia's turn all she could say was:

"Christ, son of God, born in a manger next to the cow and the oxen."

Which unsettled the rest of them because that didn't have anything to do with the gospel of the day, which was the one about the rich young man who had asked what he could do to be saved. When Botznia said this the rest of them looked at her derisively—except for María Pérez, who didn't distain anyone. And poor Botznia felt she had been censured and her eyes shifted behind her glasses. Father Roberto noticed she was flustered and said:

"Let's see, Botznia, why don't you say a prayer for us in Croatian so we can hear what it sounds like."

Then all the ladies, who had just given her the cold shoulder, said:

"Yes, yes! Pray in Croatian!" Botznia let them beg a while longer, saying she couldn't remember. Finally, once they'd gotten tired of waiting and had started the day's agenda, Botznia said out of the blue:

"*Muškarci amerike. Ni vas volim ni vas mrzim; ecke, prokleti ecke.*"

"What a lovely language!" said Father Roberto as if to encourage her. "What does it mean?"

Botznia said:

"I can't quite remember. It's about the guardian angel."

Honestly, none of them liked the Croatian language, yet they all said:

"How beautiful!"

Botznia had started to miss the meetings; it had been almost a month since she'd shown up. It couldn't be due to the cold weather—because the colder it got the earlier she came.

"Where does she live?" Father Roberto asked.

"She lives in Villa Pajarito," said Manuelita. "It's quite far from here. And Father, if you go there at night they'll give you a beating that will leave you flat on your back."

"Don't go, Father," said Mrs. Forti, who only went from her house to church and back again.

But Father Roberto got on his moped and went all the way to Villa Pajarito. It was a miserable hamlet—if you could even call it a hamlet; it was part hamlet, part wasteland. He asked a man:

"Do you know where Mrs. Botznia lives, by any chance?"

"Botznia…Botznia. I don't know the name."

"I do," said a boy walking by. "It must be the old Polish lady."

Explaining how to get there was no easy task, so the man asked the boy to walk with the priest.

"Do you know her?" asked Father Roberto.

"Yes," said the boy with a reluctant little smile.

"Has she lived here a long time?"

"Yes, a long time."

But it was obvious the boy was keeping something from him. When they arrived the boy asked him in awe:

"Are you really going to go in?"

"Yes," said Father. "Would you like to come?"

"No," replied the boy, stifling laughter. "I'm not going in there." As if the mere idea were absurd.

"Doesn't anyone come to visit her?"

"I don't know, I don't think so. She throws rocks and yells *ecke, prokleti ecke.*"

Father Roberto was starting to become intrigued by all this. He went inside and there was Botznia, sitting on the bed. She didn't have any money to buy food, or to take the bus. She had raised some chickens, but didn't have the strength to kill them. The house was a meager hut made of wood.

"Warm there, no?" she said, her eyes lighting up.

"Where?" asked Father Roberto in surprise.

"There, the meeting. Nice and warm."

That's when Father realized that she went to the meetings because she was freezing cold in her house, and that's why she arrived early on the coldest days. He gave her some money and told her:

"Come to the next meeting on Friday, Botznia. We'll be expecting you."

"See you."

Gratified, her eyes darted about and she went to the grocer's shop with her fresh money.

Every month or so Father Cheroff came to say mass at church. He was a member of the Eastern-rite Catholic priests, who had asked the Pope to be accepted into the Church. The Pope had agreed, but since the Eastern-rite doesn't prohibit priests from getting married, many of them had gone ahead and tied the knot. The Pope had to admit them with their wives and children.

Father Cheroff was married too, so he didn't live in a church, but with his wife and two grown sons, who worked in a factory. He was old, hard of hearing, thick in the head, and vertically challenged; his robe was threadbare and he was Croatian. He had lived through the war, although he didn't seem to have any opinions about it. If someone asked him what Croatia was like, he said:

"Children no wear school uniform there."

He remained silent for a while and then added:

"Some things different, everything else the same."

And he said no more. The young priests and young men of the parish made jokes about him because he was married. And to make matters worse, he didn't like wearing civilian clothes so he always wore his brown robe, covered in stains. He said mass and then went into the sacristy to get paid. Sometimes he had to wait a long time, twenty minutes even. It wasn't a manifestation of ill will—just that there were so many people they didn't see him. He got bored just standing there. He wanted to collect his five hundred pesos as soon as possible so he could go home and work in his garden.

His masses were confusing; some parts were different from the regular rite, like the consecration, for example. He turned around and announced to the congregation:

"Now, communion."

And then:

"Now, Our Father."

One afternoon when he'd come to church to ask for some money, Father Roberto told him:

"Cheroff, we have one of your compatriots in our parish."

"No compatriot," said Cheroff, who was in the habit of denying things without actually stopping to listen to what someone had said.

"Yes, yes. Her name is Botznia."

"Ah, Botznia, yes. She not compatriot. She from the North."

"Isn't it all the same country?"

"Yes, but I tell you she not compatriot. She from Breshna. I visit. Cruel war happened there."

"Let's see if you can translate something for me that Botznia says."

"Translate?" asked Cheroff. "I don't know translate."

Paying no mind, Father Roberto continued:

"She says something that starts with: *ecke, prokleti ecke*."

Father Cheroff's eyes widened in wonder and he said: "Oh!"

"What is it?" asked Father Roberto.

"Oh!" said Cheroff again.

Then recovering from his astonishment, he burst into a

peculiar peal of laughter, as if he were laughing at Father Roberto. He said:

"That no prayer."

"What does it mean then?"

"*Ecke*, damned; *ecke* terrible curse word there in my land."

Father Cheroff shifted from a panicky fear for having uttered those words to an odd shiny-eyed expression, as if somehow his compatriot Botznia had found a way to reveal her true self; then the mysterious fear came back and he said:

"Oh!"

He wanted to remedy the shock he had caused because he thought perhaps Father Roberto would throw Botznia out of the Church as a result, so he said in a compassionate tone, in the voice that beggars use when they feel sorry for themselves, almost a singsong:

"Poor compatriot Botznia, how she suffered during the war."

Father Roberto looked at him; he felt bad for Cheroff in his soiled, threadbare robe. Cheroff pained him. This time he gave him two thousand pesos.

The big day had arrived. The whole congregation—Father Roberto included—had been looking forward to it, and they'd worked so hard. It was the inauguration of the community recreation center, a large building they'd erected themselves to provide fun and entertainment for all ages. For the younger folks there was soccer, ping-pong, and a dance floor; for the older folks there were parlor games, a projector, and a sitting room. They'd been working on all this and more with great enthusiasm for two years—mostly the young folks. There were more and more young people: they went camping, held meetings, helped with the construction, etcetera. They were aglow with happiness and health—they were so happy they never sought out any other horizons beyond the parish and the recreation center. Mrs. Forti, the president of Catholic Action, had almost entirely given up on her aristocratic attitude, although she still always wore her bishop's dress. Manuelita had become as tactful as could be (for someone like her). It was all on account of people jamming the brakes on her; so often she'd been shot down that now, when she started to talk, she couldn't help but wonder whether she might be saying something inappropriate and she held her tongue. María Pérez continued to be modest; she went unnoticed. Botznia was ever-present and she ate little pastries and cakes at the parish gatherings. Botznia was a problem for Father Roberto; he couldn't get rid of her but letting her stay was difficult. She was ancient, somewhat dim by now; if a meeting was underway, going smoothly, she would interrupt by saying the most asinine things, or blurt out some word in Croatian that nobody understood. Father Cheroff no longer said Mass; he'd been retired—not that he'd wanted to retire, but they made him anyway because Mass was said in Spanish now, and his Spanish was deplorable, so no one even went to his services anymore. Father Roberto had said to him:

"You're old now, you've worked so much and it's time to get some rest. We'll help you out."

Cheroff no longer said Mass, but now and then he would get bored of working in his vegetable garden and walk over to see the progress being made at the recreational center. When he saw the size of the soccer fields he opened his eyes as big as saucers and said:

"Oh!"

His amazement never ceased.

Meanwhile, the bishop was coming to bless the building and see how everything was going. The entire congregation had been invited to the celebration. To inaugurate the building, the young people were going to play a soccer game; and in the older folks' lounge they were going to project movies about the lives of missionaries among the Eskimos and about the African Boy Scouts of Papua New Guinea. Anyone who didn't want to watch movies could stay in the sitting room to play cards and dominos.

"Listen up, everyone," said Father Roberto. "Act natural. As soon as the reception is over—which will be short, no long speeches—I want everyone to start in on whatever activity they like most. That way His Excellency will truly see the recreational center in action."

No sooner said than done. The bishop arrived, thin and spiritual as always, although he was somewhat more stooped than usual—but the curvature made him look even more elegant, if that were even possible. Everyone was waiting around the table; they were friendly and talkative, it was like a Christmas party among relatives. Botznia was sitting in a corner, and since they thought she looked gloomy all in black with her hooknose, they dressed her up in a beautiful, fuzzy white poncho over the top of her sad dress.

"It's freezing, Botznia—you'll catch a cold."

Botznia fought with all her might and good will to pull the poncho over her head and keep her arms inside. In the end she won the fight but felt trapped by that poncho and every time she lifted her arm to grab a small pastry the whole outfit went along too.

Father Cheroff hadn't been notified that the bishop was coming, but he found out anyway and went to the event, as if it were any old day, saying to everyone he ran into:

"I want to speak with the bishop. Personal conversation."

He wanted to tell the bishop that they hadn't invited him, that he was poor, and to ask if there were any other jobs he could do now for the Church. But Father Roberto wanted to keep Cheroff from talking to the bishop at any cost; perhaps because the bishop was a very busy person and had so much to see before he could possibly be bothered by whatever Cheroff had to say. Meanwhile, Cheroff anxiously paced back and forth, back and forth, all over the rectory. The bishop noticed him out of the corner of his eye, but even though they were only three paces apart it was impossible for Cheroff to speak with him. As a matter of fact, just then Father Roberto was urging the bishop to bless the table and make the obligatory toasts. The bishop blessed the table, speaking in Spanish, using an inflected tone, as if his audience required great clarity to be able to hear properly. One lady thought, *Quite short, for a bishop.* But, on the other hand, he gave the impression that—precisely because he was a bishop—his speeches should be short and sweet, without mincing words.

They did some eating and drinking. Botznia thrashed around in her poncho to an alarming extent in an attempt to reach the pastries, but then they stuck her in an out-of-the-way corner behind Mrs. Forti, who blocked Botznia with her enormous body.

Then Father Roberto invited the bishop and some of the other men out to watch the soccer game. And they left. Meanwhile, others preferred to play chess or dominos; the ladies chatted away and drank a drop of liquor. But they didn't talk to Botznia. Every once and a while someone would walk over to stuff her with cakes, sandwiches, and pastries. Cheroff walked all around endlessly by himself, half stunned, half distraught. Miraculously, there came a moment when Botznia wasn't eating anything; she was sitting still in a perfect state of bliss. Cheroff looked at her as if he had just noticed she was there, saying:

"Eh, Botznia!"

"Eh," replied Botznia indifferently.

They had both lived here for something close to thirty years and they were both from Croatia. Father Cheroff sat down next to her, grabbing a glass of wine and serving himself a sandwich; he too started to eat and drink.

"Good wine, huh?"

"*Dniet*," said Botznia.

And he asked her to hand him a slice of cake. They weren't nostalgic for their homeland, nor did they have anything to say to one another; but a spirited young lady saw them all dressed in black with their hooknoses, Cheroff rubbing his hands together as if to warm them up, and she said:

"Why don't you go into the kitchen? You'll be warmer there, and you can talk about things from back home. You can cheer up poor Botznia, she's been a little down in the dumps lately."

Meekly, they went to the kitchen; they were glad because it was warm. Botznia drank two small glasses of liquor and started to say:

"*Muškarci Amerike! Dniet scoleva ventre.*"

"No say that, Botznia," pleaded Cheroff in a sleepy voice. He was tired and he nodded off. Not long after, Botznia fell asleep too, resting her head on the table.

They didn't see what happened when the bishop came back, how he took the time to speak to each and every one of the young folks, or how they played the guitar and sang, or how they danced the zamba, or the film about the missionaries in China.

As the festivities continued and only the most intimate members of the parish stayed on with the priest and the bishop (the most virtuous, the most hardworking, and the most intelligent), someone remembered that Botznia and Cheroff had gone to the kitchen and went to find them. Much to this man's surprise he found them sleeping. He was a member of the parish, a gentleman who was going bald and had a splendid little gray car. He woke them up, gently at first but then more forcefully; he shook them a bit. They cried out and fussed before waking up entirely, because they were frightened.

He took them home in his car. It was difficult getting Botznia inside the car because she didn't understand that she had to duck her head. Graciously, he took them back to their miserable, faraway houses. He was such a good Christian that he didn't even care when his car got covered in mud. In Botznia's neighborhood, which was practically a wasteland, there was a beautiful reddish sunset coating all the houses. In that light, the small houses made of wood and cardboard looked like charming little ships.

Luisa's Friend

AT Luisa's house the chickens were kept in a dark corner and nobody looked at them. The only good thing about her house were the mandarin trees. Luisa ate mandarins when they were still green, sitting in the garden among the plants. There was a hose, too, but she wasn't allowed to wash down the sidewalks, or to spray people like it was Carnival either.

But at her grandma's house she could chase after the chickens. They had a big, beautiful henhouse. And there was a duck, too, with all her ducklings in a row. Luisa could toss mandarin peels in the henhouse and spy on the neighboring houses to see if there were any children.

And now the people who lived next door had gone away and there were new neighbors. Luisa watched them a long time to see who they were, but it was only a fat lady who scattered corn.

At her grandma's house she could throw the ball on the roof, and it rolled right back down. Once, Luisa was playing with the ball and it went up on the roof, but this time it didn't come back. The roof was low and Luisa heard a voice behind her:

"Maybe you could get it down with a long stick."

And Luisa said, without turning around:

"I don't have any long sticks and neither does my grandma."

"Maybe I could lend you a broom."

Then Luisa spun around and saw a young man who was lying down on something that looked like a gurney, but his head was propped up. It was as if he were lying down from his feet to his waist, and sitting from his waist to his head. He was much older, bigger than her cousin Ernesto, who was sixteen, and she was sure that nobody told him what to do. Luisa said to him:

"Then go get the broom."

"I can't because I'm lying down."

"Bah, I can lie down, too, and then say, 'I can't because I'm lying down.'"

Luisa lay down on the ground but then got up quickly, and the young man looked at her sadly. When Luisa got up she realized he couldn't go get the broom, and she went to ask her grandmother for one. Her grandma didn't want to give her the broom because she was busy using it and then Luisa said to the young man:

"Well, I can't play with the ball anymore so I'm going to talk to you."

He was reading a yellowish book that had drawings of skulls and legs and things. Luisa didn't really know how to read yet because she was only six, so she asked him:

"What are you learning?"

"Medicine."

"Oh, I know! Like to cure diphtheria and things like that. I have an uncle who learned medicine and now he cures diphtheria. He studied for twenty years because he had to marry my aunt, and my aunt told him if he didn't learn all those books she wouldn't marry him, so he learned them."

Then Luisa asked:

"What's your name? How old are you? Are you alone? Who's that lady who scatters the corn?"

He answered all her questions and said his name was Pedro. Luisa said her papa's name was Pedro too, but she usually called him Papa, whereas she would use Pedro for him. Pedro said he was twenty-two and he lived with his aunt, the lady who scattered corn for the hens.

Then Luisa walked around the gurney to see how it worked with springs and she sat him up and laid him down several times to see how it went up and down. Then she was called in for a bath, but promised to return afterwards.

When Luisa was home her mother bathed her, scrubbing her hands, knees, and elbows with a pumice stone. She washed Luisa's hair saying that nobody ever went blind from a little soap in their eyes. So Luisa decided to tell her grandma that she took baths by herself, and her grandma marveled at all the things Luisa knew how to do and sent her off to take a bath. Luisa took her bath contently because afterwards she was going to go see her friend. And she spent the whole time thinking about the gurney, the springs, and the book with the skull and the legs.

It was a summer day at seven o'clock in the evening. Luisa put on white shoes and a light blue dress, but she didn't brush her hair because she still had braids from the night before, and nobody could make braids that lasted as long as her mother's did. They were strong braids and she could run around in them and pull on the bows and they wouldn't come undone. Luisa went to visit her friend, who said she looked pretty. She said she didn't look her very best because she had left her prettiest dresses at home. Then she asked him:

"When did you get sick?"

"Two years ago."

"So you were twenty?"

"Yes."

"And what do you do all day just sitting there?"

"I study, I read, I look around."

"And you never get bored?"

"Sometimes, but I've always got more studying to do."

"Tomorrow we're going to play ball. I'll get it off the roof and throw it to you just right so it doesn't fall on the ground. But now I want you to tell me a story because you must know stories."

He started to tell her a story, but halfway through he didn't remember anymore so Luisa finished it. Then she told him a bunch of stories and they spent a long time like that and night-time fell before they even realized it. Luisa said:

"Gee, the stars are already out. I have to go in now, to sleep."

And then Luisa left.

One day Pedro had brought out a radio and he put it in the grass. A beautiful waltz was playing. It was morning and the sun was shining bright, and when Luisa heard the music she came over to visit him and saw that he was lost in thought. She asked him:

What are you thinking about?"

"Nothing. Did you bring the ball?"

"You're thinking about things you don't want to tell me. You should say: 'I can't say what I'm thinking about.'"

He smiled and again drifted off into thought. The radio played music and Luisa wanted to dance in the grass so she started to dance. Luisa wished she were dressed like a ballerina, or at least like a lady in a gown, but she was wearing a striped smock and had braids. Luisa danced anyway, and he watched and it made him laugh to see Luisa dancing, her hand on her skirt, which was so short, leaping from side to side like a little goat and rounding off the end of every song with a little jump, as if she were skipping rope. She turned around and said:

"You're laughing at me. I'm not going to dance anymore."

She was so tired that she sat down next to the gurney.

Being tired, she didn't notice that he was lost in thought again. Suddenly he turned off the radio and the music stopped.

"Why did you turn the music off? It was nice," Luisa said, exasperated. He didn't answer her and she went to have lunch.

They were both in the yard and it was getting dark. Nobody passed by on the street and they were silent. Luisa said:

"Were you handsome when you were healthy?"

"Yes, I was."

"Were you tall, too?"

"I was."

"Were your legs as long as that man who walked by on the street yesterday?"

"Longer."

"And are you going to get better?"

"Yes, I suppose I will get better one day."

"When you get better you're going to leave, right?"

"Yes, I'm going to go study."

"Yeah, and then you won't talk with me anymore."

He smiled and became absorbed again. Luisa had only seen him with his legs covered up and she wanted to see what they looked like. She imagined that he had two metal legs, as if he were a mechanical doll that was alive from the waist up and made of tin or iron from the waist down. She was so curious to see his legs, but he didn't want to show her. Sometimes she brought out her notebook and primer, and they wrote and drew pictures. Her friend knew how to draw really well; he knew how to draw oranges showing the individual segments. Luisa also knew how to draw oranges, but just a slice, she couldn't figure out how to draw a whole orange and show the segments.

Luisa liked to look at picture books, but he didn't have any of those. Sometimes he showed her pictures from the books about medicine; but that was only when Luisa had been good and when she didn't ask so many questions.

They were going to celebrate Luisa's brother's birthday at her grandma's house. Her cousins were coming, and her aunts and uncles too. There were going to be presents and she was going to wear a new dress. A lot of people must have been invited because the hot chocolate was boiling in a big pot; her mother was stirring it. Luisa's mother went inside and told Luisa to let her know if the hot chocolate boiled over. Luisa was standing on a chair watching the chocolate when somebody came from behind and put their hands over her eyes. It was her Aunt Catalina, who was carrying a present. Luisa protested, she wanted to open it, but Aunt Catalina took it away. It was seven o'clock; by now it was getting dark, and soon they were going to have hot chocolate with cake. Then her cousins were there, but Luisa hadn't seen them come in; she found them sitting in her brother's cart. They played with the cart until eight o'clock and they took a ride around the block in the cart. All around there were fields; there were hardly any houses. At eight o'clock they were going to drink the hot chocolate and Luisa asked if they had invited her friend. Her friend arrived at nine and his legs were covered with a blanket; he was on the gurney, sitting up. He stayed in the corner for a while, and then he was gone. Luisa didn't notice when he left. When she went to find him he wasn't there anymore, and neither was the gurney. Luisa wondered what would happen at the party now that her friend had left. They kept playing in the cart until nine-thirty and then they went to bed, completely exhausted. That night her brother threw up on the mattress.

Now her friend wasn't in the gurney anymore, he was in a wheelchair and he wheeled it around himself. Luisa thought it was so strange to watch him move the wheelchair and she wanted to push him around, but he didn't let just anyone push him. She was scared he would get angry. Luisa asked:

"After the wheelchair, where are they going to put you?"

"After the wheelchair, crutches. Then a cane, and then I'm going to be able to walk."

"Like me?"

"Of course."

Then Luisa thought for a while and asked him:

"And you're going to study that book about the human body?"

"Yes."

"Are you going to eat at the table, too?"

"Who knows?"

"What are you going to do with that wheelchair? Are you going to give it to me, or to that man with a moustache who gives you cigarettes? Why don't you smoke right now? I want to watch you blow smoke out the corner of your mouth. I told my father to blow smoke out the corner of his mouth, but he didn't do it."

"Well, now we're going to read," said Pedro.

"Yes."

And Luisa read her book and he read his book about the human body. They spent almost an hour like that, then they got tired and started talking again.

Luisa had to go back home because school was starting. Her mother scrubbed her knees and elbows with a pumice stone and cut her nails like always. There was only one girl who came to her house to play, but Luisa hated her.

Once back at home, Luisa's mother said to her father:

"It looks like Pedro's getting better. He went back to that institution."

Pedro had never told Luisa that he went to an institution. Maybe he would still be out in the yard sometimes reading his book, his legs covered with a blanket.

Luisa waited three long months until winter vacation. That whole time the same girl kept showing up at her house and Luisa hated her because she took two pastries at a time, put them in her pocket, and then ate them so slowly that she never finished. And that girl never left, not even at night.

For winter vacation Luisa went to her grandma's house. She quickly kissed her grandma and went to spy on her friend through the fence. He wasn't in the yard and the house looked empty. Luisa asked her grandma, who said:

"They left a month ago. He said to give you a big hug."

Luisa looked at the empty yard. She wanted to get the ball off the roof, the one they were going to play with before, but then they'd ended up playing with another one. She did get it down, but it was scorched and cracked from the sun. Luisa started to cry because her ball was worthless. She threw a bunch of mandarin peels in the henhouse and chased the chickens around.

In the morning she got up and went to spy on the house next door, but no one was there.

At noon she told her grandma:

"Granny, I'm going home."

And her grandma asked her to stay, but Luisa left anyway.

When she got home that girl was there, having a snack. She took two pastries at a time and then ate them very slowly. Luisa looked at her and said:

"Now we're going to play hide-and-seek."

And when the girl finished eating the two pastries in her pocket, they went to play hide-and-seek.

Bees Are Industrious

ICOME from a family of twelve children—I laugh because I'm the only one who knows my story. When I was seven years old I was sent to live as a servant for two very polite old ladies in the town of Veinticinco de Mayo. They treated me alright, but all they had to eat at their house was finger food: fancy pastries, little sandwiches, and salty snacks. They would stuff themselves silly when invited to a party, and then sneak some food home with them. I wanted a real meal, and I told my mama. She found me work elsewhere, at a hotel also in Veinticinco de Mayo, where I cleaned the rooms and ran errands. The owners were two brothers and they fought all the time; they screamed at each other and when one sent me off to sweep, the other would yell just what did I think I was I doing? I had learned to say that I was sweeping of my own accord, as if it had been my idea, to see if I could stop them from fighting, but it was no use. They kept at it all night, ranting and raging. I couldn't sleep, but I couldn't tell my mama that I wanted to leave either, so I started to scheme about how I could get out of there. And would you believe my luck? One day not long after, I saw a little old priest in the town square riding a little old horse. I went up to him.

He placed his hand on my head, gave me a holy card, and asked whether I'd like to become a priest.

I asked him:

"What do you mean?"

"To appease the souls," he said.

It sounded like something worthy and necessary. I told him I'd think about it and would give him my answer when he came back a week later, because the little old priest went out to the countryside, in search of trainees. He told me that he was exhausted, that his horse was getting old. The idea of "appeasing the souls" left a big impression on me, as did the little old priest with his horse. I was hesitant, I was eleven years old, but I felt like I couldn't let him down. He needed an assistant. I sat down to think. Just how am I going to tell Mama? I ordered a small glass of beer at the corner store to pluck up some courage and I called her, terribly afraid:

"Mama, I want to be a priest."

My mama is headstrong and temperamental, with a strong personality. I told her the story and, contrary to what I'd imagined, she said:

"If you're determined, go ahead, son."

My mama cried. I'd never seen her cry before and that changed how I thought of her. I said yes to the priest and went to live at a small seminary in the countryside. There were four of us seminarians; one of them left and then we were three. Now, let me confess something to you that I'm extremely embarrassed about. I don't know whether or not to tell you, it's so embarrassing... Because, you know what? I... I'm a priest, bah—I laugh to myself because only I get it. Can I tell you something? I'm a priest and I don't know Latin. It's because there were so few of us at the seminary that I was sent to take care of the rabbits during Latin class. Otherwise, who else was going to take care of them? Since I was so young and I didn't understand, I preferred tending to the rabbits. But now, when I say the Breviary, I'm filled with a sense of anxiety. I love the parts I understand, but saying the rest makes me feel guilty. When I listen to readings by Father Frers, who's a Latinist, I'm in awe... I'm going to confess something else: when I say the Breviary and there are parts I don't understand, I'm overcome by a strange sensation, like fear. I don't know how to explain it. A physical fear, even. I don't know if you understand what I mean.

As I was saying, there were three of us seminarians and then one summer there were only two of us: Julio and I. The other boy had gone on vacation. Julio told our superior that he wanted to learn Hebrew. The only person in the town who knew Hebrew was the pharmacist's daughter. Julio went to learn with her. He fell in love, left the seminary, and married her. That's when I got to thinking, and it ended up making me sick. I thought, *Why do I feel so bad? Could it be because I want the same thing, to get married? No. Do I miss Julio because he left? No. Do I feel lonely?* Yes, perhaps I felt a bit lonely, but that wasn't it. I started to understand that the will of God is unclear, and I learned that the will of God isn't something one can understand at first. It's only revealed long after things have taken place.

But since I was still so young, the will of God sometimes seemed terrible to me, and vague. So I told myself, "Everything that's part of the human condition, that's within my power, I'll analyze on my own, in my own way. I'll look at it from all sides. Whatever I can't analyze, whatever's not within my power, I'll leave up to God." This is easy to say, but difficult to put into practice. I was ordained alone so the hard part came when I started to hear confession. I didn't know anything about life, or about people. Nothing at all. It was as if I was forced to see people in a new light. Besides, people were always guilty of a sin different from the one they had come to confess. Somebody would come and tell me:

"Forgive me Father for I have sinned. It's envy. I'm envious."

And once I had asked them a few questions I would realize that it wasn't envy, it was despair.

Around that time I started to have dreams about my priest-hood mentor—the man who had recruited me by saying that being a priest was about appeasing the souls. In a moment of bitterness I thought the souls didn't want to be appeased. They only wanted to be soothed momentarily, then they'd dust themselves off and get back into the fight. That's when I decided it was my job to console people, to protect them, to treat everyone like the children they really are deep down, to bring them joy. I was able to form many boy scout groups, parent groups. I visited lots of houses but I couldn't leave without eating some cake or drinking a glass of wine. I would say no emphatically, that I had already eaten, but they never listened. So I would try the cake made by the little girl, I would taste the wine that had been especially set aside. In those days, back when I visited people's houses so often, I began to wonder whether perhaps I hadn't spiraled off the deep end. Sitting in front of a pile of cakes, sometimes I had to stifle my urge to break out into a fit of laughter. So I would disguise it by making a joke.

One day, a lady I often visited said to me:

"Father, don't you have a holy card for me?"

I didn't have any holy cards. In fact, among the more evolved priests we sometimes made fun of the ones who gave out holy cards.

"I don't give out holy cards," I said condescendingly.

"You've got to get one for me, alright?" she said.

"Alright, alright. I'll bring you one."

And every time she asked me I would tell her I didn't have any, that I had forgotten, disproportionately feigning my oversight. I didn't want to give out holy cards. I started to think about how strange people are. This stubborn lady, for example, who could win a fight against five truck drivers, who was relentless and headstrong, and wanted a holy card at all costs. Forgive me for laughing, but the contrast between this lady and the holy card amuses me.

Then I began to approach the matter differently: they wanted to give me something, cake or wine, and they expected something else in return—even if it was just a holy card, a token to remember me by. Apparently, the only thing I could receive were the cakes I praised, or the wine. But they wanted something, too. Why couldn't they give me something else at my visits? Because the gifts distracted me from dealing with their real problems. When I brought up something personal, trying to get to the core of it, they would defend themselves tooth and nail, so I figured, they're not ready yet. Now's not the right moment.

I was fatter and heavier by the day, and I had gotten used to giving out holy cards. An unexpected event ended up freeing me from that apathy. One of the houses I visited belonged to a couple; they were still young, almost middle-aged, and I would listen to their confession. They were some of the few people with whom I could talk freely, in confidence and with a certain degree of intimacy. They had beautiful children, were a handsome couple themselves, and had everything they needed without being rich. Their house was welcoming, their kitchen cozy, and on many nights we would get together to talk. They would invite me over to dinner on a whim, when they felt like it. I was comfortable with them because they were practically the only people who told me what they really thought of me: that I was starting to let myself go.

I don't know exactly what I liked most about that house, the confidence it inspired or that I could leave whenever I wanted—I think it was everything. The children, the dog—everything made me feel good there. Meanwhile, I worked to chip away at a hint of intolerance I sensed, a certain stubbornness of theirs regarding religious and political matters. It seemed to be a shallowness inherent in people who were well off, to those who hadn't endured a childhood like my own. Their theories about potato farmers were quite far-fetched. My whole family had been potato farmers, so I could tell them all about my own experience. But I've always found it difficult to express myself: I know what things are like, I feel them, but perhaps I refrain from explaining things because I find it hard. That's why I admire Father Frers, who speaks Latin and expresses himself so perfectly in Spanish. He has the gift of language, which is a gift from the Holy Spirit. But getting back to my story, one day, Pablo, the oldest of their children, comes to get me and says:

"José, come quickly! Papa... Papa—he wants to kill Mama."

But I couldn't move. I became petrified, as if I had been struck by a blow that shook my whole body. I started to sweat. I drank a glass of water and walked over as best as I could. Pablo kept saying:

"C'mon, let's go."

They lived right by the church. I walked through their charming little yard—it's somewhat neglected, and now it felt sinister to me. I walked inside and there he was with a gun in his hand. She was sitting on the floor, her legs spread in a daze. He saw me come in and said:

"Careful with the gun, it's silver."

I asked the Holy Spirit to enlighten me, quickly, about what I should do. I didn't have time to think. Then the Holy Spirit moved me to say this to him:

"Moron, asshole. What a nice gun you've got there. You like guns, huh? What a big man you are."

I spoke in a controlled and violent tone. It was the voice of—how can I describe it...? Like a gangster's voice. And afterwards I was surprised by the fact that I had spoken in that tone. I managed to catch him off guard, he never imagined that I could talk like that. He put down the gun and started walking around.

Pablo watched everything carefully. The wife got up, and that meant it was all over.

I told him:

"Look your boy in the eyes."

He hugged the boy and cried, then all three of them gathered together and hugged and cried. Luckily the littlest one wasn't there. Then the wife took Pablo to bed and I stayed with the husband, talking in the kitchen. I used the courage that had been given to me by the Holy Spirit—it wasn't my own. Physically I felt bad, but I had to rise to the occasion because he needed help just then. I used courage I didn't have and it was bad for me, because I felt sick. I think it was bad and good. It was bad for my body but good for my soul. I'm not sure if you can understand what I mean. My body got sick, but after it all went down I felt a sense of relief and a need to leave that place, that town. The event led me to realize that I had been wanting to leave that town for a long time. Lots of things went through my head. Even though the Spirit had spoken through me in that gangster voice to calm him down, every time I looked at him I couldn't stop thinking about what I'd said and my tone of voice. It was as if I had been struck by a spirit. Meanwhile, whenever I looked at the little houses with their perfectly trimmed grass, the stately homes with their little streetlights, I thought, *Just imagine all the disasters going on inside!* Those houses had lost the sense of peace they used to inspire in me. But despite that lurking sensation, I felt like my soul had been revived. Having regained my own soul, I was able to locate the souls of other people again because they had become lost to me, too. And even though I was in a rush to leave—and I was—even though a whole series of sinister visions appeared to me, I felt a sort of gratitude. The idea of leaving made me happy. I told my superior that I wanted a transfer, and my superior transferred me to this school, where you see me today. The truth is—I'm going to be honest here—I'm not cut out for school.

The first bell rings, we raise the flag, and when everyone goes to their classrooms I think, "Now the cattle have gone to their pen."

I have to take great pains not to say it out loud, some of the teachers would be horrified. They come and tell me:

"Father, we bought a microscope."

And I say:

"How marvelous! I couldn't be happier that you've bought something so useful, so beautiful!"

"Come, Father, come take a look."

I go over to get a glimpse. I look through the microscope for a while and say:

"How extraordinary!"

But I don't know what it is, I can't tell. The truth is my mind is somewhere else. Ever since I started at this school I've been thinking about something else, which really helps me to cope. They go on about how they've bought a telescope, how the Spanish teacher fought with the History teacher, and I try to deal with the mothers. Mrs. Luchesi sought me out five times until she tracked me down: it was to inquire why I had given her son an "A" instead of an "A+". She came ready for an argument but we ended up on friendly terms. And I'm patient, I'm in a good mood because I've decided that, as soon as I can, I'm going to go live in the countryside as a beekeeper. Bees—do you know how industrious they are?

I Don't Have Wings

WADDLING along on his short and stubby legs, Don Mascali made his way through the sown fields of the farms, carrying a basket. He stepped flatly with one foot and then the other, swaying from side to side and singing as he went. Every day he walked through the farms selling salami and fresh home-baked bread. His house smelled like smoke from the bread oven; his neighbors watched from afar as he fanned the fire with his two sons, Enrique and Leonardo. They were his assistants and he was their master: he taught them the secrets of fire, all about the bread paddle, and everything else they needed to know. He told them that on their way to school they were never to walk by the river because there was a crazy man down there. He also told them they should set aside two whole salamis and one hunk of cheese for the school principal (bless that woman's heart, may God grant her a long life!). To all these life lessons, the boys answered:

"*Sí, papito!*"

The school principal had already told him not to give the boys salami and cheese for breakfast: such heavy food made them drowsy right after morning recess, and they fell into a deep sleep. Yes, he had taken the lice medicine home with him, but his wife threw it out. She'd gotten better for a while, but before long she was back to her old tricks: she spent the whole day looking at herself in a tiny mirror under the sun. Or she put on makeup and shaved her legs right next to the chickens, the pigs, and the cow. She called herself by more than one name: María de las Glorias Argentinas, Princess, and Maribel. "My princess!" was what Don Mascali had called her while they were dating.

But it didn't take long before she decided the countryside wasn't for her: the house smelled of smoke. Besides, she wanted magazines to keep up on what was going on in the city. Whenever he could, Don Mascali went to town and bought them for her: magazines filled with smartly dressed girls sitting on leather armchairs. It all started one day when she broke into tears, ripped up the magazines, and burned them to ashes. He explained to the children:

"Mama's feeling a little sick, but she's going to get better."

There were no fashion magazines for boys: Don Mascali dressed them for school in long wide pants that had been donated to them, and besides, they tucked the pants into high boots anyway. He cut their hair nice and short so it would last, but his eyesight was starting to go and sometimes his haircuts weren't entirely even. The boys' hair was too thick for the comb, and often their father couldn't find the comb, the scissors, or even a knife. Those boys alternated between unbridled joy and snotty-nosed tears. They were overjoyed to see the principal (she knew better than to scold them because they burst into tears at the drop of a hat), but when the other children laughed at their hair, they cried. Especially little Enrique—one kid called him "baldy with braids." And they cried when they couldn't find their pencils at home: because they wrote with thick carpenter pencils, even their own handwriting brought them to tears. Sometimes you couldn't tell whether the expressions on their faces were from laughter or tears, or everything all mixed together. But they never refused to go to school because the principal was there; she assured them that they would learn and she would hold on to their school supplies for them.

Not long after Mrs. Mascali burned up the magazines, she started to say that the cow was giving her the evil eye; she wanted that cow taken away. Don Mascali moved all the animals as far away as possible, but it wasn't enough. She wanted him to go to town and bring her face powder, lipstick, bobby pins, a hairband, and fabric to make dresses. So with basket in hand, he went off to town once a month and bought her everything she asked for. At first he had trouble explaining himself to the shopkeeper, and it was almost impossible to read the scribbled notes he took to the fabric store. But since he always bought the same items, the shopkeeper nodded to his clerk, and looked the other way:

"Give him the usual."

And Don Mascali returned home with his heart in his mouth, never knowing whether the errand would be well-received, because sometimes she was happy but other times she was displeased. She would say that the face powder smelled like manure and the fabrics were so wrinkled they looked like someone had chewed on them. On those days, the presents infuriated her more than ever, and she would go on about witchdoctors who chewed on fabric. She blamed the poor cow too, which was off grazing unaware of her tirade. Don Mascali could tell when she was worse based on her clothes: the most dangerous of them all was María de las Glorias Argentinas, with her long skirt that hung to the floor and a spade she used as a scepter. In that attire she ranted and raved about the founding fathers; plus, the scepter was dangerous. When he saw her dressed up like that, he didn't give her anything. She wore the hairband no matter which outfit, and didn't remove it to take a break from Maribel or Princess. In summer, she always wore the same old slip; in winter she wore the same dress that was coming apart at the seams. She was at her best when she sewed something for a long time, and read under the sun. She jotted down notes in the margins of the magazines. But one time, she seized the knife and started cutting up the cheese and salami. Ever since then, he began hiding the basket behind a tree and buried the knife in some ashes. Once he spoke with a doctor in town, who told him:

"She needs to be put away."

So he ended up having to leave the children alone for quite some time. How he wished to have wings so he could fly from here to there! By the time he went to visit her, her skin had almost turned black: she'd stayed out in the sun at the hospital, refusing to get up from her bench. She told him:

"Take me home, I promise I'll be good. Take me with you, I don't like this school."

Seeing her all burnt by the sun, he took her back home. Besides, he couldn't up and leave everything to go visit her. The place was so far away; he had to sell his goods to make a living. He'd left the boys alone, his feet were tired, and he thought, *I don't have wings. If I did have wings, I would first make my rounds and then go visit the hospital so she wouldn't feel so alone.* That way he could sell in town too; he would make so much more money; with his earnings he could build a room for her—no, not just a room, a whole house behind the main one. No, not just a house, a palace, so she would be comfortable, to make her happy. That way they could be together and separate at the same time.

Every now and then he went to the principal's house to see whether she'd buy his goods. Sometimes she told him:

"Not today, I don't need anything today."

But he wouldn't leave; he stayed chatting about the children for a while, about their progress. One day she said:

"Leonardo is learning, but Enrique is a lost cause."

And his eyes filled with tears. Lately, he found himself shifting from laughter to tears in a split second, and the principal thought to herself, *What an admirable, hard-working man! How does he manage it all? What a good father! He could teach the rest of us a thing or two. He could use a break. Plus, he's so sensitive. I wonder, that expression of his—when you don't know whether he's about to burst into laughter or tears—it must run in the family, because Enrique has exactly the same expression.*

Then she gave him some advice about life: you've got to carry on, God willing. But you must also take care of yourself—eat a diet with fruits and vegetables, fruit is very important. And the children don't need to be so bundled up: they're always running around during recess, they get so sweaty and, well, you know…

But Don Mascali just stood there. He wanted to ask her if maybe… Just until his wife got better, just until they found the right cure, the right medicine—whether the principal couldn't possibly take care of the children for a while… Even if they were to live right there in the school, they knew how to sweep and clean.

He started to say:

"I wanted to ask you…"

But he didn't finish. There's that face again. Oddly enough his skin looked yellowish in some spots, tinged with red and purple splotches in others. It contorted as if on the verge of something.

The principal didn't know what else to say, so she told him:

"Alright, chin up. Even the longest night comes to an end. God who gives the wound gives the salve." And then:

"Excuse me Don Mascali, but I've got some things to take care of…"

And she gave him some lice medicine.

He put the medicine in his pocket and left. He was overwhelmed by so many battlefronts. For starters, the pocket had a hole and he had to make sure the entire way home that the medicine didn't fall out. The principal had given him so many instructions he had already started to forget them. Plus, he couldn't help but worry about what state he would find his family in when he got home. He didn't have wings to get home more quickly. The walk seemed neverending.

Don Mascali had always sold his products at the only market in town. The locals gathered there, drinking grappa or Cinzano.

He used to peddle his goods at the door, but recently they'd called out to him:

"Come in."

But he didn't sit down with them. He sat at an empty nearby table and they conversed from one table to the next. He ordered grappa and downed it like a shot, as if it were cool refreshing water. The most insolent of the locals said:

"Looks like we're thirsty."

And his sidekick added:

"Yep, parched."

"Don Alfonso," the first man said to the owner. "Another grappa for the gentleman."

He said "gentleman" wryly. Don Mascali protested: No thanks; he was just on his way out. That's when the insolent one told him:

"Got you on a short leash, has she? Yesterday your princess was in here."

"Yesterday when?" he said alarmed.

"As far as I know, yesterday was yesterday. All decked out when she came in. Looking real snappy."

"Yep, above all, real snappy," said the sidekick.

Don Mascali wore that face like he had just stopped laughing and was about to cry all at once.

"Now, here's a tip: I wouldn't let her go out with such a short skirt, or that bright red bow…"

"What…What did she do?"

"Nothin'. She sat over there and downed a shot of grappa, just like you did. Shows she's your kin."

"Yep, yer kin," said the sidekick.

Don Mascali left; he sensed he'd better get home quick, but his legs thought otherwise. He hadn't had a good foot bath in quite some time, a foot bath to ease his aching feet. With so much going on he'd forgotten. He sat down to rest in the middle of the road, noticing some low clouds, the kind that don't just threaten rain—it looked like the clouds were about to swallow him up. He hurried the best he could and from afar saw the children running toward him. No matter what they say, there's no place like home. Everything was alright. Everything had been normal until his wife, in her role as Princess, had started chasing after Enrique with a knife all through the fields. She never did love him: in her own way she always loved Leonardo more, but the slightest shift in his mother and he kept his distance. Luckily, Leonardo was able to grab his brother and pull him out of the way, because Enrique had become practically paralyzed next to her, saying:

"Mamita, mamita!"

And she just kept getting angrier.

Leonardo told his father everything. No sooner had he arrived, Don Mascali built a bread oven as far away as he could, next to the dirt road, using some bricks he'd been saving for quite some time. He worked day and night with his two assistants. Don Vicente, who lived across the way, just about two blocks down, watched as Don Mascali built the oven right by the road, confirming his suspicions: the people who lived in that house were not up-and-coming. They didn't have a vegetable garden or a sulky to drive to town, and besides, the people who lived in that house spent all their money on rags: there were always clothes of every possible color hung out on the line, and when a man lets a woman spend money on such junk, he's a lost cause.

When Don Vicente saw Don Mascali and the children eating down by the road, practically out in the street, he pointed them out to his wife and said:

"Didn't I tell you? Can't you see now that I was right?"

Coordination

ONCE, I was asked to be on the organizing committee for the Buenos Aires Book Fair and to coordinate a round-table discussion among writers. The topic had already been chosen: rural and urban literature. The invitation was printed on the letterhead of the Ongoing Commission for the Organization of the Book Fair: from Authors to Readers. It was a great honor but I was reluctant. I didn't know anything about the subject, I don't know the first thing about coordinating, and one of the writers invited to take part in the panel was a priest who talks on the radio and travels from province to province on an evangelical mission. He wants to do away with the antiquated stereotype of reactionary priests, so he tries to copy the way kids speak nowadays. He says, "Christ loves you to pieces," or, "When you hit a rough patch," and sometimes he talks like he's from the countryside, telling stories about animals—like that one about the parrot that doesn't want to share. All his stories have a moral. It's really just a bunch of mumbo jumbo with words like *paranoia* and *identity* mixed in. In my opinion, he's a fraud who sells a ton of books and his breath smells like rotten eggs and he's sneaky.

I hope he doesn't show up, I thought.

Besides, I've never been able to coordinate anyone. If I'm with two people who start to argue or dig in their heels about something, I immediately come up with a third alternative to appease them both: I know how to mediate, but not how to coordinate. I'm not capable of cutting anyone off. I can't look at my watch to let the other guy know his time is up, because I don't wear a watch; and if someone tells me to do something, I do it.

We were gathered in a small conference room at the book fair. A lot of people were there. To my right, a very elderly writer was reading an excruciatingly long story. She kept pausing because she kept losing her place on the page. She had the voice of a convalescent—no, it was more like the voice of someone who had lived alone in a cave for a long time without speaking to a soul. I would have offered to read the story for her, but her handwriting was so cryptic that only she could make sense of it. The text was covered in scribbles and words that had been crossed out. *Besides*, I thought, *taking the paper away from her would only make her seem even more defeated. She could break into tears right here in the middle of the roundtable discussion.* The writer to my left—a man itching to get involved—said to me, "Cut her off. Tell her to stop reading, to wrap it up."

I gently asked her to summarize the rest of the story and tell it from memory. A minute later the guy on my left tapped my shoulder again: "Cut her off. Her storytelling is worse than her reading."

Luckily, she was interrupted by the woman sitting next to her—a lady who wrote stories about the countryside. It was one of those stories in which the sorrel gallops, the morning birds warble, and the farmhands drink yerba mate around the fire. Everything was as it should be. At one point she said, "Because he who possesses the countryside knows it best; it's been passed down from generation to generation."

You wouldn't believe all the fuss! Enraged, a woman in the audience stood up and said, "What—you think only the land-owners know how to love the land and write about it? You've got some explaining to do," with a look like she'd shoot the writer lady dead if she didn't explain herself.

The writer did the best she could, but people were already on edge. I don't know how we ended up talking about the Desert Campaign, which led to how poorly the lands had been divided up in the previous century, and the massacre of the natives. Then somebody pointed out that gauchos and natives were not the same thing, and somebody else said that actually, they were entirely related. By that point, I had completely given up hope on coordinating anything; I just sat there watching them all as if I were at the movies. I even ended up wishing the priest had shown—anything to unite all those people so it wouldn't be all on me. I realized, levelheadedly, that I never should have accepted the honor. Still, I kept my cool—I didn't blame myself or anything.

From way in the back of the audience a man said, "Until now we've spoken only about the Buenos Aires countryside. Have you all forgotten the provinces? San Luis exists, too." (Three people stood in solidarity to show they were from San Luis.) "We provincial writers are here, too, but the capital—the bigheaded monster—feasts on everything."

Fortunately, by that time they'd stopped fighting. It was as if each and every one of them wanted to voice their anger, but in isolation. The shit really hit the fan when a writer from the Pampas stood up and spoke of the drought, reminding us that the Pampas also exists. To pacify everyone, I came up with something amiable and flattering to say. I recited some lines from a famous tango:

Y la pampa es un verde pañuelo,
colgado del cielo,
tendido en el sol.

And the Pampas are a green mantle,
suspended from the sky,
lying in the sun.

The writer from the Pampas looked at me grimly and said condescendingly, as if talking to the stupidest of all his students, "But that song is about the Humid Pampas. The Dry Pampas have giant cacti."

I said, "Of course, of course."

And while he elaborated on the *cardón* cactus and its mythology, I was reminded of an obscene poem I'd read at the age of twelve about the Pampas and giant cacti.

I was never invited to coordinate—or do anything else—at the book fair again.

Paso del Rey

THE type of thing overheard at Aunt Elisa's house:
"Blue is a fine color. Beige checks are more slimming than
red checks."

It was the kind of house where melon with prosciutto was
served, and once Aunt Elisa had gotten a thorn stuck in her
eye. It remained an absolute mystery how a plant had dared
to prick Aunt Elisa in the eye because Aunt Elisa wore gloves
when she traveled to Buenos Aires and carried a purse with little
compartments containing only the essentials. All charm aside,
Aunt Elisa's house was as dull as dishwater compared to Aunt
María's house. For the longest time Grandmother had lived with
Aunt María, but then some terrible calamity had ensued to pre-
vent her from staying any longer. Now Grandmother lived in
the house next door with her son Esteban. Nothing in Grandmother's expression had changed now that she'd moved: seen
one house, seen 'em all. No matter where, she slaughtered the
chickens, boiled them into a nice broth, and once they were good
and cooked she stuffed them with some sort of green paste all
chopped up like grass (which looked like something the chicken
itself might eat). Nobody cooked at Aunt María's. Aunt María
either ate the food brought to her by Esteban, or otherwise she

made fritters. She didn't cook out of necessity, only when she was in the mood. Fritters, which at Luisa's house were dismissed as an unwholesome privilege granted to children—a treat to put a smile on their faces, but not the adults' faces—that's what Aunt María fried up any time she pleased. They were flat and wide like lily pads. Aunt María formed them impetuously, blabbing nonsense the entire time. Her knack for making fritters no doubt came from an era long gone.

Once Luisa had gobbled up the fritters—without anyone checking whether one of her knee-high socks was sagging or her coat was dragging—she would go visit the chicks. Aunt María kept them under lock and key in a damp room, where she bathed them. They got a proper bath right after they were born; every now and then a chick would actually survive.

All of Luisa's other aunts and uncles—even her own mother—reproached Aunt María for this habit, saying:

"They die."

Not that they felt sorry for the dead chicks—they just enjoyed observing how ineffective the practice was and showing off how smart they were. Who knows how they got so smart? That's why Luisa liked visiting the room where the chicks were kept: perhaps her aunt was conducting a special experiment in there with them. After all, some of them lived. She locked the door with a key, but you could still hear them cheeping inside and Luisa pleaded with her aunt to let her go in and see. Aunt María only rarely opened the door, so when the chicks were confronted by people they became frightened and fluttered around, cheeping louder than ever. Aunt María scolded Luisa for riling them all up. She yelled:

"Troublemaker!"

Luisa ran out and María said:

"Now where are you off to? Troublemaker! Trickster! Busybody! Come back here this instant!"

Luisa ran off to tell her Uncle Esteban how María kept the chicks holed up, cheeping. Uncle Esteban said:

"Wear a hat if you're going outside, the sun is strong!"

Luisa ran off to the swings at the playground. Between María's house and the playground was Uncle Esteban's market. He was a watchdog to steer clear of—albeit a distant watchdog. He yelled:

"Don't go in the sun! Don't run so much, you'll get all sweaty!"

But from afar. He was always sweeping the big dirt and flagstone patio where there were some little cement tables bolted to the ground and some aluminum chairs. Uncle Esteban was weighed down by life, he never held his head high. He swept like a maniac, his lips pressed together tightly. If it was Saturday or Sunday Uncle Ernesto would join them from the city to help out. He didn't sweep; he got drinks for the regulars and poured liquids into bottles with a funnel. Uncle Ernesto would say to Luisa, sweetly and absentmindedly, as if all little girls were made of sugar and spice:

"What does my little girl have to say for herself?"

This he cooed without even looking at her, holding up a bottle of beer for one of the regulars.

On the far side was the playground; there were swings, a seesaw, and a bar for practicing gymnastics. Luisa ended up choosing one swing as her own, it was tied with chains to the branches of two thick trees. The chains had been tied at an angle and there wasn't enough space between them to go very high, but you could do all sorts of tricks without falling off. If you sat sideways on the swing it was like a boat, rocking around in a circle. Sometimes Luisa felt like there was something wrong with that swing, like it was crooked. But the swing was so solid, its chains were so thick, that you could whack it and kick it and it would bounce right back. After sitting on the swing like a boat, then standing on one end to throw it off balance, she would get bored and walk off. The swing just wobbled back and forth on its own, lopsided. Then Luisa would go to the playground gate to watch the cars pass by on the road. One after another they drove by. She wished one would stop and take her somewhere else, to some other house.

The park was comprised of the playground with swings, the regulars' seating area, which was next to the market, and another vast space with a fig tree and a bunch of grass with lots of criss-crossing paths; that area bordered on a big henhouse.

Since it wasn't enclosed, the chickens were constantly walking around the area by the fig tree, which was next to the bathrooms. The vacationers wandered around the fig tree too. The park became truly lovely when the vacationers came. They were people who weren't used to living in nature. Nature unsettled them, making them want to enjoy everything right then and there. The vacationers' children chased the chickens, used sticks to prod the broody hen who sat peacefully on her roost, and then ran off to drink orange soda. When Uncle Esteban noticed, he threatened them from a distance. They ran off, and no one knows how they found their families again. Families were always getting lost in the park.

The men on vacation claimed if it were their land they would plant potatoes, tomatoes, and squash and they could live off chicken eggs. Every once in a while they'd kill a hen. No pigs though—they wouldn't breed pigs because they're dirty. In other men the contact with nature would awaken their desire to set up industries, poultry farms, and flower shops selling wildflowers—all those aromo flowers going to waste.

But then they would arrive at the conclusion that chickens get roost mites, and since their children would come running to tell them how they'd been scolded by a man just for playing with the chickens, they'd say:

"Don't mess with the chickens, they're dirty birds."

And the vacationer fathers would do a spin on the gymnastics bar.

The vacationers drove Uncle Estaban into fits of hatred, while Uncle Ernesto was bursting with friendliness. Someone would come up and say something like:

"Don Esteban, could you please heat up this kettle for me?"

"No. No can do."

Then they would ask Ernesto:

"Don Ernesto, would you mind?"

"Why, of course. Bring it right over."

It was the same with heating up bottles of milk for their babies and chilling bottles of beer. Later, Esteban would bicker with his brother for being so good-natured, but these discussions always took place while the two were out on walks. Esteban started to make *empanadas* and *matambre*; he was old by then, his mother had taught him. They turned out so well he decided to sell them. Then the vacationers started in with:

"Don Esteban, could you please sell me some *matambre*?"

And if he was in a bad mood or didn't like the customer's face, he would say:

"Nope. I'm all out."

Quick as a squirrel, Uncle Ernesto would beckon them over his way and sell everything in sight.

There were so many vacationers who descended upon the park. They were so unruly, and always asking to heat up so much water and chill so many beers, that Luisa stopped going to the playground. But on Sunday afternoons the park was different; neither the regulars nor the vacationers sat around the little tables outside. Instead, the place filled up with peaceful folks slowly sipping on a beer. That was the day the Shuets came: Old Man Shuet and Old Lady Shuet, who may have been his sister or sister-in-law, or perhaps they were siblings or cousins. They were ancient, but there was nothing haggard about them. The other lady was somewhat younger, and she came off as easygoing and whimsical. The three of them chatted jovially, they seemed grateful for something, as if it were their last Sunday on Earth. They smelled the jasmine, inhaled the fresh air—because they drove in from the city—and left early, before nightfall, because the road got dangerous. The old man drove. When Luisa saw them, she cheered up. She approached them and talked with them for a while, they regaled her with smiles and a pat on the back.

Deep down, Grandmother knew something good when she saw it. She took off her apron, smoothed down her hair, and stepped out to welcome the old folks. They greeted her warmly and respectfully, and Grandmother treated them with a charm and politeness that Luisa had never seen her use among the family.

Luisa started to take the bus by herself to Paso del Rey. She went to visit Aunt María and brought her what she had requested: Rachel face powder, bobby pins, and sewing thread. She first stopped by Uncle Esteban's market asking for two chocolate bars: one for herself and one for María. He said:

"Chocolate bars are junk."

All the food and drinks at the market he regarded as junk. He didn't think much of the regulars either because they drank his wine and ate big salami sandwiches; and like everyone knows, there's nothing refined about salami. And the conversations he overheard were abominable: Don Juan Ventura said that all governments are garbage, that every president on Earth should be hung to rot forever in hell. One day Don Juan Ventura even went as far as to say that the sun is the real God and father of us all because it shines its light on everyone. Don Servini said that up until the Battle of Abyssinia, Il Duce had been right; and that Arpegio, foal born to Parejero and Rosalinda, had a better pedigree than Yatasto—but they'd never let him show his true potential because of the political interests involved.

Luisa insisted; she got the chocolate bars and sometimes even a notebook to draw in. Uncle Esteban knew the future of that notebook would be bleak. Luisa gave half of it to Aunt María, ripping the pages out. On her pages, Aunt María drew young ladies with curly locks, hats, long dresses, and handbags. As she drew, Aunt María said: "This is the young lady of sport and ruffles. How charming!" She drew another just like the first and said: "This is the young lady of sport and surf." There was another she called the lady of bidet and toilet, but they all looked the same: little ringlets and faces like a dead fly.

Around that time a southern screamer showed up at María's house. Nobody knew where it came from or why. The southern screamer is a bird with spikes on its wings that it only flaunts when nervous. The bird chose to maintain a safe distance from the house, but since no one ever visited Aunt María, the first time Luisa walked through the gate the southern screamer became startled. Luisa watched as it exposed the spikes, drawing closer; her heart raced.

She didn't mention it to Aunt María, who wouldn't have had the slightest clue how the southern screamer had shown up anyway. Luisa presented the face powder to her aunt, who said:

"It's not Rachel."

"I'm telling you it is. It's Rachel," Luisa said. "What does it say here? What's that word?"

"Liars! Troublemakers! Tricksters!" María said.

That day she didn't draw any young ladies of sport and ruffles. She didn't make any fritters either. She maligned all the filthy people and troublemakers of the world.

Luisa ran to the playground. She told Uncle Esteban:

"I'm going to the playground."

She played on the swing for a while, halfheartedly. More like she sat on the swing. She was bored.

She wanted to stop by María's before going home to say goodbye, but the southern screamer was there; still, the idea of facing the bird gave her a sense of satisfaction. She couldn't let it scare her. She'd approach the house casually, as if invisible. When she opened the gate, the southern screamer played the fool. Luisa said to her aunt:

"I'm leaving."

María heard her but it just set her off again:

"They're not honest, they're not honest people. They're a treacherous, bloodsucking race!"

Luisa conjured up a terrible race of bloodsuckers and treacherous individuals, but then she realized that some of the comments were directed at her, for example "troublemaker," which made Luisa feel a little bit naughty.

This time, when she left, she had a pleasant surprise: it wasn't Saturday and yet Lili was there. Lili vacationed in a nearby house and had a romantic past: her parents were poor and she'd been adopted by a well-to-do family, the ones who took their vacations there. Lili had met her poor parents and siblings, but it seems that she was something of a nuisance to both her poor family and her rich adoptive parents.

They wanted her to be a concert pianist and Lili practiced for four hours a day, but when she went to the playground, she made mischief. Luisa really liked Lili, but she also figured that a concert pianist—even if only eleven years old—should be more reasonable than someone like Lili, because when they were sitting on the swings Lili told her a flat-out lie. She told a story about an aviator's plane that malfunctioned: the aviator ejected from the plane into the sky and fell, making a pit six feet deep in the ground. Then, alive and kicking, he stood up, brushed himself off, and walked home. Luisa knew it couldn't be true and she said:

"No way."

"I swear over my own dead body," Lili said, crossing her fingers. Luisa figured it was worthless to keep arguing.

She pretended like she believed that the pilot had gotten out safe and sound, but afterwards she felt lonely and pensive. She decided it wasn't worth it to lose Lili's friendship over an argument about a hypothetical pilot. Besides, she found Lili to be both admirable and despicable: despicable because such a ludicrous fantasy was shameful coming from an aspiring concert pianist—*or perhaps*, thought Luisa, *playing the piano was mechanical for Lili*; she banged out the notes and got better and better without even realizing it, like a talent she possessed in spite of herself, as if she were an acrobat. And admirable because such an outlandish fantasy, together with the fact that she'd been adopted, made Luisa think Lili was some type of gypsy.

The house where María lived belonged to Uncle José.

It had a front porch with mosaic tiles decorated with fleurs-de-lis and the Page of Wands. The land around the house used to be a yard, complete with grass, but now tall weeds grew because Aunt María hated the lawn mower, and she especially hated the scythe. There were rosehip bushes, a jasmine plant, an apple tree, a persimmon tree, orange and lemon trees. You used to be able to see the train pass by from the kitchen, back when the hedge had been trimmed. The kitchen was huge and it was next to the damp room with the chicks.

Then there was a big dining room and three lovely bedrooms. Uncle José had wanted to contribute by letting Aunt María live in that house in Paso del Rey; but every time he came to visit from Buenos Aires he spluttered with rage. Since the hedge hadn't been trimmed in a while, it had grown into a thicket of tall trees; you could no longer see the train through the hedge. María was on friendly terms with José because he was a "visiting brother" and not a "resident brother" like Esteban and Ernesto.

She let José enter the kitchen.

"Hello José dear," she would say to him. "Where have you been?"

"I'm in from Buenos Aires."

"What do you mean—all the way from Buenos Aires!" said María. "How silly!"

José started to stutter and he showed her his train ticket.

"I'm—I'm telling you that I came from Buenos Aires."

José was active, he had a long list of home improvements to make. He didn't stay talking to María for more than two minutes. Just looking at the hedge made him flush. He kept getting redder and redder and he couldn't stop walking in circles. There were red ants; the big rose bush was cankerous; the southern screamer strutted around smugly like an absurd little monster. The small room with the chicks was dank and musty; they were pecking at the lime on the wall for food. María was always forgetting to feed them, especially when she was filled with prophetic inspiration. The bidet was black and there was no heater in Esteban and Grandmother's place. Uncle Esteban suffered from chilblains and they weren't the normal kind. His hands were entirely deformed and he couldn't get rid of them. Meanwhile, Uncle José put out ant poison, muttering about neglect, backwardness, and moral misery. He unclogged pipes that had gotten backed up, and found the ant nests right away. When José arrived, pesticides and ant poison materialized miraculously. He went after the poultry mites and if the weasel was in range, he killed it. José agonized over that house, but more than anything else he wondered what he would say to his wife; she was so neat and careful. She knew how to wrap up packages just like they did at the shops, she painted folding screens, and she used to play the piano. Then she stopped because she thought she'd forgotten how. She feared she would make a mistake—and no matter what, she never made a mistake.

The Saturday-afternoon crowd created so much work, there were always so many baby bottles to be chilled and kettles of water to heat up. More and more of them kept coming; they came in droves, in truckloads, they were like nomads who moved into the park. Now they asked to use the telephone too, and they wanted to go to the river. The river was three blocks away and Luisa was never allowed to go swimming there. It was a dirty and dangerous river. Only once in a while, with Lili and a grown-up, could she walk along the bank. The vacationers went to swim in the river; they came back overjoyed, asking for more beer. Uncle Esteban scoffed at them, treating them as if they were an inferior caste deserving of that river. Plus, they invaded the area used by the regulars. One day, after his second glass of wine, Don Servini (for whom the bar was his home away from home) didn't bring up Rosalinda the dam or whether King Umberto I had been a good ruler. He got up from his little aluminum chair, walked up behind Ernesto, and said:

"Just look at this place, Ernesto. It's a regular dance hall. A regular dance hall."

Ernesto, who was just in the midst of watering down Don Servini's wine, said:

"I'll be right there, I'll be right with you."

Don Servini walked up and took a look around. There was a gazebo and a perfectly level dance floor, painted pink.

"Ernesto, the gazebo is for the orchestra. That's it! That's it! Let's see, but it's broken here. Tomorrow I'll send a man over to fix that gazebo."

"Alright, Don Servini."

Uncle Ernesto was capable of filtering the water and wine—or transferring certain drinks into different bottles—right in front of the regulars. The regulars already knew about it, which led to all manner of jokes and teasing.

To a certain extent, Don Servini had the power of decision; he came every day and didn't care for the Saturday vacationers. A dance is much easier to control, like Don Servini said. You can charge for tickets at the door and hang a sign that says: "This establishment reserves the right to deny admission."

Uncle Esteban began sweeping furiously. If he was put off by the Saturday vacationers, the regulars, and the river, he loathed the idea of putting on a dance.

"A dance hall," he said sarcastically. "A fucking dance hall."

Don Servini knew that he couldn't discuss the matter with Esteban, so he followed Ernesto around as he performed his distillery duties, Don Servini even trailed him to the telephone, where he would call his family in Buenos Aires. Ernesto listened to the scheme without much interest. In fact, he was just pretending to listen because Ernesto was always caught up in his private affairs, but he never said no.

Records they already had; they'd been dumped into a corner a few years back. Luisa had listened to them when she was around six years old. There was one that went:

Los gitanitos tenemos todos
El alma alegre y el cuerpo loco

All us little gypsies have
A happy soul and a crazy body

When Luisa heard it for the first time, she went nuts. That record made her want to dance immediately. Then there was another one, with strange lyrics:

Ven a ver la ola marina,
Ven a ver la vuelta que da,
Tiene un motor que camina p'alante,
Tiene un motor que camina p'atrás

Come and watch the ocean tide,
Come see how she spins about,
She's got an engine to move her forward,
And an engine to move her back

Luisa felt like that song embodied the spirit of investigation. It wasn't so easy to decide how to deal with admission to the dance: Was it going to be exclusive? Could Antonio come? He brought around the vegetables every day wearing tennis shoes and the regulars constantly teased him about his family, and especially about his brother. Antonio had a brother who took care of the cows; he didn't know how to speak. Luisa and Lili saw him walk by sometimes, behind a couple of cows. He was half man and half monkey. His entire body was covered in thick hair. He had a fleshy, toothless mouth and he only knew how to cry out to get the cows moving along. Lili said that he must have turned out that way because his mother had gone to bed with a monkey, but Luisa didn't believe it. No, he wouldn't even find out about the dance. But Antonio did come, wearing a suit and a tie—he was barely recognizable—and with him, a petite brunette. The regulars kept their mouths shut, expectantly. It wasn't the time or the place to mention his younger brother. Antonio and the brunette lined up outside the market. On the patio, the regulars started playing cards; they had more important things to do than watch what Antonio was up to. But Luisa followed him in. She adored Antonio, who always smiled at her and treated her nicely. To Luisa's surprise, the brunette eagerly approached the candy jar. Uncle Esteban would never let Luisa eat those candies because he said they were old. At this point Luisa wouldn't have eaten those candies even if she could have (because she bought bigger, better candies in Moreno), but they'd caught the eye of the brunette, who was around eighteen years old.

Antonio smiled, realizing he could indulge her, and he urged her to ask for more. She did and gave some to Luisa, who accepted. It dawned on her that Antonio and the brunette were treating her as if she were grown-up, or at least as someone deserving respect. Then Luisa asked her:

"What's your name?"

"Aurora."

"Aurora what?"

"Aurora Lipzchi."

"Write your name here."

Aurora smiled but she didn't say anything. Antonio took her by the arm and said:

"She doesn't know how to write. She's illiterate."

He smiled and gazed into Aurora's eyes. She said pleasantly:

"My mamita couldn't send me to school."

And he led her, sucking on candies, to the dance floor.

It didn't make any sense to Luisa. How could such a big girl, eighteen years old, be so enchanted by a jar of candies?

She told her mother, who was reading the newspaper, about the incident. She said:

"They're girls from the countryside. They don't know anything."

Luisa couldn't imagine what it would be like not to know anything. And just how was it that adults knew so much without even getting up from their chair or looking up from their paper? She decided that even though the brunette was much older than her, it felt like she was younger.

They decorated the dance hall with colorful garlands and even hung some out on the patio too, where the regulars sat. They had a great view of the dance. Luisa didn't know where to stand, she didn't know how to dance but she didn't want to stay too close to the adults either. When she heard that song she loved:

Los gitanitos tenemos todos
El alma alegre y el cuerpo loco

She was struck by a feeling of sadness and a fear of the unknown, at the same time. So she went out into the darkness, under the fig tree, and watched the dance from there. She would have liked to watch it all from up close, but only if she had been invisible. If Lili had been there, they would have watched from afar together, but she wasn't.

Luisa felt ashamed of herself for wanting to dance and not knowing how. No, she couldn't dance in front of everyone now like she had at age seven when she danced to "Los Gitanitos."

Then she forgot all about her problems because something unusual happened: Aunt María had gone over to Grandmother's house and there, with the dining room door wide open—which was visible from the regulars' patio, the dance floor, and even all the way from Mars—her aunt was dancing alone. She held her hands on her head and took small steps, dragging her feet, a little bit forward and a little bit back, like the ocean tide.

Uncle Esteban was beside himself. He called out: "Alright! Enough!"

But it was obvious that she couldn't stop dancing, she was possessed by her role as a dancer. There she was, a stout woman over the age of fifty, holding on to her skirt. Strictly speaking, there's nothing wrong with a stout woman over the age of fifty holding on to her skirt, but you should have seen Aunt María. She kept placing her hands on her head, lurching forward with such determination and disregard for others—as if she might even shimmy all the way over to the dance floor. But then they realized she didn't have plans to go anywhere; there she stayed, as if inside a magic bubble.

At first, Luisa laughed at her aunt's dance; she felt irritated, embarrassed, and ashamed by her aunt's persistence. María had violated an unspoken agreement until then respected by all the other dancers on that calm and enchanted dance floor. They could all see her and yet she couldn't care less; she didn't manifest any hopes or desires of dancing with anyone else.

Luisa went back out into the darkness, by the fig tree, to watch the dance floor from afar. She knew her aunt was there too, dancing with her hands on her head, and Luisa couldn't push that image from her mind.

She was momentarily repulsed by her aunt's dancing, but then she felt bad about her disgust. Aunt María would just have to learn to dance the right way—a more normal dance, like everyone else. She looked like she was under some sort of spell; perhaps one day in the future Luisa's aunt would become more discreet and prudent. She couldn't possibly dance like that forever.

So Luisa accepted it, temporarily. She thought to herself: *In the end, the only ones here who truly love dancing are Aunt María and me.*

One day Luisa was standing outside the front door with her Aunt María when a man walked down the sidewalk. María yelled:

"Cross to the other side of the street, you thief! This sidewalk is mine! This is my street—all of this belongs to us!"

The man left quickly, sheepishly.

Luisa was embarrassed. How can anyone rightly say they own the sidewalk?

"Why did you say the sidewalk is yours?" she asked.

More furious than ever, María replied:

"It's mine! They're all thieves, murderers, fucking gold diggers!"

Where María had come up with those insults, no one knows. After yelling she muttered to herself, as if repeating a mantra: "I'm right. I'm right."

Luisa half believed her aunt. Perhaps there was some history around that block and the street, a dispute. Otherwise, who would make such heated demands about something that wasn't theirs?

But that part about owning the sidewalk, it just didn't make sense... Besides, María's foul language tainted the street. It cast a gloom over the cottage across the street, which was small and well-kept, and some nice old folks lived there. The entire street, which was now paved, wide, and smooth, became imbued with a sort of uneasiness. By now María had ventured as far as Esteban's yard and she was right up against the fence, yelling where the regulars sat. She started making demands of her mother, she wanted her mother to live with her—not with the fucking gold diggers, as she called them. Grandmother spent most of her days in bed now. All she could do was pray; she prayed for her family in Italy and for her family right here. She found it hard to remember the names and faces of everyone in Italy, and she didn't want to leave anyone out.

Aunt María walked over and yelled in her face, interrupting the prayer. If Grandmother concentrated she was able to recite a whole string of names: Joaquín, Carolina, her own mother who was in heaven, but when she lost her train of thought she screamed:

"Shut up!"

This only made María yell even louder, saying more and more bad words to offend God and all the peaceful inhabitants of Heaven. Her words did not please the inhabitants of Heaven. Joaquín disappeared from Grandmother's mind; her own mother faded from view. After concentrating so much to remember them all, after so many years; she screamed at María from her bed:

"Madwoman! Fucking lunatic!"

Now María was yelling and crying too; and when Grandmother felt like María's sobbing had become strange—they weren't tears of relief, they were bitter tears from an unhappy person, the kind of tears that no one can take pity on, the kind of tears that don't convince anyone, they're just annoying—that's when Grandmother started crying too, holding her head in her hands to make sure no one could see so they didn't come over to console her.

Uncle Esteban wanted to grab María by the arm and push her back into her house, but she got loose. Esteban held up one of his arms menacingly, as if he were going to hit her, and she retreated back to her house, but she kept turning around to holler out excuses in an attempt to leave with dignity, as if she were professing her reasons not to be thrown out. The regulars watched the whole show. Don Servini offered to give her a good beating to stop her from mouthing off once and for all, and Don

Juan Ventura said he would tie a rope to her neck, throw her in the sea, and let her sink to the bottom.

After a while, Grandmother sent Uncle Esteban over to spy on María and find out how she was doing. This was practically a diplomatic mission, because Esteban never entered María's house. He spied through the fence, near the southern screamer. He had to stay hidden, to keep María from getting angry. This wasn't a problem because there were lots of trees and the thick hedge.

If he heard yelling and pounding on the table, or the sound of large buckets of water being tossed all over the house—especially if there were large buckets of water—this was a sign that everything was alright. Uncle Ernesto and Uncle Esteban never entered her property but José did—to check on the rose bushes and the persimmon tree.

Uncle José, however, didn't know the real condition of his house because he never went beyond the kitchen. His sister didn't permit it; in fact, she only let him into the kitchen when she was in a good mood.

José came a few days after this episode; he was already nervous when he arrived. When he was nervous his head filled with blood, he stuttered, and he continually stuck his hands in his pockets and then pulled them back out. When he arrived, she was in a good mood and he walked into the kitchen. He wanted to pour himself a glass of water from the sink. There was no water. Some sort of intuition led him to flip the light switch. There was no electricity either. He turned redder and redder.

María became restless:

"What are you doing? What are you getting into over there?"

Uncle José walked into the bathroom and she followed him. She started to get worked up. She didn't allow men into her bathroom, not even her brothers. José already knew this—he didn't dare use her bathroom, he was just checking whether there was water and electricity in the bathroom: no, there wasn't—which intensified his fury and made him unstoppable. Then, to prove her competence and goodwill, María said:

"Every once in a while, I flip the switch to see if the light comes on, and it does."

She said it tentatively, as if electricity were a mystery of nature. Her tone made him even more irate and he went to the bedrooms. Everything was damp because María threw buckets of water on the walls. A pungent stench arose from the house, but it wasn't the usual smell of cigarette smoke or filth; it was a very clean smell, like damp lime, as if winter were sprouting from the walls. Livid, Uncle José then walked over to Uncle Esteban's house and María said:

"Where are you going? Busybody! Gold digger! Backstabber! That's what you are, a backstabber."

And, like always, José was back in two minutes, his clothes changed, carrying a pair of pruning shears—where he got them, no one knows. Then, acting as if nothing had ever happened, he doggedly started trimming the hedge. The branches had grown as big as tree trunks and there was José, lost and small, trimming that forest. María went berserk and the whole time he was trimming, she yelled:

"Backstabber! Thief! Hooligan! Traitor! Gold digger!"

And after he'd trimmed the entire hedge without looking up at her even once, he took the pruning shears back over to Grandmother's house and changed his clothes.

He asked her weakly, in an angry yet conciliatory voice, how any of this was possible, counting off his troubles on his fingers: the electricity, the water, the hedge, the chicken mites, the plague-infested rose bushes, the southern screamer. José started to pace back and forth in circles as he said:

"The list goes on and on, there's no end to it."

Tentatively, Uncle José then said that in his modest opinion—it was just a suggestion, all things considered—perhaps Aunt María should be hospitalized, even if it was just for a short time, and then we could take it from there. He said all this without looking at anyone, but it was Grandmother he was addressing. Esteban didn't say anything; Uncle Ernesto never said no, he was always accommodating. Cautiously,

Grandmother asked whether perhaps some sort of new product with curative properties hadn't come onto the market. If penicillin had saved her life, there must be some sort of medicine to try on María, something like linden tea but much stronger. Grandmother wasn't convinced that such a product existed, but she wanted to try something else before hospitalizing María; because Grandmother had prayed for God to take her so many times, so that she could accompany María when she died and not have to leave her in the hands of strangers.

But it seems that God didn't want to take María; the will of God was for her to live. So first they were first going to try some sort of treatment and if that didn't work they would hospitalize her, even though Grandmother wasn't so sure that it was God's will.

Gina

LATELY I'd been feeling mildly fatigued, I couldn't figure out what was causing it. Work more than anything, I supposed. I kept thinking it over, but I couldn't find a way to lighten my load. Housework took up a lot of my time. It wasn't because I wanted to have a charming, tidy house. Just that it was a big house with a big old yard—it was one of those houses with high ceilings that collect lots of cobwebs, and the floorboards were disintegrating around the edges. Sometimes a gardener came around, but it wasn't enough. He trimmed the hedge but left all the cuttings on the ground until they rotted and shriveled up. Then I could easily gather them together and throw them in the garbage can. *How will I ever find myself a break with all this work?* I thought. *The house is too big for me, I can't do it alone.* Then one day when I was glancing through the newspaper I got an idea: *I'll hire a girl to come work here, that's what I'll do. She'll help me with so many things—maybe she'll even know how to cook. I'll teach her to make walnut cake (which is the only thing I know how to bake). I'll give her all my old dresses—except the navy blue one. I know it's old, but I'll keep that one for myself.* It had to be someone without children because if she had children they would break the silence, and by now I'd gotten used to things being quiet. Keeping that last bit in mind, I went right out and published an ad in the local paper. It read: "GIRL WANTED FOR FULL-TIME LIVE-IN MAID. NO CHILDREN PLEASE."

When I got back from placing the ad I sat down on a bench outside to eat the rest of a walnut pancake left over from the morning. There were lots of leftover pancakes and I thought: *She'll be able to keep me company, too. I've been so lonely lately.* I hadn't exactly wanted my life to end up like this, it just worked out this way and I hadn't done anything to change it. Besides, let's not forget that my routine had been the same for something like twenty years: get some work done, go out for a stroll—never too late—and then back home to make sure everything was ship-shape.

Nevertheless, it's not that I was entirely alone because I had a friend—a man of a certain age, like myself—whom I seldom saw, maybe three times a year. Together we would sit out on one of the benches in the garden, read the newspaper in each other's company, make the odd remark about what was happening in politics. I was quite fond of this friend and perhaps I would have preferred to discuss something other than politics, but that never happened. I took things as they came. Anyway, I couldn't help but feel pleased thinking of what great company the girl was going to be. In fact, I was so glad to have placed the ad that before I went to sleep that night as I dusted the floorboards and removed a huge chunk of flaking wall, I surprised myself by singing a tune that was very dear to me; I thought I'd forgotten it because it had been so long since I'd sung. But I caught myself right away; I stopped singing and set down the duster. I went to bed early that night.

The following days were a blur. I'd been given a long project at work; it was a census with spreadsheets that took over my entire desk. I had to give it my full attention to get it done accurately, and any little noise distracted me and put me in a foul mood. I couldn't deal with the birds chirping, let alone the sounds from the street, even though they were pretty subdued. Like I said, I was working on the spreadsheets when the doorbell rang. The doorbell hardly ever rings at my house. I got up quickly, leaving everything just the way it was and went to see who was there: I knew it would be someone about the newspaper ad. It was a fat lady with a high bun on the top of her head. She was no girl—far from it. The loose bun shook whenever she moved her head, and she kept her hands by her sides. She wasn't anything like what I'd expected. Plus, I was in a bad mood because of the spreadsheets and I don't think the look on my face was too kind, because she walked in apprehensively. She sized up the house as if she were a prospective buyer; I could tell she was taken aback by the size of the patio and by how hard it would be to clean that filthy tile floor—the mosaics were almost black—

and then she shook her head as if to decline. I think she added, although very faintly:

"At my age…"

She toured the whole house anyway, even the chicken coop, but she did so with indifference. I didn't say anything to convince her otherwise and we walked through the entire house in silence. After a while she said:

"It's quite big."

I replied:

"Yes, it is big."

She asked if there were any children and I said no. She stopped to think and said either way she'd get back to me, but I never saw her again. I went back to my spreadsheets begrudgingly, but that woman's visit had given me some food for thought: *How is it*, I wondered, *that when my ad says "girl" this lady comes along, who couldn't be farther from a girl?* I contemplated the tenderness people start to feel toward themselves when they get older while still thinking of themselves as young. *But*, I thought, *it's also possible that she just didn't notice that part: "girl" is just a figure of speech, like any other expression."* I mean, who actually stops to think about the image conjured up by an ad: she read "girl wanted" as if it had said "woman wanted." She just hadn't paid attention to the part about being a girl. *The same thing happens with errand boys*, I thought. *People say "girl wanted" the same way they say "errand boy wanted."* Besides, it made me happy to think how that lady—who was two or three years older than I was as I'd just turned forty-two—still thought of herself as a "girl." It gave me a vague sense of hope. While I was distractedly mulling over these thoughts I made a huge ink stain on the spreadsheet, which blotted out a very important data set. I couldn't remove it with an eraser or with a metal scraper. I was worried the whole page would tear, so I went to buy an ink eraser. It took me a while to get the ink eraser and when I left the stationery shop I noticed someone ringing the doorbell at my house, someone with her back to me who didn't see me walk up behind her. It was a girl who had no doubt come because of the ad, although once I got closer I wasn't sure because there was something fearless about her: she seemed demure yet cheeky at the same time. She wasn't expecting me to approach from behind and I felt somehow intimidated, as if it weren't actually my home and I had just ended up there out of some sort of mix up. I asked her:

"Did you come for the ad?"

"Yes," she said and lowered her head.

She had blonde hair that on first glance didn't strike me as anything special, but when I looked again I realized it was beautiful. Her hair was downy and soft, like a young child's. There was nothing unusual about her face, except that she was blushing a little. I don't know why I didn't realize how pretty she was at the time. Perhaps because there was something even more striking about the way she spoke and how she dressed and in her posture: as if she'd spent time in an orphanage or a nun's school for poor girls. It showed in the way she held her jacket in one hand and also in her choice of words. In fact, when she spoke I noticed she pronounced her words slowly, shyly, a little distrustingly, and with a slight lisp, the way the children spoke at an orphanage not far from my house. We talked about the pay and walked through the house; it didn't seem to make much of an impression on her: not too big or small, not too old or new. She tucked her jacket under her arm and kept her purse concealed. Since she didn't ask anything else I assumed that she had accepted the job and I showed her to her room, a little room upstairs that was nice and neat. I had to point it out to her several times because she kept her head down. I offered her soap and water to wash up in case she was tired, and I took the opportunity to ask whether she'd traveled far and where she'd come from, but she didn't answer me about the water; she just went to her room. I decided to erase the big stain on the spreadsheet but as soon as I went back to work I could sense something. When I turned around, there was the maid, on the second step of the staircase, just staring at me. She smiled and blushed a little and scurried off to her room. Then I heard her turn off the light.

The next day we went over how to clean everything, where I kept the feather duster, the dustpan, the mop, and where to toss the garbage. Every time I showed her something she nodded her head like someone who really wants to learn and whatever they learn becomes a revelation. But when she went to fetch the cleaning supplies she got it all wrong, and I realized she didn't know where the duster or the broom were. At first she didn't say anything, but then, little by little, instead of smiling when she went to look for the duster she'd ask me:

"Could you remind me where the duster is?"

And I told her as many times as she needed. Meanwhile, I started working on another spreadsheet that was shorter than the first one. Distracted, watching her walk back and forth, I used blue ink instead of red and I blurted out:

"I did it again!"

My voice sounded disgruntled and nervous. She must have overheard because she said the strangest thing in a voice that was also remarkably peculiar, accentuating the orphanage accent:

"Life takes its twists and turns."

I was surprised she'd used that expression and I expected her to follow it up with a whole series of explanations about how her life had taken twists and turns, filled with unpleasant details about the death of a sick father or her younger siblings, or what have you. But she didn't elaborate any further; she just kept dusting. In other words, the details must not have been so unpleasant because then when I deliberately said (anticipating the possibility that she would talk about her life, and wanting to console her): "Yes, we're all in the same boat. Life takes us all by surprise," all I got was a weak smile. She said no more. I noticed her face wasn't as flushed as it had been the day she'd arrived, but her hair was wet and plastered to her face.

Then she turned around and asked:

"Shall I clean the dining room?"

"Very well," I answered.

But she'd already rushed off to clean the dining room, without waiting for my reply.

One day she must have had breakfast before I awoke because when I got up she'd already piled all the cleaning supplies in the middle of the room. When she saw me she called me over and said, in that mysterious orphanage tone of voice:

"There's dust under the beds. There's dust under the furniture, too."

The truth is I already knew about the dust, but it didn't really bother me. Nonetheless here she was, reminding me about all the dust under the beds. I couldn't play dumb; it had to seem like I cared, so I said:

"Yes, it needs to be cleaned up. I just got back from a trip."

That's how I excused myself. Then, to show my concern, I went to look at the dust so she would get rid of it. That afternoon while I was checking that everything was more or less in order I noticed that she had cleaned everything except the dust under the beds and the furniture. It was still there. She'd mentioned it at least three times, yet she hadn't cleaned it up. I went to look at the other room where she was still dusting, but she hadn't cleaned under the bed there either. I didn't want to be the one to remind her that she'd been the one to notice the dust under the furniture and then hadn't bothered to clean it up. So, just to prove my point, I cleaned it up myself—it had been so long since I'd done that type of chore. Afterwards, my lower back hurt. That night at dinner I asked her what her name was. She told me:

"Gina."

What an exotic name, I thought, because Gina was the name of an actress who was all the rage at the time and this girl was nothing like her: Gina the actress was cheerful, happy, and outgoing. I wondered whether my girl just wanted to be called Gina. Maybe it wasn't her real name; perhaps it was Maria, for example. Even though I knew I ran the risk of appearing rude, someone who gets easily distracted when they're being told something important, like a name, I asked her again:

"What's your name?"

"Gina," she answered plainly.

She didn't have any sort of ID to prove whether or not she really was Gina, but I was sure it wasn't her real name. After that I always called her Gina to her face, but I was suspicious. At the same time I found myself laughing about it. She didn't seem to notice anything strange, and when I called her name she always walked in wearing a straight face.

I had a friend, as I mentioned, who came to visit me once in a while. He always came unexpectedly, around eleven o'clock in the morning. This time he arrived somewhat earlier because he had taken his watch to get fixed. There was something different about him: he looked taller and his clothes were a shade lighter. I told him there was a new girl working for me named Gina— at least so she claimed—and we spent a long time talking about her before she appeared. When she did walk in, all of a sudden, I decided to pay close attention to how she behaved around my guest because we hadn't had anyone over since she'd started. I was surprised to find how cordial she was, and my friend just gave me a look as if to say: *What's wrong with you? Saying all those cruel things about her.* She was still nice to me—but it was more of a generic kindness. In fact, it even seemed like her orphanage voice had changed. My friend and I spoke enthusiastically about politics and she listened. At one point she even sat down in a little chair and listened in silence.

My friend was talking about someone who had taken an unnecessary risk for a cause and suddenly I heard her say:

"You made your bed, so you must lie upon it."

She kept saying all these cryptic things throughout the entire conversation. Her comments weren't entirely relevant, but you couldn't say they were complete nonsense either—perhaps a bit foolish, but only a little bit. My friend agreed with her and Gina's face started to blush, which really suited her. That's when I discovered she was pretty. Her hair was lovely and she had a pretty face too, even if it was a little bland. At eleven o'clock she said she was tired and wanted to turn in, and asked my permission to do so. I consented, but noticed her light was on until much later and I heard footsteps, too. My friend remarked that that girl had real common sense—that she must be from a village. And then he noted how beneficial it was to discuss politics with a villager. He also said he'd quite enjoyed our conversation that night—a conversation in which "the people" had taken part too. I agreed and we continued to talk about Gina for a long time, until three o'clock in the morning. That's when it dawned on him that he should have remembered to pick up his watch, but it was too late. I promised to get it for him and he promptly left in good spirits.

We had been having a pretty good time of it, without much work, when I told her:

"Today we're going to wax the floors."

She went right out and bought some wax—a type I don't like because it has a reddish tinge to it—but I didn't say anything. She got down on her hands and knees with an old rag and started scrubbing the floor with such vigor that the whole house shook. She worked doggedly, without stopping, and when I approached her to see how it was going she stood up, as if waiting for something, but she didn't speak. Then when I went into the other room she asked in a low voice:

"Who was that gentleman?"

I didn't answer right away; then eventually I said:

"He's a friend of mine."

I guess she was satisfied with that answer because she continued waxing the floor with the same gusto, and again the sound of the rag rattled everything.

My friend showed up at eleven o'clock in the morning: he hadn't trusted me to pick up his watch so he'd come to get it himself. When he saw her kneeling on the floor waxing, he said:

"That's so old-fashioned! We'll get you up to speed in no time."

He set right out to a nearby store that sold household appliances and asked the owner (they were friends) if he could borrow a buffing machine. Then he came back with the machine and showed her how to use it, but the girl didn't understand so he went ahead and waxed the whole house himself. Happy, wiping the sweat from his brow, he said:

"Let's take advantage of the extra time now. What could we do? I know! Let's play cards."

He took out a deck of cards and nimbly dealt them into little piles on the table. Then he asked the girl:

"Do you know how to play cards?"

"No, I don't," she replied blushing.

I knew how to play cards, but not very well—it was something I mostly did just for fun. Inevitably I would get bored and stop caring which card I played, but every now and then I would play, particularly solitaire. My friend started explaining the game to her and she listened to him as if it were a matter of life or death, but it didn't make any difference because either way she didn't understand, she just blushed and then smiled. We started to play anyway, my friend directing the game because he knew the rules and besides, he really enjoyed playing cards. He said since she was just learning the two of them would play as a team, against me. Needless to say, they beat me at every game—he played for her and told her which cards to play. We played *escoba*, making groups of cards that add up to fifteen. He showed her how to make fifteen points and she seemed pleased, as if she'd gained a new perspective on life. After they'd beat me over and over again my friend said he'd lost interest in the game because it was unfair—we would play a different way: just me against her. It was almost as if Gina had a delayed reaction because then she said triumphantly:

"We beat her."

I was surprised because her claim came a touch too late. Then my friend said:

"We sure did. Now we can beat her again."

He stood behind her telling her every card to play, and when she didn't catch on he kept saying: "You've got to practice, you've got to practice." And she would smile and play her cards attentively. By then I'd gotten to the point where I end up throwing any old card down and I began to yawn. I smiled and said:

"I'm tired. It must be bedtime."

It had gotten quite late and my friend promised to come back soon, which sounded nice to me—albeit unusual. When he left Gina closed the gate, making sure the inside doors were locked and, before going to bed, when she asked which type of meat to buy the following day, she added:

"Another day you can win."

"I hope so," I said smiling, "but now it's time for bed."

It rained for the whole month of February: you couldn't even step outside unless you were wearing boots. There was too much mud and we spent practically all our time indoors. One afternoon I got up from my nap and found Gina sitting at the table with all the cards spread out before her.

"What are you doing?" I asked.

"I want to play solitaire," she said, "but I don't know how…"

Strictly speaking, she hadn't asked me to teach her, but I did. She picked it up right off the bat, perhaps because of her previous experience playing *escoba*. After that, whenever I was napping she would play solitaire. Once, when I got up and it was raining like usual, I found my friend there showing her how to play. He was amazed by how much progress she'd made. He opened a bottle of wine he'd brought along and we all had a glass. We made a toast to something—I can't recall exactly what it was we toasted—but the atmosphere was fairly lively. Still, my lower back was hurting a bit. I got a sharp pain and I didn't want to say anything right then so I went out and sat on the bench on the patio. I ended up staying there for a long time. When I came back in, there they were, still talking and laughing. I said:

"I'm a little tired. I'm going to turn in."

Then I added kindly:

"Please clean everything up when you're done."

And my friend answered for them both:

"Rest assured. Good night and sweet dreams."

By the time I'd given them instructions on how to clean up and we'd said goodnight, a while longer had passed. I went to my room but I couldn't fall asleep because my back hurt too much.

From that night on, Gina started asking my permission to go out every evening after six o'clock. I presume that had I denied her she would have gone anyway. She left with her jacket in hand—but not stiffly like she had the first day, she was more relaxed now. She tucked it under her arm carelessly, or slung it over her shoulder. Once I even saw her drape it over her shoulders, like young athletes do. These days she powdered her face, and she'd bought rubber gloves. They were enormous gloves meant for some lady with monstrous hands, but she was convinced the gloves were practical. One afternoon when Gina was finishing her regular game of solitaire, she said to me in a voice feigning indifference, but tinged with the severity of the orphanage:

"I'm going to get married."

"Sounds good," I said to her, "sounds very good."

She turned red and smiled like she always does when I say that to her. She hesitated and then she said:

"We're going to rent a house. Be sure before you marry, of a house wherein to tarry."

"Sounds good," I repeated.

Then she didn't say anything else.

And so it went: Gina got married to my friend—of all

people—and went to live in a house they rented together in a neighboring town. Meanwhile, as I look back in retrospect over all that's happened I've forgotten the point. I have to find another girl, because all this work is too much for little old me.

Hello Kids

AT the zoo in Buenos Aires there's a baboon cage. The sign says: Sacred Baboon of India. I've been to visit three times and I'd go a fourth. Whenever I go, I first stop in front of the brown spider monkey, who's the best acrobat I've ever seen. He splits his time between resting up after his balancing acts (slumbering with limber passivity), and spending long spells watching the endless source of enchantment parading before his eyes: a seesaw next to a sandbox where children of all shapes and sizes play; up and down, laughing and swinging. He seems fascinated by the spectacle, but every now and then remembers that he's got his own show to put on. Then he scampers back and forth at full speed along the narrow ropes without a hint of vertigo, as if it were a cinch. I figure a human athlete would have to train for something like ten years to do even a quarter of his tricks.

Next to the baboon cage, separated by a fence, is the southern pig-tailed macaque. Like the spider monkey, he's alone, but the macaque has less fun because he doesn't climb, he doesn't have anyone to groom him, and he doesn't get to groom anyone else. He spends his life spying on the baboons. There's around twenty of them and they don't pay the slightest attention to him—except once when all hell broke loose. It was fantastic. The whole troop of baboons, who are really rowdy, swung into motion. They rapped on the pig-tailed monkey's fence three times, as a warning, as if to say: *Careful, you're not going to get off so easy.* One of the chiefs kept passing by and smacking the fence on purpose. But when the troop is peaceful, Mr. Pig-tailed can watch the baboons all he wants. Once I saw them grooming each other in circles of three, one behind the other, meticulously parting each other's hair into sections like a hairdresser getting ready for a dye job. As one chief offered up the other side of his body to be groomed, the expression on his face was a mix of arrogance and vanity. Another monkey was absorbed in studying his long, dark hand.

They must have inspired Modigliani to make his stylized figures; the eyes of these monkeys are two lines; their breasts, two pink tips; and the penis, a long, red sheath. They cough and sneeze. One of the monkeys made a little noise and a girl said:

"Mommy, he's got the hiccups."

They chew forcefully and conscientiously when they eat, as if following advice from a magazine for humans on how to aid digestion. There's one main chief and other minor ones; you can pick them out by their hair: it's long, white, and slightly wavy. Leadership seemed to be granted based on hair. If their hair falls out, the other monkeys no longer obey. One girl said about their hair:

"Mommy, he got a blow-dry."

Perhaps the notion of strength—which for us is different from beauty—is an all-encompassing concept for them, some sort of fascination. The foremost chief stands out because he's the most indifferent of them all. He climbs up on a high rock to keep tabs on all the persecutions he witnesses daily. Not surprisingly, the biggest skirmishes occur in the back, behind the scenes, where he can't see. He's more tireless than Zeus, who likewise climbed atop a mountain to observe the end of the Trojan War and wearily said to himself: *Go ahead and do whatever you like—I've had enough*. But this chief never tires, and when the fight gets dirty he doesn't hesitate to run over and let 'em have it. When it comes to mealtime, however, he's no different from the rest—he shakes the fence nobly and pounds on the food chute, too. Like they say in Mexico: *Mendigo y con garrote*—beggars can't be choosers. After the chief has made his plea, another very different beggar comes along. Perhaps he was once the chief but his hair fell out, taking his confidence along with it. He tries to jiggle the fence but to no avail, as if to say: *Anything for me?* No crown of hair, no attitude, no conviction. He doesn't score so much as a scrap.

And then there's the mother monkey with her little baby, who is around three months old. Sometimes she gives him a piggyback ride, or she holds him in her hand like a tiny package. She shepherds him around, but when he's dying to play with a monkey who's bigger than him she carts him off, like a suspicious human mother around an older kid. Once, the baby monkey climbed up the fence but then didn't know how to get down. And his mother didn't help—it was an aunt or an uncle or simply a neighbor who rescued him.

There are a lot of people watching and some of them are impressed by the baboons' behinds—they're so prominent. A girl around the age of nine says:

"He's got a brain in there."

And the parents, the grown-ups, don't seem to understand that a baboon's behind is an integral part of the species. They've all got it, it's their hallmark. Some of the people say:

"He's got hemorrhoids."

They must subscribe to some sort of creationist theory. God would never have conceived of such a deformity; there'd have to be some element of perversion in God's mind for him to design a creature with such a large rear end. But like Spinoza said: "Any one thing considered in isolation and not in relation to anything else encompasses a perfection as far-reaching as its very essence."

The mother monkey has a suitor. It's one of the minor chiefs and he stands before her expectantly; I saw him at all three of my visits. Sometimes, she quickly hides her playful little baby behind her, but I can't figure out why she periodically lets him stay only to shield him from the suitor later on. She doesn't dislike the fellow, she just sits there, facing him. Now and then he goes to fulfill his duties as a vigilant minor chief, but he remembers to come back to his girl, perhaps awaiting a moment of weakness.

The last time I went, a boy around the age of three said to them:

"Hello, kids."

The Old Man

It's not that I'm selfish, I told myself. *That's not why I don't want to give up my seat. Giving up one's seat involves a considerable change in position: here I am sitting down, then suddenly I'd have to get up, reposition my newspaper, or reposition myself to read the newspaper. Meanwhile everyone's staring at me. I'm just going to stay put.*

The person waiting for a seat was an old man with a bowler hat, the type nobody uses anymore. He was wearing one tennis shoe and one dress shoe, which didn't seem to bother him. When I noticed he was wearing two different shoes I figured his feet must really hurt, so I gave him my seat. I was tempted to move down the aisle to get away from him, in case he became too friendly, but that didn't happen. He sat down with a little sigh. Anyway, it wasn't just in case the old man became all chummy: I wanted to watch him. I couldn't quite tell why he was wearing two different shoes. I figured that someone dressed like that would feel insecure, but that didn't seem to be the case. He looked out the window of the train, watching the houses pass by. At one point he looked at a construction site with great interest, squinting as if he were short-sighted. When the lights of the train flickered on in the tunnel, everyone got up to get off. But the old man just kept sitting there, and I just stood there next to him.

When I saw that he wasn't getting up, I gave him a little nudge on the shoulder and said:

"We're here."

"Ah, yes," he said, visibly moving his head to answer, as if our arrival meant nothing to him. He prepared to get up and I realized he couldn't: it was causing him great effort. Then he held onto my arm, grasping my elbow. To be more specific, he tugged on my sleeve. Honestly, I didn't like him tugging on my sleeve so I pulled him up, grabbing on to his arm forcefully. He started taking tiny little steps and I thought to myself, *I'll walk him to the subway station and then, sayonara*. But I had to take the subway, too, and I asked him:

"Do you suffer from a foot condition?"

"It's my heart."

He said this without looking at me, his head somewhat bowed. I found myself wondering whether there was anything beautiful about this old man, whether he was wearing a beautiful hat, for example, or whether it was a beautiful day—for a Monday morning. And I asked myself why that should matter. Maybe because everything that happens to me has to have some trace of beauty. I looked at the old man and realized my thoughts were dumb and pointless. Then I had two more thoughts, simultaneously: how sad life is and how pathetic the social system is—letting a poor old man with a heart condition walk around with two different shoes. But I also thought, in disgust: *Why did he tug on my sleeve? Besides, his neck is all sweaty with those little lines that form on the necks of bald men, inevitably giving off a bad smell.* When we got off the subway I wanted to hand him over to someone else, so I asked him where he was going.

"To the Ministry," he said.

I asked him which ministry and he didn't know what to say: he kept pointing insistently with a shaky finger in a vague direction. I figured it would be extremely difficult to get him down the stairs, so before starting down I said:

"Wait for me here, I'm going to ask where the Ministry is."

I walked off solicitously, like a helpful citizen, and I noticed he was looking at me as if I really were. I felt invigorated as I walked down the stairs, but when I got to the bottom I asked myself: *How am I going to ask where the Ministry is? They're going to ask me which one. I can't just point with my finger like the old man.* This worried me, but then I tried to regain the demeanor of a helpful citizen. I asked a worker, pointing with an air of complicity at the old man, alone at the top of the staircase. He wasn't attempting to walk down.

"Excuse me, the gentleman has to get to the Ministry and he doesn't know which one. Could you..."

"Ah, yes," said the man, and he gave me the address.

How did the worker know which ministry the old man was going to? He didn't even bat an eye. He didn't seem surprised. But I was, and I couldn't help but think about that, because it's happened to me before: people know things that seem otherwise impossible, like now, the relationship between a ministry and that old man. But I didn't pause to think because the old man was up there waiting. I hastened to get back to his side, eager again, and I thought: *In case somebody else... In case somebody else does what? Offers to take him there? And then what? As if I had first dibs on him!* But nobody came along and we walked slowly down the stairs. At some point I said to him,

"It's really hot."

"Ah, yes," he said.

But it didn't seem like the heat bothered him. By the time we reached the bottom, scores of people had gone up and down. We ended up in a big plaza with a pond in the middle. The old man grabbed me by the elbow again and, without saying a word, walked me over to a bench. I figured he was tired, although he could have spoken up. I asked him:

"Weren't we going to the Ministry?"

"Ah, yes," he said.

He didn't say anything else. People walked by and looked at us and I wondered, *Do they think we're related?* And I realized I didn't want them to think we were related. On the other hand, it didn't really matter. I kept looking at him sympathetically—much too kindly for a relative. *Furthermore,* I told myself, *he doesn't look like he has any relatives. At least I couldn't imagine it.* This made me feel better and I asked him politely,

"Are you retired?"

His face lit up and he said:

"Yes, yes, retired."

I suspected—because my question seemed to provide him with an answer to justify himself, and because I figured he wasn't actually retired—that perhaps when he was younger he had been a bum. But I couldn't have actually asked him that, although something told me that if he had been, it wouldn't have mattered anyway. Clearly, the old man wouldn't have paid any mind to the question.

"So," I told him, "now we have to go. The Ministry is really close."

"Yes," he said, and he got up. Then I realized he would have been impervious to anything I said: he had lost faith in everything, so now he could place his trust in anyone, that's why he had pulled on my sleeve. I felt his hand on my sleeve again, as if to confirm my thoughts, and we started walking to the Ministry.

There it was, before our eyes. Suddenly it hit me: the Ministry had been newly renovated. There were bright marble walls and benches where one could sit and wait, the employees wore such elegant ties. What were we going to do at the Ministry? I wasn't sure and I figured I should ask—he wasn't going to know what to say. And it's not like I'm well versed in the type of thing one says at a Ministry, but I could articulate it better than him, whose hands were starting to shake. So I asked him:

"What are we going to do at the Ministry?"

He didn't answer and, his hands still shaking, he took out an old piece of paper. It was all folded up, but you could tell it was valuable to him: it hadn't been crumpled or torn. It said: "Laguna's widow," and something else, something entirely unintelligible. What were we going to do with this? What was it for? I racked my brain wondering just what would happen next. In the end, fed up, I made up some nonsense: *Laguna's widow was a real good kiddo.* I laughed, but then I thought perhaps it was inappropriate. We walked into the Ministry and once inside the old man's stride became lighter, as if he had gathered new strength. He touched one of those employees wearing an elegant tie and said,

"Toranzelli."

"The lawyer Toranzelli isn't with us any longer," the employee said. "Now Rodríguez is working with us."

I was amazed that, despite his elegant tie, he treated the old man with such respect. Then I reproached myself for not having wanted to be related to the old man, and I decided I should treat him with the same amount of consideration.

"Come back on Tuesday," he said.

The old man cupped his hand to his ear to hear better and the employee repeated:

"Tuesday."

Then I thought: *Alright, now I'm leaving. I'll call an ambulance for the old man and be on my way. That's fair*, I told myself. *Yes, that's just what I'll do.*

As soon as I walked out onto the street, leaving the old man sitting on a bench (he seemed entirely ambivalent to whether I stayed or left, anyway), the first thing I saw on the street was an ambulance. *How is that possible? Is that the ambulance I'm looking for?* I asked myself. *Could the man in the tie have called an ambulance without telling me? Could this be another case of someone knowing things that seem otherwise impossible?* What a ridiculous notion. I walked the old man out to the street and we tentatively approached the ambulance. There was a man and a young woman in the front seat. The man was making a joke and she was flirting with him. He was saying:

"We should get some gas."

And then they drove off at full speed. The old man didn't notice a thing and I silently resolved to take him home.

It ended up getting really late on our way back; there were

hardly any buses. I was distracted, standing next to him, looking around, when I vaguely noticed that he held his hand up to his chest. I saw it, but I didn't pay much attention. Like I said, I was somewhat distracted and it didn't seem to mean anything—but then he put his hand to his chest again, which startled me. It's a quirk of mine not to notice when somebody's in pain. I could spend two days with someone whose face is just pure agony and I wouldn't even realize it; but if they told me, I would take charge right away. Honestly, I just need them to spit it out. But my mother always says sharply:

"I shouldn't have to say anything."

I asked him:

"Are you in pain?"

He signaled again to his chest and I noticed that he was having trouble breathing. We got a cab and I took him home. He didn't say anything on the way there, he just gave me the address. When we got out I asked him:

"How do you feel?"

And he made a gesture with his hand, like when you're shooing the chickens away or fending off a busybody; the gesture was rather impatient. I noticed, however, that as he approached the house, and especially when he opened the door—he opened it by himself—he perked up and became more confident, he wasn't as hunched over. I'd already seen this change in behavior at the

Ministry, when he asked for his lawyer. He told me to put the kettle on and I did. I didn't ask what for. I told him:

"I'm going to give you a rubdown."

Strictly speaking, I wasn't convinced about the effectiveness of rubdowns. I'd seen them done when I was a kid, and I remember once being surprised by how the flesh and skin continue to be exactly the same after a rubdown, they don't change color or get stronger. Plus, the adults always said: "You're going to feel much better now." It was the only type of treatment I knew how to do. I removed his black hat, which smelled old, and I started the rubdown. Every once in a while I would ask him:

"Any better?"

And he moved his head a little, by which I imagine he meant yes. Around ten minutes into it he threw up his hands as if to say: *Enough already*! So I stopped and got ready to leave. On my way out, he called to me and uttered the first complete thought I'd heard since we met:

"I don't have any neighbors. I can't call the doctor. Stay."

The truth is, I live alone. I didn't have anybody to call, so, on that front, staying wasn't any sort of imposition. But still, I felt a certain uneasiness and I didn't know why. I kept going to look out the window. I looked at the trees, the sky, and the houses. At some point I turned around and noticed this: he had prepared water for a foot bath and he was putting a lot of mustard in it. I thought, cruelly: *He suffers from a foot condition, just like I thought, and he didn't tell me.* So I asked him:

"Do you have a foot condition?"

"It's my heart."

"Couldn't it be your heart and your feet?"

He didn't answer. He was contemplative, soaking his feet in the water, and less agitated. The sun was rising so I got ready to leave. He grabbed on to the sleeve of my coat and said to me:

"Tuesday."

"What about Tuesday?"

"The Ministry."

And he gave me the smudged piece of paper that said, "Laguna's widow," so I would go back.

"I'm not taking this with me," I said.

I'd never done anything of the sort—going to a place like the Ministry with a tattered old scrap of paper! There was no way I was going back with that piece of paper. I told him to explain the matter to me and I would relay it to the lawyer. He didn't say a word, but he stuck the piece of paper in my pocket. Storming out, I said in a purposefully hostile voice:

"Good night."

He raised his hand to say goodbye as he splashed his feet in the water.

All Tuesday morning I had that disgusting "Laguna's widow" piece of paper with me. I would be walking along, peacefully, and then suddenly remember it: my hand would brush up against it in my pocket and then I'd recoil as quickly as if I had touched a toad. At one point I thought: *I'm going to throw it out, I'm going to rip it into a hundred pieces.* But I knew I couldn't throw it away, it wasn't my piece of paper. And even though I'd said no, I did end up going to the Ministry that afternoon. I sat in the back corner, humiliated, hunched over. And when the employee with the elegant tie walked by I asked him if the lawyer was there. To my surprise, he was, and they called me in shortly. I tried to assume the most impersonal air I could and I reminded myself that I was smart, I had gone to college. But I couldn't help thinking it didn't matter how many degrees I had, with that smudged piece of paper... When I finally took it out of my pocket it was entirely unplanned: I did it without even realizing it, but I blushed when I gave it to him. He looked at it matter-of-factly, handed it back to me, and said:

"This could take a while."

I thanked him—even if it would take a year—because I had secretly been expecting him to say: "Where did you get this ridiculous piece of paper from?" and thought he might give me a funny look. But he didn't say anything else; he kindly bade me farewell and I left quickly because I needed some fresh air.

I sat on a park bench for an hour; I really needed that fresh air. I looked around and everything I saw seemed beautiful to me, but too distant. And I was tempted to lie down on that bench and stay there for a long time without thinking about anything in particular; but I didn't. Now I think maybe I should have. Instead, I said to myself: *I thought everything was going to be more complicated. In fact it was rather simple; so simple that I almost didn't even realize when I took out the piece of paper.* Then I thought: *Now I should go tell the old man*, which put me in a foul mood. Although, it wasn't exactly a foul mood, it was like a vague desire to curse. I started to say "Goddamned—" and then I didn't go on, I waited for someone to come along and tell me who was goddamned. And again I said, "Goddamned—" and then I shut my mouth. I started to look around and I ended up saying: "Goddamned sky." But that seemed wrong, so I chided myself: *It was only a game.* Then I had an idea. I repeated several times: "Goddamned piece of paper," which made me happy, but then I thought: *If I curse the piece of paper, how am I going to do the paperwork? Do I truly want to get the paperwork done?* I didn't want to answer that question and I managed to distract myself by looking around again, but there was nothing interesting to look at, and I started to feel bad. I felt like when you eat breakfast and you know that after breakfast there's nothing else worthwhile, so you have to slow down, eat lots of things and read the newspaper. I couldn't find a way out now, like I do when I eat breakfast, but suddenly I thought mournfully: *I'll buy a cake. I'll buy a cake and we'll eat it together. That's how we'll forget about that disgusting piece of paper.* I said "we'll forget" without realizing that the old man didn't have anything to forget: for him the piece of paper was perfectly in order. When I went to buy the cake I tried to cheer myself up by choosing one with lots of cream and chocolate, and if the old man had some wine (I had a sneaking suspicion he would), then we could eat the cake with some wine. It took me a while to get the paperwork done, and I left the cake in my house for two days before taking it to him. Then one afternoon, opening the cupboard, I found it. (I didn't need to open the cupboard, I knew the cake was there.) I thought: *This cake is going to turn stale*, so I took it over to him. I told him about the paperwork and I unwrapped the cake. The old man was happy, he took out a big knife and cut huge portions. He sliced up half the cake and put the other half in the cupboard. He started wolfing it down. I wasn't at all interested in eating and I couldn't help but think: *Sure, sure, he says he's got a heart condition but just look how he's gobbling up that cake.* This reminded me of something my mother would say when I was a child, which always seemed outrageous to me. When I felt sick and I couldn't deal with something in particular, she would say:

"Sure, you say you're sick, but—"

Then not even the cake was enough, not even a newspaper would have been enough. I had the overriding need to stop watching the old man as he ate his cake. I sat there another five minutes without looking at anything in particular, then I suddenly got up and left. Once on the street, I absentmindedly stuck my hand in my pocket and realized that I had forgotten to give him the piece of paper about Laguna's widow.

By now I was going over every night to give him updates about the paperwork I'd submitted that day to the Ministry. I had to repeat things to him several times because often he didn't understand. When he did understand he would get upset; he wanted everything to go more smoothly, he didn't understand all the inconveniences inherent to paperwork. Every night while I was there he would soak his feet in a bucket with mustard and he had started to address me with the informal "*tu*." That is, he had used "*tu*" a couple times when specifically addressing me, although he never called me by my name. In fact, I don't think he ever asked me my name. One night, when I arrived later than usual, he was waiting for me outside. His light blue eyes followed me closely, which was rare. He was clearly angry; more than angry, he was outraged. He asked me:

"Why are you so late? You're going to give me a heart attack."

I looked at him in dismay and sat down to think. Undoubtedly, I really needed to think and I said to myself: *I can take this in two different ways: either I can assume the possibility of my own guilt if he has a heart attack, which is a big responsibility* (although I didn't feel at all responsible) *or I can take it ironically.* I can say: "Sure, sure, you say you're going to die from a heart attack, but—" *Or I can find some middle ground.* All this I said to myself almost out of breath, and I noticed I had tears in my eyes even though I tried to fight them back. *Some middle ground. I could assume you're just bewildered, that you'll be over it in a couple days. That sure, you might feel some mild heart pain, but it's not an outright attack.* Nevertheless, the mere suggestion of the word "attack" filled me with terror. I didn't say anything. I turned my face away so he wouldn't see me cry and I went to the backyard. I couldn't stay inside any longer.

I didn't leave his house. Stubbornly, I stayed in a corner and said to myself: *I'm going to spy. I'm going to lie in wait.* Who knows what I was going to lie in wait for; but sitting there in the corner, I discovered that the old man was friends with some of the neighbors who were out back, behind the chicken coop, and that's why I hadn't seen them before. He was friends with one of those men who live in a wooden shack. Together they shared the newspaper and when the weather was nice he went to the corner store and they stood in the doorway chatting. I can't remember what I ate that whole time; I only remember what I've mentioned here, and how once when the old man seemed surprised to find me sitting there so still, he said something strange to me, so completely unexpected from him:

"Aren't you going to get a bit of fresh air?"

But I didn't answer him. And I stayed there another three or four days longer without moving. I thought about the neighbors almost the whole time. One afternoon when the old man was soaking his feet in a foot bath and I was sitting silently across from him, I said:

"Alright, I'm leaving."

"Alright," said the old man, "come back soon."

And that's how it went. I go visit him all the time, almost every day. Sometimes I bring him something. The other day I heard him say to the neighbor, the one he chats with at the corner store:

"My son comes to visit me a lot. You should see how smart he is."

My New Love

I'VE got a new love and I've learned lots of things from him. For example, boundaries. So many years of going to the psychoanalyst to hear him tell me over and over again: "But you dive head-first into an empty swimming pool." I was horrified by that image because an empty swimming pool is the saddest thing there is. Or he would say, "Make yourself feel worthwhile, you have such low self-esteem. You're intelligent, you're creative." This gave me a momentary glint of self-worth but then ended up sounding like a consolation prize, like when you introduce a friend to a man or woman who's entirely unsuited for them and then try to fix it by saying, "He's a historian," or "She traveled to Tangiers." And since I think I've found true love, I don't need to be pretty or creative or travel to Tangiers: he loves me for who I am. And he doesn't care if I'm a little old because it's almost like he doesn't even notice that type of thing. To my surprise, he loves me unconditionally. With him, I've learned how to express myself with just a look, which is worth a thousand words. I'm not scared if I see a hint of hatred in his eyes. I know it's not directed at me, like I used to think. Or perhaps, in retrospect, all those years of therapy have actually made a difference. A flash of hatred can come across your eyes all of a sudden, just by remembering things, for private reasons. I know when to approach him, when he won't reject me brutally, and so—and this is something I've always considered to be a test for living with someone, my analyst would be proud of me—we can each be in a different room, lost in our own thoughts, without having to pester one another by asking, "What are you up to?" and losing our patience with each other. With him, an unexpected femininity has arisen in me, because his simplicity—he has regular habits and straightforward desires—has led me to put an end to any rivalry or competition. We share that neutral quality that's formed over time, after a certain age, in which there are no terrible days or dazzling celebrations, because our days have become about eating, sleeping, working, and watching a bit of television.

To tell the truth, he doesn't actually watch television. At night, to separate one day from the next, we rub our foreheads together. The only problems are his diet and one particular bad habit, because otherwise he's quite mild-mannered: he only eats ground beef and he scratches his fleas in front of other people.

Events Organization

I WAS on the steering committee that took care of the artists and scientists invited to San Andrés. It's sponsored by the university, and I gave several years of my life to the committee without asking for a penny. They chose me because I know all about literature and painting, but also because I'm profoundly discreet: I don't discuss subjects I'm not familiar with, but I'm very good at disguising when I'm ignorant about something. It's remarkable how you can string people along with a "sure," "of course," or "could be." But once there was a man who had a face that looked like it was carved in stone who said to me:

"Did you really listen to what I said?"

And I thought, *now he's going to ask me to sum up what he said and I haven't got a clue.* I don't know how I got out of that one, but I did. They also chose me because I'm so tall and I'm good at picking someone out of a crowd: when our unidentified visitors get off the plane or the bus, I have to pick them out. Lately, I'd gotten so good at it that as soon as they stepped out, as soon as I saw a person craning their neck and looking all around, I would say, "That's him." Right after I was appointed, Nicolás di Marco started giving me the cold shoulder, and when he can get away with it he snubs me on the street. He must have figured that he would have been a more qualified guide because he's more knowledgeable than I am in just about every field. But he's also blind as a bat and besides, he's liable to make friends with the visitors. He's even gone so far as to invite them to stay at his house after the event is over, which is unwise: you end up running into our illustrious guest, who's out and about, and then they expect us all to go along with some harebrained scheme. If it's a woman, she wants to go pick flowers in the countryside; or some guy will inevitably want to go to the casino when he would never dream of going to the casino in his hometown, and then you have to explain the rules of roulette to him. I've always been of the mind: show the guest around, then get the guest out of town. Not that I could do entirely without Nicolás di Marco, because he's useful during the debates. After each lecture he asks the best questions—I'll admit that—but he sits in the back with his tormented face, like a poor abandoned gaucho, and he makes me uncomfortable. He never stays to have dinner with the steering committee. True, he's barely scraping by, but he never lets us buy him anything—not even a beer.

I could write a book about all the people who have come to give talks in San Andrés, because each and every one of them is a novel of their own; but there are a few cases I will never forget. One man, who came to talk about new technologies in copper work, stepped off the plane drunk as a skunk. Our airport is tiny; the one and only airplane lands every afternoon, and while you're waiting, the plains reach as far as the eye can see; the littlest detail stands out. When I saw this guy get off the plane and realized he was my guest, I couldn't believe it: he was the last one off and he stumbled out as if each foot had to ask permission from the other just to move. If he hadn't taken the stewardess's arm he would have plunged right off the airstairs. He didn't have a portfolio, which people usually bring along to keep all their lecture papers organized, only an old bag slung across his chest. When he got off I told him:

"If you'd like, you've got time to go to the hotel and rest a little. I mean... To freshen up. There's plenty of time. I'll give you a wake-up call."

He didn't seem to understand anything and I was going to add "to change your clothes," but how was he going to change if he didn't even have a suitcase? If it had been up to me I would have sent him back that very night, because we ended up having to postpone the talk until much later that evening: he didn't wake up. Half the people left and I had to wait it out with the ones who stayed, paying their way at the café on the corner. When he finally did show up—his hair all wet and slicked down and his bag slung across his chest—it didn't turn out so badly, but if it had been up to me it would have been "game over" that very night.

Women are difficult and older women are the worst. Some-times they're deaf, they lose their bag, and the door to the taxi gets stuck; or they want to go see the river at eleven o'clock at night. Once a woman came (she wasn't that old) and said she wanted to see the poor neighborhoods and eat what they ate, because only then can you really understand a city. I showed her a humble neighborhood, but she said surely there must be a more destitute part of town. Reluctantly, I took her to the slums—it's not like I wanted to march around town show-ing off squalor. I'd never gone out to eat around there before. I put on a tough face so that nobody would mess with me. She wanted to eat at a hole in the wall where the "door" was just a bedsheet hung up like a curtain. She saw some fellows eating some sort of stew at the table next to ours. Nobody—not even she—knew what the dish was called, and she said to the owner:

"I'll have the same as the gentlemen over there."

It was a disgusting stew with some bones in it. The place was cramped, the air was thick. I pretended to eat while the two men glanced at us out of the corners of their eyes when no one was looking. She had come to give a talk called "Integration Pro-cesses in Poly-classist Cultures." When we left, we hadn't gone more than three blocks when somebody hurled a rotten tomato at the front windshield of the car. Splat! I was almost glad. I thought, *serves her right*. Now she'll learn not to eat where she shouldn't. But she didn't take the hint, she said:

"When the processes of symbolization haven't been developed, the starkness of the facts becomes as clear as day."

She should zip it, I thought. I'm never taking anybody there, ever again. Because the thing is, I'm not just in charge of picking them up and taking them back: I have to make sure the microphone works, or keep tabs on some group rehearsing for a boisterous *murga* in the room next door at the exact same time as the talk. If there aren't enough people in the audience, I have to rustle up some high school kids (sometimes they don't want to come). Plus, people tend to show up late because they eat first and also because of the weather: the warmer the weather, the later they turn up. And then I'll get a call from the lecturer, from some public telephone, saying they went for a spin to check out the city and they'll be waiting for me at such and such café—not like they've got the slightest notion where they are or what it's called. Sometimes I have to sniff them out on the street like a hunting dog, and to top it off, I have to put on a face like "What a pleasant surprise" when they decide to stop and buy some donuts because they "just feel like eating donuts."

Once we hosted a Mexican professor; we'd decided at the steering committee that we wouldn't just invite people from around the country; every now and then we'd invite someone from abroad. That visit resulted in my first brush with the steering committee. I remember the name of the talk because it was so long: "Different Interpretations of the Cartesian Cogito in the Context of the Process of Globalization." When she got off the airplane—the distance from the plane to the main hall is only fifty feet—I noticed that her slip was hanging out from her skirt, and she had hairy legs. Being a man, I couldn't say anything about it to her, but I told Mimí and Chichi, who were part of the decorations committee. They told me they weren't about to mention it to her because it was so embarrassing. And Nicolás di Marco—that know-it-all—said that in Mexico women don't shave their legs. Bottom line, when she gave the talk, sitting there with her legs uncrossed, her slip hung down even more. Or at least it seemed that way to me.

From then on, I started to think of each guest as a little animal with their own little habits, and it was my job to guess their type: when I saw a woman wearing a floral print dress with red shoes and windblown hair, who wasn't very quick to pick up on things, I would say: "I bet she wants to go to the river." And if I saw a man wearing the right clothes, but who seemed to have put them on haphazardly, the garments somewhat faded and worn, in shades of gray and brown, I would think: *Roulette*. And I was almost always right. But the one who really took me for a ride was a sociologist who came to give a talk about "Tensions

Inherent to the Present Day." He seemed like a great guy: he asked to tour the city, we took a town car and ended up talking about the increase in drug use, the power of the cartels, and how the youth today need to channel their energy into sports. The guy knew a hell of a lot. Now, looking back, he spoke kind of like a politician—like he'd known everything since the day he was born, like someone who never asks any questions or has any doubts about anything. This guy knew all the tricks and he knew them well. When we drove by a little pink house I told him:

"They sell drugs over there. The guy in charge is called El Chino."

He asked me, "Do you think there's anyone there?"

"Probably."

"Hold on, I'll just be a minute."

He got out, rang the buzzer, and out came El Chino. They spoke briefly. When he came back he said:

"I'm just doing some research."

But I don't think he was doing research: he was bullshitting me so he could go back later. It's too bad that Marilú, who lives the next block down, was on vacation. Otherwise, I would have been able to confirm my suspicions. Personally, I'm 98 percent sure it was bullshit. And from then on, I didn't believe a word anyone said to me. I barely listened, and I became much more guarded than I'd been before. I would say, "aha" or "could be" to everything.

But not everyone who came was a disaster. After the sociologist there was one lady who, compared to the local women, the ones we all considered to be ladies—they couldn't hold a candle to her: she was the real deal, from the tip of her head down to her toes. Her hair was shaded a striking ash blonde. She wore barely any makeup, just a hint of light pink, and her dress went with everything. It was a dress that seemed inconsequential at first, but then you realized it was proper, practical, and perfect. And even though the idea was farfetched, everything about that lady was so exquisite and refined, just like her clothes, that I could have fallen in love with her (although she must have been twenty years my senior). She came to speak about "Life as Artwork" and I remember the entire talk, especially a quote from Goethe: "One cannot think properly with a poorly combed head of hair." Her talk had a big impact on everyone. When she said that she only ate macrobiotic products (whole-grain bread, wheat gluten, chicory coffee, and stuff like that), we brought Mónica Gaucheron onto the committee because she was the only one who ate that type of thing back then. And from then on Mónica was in charge of ordering specialty foods for anyone who wanted them. This led to a discussion at the steering committee because they took the opportunity to dismiss Chichi and Mimí, who had been entirely useless of late—not even asking their silly questions during the debates. That lady marked an era: after her visit people ate macrobiotic products for quite some time; then they got tired of it. I started to get tired, too, especially of having to wait for people at the bus station. Those dogs are always there lying on the ground; it looks like they've been there for a hundred years. And if it's hot, the street sweeper makes it even hotter by sweeping with a dirty broom. And I don't know why, but there are flies. When the buses roll in from the countryside, people get off with packages and more packages, as if they were carrying their house on their backs. Truthfully, everything started to rub me the wrong way, but especially the dogs and the packages. The dogs are almost always just lying around, and if they do move it's only out of pure necessity. Who they belong to, nobody knows. And the packages pissed me off because their owners' faces were filled with hope, as if they'd just arrived in a big city, like Buenos Aires or Paris. What do I know. By that point, I was showing up at the last minute. "I'm here, then I'm outta here," I would say. Soon enough, going to the airport started to get old too: the lone airplane in the middle of the prairie, the starkness all around. It's a small airplane, like a toy plane. To think that when I was a kid I wanted to watch that airplane everyday. I started to get tired of going to pick people up and I would call them "freak," as in: "The freak said he was getting in at ten o'clock." I would get up in a rush, arrive at the last minute—or even a little late, worried that they had already left and, sometimes, hoping nobody was there. Then I started calling Nicolás di Marco "freak" too, because even when I didn't know what the talk was about, I knew exactly when he was going to ask a question, even before he opened his mouth. Since I was in charge of organizing the debate, I started cutting him short. I would only let him ask three or four questions, and then: game over. That's when Nicolás di Marco and I had it out. He said, "It's authoritarian to interrupt people during the debate." No wonder he says that, debating is the only thing he knows how to do. Once they even asked him to give a talk and he said no, poor idiot! He thinks the talks are so special. After he lost his chance, he started to ask even longer and more complicated questions. Eventually, I began to distance myself from the steering committee: they kept complaining about me cutting people off during the debate, and whatnot. That squabble helped me to realize that I wanted to leave town; I'd been so indecisive. A while back I had started searching on the computer for some sort of grant that was up my alley. And I found a one-year fellowship in the Netherlands for events organization. I leave tomorrow.

Boy in a Boarding House

ARTURO'S godfather said:

"Send the boy to Buenos Aires? How could you! All that traffic, everything's overpriced, and all those non-believers!"

Arturo's godfather always knew what he was talking about: he'd been to Caracas, he'd experienced the big city. Arturo's father wanted to send the boy to Buenos Aires because he liked the tango, especially one song in particular called "Vida mía." Once a blonde-haired singer came to Portofino and sang "El día que me quieras," "Mi noche triste," and "Vida mía," but it was that last one that was so memorable. Besides, the exchange rate favored going to Buenos Aires, and if everything stayed the same for a year or two, he could meet up with Arturo—who would be a real young man by then—to go see that singer or some other girl just like her.

His godfather continued:

"Pastor sent his son to Rosario. So did my younger sister-in-law's brother. Those kids are really getting a leg up on life. You wanna stand out? That would make three from Portofino in Rosario."

As always, Arturo's godfather was right. He would send the boy to Rosario that same year, and the following week they would go in to Portofino and have two suits made: one navy blue and the other gray, which both go so well with gray socks.

Arturo listened to his destiny from behind the door and what struck him most was the part about the suits. Would he feel comfortable in those suits? Would they be made right? Tailored to fit him? Or would he end up in very long trousers because they hadn't taken his measurements? He was quite short with dark skin. One day he asked Father Esmeralda, who came to collect the tithe:

"Father, how come I'm not getting any taller?"

"Because of the solitary vice," said Father Esmeralda.

Father Esmeralda came every month to collect the tithe: pumpkins, tomatoes, and fruit. Arturo watched from afar how his father arranged everything carefully in the priest's truck. His father—who never got on anyone's case about anything—mistreated the boys who helped him stack the fruit in the truck.

Arturo thought even if he were to give up the solitary vice for a while it might not take effect because the decision had been made in haste....

The Rosario boarding house was far from downtown, two blocks from the bus station. With all that noise at the bus station it was just as wearisome as Buenos Aires. The loudspeaker belted:

"Bus departing for Mendoza," "Bus from Cordoba arriving at platform 102." What if he didn't make it on time? What if Pastor's son, the fellow from Portofino, couldn't find him? There would be no one to ask. No one knew that he was waiting for Pastor's son, from Portofino. Pastor's son found Arturo sitting on his suitcase. He wasn't wearing a suit; he wore blue jeans and a leather jacket. He chided affectionately:

"Arturo! What're you doing there?"

"Nothing. Here I am."

"Yeah, I can see that. But let's go, man," he said and grabbed the suitcase from Arturo's hand.

Pastor's son was tall and dark, but lighter than Arturo. He carried the suitcase carefully, as if there were a treasure inside. Arturo didn't say anything; he was slightly annoyed at having his suitcase taken from him but he wasn't about to bring it up. Pastor's son took one look at Arturo and said:

"There's no vacancy at my boarding house. I'll take you to a nice place."

Fortunately, the din of the terminal began to fade. They entered a neighborhood with one-story houses unlike those in Portofino. Back home, the houses were yellow and azure with blue trim. Here, it seemed like the residents didn't care about what color the houses were—or about anything else for that matter. This notion was reaffirmed when he saw a man watering the patch of land in front of his house: he was tossing big buckets of water on the ground without bothering to look where they landed. And the people who had set their chairs on the sidewalk, they weren't like the people from Portofino either. In Portofino people greeted everyone who walked by, and if a stranger happened to pass they wouldn't look at him so suspiciously, like they did here, without so much as a "good day." Plus, people here didn't sit calmly by the door; they went in and out, and the children wearing skates and riding bicycles on the sidewalk didn't get out of the way or look at anyone.

When they got to the boarding house they were met by a lady in her forties and Pastor's son requested a room for Arturo. Behind the lady there appeared an elderly woman who made gestures and movements with her mouth, as if she wanted to say something. The movements were constant, automatic, as if she were trying to speak very softly without using her voice. Maybe the daughter didn't let her speak. The younger lady looked at them in a not-too-friendly manner and said:

"It's one thousand five hundred pesos a month."

Pastor's son said:

"That's expensive, for one thousand two hundred you can get…"

"Never mind then," said the lady.

The old woman followed the conversation with her eyes, intrigued. Arturo addressed the old woman, without looking at the younger lady:

"I'm Arturo, Ma'am. I'm a good fellow and I have some money. I'll take a room."

The old woman moved her head. Arturo wasn't sure if she was nodding yes or no, so he looked for some positive cue on her face.

"Just a moment," said the daughter and she took the old woman inside to talk alone.

Pastor's son pinched Arturo and said:

"It's expensive. Let me do the talking."

"I'd like to stay here, if they'll have me," said Arturo, and he started to pull out papers: his ID card, transcripts, high school diploma with a photograph of all the students. He also took out a photo of himself with his little sister and their cat. When Pastor's son saw the photo he said:

"Put that away, man!"

But the two women reappeared and Arturo showed them all his paperwork, just like he wanted to. The old woman liked the photo of the kids with the cat and her daughter said to him:

"Come in, Arturo."

Pastor's son was annoyed and told him:

"Do whatever you want."

Arturo grabbed his suitcase. Pastor's son looked at the room and said:

"It's not bad. If you need me, here's my address. What's the number here, Ma'am?"

"The telephone is for incoming calls only. You can't make outgoing calls from here."

"Alright," said Pastor's son. "I'll call you once you've settled in."

Once Arturo was alone he sat on the bed and looked around at everything: the bed, the mattress, and the bedspread were all hard, as if they were meant for business-minded people. He had a little table all for himself! The table had a drawer, and right now he was going to take out his two-volume dictionary. His father had told him:

"You'll find all the words in our language there. When in doubt, turn to the dictionary."

As he was setting the dictionary on his table   he now referred to it as *his* table—there was a knock at the door. The lady said:

"Do you need an iron?"

" … "

"I'll leave it for you."

He accepted it because he didn't want to say no. He didn't know how to iron but he didn't want to say anything; maybe here in Rosario men ironed. He hung his suits and balled up the rest of his clothes using a big towel his father had given him. As he gazed out the window at the vast sidewalk there was another knock at the door. This time it was the old woman. She asked:

"Have you finished ironing?"

Her words seemed to keep time with the movement of her head. He said:

"Yes, thank you."

"Let's see," said the old woman.

He didn't know what to tell her. Finally, quite embarrassed, he said:

"I don't know how to iron, Ma'am." And he showed her the bundle of clothes.

She seized the bundle and the iron in a huff, saying:

"Fancy that! Did you ever! This boy!"

On her way out with the iron and the clothes the daughter stopped her, saying:

"But mother!"

He closed the door, but an argument ensued between the daughter and the old woman. The daughter was saying:

"This is the last time."

What was the last time? The last time he would see his clothes? The last time in the old woman's life that she could iron? Maybe ironing aggravated her illness?

At the boarding house, dinner was served at nine o'clock. It's a good thing that Arturo got his clothes back before the meal. The lady came and said:

"After ten o'clock food will no longer be served."

He didn't understand why she'd told him that. He didn't plan on breaking the rules. At nine o'clock sharp he sat down at the table: the bread was set out, but bread shouldn't be eaten before a meal begins. At ten after nine a very pale girl arrived with her head held high and her nose in the air. She started eating bread straight from the breadbasket. Arturo was hungry, but he didn't follow her lead: perhaps she had some special privilege.

She asked him:

"Where are you from?" She had a funny accent.

"I'm from Portofino. Well, actually, about eighteen miles from Portofino."

"And where's that?"

"It's in Ecuador, in the northern region, but…"

She interrupted him:

"Far from Quito?"

"Indeed! That's a different region."

She seemed to lose interest when she found out he didn't live near Quito. She walked over to a room and called out:

"Mabel!"

Instead of Mabel a skinny, dark-skinned guy appeared from the street wearing a yellow T-shirt with red patterns. The dark-skinned guy asked Arturo, with a hint of arrogance:

"What's your name?"

"Arturo, at your service."

"Service? Forget the service, man! Are you from my homeland? I'm from Maracaibo, which should rightfully be the capital but it's not because the usurpers from Caracas won."

"Why did the usurpers win?" asked the white girl named Ana.

"It's a long story and right now I'm hungry. In Argentina there are no beans, or mayonnaise, or chicken with French fries."

Ana had already heard the Venezuelan from Maracaibo mention this several times: the night before she'd heard him say that in Argentina there were no melons. She grabbed a book and started paging through it. Arturo thought it was rude to read during a meal. Perhaps the landlady would scold her; in fact, he almost wanted her to get in trouble because that girl was so pale, wearing shoes with no heels, she looked just like a North American girl he had once seen when he went to Quito. And like everybody knows, North American girls are from outer space.

When the old woman's daughter started to serve dinner Mabel showed up. She was around thirty or thirty-five years old. Her skin was the same color as the Venezuelan's from Maracaibo, but hers was radiant and her dark eyes were shiny, too. She was wearing a bathrobe; her lips slightly tinged with lipstick and smiling, she said:

"Good evening everyone." She looked at Arturo and said, "Welcome."

"Thank you very much, Ma'am," said Arturo.

Ana and the Venezuelan laughed. Calling Mabel *ma'am*!

"What's so funny, you two?" Mabel asked.

"It's just that Arturo is so polite, that's all," said the old woman's daughter. Upon hearing the word "polite" the old woman perked up, nodding her head:

"Yes, yes! You see? Manners come first. Always, always."

The daughter picked up the soup tureen and walked back to the kitchen with her mother. The Venezuelan from Maracaibo said, specifically addressing Mabel:

"Now, seriously, I've noticed incredibly bad manners here in Rosario. Nobody stops to give you the right of way, they don't walk on a lady's left side…"

Mabel smiled as if she were thinking of something beautiful, something she kept to herself, and said:

"They're just different ways of life…"

Arturo ate his soup and didn't speak up. That lady, who was so pretty, had looked at him and said, "Welcome." They'd all laughed at him, but then the old woman had redeemed him. And maybe someday he would get used to addressing her as "Mabel," that lady who was dressed as if she were ready for bed. Did she wear lipstick to bed?

When it was ten o'clock at night—the time when food is no longer served—the loud bell of an approaching bicycle rang out. Seated on the bicycle was a fellow with a straw hat cocked jauntily to one side. He came right into the kitchen with the bicycle, tasted the soup of the day—straight from the pot—and the landlady's voice resounded with mock alarm:

"Jorge!"

After Jorge arrived on the bicycle the meal became more lively. No, he didn't want any soup. (Arturo noticed that Ana hadn't wanted soup either. How could they turn down a dish that helps a child to grow, and a grown-up to thrive?) Jorge wanted a steak sandwich and then he was leaving because he had a political meeting at the regional convention. He was going to battle it out until they won. Jorge said to the Venezuelan from Maracaibo:

"How you doin', man?"

"Alright."

Jorge was Venezuelan, from Caracas. He made himself a steak sandwich and while he ate, still wearing his hat, he said:

"If we win the primaries we won't stop until the regional election. We're just one vote away and we don't plan on budging an inch."

He yelled to the kitchen:

"Isn't that right, Granny?"

It was obvious that the old woman paid no attention to the primaries or the Student Regional Convention, or how to get more votes, but when Jorge went to the kitchen and took some jam from a nook in the corner where the old woman kept it hidden, she yelled:

"How dare you!"

Jorge grabbed a hunk of bread with jam, got on his bicycle, and went to the primary convention. Mabel looked at herself in a little mirror and said:

"I look so tired and haggard. I'm going to sleep."

Ana went to read on the patio. If Mabel was going to sleep Ana couldn't read in the room, nor would she want to chat. Arturo stayed with the Venezuelan from Maracaibo, who said to him:

"The women here are no good. I don't know what they're like where you're from, but where I'm from they grow their hair down to their waist. White girls have brittle hair. I've seen bald ladies here in Rosario. And when they get old, little blue veins appear in their legs. They're called varicose veins, did you know that? Back in Maracaibo I'd never seen it before. Have you seen them?"

"No," Arturo said.

"Look at that girl," he said, referring to Ana, who was at the far end of the patio. "Look at those white legs, do you see?"

"Yes," said Arturo.

Arturo only saw a girl reading in a corner.

"Well those pretty legs will be filled with varicose veins in ten years. You'll see what I mean."

The Venezuelan from Maracaibo went to the bathroom and on the way back he said to Ana in a gruff voice:

"Always reading, you. You're gonna ruin your eyes."

Ana looked up for a moment and then turned back to her book without saying a word.

"Did you see that?" the Venezuelan asked Arturo.

"Uh-uh," said Arturo.

"I talked to her and she didn't even answer me."

Now Arturo looked at her differently. That girl was somebody you couldn't talk to: if you talked to her she didn't respond.

"My name is Gualberto," said the Venezuelan, "but everyone calls me Freddy. You can call me that, too."

"Alright, Gualberto," said Arturo.

Gualberto looked at him strangely and said:

"Good night."

Why? Why had he looked at Arturo like that? Now Arturo had to go to his room and whereas before he'd been content with his table, a little table all for himself, he now looked at it differently. Maybe because of the climate in Rosario the table would also deteriorate, just like the women, like that Gualberto had said. He seemed like a short-tempered guy. Back in Porto-fino Arturo imagined it was seven o'clock in the morning. His father was loading the truck and saying to him, "C'mon son, come help me out." His little sister didn't want to get up and go to school and his father said, "Go wake her up. Make sure she gets dressed. Set her books out for her, boy." He couldn't sleep. He started to think about Mabel. She smiled at him, exposed one of her breasts from her bathrobe and offered it to him. Then she seemed annoyed, because what right did he have to look at her figure? But it only lasted a moment, then she smiled again. She took out a little mirror and started to look at herself. She left her bare breast exposed as if to suggest that she wasn't the least bit bothered by what he did. He locked the door, succumbed to the solitary vice, and fell asleep immediately.

Jorge, the Venezuelan from Caracas, was talking on the tele-phone in a low, clear, serious tone of voice. He wasn't acting like the same person Arturo had seen on the bicycle with that fancy hat. He made call after call and then suddenly the phone rang. He said to Arturo:

"It's for you, it's Pastorcito. Make it short."

Arturo thought, *what a sharp tongue! And if Honorio Pastor had heard what he'd said? The nerve! Referring to Dr. Pastor's son that way!*

Honorio told him:

"I'm coming by to pick you up in half an hour. I'm going to show you around the city."

Arturo put on his two-piece suit and his gray dress socks. He scrubbed his face, his head was filled with lovely thoughts. Honorio was going to show him around! He had a look at his socks, they were straight. His jacket was brushed. He took a seat on the wicker armchair on the patio and saw Mabel rushing out on her way to work. The old woman was chopping onions and something green for a long time; she hadn't seen him. The house was silent, it didn't seem like a boarding house. The old woman's daughter wasn't around. It was hard to believe the day before that same room had been filled with people and laughter. Honorio showed up wearing a checkered suit with black, purple, and yellow stripes. He looked at his watch and said:

"Let's go, *ándale.*"

Arturo said to the old woman:

"Granny, I'll be back soon. I'm going out with Honorio."

The old woman didn't know whether Arturo was on his way in or out. She looked at him as if trying to remember who he was and said:

"Good morning, boy."

"*Vamos*, let's go, man."

The old woman said something Arturo didn't understand, but he couldn't stop now because Honorio would get upset.

"Should I bring some money?" he asked Honorio.

"No, let's get going."

Arturo recognized the street, but not the way back to the bus station. He would have gone the other way. They took a bus and Honorio told him:

"To go downtown ask for a one-hundred-peso ticket. Take the number 30 that says 'City Center.' Don't get it mixed up with the other 30 that says 'Cemetery.' Don't forget."

What if he couldn't get a good look and he took the 30 that said "Cemetery?" This was a problem he'd have to figure out. He would ask a hundred and one times—the more eyes the better. Plus, both buses started with a "C."

On the bus Honorio showed him the local currency.

"The bright red bill is a one-hundred peso note. This greener one with San Martín printed on it is one thousand."

"Who's San Martín?"

"Look, this guy right here. Remember this face."

When Arturo went back to his room he was going to separate all the brown notes from the ones with San Martín and study them. Honorio said:

"We're getting off here. This is the Grain Exchange. Remember it so you know where to get off."

It was a gray building with a black marble base; a lot of buildings looked the same. They walked down a pedestrian street. Honorio pointed out a dead-end and said:

"There's the restaurant. If you're downtown and you don't want to go back you can eat there for cheap."

"I'll keep that in mind, Honorio. Tell me, is there a lot of mold in Rosario?"

"What kind of mold?"

"The kind that spoils women and things."

"Cut it out, man! Let's go to that café."

At the café there was a waiter who looked like a prince: blond with slightly wavy hair; he was wearing a green jacket with black lapels. Would such a prince come to their table if he were called over? Amazingly, he would. Honorio gestured to him and over he came. Honorio said:

"Two coffees. Do you want anything else?"

"No, Honorio."

"Now, listen up," said Honorio, gesturing vigorously with his arm to get a look at his watch. "I'm going to give you three golden rules to live by. One: Don't go out on the street all the time. When do you go out, be smart and do everything you can to run all your errands in one trip. None of that, 'I've got to find my notes,' or 'I'm just running out to the kiosk,' or 'I forgot a book and I'll be right back.' Procrastination is the thief of time. Two," he said as he stirred his coffee with an odd little spoon—it wasn't like the spoons in Portofino. "Set a schedule, a time for studying. You'll get the best results by working for fifty minutes and then relaxing for ten. Did you know that?"

"No, Honorio."

"Well, now you do. Three: When you have a serious exam, lock yourself in."

"What do you mean, Honorio?"

"Stay inside until you've memorized everything you need to know."

"It must be tough. Is it, Honorio?"

"You bet," said Honorio in the voice of an experienced man. He called to the waiter, who didn't come this time. No, the fact that he'd come earlier had been one in a million. He was serving a nearby table with two blonde women who were pretty and chubby with light streaks in their hair. A boy, probably one of their sons, was running around the table with a toy gun and holster. One of the blondes said to him:

"Cut it out. You're driving me batty!"

The boy walked calmly out to the sidewalk but Arturo was shocked because she had said "batty." A bat is a filthy animal, like a rat, something that festers, it stinks. Maybe that Gualberto or Freddy guy was right; maybe in Rosario there *was* something about mold and sickness. When the princelike waiter miraculously came over to charge them for their coffee, Honorio told Arturo:

"I've got to go. Just walk straight back about five blocks and then one block to the left to catch your bus."

When Arturo went outside he discovered a sea of people, as far as his eyes could see, walking down the street. It was a very wide street and the light was blinding. No sooner had he taken his first steps, he immediately bumped into a woman.

He said to her:

"Excuse me, I didn't mean to."

The woman continued on her way and said nothing; she looked at him as if it were perfectly natural to bump into one another. He took a few more paces and bumped into a tall fat man. Arturo thought, *it must be because I'm so short. I should pick up the pace and pay more attention.* For the time being, he discovered there were three streams of people: one that went toward the boarding house, one going in the other direction, and in the middle a fluctuating, more peculiar mass. He would join the people walking toward the boarding house. But then, across the street he saw a bookshop like he'd never seen in his life: books as far as the eye could see. He decided to cross over and get a better look; slowly, so no one would bump into him. He looked around; there were people everywhere. Just when he was about to cross, a man wearing a blue uniform stepped in front of him and said:

"ID."

"Oh, I don't have it with me, sir. It's at the boarding house. I'm Arturo Zaldúmbide, from Portofino. I'm a studious, obedient young man and—"

"How much money have you got on you?"

"Well, I just realized that I don't have any money with me, sir. Honorio was carrying it."

"You think this is a joke?" he said, somewhat louder. People drew nearer and another blue-uniformed man appeared.

"*Pues*, I came from Ecuador to study, sir. I'm a well mannered boy. The old lady and her daughter at the boarding house can—"

The other uniformed man walked up and said to the first:

"Greenhorn."

"If he's got money hidden on him, I'm booking him," said the first guy and frisked Arturo right there in front of everyone.

Arturo was on the verge of tears. While he was being frisked he started to say:

"I'm a good person, sir. I've never done anything to anyone."

"Shut up," said the man in blue. The other uniformed man said impatiently, in a derogatory tone:

"What did I tell you? He's a greenhorn."

The first uniformed man told him:

"Get outta my sight."

Arturo couldn't move. How could he instantly get out of the man's sight when the man in uniform could see so far in the distance?

"C'mon, move along," he said.

Arturo was paralyzed; a nearby gentleman took him by the arm and led him to the other side of the street. He seemed nice, but where would he take Arturo? He led him far from the police and Arturo said to him, almost in tears:

"I swear I'm a good boy, sir. I didn't do—"

"It's alright," said the man. "Don't worry."

"I ..." said Arturo. "Now I don't know where to take the bus."

And that man—who was a regular Saint Gabriel the Archangel come down from heaven after witnessing such terrible injustice—walked Arturo over to the bus, entrusted him to the driver, and gave him a brown bill for his ticket. As he led Arturo to the bus, Saint Gabriel the Archangel said:

"I don't know who you are and I don't care, but that cop was a real son of a bitch."

Now Arturo was in the kitchen, where the old lady was chopping up green onions. Over the course of that week Jorge, the Venezuelan from Caracas, won the primary conventions; Ana studied the difference between the transcendent self and Kant's transcendental self; the Venezuelan from Maracaibo added seven things to his list of what Argentina was lacking; and Mabel went out wearing a white dress, then a red one, then green, and finally white again. Only Arturo stayed holed up in the boarding house. He went from his room to the white sofa on the patio. He held his head, saying:

"Granny, my head hurts."

"Didn't I tell you? That's from drinking too much beer."

Protesting weakly Arturo said:

"I didn't drink any beer, Granny."

"Beer bloats your stomach and gets to your head," said the old lady.

She chopped energetically and turned around, bobbing her head as she tended to do, and said to him:

"Poison, that's what it is."

She turned back and continued chopping confidently. No one else was home. The cat, free of the residents, studied in the corners. Arturo waited a while to see if his headache would go away, keeping still. Then he said again:

"Granny, my head really hurts."

Mister Ludo

MISTER Ludo turned up in fairly unpopulated places. He had a wife and six children who walked like young camels. The first time the town neighbors got a glimpse of him, he was hammering four stakes into the ground, fastening a canvas on top. They were dumbstruck. One neighbor came up and asked:

"Is this a circus?"

"No," replied Mister Ludo. "It's my house."

The following day they noticed the family didn't prepare any food—they just shared one big *alfajor* cookie cut into pieces by the father and divvied up. Meanwhile, the mother stayed in a corner. They never ventured out on their own, but sometimes one of the children would stick his head out from under the canvas and then quickly draw it back underneath. Nobody asked them anything, although everyone kept an eye on them.

Mister Ludo had a long brown beard and he was bald. Three days after his arrival the neighbors noticed a large animal—it looked like a dog and walked like a duck—but soon enough a hand pulled it back under the canvas. Several days passed and no one saw any movement. Everyone had all but forgotten about them until they came out on the street. They walked in a line with Mister Ludo at the front, wearing sandals. When one of them spoke they didn't stop to listen—they simply repeated the words down the line to the person behind them, from Mister Ludo all the way back to the smallest child. They walked up and down every street in town and then back home. They never bought anything and all the people stared at Mister Ludo's children, who looked like little camels. Then the mother, who was bashful, said to Mister Ludo:

"They're staring at our children."

Mister Ludo told her, "Our children are strong."

And they kept walking, barely uttering a word. Only Mister Ludo spoke, to tell them when to turn or to rest. They rested standing up, and Mister Ludo wiped his brow with a purple handkerchief. Then he said, "Fall back in line."

And they marched until well into the night. Then they walked back to their home.

One day they were walking down the street; Mister Ludo was at the head and the smallest boy was last of all. When they turned the corner, the little boy said:

"I lost a shoe."

The child in front of him repeated this to the next one, and so on and so forth, until the news reached Mister Ludo. Mister Ludo thought for a while, but he didn't say anything. After he'd stopped to think he said:

"We've got to look for that shoe."

So they all turned around and went back to look for the shoe. They searched every street in town but it was nowhere to be found. The littlest boy was limping, he looked like a cripple. So when they walked by a shoe store the mother said humbly:

"We could buy new shoes."

Mister Ludo didn't hear her, and they searched for the shoe until well into the night. By the time they were all tired Mister Ludo said in a serious voice:

"The shoe is gone."

They all repeated this down the line, and then they walked home.

Mister Ludo told this story to his children:

"Children, your father was an Alpine legionnaire. He was on the frontline of the mountain army. Back home, we fought and we won. We hunted wild ducks, but now, here we are. We won't stay here forever—one day we will return to the Alpine mountains.

The mother nodded her head, but the children had never been Alpine legionnaires, so they just peered at their mother curiously. The father continued:

"Back home, no one has to forage food from the ground and

anyone who eats a wild duck with a wounded eye is shot by a firing squad in front of everyone."

The littlest boy said, "What if the wound is just near his eye?"

But Mister Ludo didn't answer him. Instead he said, "Back home, people sing songs and no one rests. Everyone marches along and they relieve themselves without falling out of line."

The children were in awe, imagining so many active people walking. The littlest boy was tired and he wanted to go to sleep. Finally, it was bedtime, but Mister Ludo stayed up to keep the fire going. Once they'd all fallen asleep and no one was looking he took out a book with red letters. He made strange gestures, and when he started to nod off, laying his cheek on the book, he slapped himself to stay awake and kept reading. But no one— not even his wife—ever knew what that book said. No one even knew that he had the book.

Mister Ludo wasn't home during the day and his wife had to go fetch water at the neighbors' house. At first his wife went, but then she started sending the littlest boy, who was happy to fetch the water. One evening Mister Ludo came home early and saw the boy carrying a bucket of water. He said to his wife:

"Whose job is it to fetch the water?"

She lowered her eyes and said, "Mine."

Raising one finger Mister Ludo said, "It's not his job to fetch water. He will be an Alpine legionnaire."

Then the boy, who was waiting with the bucket of water in his hands, asked: "What should I do? Should I toss it on the ground or give it back?"

Mister Ludo looked at the boy. It was nighttime; the neighbors' houses were dark, only a few lights shone in the distance. Raising one finger he said: "Bring the water inside, just this once."

One day the neighbors watched as the family took down the canvas and walked away, carrying their house as if it were a banner in a procession. They all carried a bundle on their back and seemed quite serious. They walked to a new plot of land and set up their house. A ruddy-faced man came along right away and told them to leave. The father solemnly took out a medal with some very old pearls. The ruddy-faced man looked at the pearls and then said:

"I don't care."

So Mister Ludo and his family continued to lug their house around until they found another empty field. When they found one, tired as they were, they quickly set up the house. But once they were inside, with the canvas up, they realized the field was covered in horse manure, so they had to go elsewhere. It was nighttime and they erected the canvas on someone else's land. The following morning, the first neighbor who awoke to find them called everyone else. They spied on the family until the first head peeped out from under the canvas. It was the littlest boy, and he quickly drew his head back underneath. Later his mother sent him to fetch water, but the neighbors refused. That night they had to move again.

Mister Ludo ended up selling his pearl medal for a plot of land, which they had to share with two horses and a rabbit hutch. The littlest boy made a hole in the canvas to spy on the horses and the rabbits, but the hole was almost impossible to notice. They had new boots by then too, and Mister Ludo even bought a perfume spritzer. Every afternoon he spritzed perfume all around the house; sometimes he even spritzed it into the fresh air outside. They all reeked of that perfume, and they were happy—even his wife was happy because she had a new rug and had bought some fish. They ate the fish raw. Mister Ludo broke it into pieces and poured the blood into a little bucket. Afterwards everyone got cleaned up, although in their house they almost always washed up only with water and never with soap.

Once they all went out walking, one behind the other, carrying small bags. The littlest boy had the largest bag—it was because he had grabbed a rabbit from the hutch. He'd looked at the hutch and said to himself:

It's been forever since I got to have a rabbit.

So he nabbed one and stuck it in a bag. As they walked down the street he opened the bag to peek at the rabbit and it escaped. But he couldn't tell Mister Ludo that his rabbit had escaped. So, on his tiptoes, without saying a word, he went off to look for the rabbit. He said to himself:

I won't come back until I've found it.

He searched and searched, but he didn't find it. The other children didn't tell their mother that the littlest boy had left. Instead, as if they'd silently made a pact together, they just turned around and started walking in the opposite direction. When they turned the corner, it dawned on the mother what had happened and she covered her eyes. She started to cry and moan and Mister Ludo, without even turning around, told her:

"You can go too, if you want."

So the mother left, crying and moaning.

Mister Ludo went home. He spritzed everything with perfume and right there, in the middle of the day, started reading the book he saved only for nights. He read for a long time. When night fell, he went out and ended up in the plaza where a man sat reading the newspaper on a bench. Mister Ludo sat down next to him. The man with the newspaper looked up and Mister Ludo said:

"Soon we will go to the mountains and fight against the tribes who wear feathered headdresses. I am an Alpine legionnaire."

"Ah, you're an Alpine legionnaire," said the man with the newspaper, which he continued to read.

"Back home, anyone who kneads their bread without yeast is sent to Siberia," said Mister Ludo proudly.

And the man with the newspaper said, "To Siberia, eh," and he kept reading.

"People on their deathbed are all taken to one place, to find solace in the other dying souls," he said, looking off into the distance.

"Of course," said the man with the newspaper, and he left.

Mister Ludo stayed on the park bench in the plaza for a long time, then he slowly walked home. He didn't tell anyone to follow him, or to turn at the corners.

When he got home he heard a noise inside and thought perhaps it was thieves.

He stood there for a while contemplating whether to go in or not, but finally he did. There he found his smallest child, sleeping next to the rabbit. He wanted to gently remove the rabbit, which was also asleep. When he tried to move the rabbit, the boy woke up and pressed the rabbit against his body. Then he fell back asleep.

That night Mister Ludo took out his book with the red letters again, the one from that afternoon. Then he stoked the fire.

The Light of a New Day

for my mother

IT still didn't make sense how she'd fallen down. She'd gone out on the terrace to hang a bedspread to dry and on her way back down the stairs she'd missed the last step. It was dark and although she'd had the feeling that she was stepping into thin air, it was as if something, the spirit of that darkness, had forced her to do it. Then she fell and couldn't get up. For some years now there had been something about the last step of that staircase—especially when the hallway was dark. When she placed her foot on the second to last step some sort of vertigo led her to miss the last one. Who was going to help her up? Doña Herminia was just as old she was. Genoveva called out for help and some young folks—thank the Lord, a young couple, may they have ten children and live a thousand years—came to her assistance and took her to bed, where Doña Herminia was waiting. Young folks are good; middle-aged folks are not. Young folks like that couple are good, like her granddaughter. But her granddaughter was always studying all that stuff people study nowadays, and personally, she never much liked studying. Doña Herminia had taken her in and always explained everything to her patiently, because she had studied.

Doña Herminia took in everyone who needed help. Ever since Genoveva's children had been young, they'd always had a parallel family at Doña Herminia's. When her children were young, before the others ate they would have a bowl of soup in the kitchen. Four silent children who spoke only when they were asked a question, and even then in faltering voices, muffled tones, as if speaking directly into someone's ear.

One of them, with a cloudy eye, had been given the affectionate nickname "Rosita" by Doña Herminia—she never used a diminutive for her own children. Later on, Walter Lioy Lupis became her godson, known as "Badass" to his classmates. Badass cut the rope of the school flag, kicked over the classroom chalkboard, and turned up one day in the Palermo Woods, even though he lived a long way away.

The four children also had to practice reading, which they did in those barely audible voices, the cleaning lady in a fit of rage because she wanted to finish washing the dishes already. Now, since it was impossible to get Walter Lioy Lupis to practice reading, because it wasn't in his plans, and since that boy infuriated the cleaning lady, he got an apple, a chunk of bread, and some useful advice on life. Doña Herminia's motto was "Good folks can take care of themselves," applicable to children and stepchildren. But don't go thinking that made her some sort of Saint Francis of Assisi—she had her Saint Francis of Assisi side, but she had some Borgia in her, too. Because if a canary sang early in the morning she'd say, "I could just wring that canary's neck."

If she heard that someone had been scammed she'd say, "You've got to be a dimwit to let yourself get taken for a ride."

And if she heard that a woman happened to be in love with a man who was a bit of a slob she'd say, "I'd rather clean up after a pen of piglets than give that bum the time of day. Women these days haven't got a shred of dignity; it's no surprise they let themselves get walked all over."

Doña Herminia prayed for two hours a day and went to mass every day, too. She prayed for travelers, for seafarers, for those who lose their way—but above all she prayed for the dead, and among the living she preferred those with a heavy burden in their family, for example an old blind mother with a retarded son.

She lent money to Doña Josefa, who took a taxi to the clairvoyant's house so he could tell her fortune. She also lent money to Doña Josefa for custom-made orthopedic shoes, which instead of correcting her bunions made them bigger. Josefa complained about her bunions and about how she had been scammed, but since she rambled on about her miseries it was hard to tell when she was complaining about the bunions and when she was complaining about the scam. Personally, Genoveva didn't much like Josefa and when she saw her on the street she would stop to look at some shop window, but Doña Herminia would walk side by side with Josefa and every so often say to her, "Of course."

Another person who came to Doña Herminia's was that fat girl Silvia, the paralytic in a wheelchair. She got everyone to help her cross the street, mainly she would ask men to help her cross. Once there was a man who wanted to charge her for crossing.

Silvia talked. She talked with Doña Herminia because she had studied, and at night she never left. When Genoveva got bored and tired she would say, "Well, Genoveva's off to bed."

And she'd leave them to it. Old folks and young folks are good. Middle-aged folks are not. Now her daughter-in-law was going to ask her why she'd fallen and just the thought of it made her feel to blame. Lying down on her bed, Genoveva thought about what she would say to her daughter-in-law, because she was going to ask. It was because the staircase had been waxed and the wood was so slippery, that's why. She'd been paying attention and was sure she had placed her foot on the last step. She hadn't been distracted—if only it were so simple. It's as if her leg hadn't reacted. Shame on that leg!

As for Doña Herminia's daughter, it's not that she was all bad, but if she came over for a meal she would read the newspaper at the table, and once she watched boxing on television— boxing was something Genoveva did not tolerate or understand. Furthermore, middle-aged folks clear the table as soon as they've finished eating, they speak in loud voices, and they ride roughshod over everyone. Had she known, she'd have let the bedspread stay dirty forever. Damn the moment it occurred to her to hang it out to dry. Deep down she had never liked it anyway, and it brought her bad luck. That's what she was going to tell her daughter-in-law: that the bedspread brought her bad luck.

"Doña Herminia," she said.

"What is it Genoveva?"

"I can't move. Where are they going to take me?"

"You'll have to be admitted, Genoveva. It might be a fracture."

"Oh my, heaven forbid! I have to go to the hospital—pardon my language. When I get back I'd like to come here. Oh! I can't move!"

"Calm down, calm down. My daughter's on her way."

It wasn't her daughter. It was a doctor who sprouted up from Lord knows where. He came in and scanned everything quickly while Genoveva said to him, "I went to hang out the bedspread and just as I reached the foot of the stairs…"

He said to her, "Pull back the covers."

He looked and said, "It's a hip fracture. You'll have to be admitted. That'll be twenty million pesos."

Genoveva, who had not understood properly, said to Doña Herminia, "What luck that he left so quickly! Surely it's nothing because if it were serious he would have stayed longer."

"No, Genoveva, it's…it's…"

"What is it Doña Herminia?"

"It's a fractured hip."

"Oh!" Genoveva said, disappointed.

And she started to feel tired, sluggish, uninterested. Then her daughter-in-law came in and asked, "Why did you fall?"

But Genoveva had succumbed to some sort of fever and she was talking about meatballs. Suddenly, there was a slight improvement and she reconnected, she asked for water. The daughter-in-law asked her again, "Can you tell me why you fell?"

"Oh, I don't remember," Genoveva said.

Then Doña Herminia's daughter came in and asked in an alarmed, somewhat dramatic voice:

"However did you fall?"

And then she turned to Doña Herminia and said, "She fell again?"

"Anyone can fall," said Doña Herminia.

While Doña Herminia stayed with Genoveva, the daughter and daughter-in-law—both middle-aged—discussed who would take care of what.

The daughter-in-law said, "I can take her to the hospital tomorrow—not today, because today I have ikebana flower arranging and my physical theater class."

Doña Herminia's daughter didn't have any classes, but she didn't want to be outdone so she said she had her Precambrian Welsh class that evening. Finally, they both took out their calendars and compared schedules. Doña Herminia spied on them to see what they were plotting. She was of the opinion that middle-aged folks only think about money, and that any middle-aged folks who *don't* think about money are fools. *But,* she thought to herself, *they are useful for requesting things from the authorities, for all those tedious little procedures involving ID cards and such.* They always devise a way to get things done so quickly.

The daughter-in-law couldn't miss her physical theater class because that day she was going to learn a certain movement that was the culmination—the compendium—of everything they had learned throughout the entire year. Which is to say, missing that specific class was equivalent to missing more than one class; but it would take much too long to explain all this and only a person who had actually done physical theater would understand it. She looked at the clock and said: "For goodness' sake! Just look at the time!"

And she offered to help the following day.

Of course, thought Doña Herminia's daughter. It would be up her to admit Genoveva to the hospital. She looked for all the right documents and ID cards. Doña Genoveva had a stylish wallet with four pockets to store ID cards, but unfortunately it didn't have any of them inside. The first had a beautifully colored landscape; the second, a photograph of a shaggy white dog in the doorframe of a house; the third, some children on a beach; and the fourth—neatly folded so that it fit perfectly into the flap— contained a cooking recipe. Genoveva's documents were spread out in random old handbags, which were all in good shape but it was obvious she didn't use them much. They were successive handbags, all similar and interchangeable, filled with ID cards, dried olive sprigs, and little lost mirrors.

Rummaging around in Genoveva's handbags and clothes gave Doña Herminia's daughter a sense of ambivalence. On the one hand, she felt some affection and protection for such a defense-less woman; but she was also annoyed for the same reason. Genoveva lay meekly in bed while others took care of her in the other room.

Some days later, Doña Herminia's daughter went to the hospital to visit Doña Genoveva. "Please," said Genoveva, "could you remove that sweater wedged between my legs?"

Doña Herminia's daughter looked but there wasn't any sweater. There were some wounds that looked like they came from stitches.

"It's not a sweater," she told her. "They're wounds. Did they operate on you?"

"Not that I'm aware of. Heavens above!"

"Yes, Granny had an operation," said a seemingly healthy young woman who was wearing a nightdress in bed.

"An operation?" said Genoveva, astonished. "But how come I didn't notice?"

"Because they gave you anesthesia, Granny," said the lady, who was very understanding.

"Oh," said Genoveva, but as if there was something else, something more perplexing than the operation. She seemed to be in a state of constant shock.

"How's your mother?" she asked then.

"She's good."

"Take care of her and don't let her break a leg, for goodness sake."

"She's going to come visit you."

"She shouldn't come. Lord have mercy, what if she falls! No, it's unsafe... There are dangers: the street is slippery, the spiral staircase..."

Doña Herminia's daughter had the tendency to ask metaphysical questions at inopportune moments. And so she said, "What's so dangerous?"

"Exactly, dangerous," said Genoveva, as if she were thinking about something else through her smile.

When the seemingly healthy young woman saw Genoveva smile she said to Doña Herminia's daughter, almost as a reprimand, "Put the bedpan in place. It's been a while since she's done her business."

Once she'd relieved herself, her head worked better. Besides, there was no doubt that Genoveva was a sensible person. She rightly complained that the nurses didn't come when she called them, and even though she sometimes talked nonsense, she had the tact not to criticize out loud if there was a nurse nearby, and when they cleaned her up she said, "Thank you, thank you," and smiled like a little bird.

One day she received a visit that made her feel better. A sweet young doctor sat on her bed and said to her, "How are you, Granny?"

"Very well, thank you. When am I going to walk, doctor?"

He said to her, laughing, "Are you ready now? Shall we get up and walk?"

"Bless my soul! May the Lord hear you and grant you another hundred years of life!"

Then Genoveva tried to get up and he said to her, half chuckling to himself, "No, dear. You'll have to wait another two weeks or so."

"Two weeks?" Genoveva said, surprised. "That seems like a long time if you ask me."

She was working on a difficult calculation. She couldn't remember which month or day it was; she didn't want to ask. But the doctor realized and told her, "Today is September 20th."

"Come again?"

"Today is September 20th."

"Oh, thank you, thank you," she said, as if September 20th were something valuable in of itself, some sort of gift.

It was around six o'clock in the morning and it was getting light out. Genoveva stood up trying not to make any noise, and she got as far as the nearest chair. The chair would help her walk.

It took all her concentration, determination, and strength to get to that chair; she thought of nothing else. No sooner had she moved it, the chair made a noise and the seemingly healthy young woman in bed next to her said, "What are you doing, Granny?"

"Good heavens! You startled me!" said Genoveva.

The bed-ridden young woman meditated on whether to call the nurse or not. Making an uproar in the hospital was a crime of its own, and she was trying to decide whether she could fix it, or whether calling the nurse would make the commotion even worse. She decided it would be out of line to call the nurse and continued watching Genoveva, trying to figure out her intentions. Genoveva took a few steps using the chair for support, her legs were stiff. Finally she reached the door. In her effort to move silently, she managed a few steps in silence until suddenly, when she most wanted to avoid it, the chair made an awful screeching sound. When she got to the doorway, which led to the corridor, she saw a bulky shape: it was the head nurse, the fat nurse. Seen from afar in that early morning light that makes everything hazy, the nurse was so round and so thick that after peering down the hall—and without even knowing it was the head nurse—Genoveva went back to bed. But she was content because she'd walked and, furthermore, that big woman wearing white hadn't seen her. Still, her legs were stiff. She would have to whip them into shape. At night, once everyone had eaten their dinner and gone to bed, she decided to go out again, but this time she propelled her legs energetically. She insulted them—one in particular, she told it, "C'mon! Walk, stupid. Don't you gimme that dumb act. Who do you think you are, huh?" And it seemed like her legs understood, because they took her a little further. "Well, fancy that! You don't want to walk," she scolded, "Keep moving, keep moving now."

When she got a bit further—always with the help of the chair—she started to think, *Yes, she would be able to walk and go back to Doña Herminia's house, where only the choicest cuts of meat were bought; and where the mattress had to be turned over because Doña Herminia couldn't do it alone; and what about the mashed potatoes?* Doña Herminia liked Genoveva's mashed potatoes. Since Doña Herminia had studied, her mashed potatoes came out lumpy, while Genoveva's were fluffy; she always let Genoveva make them. Who was going to make Doña Herminia the mashed potatoes now that Genoveva wasn't around? And in the afternoon Genoveva would read her lectionary by the window, near the banana tree. The banana tree didn't bear any fruit, but it had wide green leaves that looked edible. She was going to go sit by the banana tree, God willing, if that fat nurse—God forbid—didn't stop her from walking with the help of the chair. That fat nurse mustn't see her. If she saw Genoveva she'd give her an earful, and then her legs would give out from fear.

One day she got up to walk down the corridor, like the previous days, but the main hall was livelier than usual and she wanted to get closer to have a better look. All that hoopla made her dizzy. There were people walking by with bottles of yellow liquid; others pushed wheelchairs. There was a man wearing pajamas and a nurse with a cake.

Terrified of falling down, because she had gone so far, Genoveva kept walking and insulting her leg so it would move. She said, "Move it leg, or I'll teach you a lesson," and all the while she thought about the mashed potatoes she was going to make when she went back to Doña Herminia's house. At the same time she felt dizzy and scared, as if everything around her were a blur. But when she got to the middle of the hallway she heard a voice saying, "Good job, Granny. Good job!"

And another voice added, "Would you look at that! Granny's out for a walk!"

She smiled her humble smile and said, "Thank you, thank you."

And the fat nurse had to watch it all with her arms folded, that infraction of hospital law, because everyone was gathering around her and celebrating.

Doña Herminia wanted Genoveva to live and she wanted her to come back, but she knew she would have to accept God's will. And since perhaps God's will was for Genoveva to die, Doña Herminia was going to pray to Saint Anthony of the Miraculous Medal to intercede on her behalf.

Saint Anthony of the Miraculous Medal was not the type of saint you could bother on a daily basis; he had to be reserved for special circumstances. He was only to be summoned when one felt like the other saints were playing dumb. Now, how was it possible that someone like Doña Herminia—who had studied, who could, in a pinch, correctly explain Boyle's experimental gas law, or place, according to the logic of events, the date of the Battle of Maipú—how was it possible that she could believe in Saint Anthony of the Miraculous Medal? It had to do with where one lived and jurisdictions. San Martín had lived in the Andes, that was his jurisdiction. The jurisdiction of Boyle's law included liquids; and Saint Anthony of the Miraculous Medal worked, from his spiritual realm, in difficult cases, as long as you didn't bother him too often. Besides, everyone does as they please in their own home, and takes on whatever they can. Saint Anthony of the Miraculous Medal wasn't like Saint Anthony the patron saint of lost things, who you invoked, for example, when searching the entire house for the feather duster. That was a cheerful, carefree search. You would check all the nooks and crannies, come across some dust and be reminded how the place needed a good sweeping. No, Saint Anthony of the Miraculous Medal required all your strength, you had to concentrate all your thoughts into the request. Once Doña Herminia had finished praying and put in her request, she felt her body slacken with fatigue and she waited patiently for the saint to do his part.

She was about to make breakfast: the comfort of a glass of milk and crackers that give strength to weak legs, when the doorbell rang. The doorbell rang and she heard from outside the drumming of fingertips on the windowpane. She could see the blurry outline of a face, a little hand waving goodbye and a car driving away. Who was it? She didn't know. Then the doorbell, insistent. She opened the door and it was none other than Genoveva.

When Genoveva saw Doña Herminia she said, "You're a sight for sore eyes!"

Doña Herminia couldn't say the same. Her own eyes had been entirely domesticated for quite some time: nothing surprised her anymore. Doña Herminia thought, *What luck, the coast is clear.* The daughter-in-law had already left and fortunately her own daughter hadn't stopped by that morning. Her daughter had already told her, in a somewhat ominous and threatening tone, that in order for Genoveva to be able to come back to the house she would need to bring a document verifying her physical health, another stating her homeostatic balance, an electroencephalogram, and a short- and mid-term prognosis of her disease.

Doña Herminia noticed that it was hard for Genoveva to walk. She looked like she was in pain, and the pain from walking was making her turn pale. *So what?* she thought. *She's not going to run a marathon. If she can walk from her room to the bathroom, that's enough.* Then they greeted one another and she took Genoveva's purse and asked her solicitously, "Have you eaten breakfast yet?"

"I think so," said Genoveva.

"What do you mean you *think* so? Really Genoveva, did you have breakfast or not?"

"I guess."

"And what did you have for breakfast?"

Genoveva thought and thought and then she said, somewhat alarmed, "Would you believe that I don't remember?"

"Well, come now, it doesn't matter. Would you like to have breakfast again? Or, I mean, have some breakfast?"

"If it's not too much trouble," said Genoveva with a pleasant smile, like someone who's done something slightly mischievous and good.

And so what? thought Doña Herminia. *She can't remember. What did she need all that memory for anyway? It's not like she was going to become a historian. Bah! And sometimes, when a person has suffered a lot in life, it can be a gift to lose your memory. Our Lord works in mysterious ways...*

Genoveva washed her combs, took a nap, and later, in the afternoon, they made a fruitcake together with lots of candied fruit, walnuts, and raisins. At night, before they went to sleep, each in her own room, Doña Herminia bid Genoveva goodnight, standing in the door frame, saying, "Let the Lord grant us the light of a new day."

But before they went to bed, they joined the palms of their hands and smiled at one another, looking into each other's eyes lovingly, without even a hint of resentment.

Homeowners Association Meeting

THE Homeowners Association Meeting of Calle Encarnación no. 375 is always held in the foyer of the ground floor; almost everyone present has to stand. Only the building superintendent sits at a little table (normally kept in the basement), and the President of the Homeowners Association sits at the other end (jotting down the minutes). Two elderly ladies, Azucena and Francisca, bring down little stools from their apartments. The super isn't an ugly woman, but she is a bit hunchbacked and short-sighted from all the paperwork she has to read and sign. And her face is somewhat misshapen from listening to so many complaints from every tenant in every apartment, and from all her dreams about them at night. The President of the Homeowners Association has a tan no matter what time of year it is. He's wearing a tracksuit and tennis shoes. He's the only one who's on a first-name basis with Mary, the super. She calls him Carlos. Azucena and Francisca are always the first to arrive at the meeting, but for different reasons. Azucena—always with a smile on her full-moon face—wants to be informed, in the know. Francisca has a long list of topics to raise and she's prepared to give everyone a piece of her mind. Azucena admires and looks up to Francisca because Francisca knows everything: she knows which days the garbage man comes; how to procure calcium by chopping up eggshells (they're good for the bones); and where to buy the most comfortable shoes.

The super glances at her watch and says in a condescending tone of voice:

"Unfortunately, people in this country are not very timely. Carlos, please buzz the man from 4-C. He said he was coming."

The man from 4-C, a newlywed with large bashful eyes, leans up against the corner of the wall. The super asks him:

"Did you bring the authorization, Mister…"

"Martínez."

The super checks his name against her list and says:

"Indeed, here it is."

The man approaches the table with the authorization as if he were standing trial in front of the court. The super says, didactically:

"Very good, Mr. Martínez. Let me remind you that our tenants must always bring the authorization. And, furthermore, I'd like to insist that everyone be punctual. That way we can settle matters in a timely manner."

Mr. Martínez thinks perhaps this lecture was meant for him and he doesn't move, he's all eyes.

Just then Roque walks through, in a hurry, as if he were preparing for a long trip. He's muttering and carrying something in his hands, as always, and the super asks him:

"Are you staying, Roque?"

It sounds vaguely like he mentions the word "shopping." They assume he'll be back, but it's not clear—when it comes to Roque it's hard to know whether he's coming or going. And he often starts in one direction only to turn back around. Francisca says to the super:

"Ma'am, I think you should know, that gentleman has several cats in his apartment. He's never admitted just how many, but I feel his apartment should be inspected. If you don't take the appropriate measures I won't hesitate to bring in an inspector myself."

The super says:

"That's exactly the first topic on the agenda: 'Pets.'"

Francisca says:

"But it's not just cats. Some people take their dogs up on the terrace. They soil everything—not to mention the racket..."

The super says:

"That falls under 'Noise Problems.' We'll discuss that later."

Francisca:

"It's as if nobody sees anything around here—nobody hears anything, nobody smells anything. But the elevator reeks of dog, and it's all scratched up. Who scratched it? I bet it was those kids who sit out on the sidewalk, which actually belongs to everyone. Just who do they think they are? The guardians of the doorstep?"

The super says, in a weary voice:

"Remember, one person's freedom ends where another's begins."

Francisca:

"What freedom? With all the hubbub in this building! There's so much noise and confusion that a thief scaled his way up to the third floor, like a regular Spiderman. Nobody saw him! Nobody heard him!"

Carlos says:

"What should I write down, Mary? Noise or pets?"

The super:

"What a mess! Spiderman? We'll get things in order, Carlos."

Azucena says, smiling:

"There's something wrong with my left ear. I can't hear much, but I can see alright. I mean, I'm sorry, I don't know if it's the right moment but… It's just that little rug in the foyer was new, and now it's all trampled and…"

The super replies, also smiling, "Azucena, there are other priorities. We'll get there, we'll get around to your complaint."

Francisca:

"Priorities—that word is always getting thrown around, but

it's never my turn. And I pay my dues religiously on the second of every month—not like some people who have a six-month debt! I hear everything, and I can tell you where the noise is coming from. It's those kids in 5-C who play their music at full blast. Bah, if you can even call that music. Then there's the lady who lives above me, who slams the elevator door at three o'clock in the morning. Is it my fault her life's a wreck? And to top it off, now there's shoes that make noise. They invent such junk these days. The girl from 1-B has shoes that play music. I know she doesn't go upstairs that often, but still…Freedom? What freedom!"

Carlos (boasting): "Personally, I don't have to worry about that, Mrs. Mastropiero. I soundproofed my walls with paneling."

Super (in a sad voice): "What a good idea, Carlos."

Just then Roque comes back from the street carrying a bag filled to the brim, hugging it to his chest as if it were a baby and muttering to no one in particular about how he's just going upstairs to drop off the package. At the same time, Florentina comes down wearing an alluring velvet skirt and a dazzling blouse with sparkles. The super says to her:

"We've been waiting for you, Flor."

A hush descends with Flor's entrance. Politely, Carlos asks her:

"Would you like a chair?"

Flor declines the offer and stands next to the young newly-wed who's becoming increasingly tense. She says:

"May I propose something very specific?"

The super nods.

Flor:

"I've been concerned about the doormen for some time. They both sit on chairs on the sidewalk—I know it's more during summertime and that's a long way off—but we must anticipate these things. They greet everyone under the sun and give the impression of a commonplace building. Once we've lost our standards everything else is out the window, too. I think they should be made to stand and wear a uniform, that's the way it's done. I've seen some very discreet uniforms—nothing too silly—on Calle Tacuarí. I've already picked out the color.

"Now, the entrance hall isn't up to par either, with that relief or whatever it is with the pregnant lady on the wall. That's right, you're all looking at it. Just what is a pregnant lady doing on the wall of an apartment building? It really upsets me on my way in and out; it's disturbing. Our building should be a peaceful refuge. Now, there are some marble wall coverings, they're sold right down at Quadri. I've already picked out the color. I've got a real eye for these things and—"

Super:

"But Flor…"

Flor:

"Let me finish. The doorman's manners contradict his job as a caretaker. He told my mother—none other than my own mother—that he knows which people live in each apartment based on the trash they throw away. What is this, espionage? If you ask me, I don't want a spy in my own building. My mother's blood pressure spiked because of him, because it's like living with a spy. And if he continues down that road I'm going to take him to court for damages. People's health cannot be taken lightly and—"

Francisca:

"She's right, she's right. The doorman flings my letters under the door as if they were paper airplanes. Once one of them slid all the way out to the balcony! I'm going to send a registered letter and if that doesn't make a difference, I'll take it all the way to the ombudsman."

Azucena (as if this were pleasant news):

"Ah, is there an ombudsman?"

Roque comes down with an X-ray and walks toward the front door.

Super:

"Roque, aren't you staying?"

Roque (muttering as he holds up the X-ray):

"I'm going to the doctor down the street. Maybe he'll see me... Maybe he won't."

Francisca:

"Stop right there! Just how many cats do you have?"

Roque, at the front door:

"Cats are very clean animals. I hope the dog owners don't take that the wrong way. Dogs have some charm, no doubt about that. Oh, I just remembered something. See that latch on the door outside? The guy from 8-H comes along and forces it, then the guy from 1-D, and so on and so forth, and so on and so forth... The latch is all worn out and—"

Francisca:

"He's got a point, but—"

Flor:

"He may be right but he spends his time spying on the lives of others. My philosophy is: Live and let live."

Carlos:

"Mary, what should I write down?"

Super:

"We'll smooth out those details at the end. Listen up: we're all on the same ship and we have to hold course together if we want to make fast. We all want to be number one, don't we? We simply cannot lose sight of our objective, because we are forgetting the core issue: Safety."

Flor:

"Considering the state of this country—I'm no stranger to the state of affairs—our building should have a night watchman all night long. I always, *always*, keep a stun gun in my purse so I'm not caught off guard. It works for sexual assault too. I've kept it on my person ever since I had an experience that I would sincerely never wish on anyone. I propose that the board gives each proprietor a stun gun for self defense. I don't know if that's an option, but life is first and foremost. Even if they just break in and no one gets killed. Robbery is one type of violation, let's not deny it…(Not to mention other equally terrible things)."

Azucena:

"And that…gun…How does it work?"

Super:

"One minute, Flor."

Francisca:

"Also, I had my newspaper stolen."

Azucena (contemplative):

"I heard a shirt was stolen from the clothesline on the terrace."

Francisca:

"It was a sheet. But what's this? First, it's badmouthing, and before you know it, thieves right here among us? I never!"

Flor:

"I've already raised my concern. I'm going to bed, I've got a hard day ahead of me tomorrow."

Super:

"Sign here, Flor. Go on, get some rest."

Flor signs and goes quickly upstairs. Roque comes back with the X-ray under his arm.

Roque:

"He wouldn't see me."

Francisca:

"Come over here. Just how many cats do you have anyway?"

Roque:

"I'll be right there. I'll be right with you. I just have to go up because the X-ray belongs to my wife, poor thing. What can she do?"

The newlywed starts biting his nails.

Francisca:

"The lady in 3-G opens the door for anybody, day or night. And besides, her awning is not the approved color. We should send her a registered letter."

Super:

"But, Mrs. Mastropiero…"

Francisca:

"And then there's the fumigator. I'm not letting him in. Does he have some sort of license, or anything at all to prove he is who he says he is? For all we know he could be some sort of charlatan, because he just sprays Lord knows what in the gratings and meanwhile he traipses dirt all over with those galoshes of his…"

Carlos:

"Mary, shall I write down 'safety'?"

Super:

"Yes, Carlos, record that tidbit."

Somebody knocks on the glass door and Francisca opens it. It's the taxi drivers from the adjoining premises. They're led by a fat little man who looks like a tapir. He addresses the superintendent without saying hello to anyone:

"I had to come over here myself because when I go to the office you don't give me the time of day. I call and I call and I just get that little music, and I don't want to go over there again because that guy who works for you is a fucking snob. What's the deal? What, you're better than us because we're cab drivers?"

Carlos (in a neutral tone):

"Lower your voice, please."

Cab driver:

"I'm not gonna lower my voice, it's raining in there, brother! There's water pouring down from the ceiling. I've got the whole place filled with buckets, and if it's not fixed this week I'm sending a registered letter. To hell with that fucking music, to hell with that good-for-nothing moron you've got working there."

Super (in a weary voice):

"Please understand that the terrace will only be fixed once the rainy season is over—"

Azucena:

"That's for sure, it's been so rainy. I've never seen anything like it!"

Super:

"Isn't it something, Azucena? Can you believe all this rain we're having? Well, as we all know the climate is changing, the planet is changing—"

Cab driver:

"Which fucking terrace are you talking about? We're on the ground floor! And something else: it's a good thing that guy isn't here, the one who calls for a cab at night and then doesn't show up. Lucky for him he's not here. Well, now you know." (They leave.)

Super:

"What manners! How rude! Look how late it is!" (To Carlos:)

"Did everyone sign? Alright, you can all go. We'll stay here to write up the minutes."

The newlywed:

"Um…I, I've got…uh…There's mold growing on my ceilings and—"

Carlos:

"Never buy the top-floor apartment. We'll deal with that when the rainy season's over."

Azucena and Francisca, each carrying their stool, go upstairs with the newlywed.

Super:

"Good night everyone. Get some rest."

She and Carlos stay in the foyer to write up the minutes.

The Uncle and the Niece

I HAD an aunt and uncle who lived pretty far away, in Casilda. They were always the subject of conversation at my house, and I was going to visit them soon. Everyone said that my aunt had suffered a lot with her first husband and now she was married to my uncle, who was her second husband—but you weren't supposed to mention that in front of them. They said that my uncle had aged a lot lately, that he was practically a shadow of himself, and that my aunt, despite all the pain and suffering, was twice as fat. She was a self-sacrificing person because she gave my uncle massages with all sorts of ointments and stayed up with him until late at night because he had a lung problem. I had also overheard someone saying, one summer afternoon during siesta time, "Before, at that house? You would walk into a room and the hats on the coat rack, a napkin on every lap, and not a fly to be seen. But *now* ..."

It took me a while to figure out what it would look like: a hat on every lap...no, I knew perfectly well. The hats on the coat rack and not a fly to be seen. I was just avoiding the idea of what it looked like "now" because it tortured me. What was it like now? What would become of all those flies there, tons of flies on the table and in the air? And despite all her self-sacrifice, wouldn't my aunt be tired? Would she stay in bed? And since she was so fat, would she even be able to get up? I would be going there soon and my mother told me:

"If they ask how we're doing financially, tell them we're fine."

"Okay," I said.

"And don't ask for a cent. Don't accept any money, even if they give it to you."

"Alright," I said.

It was practical advice, I had already heard it many times before; but her face was so strange when she said it. Why wouldn't they give me any money? Do they have to spend it on injections? And even if they did, why couldn't I accept it? They might be offended, they might think I turned them down because I think they're poor. My mother told me to say that we're doing alright financially. Why? If we have more money than they do, that's obviously boasting; and if we have less, why would it be a problem for them to give us money? Are we too proud? I didn't ask my mother even though I've always wanted to know whether we're rich or poor, but I've never gotten a straight answer and I realized I wasn't about to get one this time either. The two days before I left I kept running it all over in my head. They hadn't told me to be mindful at meals and eat everything on my plate. Why not? Why hadn't I been told to show them my good grades, either?

I was going to take along my report card anyway, on my own. I would take all my tests with the highest grades to show them one afternoon. But it was strange that no one had suggested it to me.

"Shouldn't I take something to play with outside?"

"You don't play much outside."

"I'll take a ball with me."

"Alright, go ahead."

Don't be so accommodating, I thought about saying. Remember the time you wouldn't let me take it along? Besides, she said "alright" like she didn't care whether I took it or not. In other words, I was free to take it but it came with a price: she was letting me take the ball in the same way that I wouldn't get a beating if my clothes got stained, for example, because right now there were more important things. It was the first time I was going off like that, with a suitcase, far away, and I had packed it myself. I asked,

"Should I take some perfume?"

She replied absentmindedly,

"Perfume? No."

"Alright, then I'll close it up," I said.

"What do you mean you'll close it up? You haven't packed your socks, your scarf, your cape—Lord knows what else!

"If I'm not taking any perfume, I'll just close it up," I said.

Even I knew there was something secretly wrong with closing a suitcase before packing socks, but I did it anyway. *I'm not taking any perfume*, I thought that afternoon, *it's better that way*. And that night I couldn't fall asleep until late, I got up to see if the suitcase was still there.

The first thing I saw when I got to my aunt's was a woman who must have been a neighbor. She had her back to me, she was drinking yerba mate and talking with someone who I figured was my uncle. "What's different about him?" I asked myself. My uncle was a thin man, by all odds, but compared to the ringmaster at the circus he looked like a whale. I'd seen my uncle before, when I was really little, so I didn't notice anything that different. After chatting awhile—he didn't ask how we were doing financially—my aunt came in. She was pretty fat, but it was nothing out of the ordinary. She had just gone out to the store to buy salami. And she was smiling and wearing earrings. *She doesn't seem so self-sacrificing after all*, I thought. *She even goes out to buy salami and stuff...* I always imagined a self-sacrificing person to be someone who's shut up in a small space with no windows. She patted my head and fiddled with something that was falling out, a clip I think. That's when the neighbor left and my uncle coughed. He coughed a bunch of times, uncontrollably, and my aunt asked him in a gentle voice, an early-morning-before-breakfast voice:

"Shall I get it ready for you?"

"No, not now. Later."

It was like when someone asks you if you're going to have breakfast now and you say, "Not now. Later." That's how my uncle answered. And right away he added, when she came back with a glass of water and a little pill:

"Where's the new charm for your bracelet?"

"I lost it. I don't know where I could have put it."

"We'll have to look for it," said my uncle as he stirred the little pill into the glass. "It was the prettiest of them all."

While I arranged my things in the wardrobe, he looked all over for the charm and my aunt hummed some tune. It was late and I thought, *We'll see tomorrow.* But I didn't know what tomorrow would bring and I fell right asleep.

The next morning my aunt said:

"Luisa, would you like to play checkers with your uncle?"

"Alright," I said. "I don't know how to play that well."

I assumed it didn't matter whether I was good or not, it was just a way to kill some time in the morning. I was distracted and my uncle won every game, even when he gave me a head start, and then he looked at me and smiled. That's when I realized I should have tried harder, that he'd been beating me on purpose. I said:

"Now the last game, the last one of all."

"I'm done for now," he said. "Tomorrow or the next day."

My aunt told me to go buy some eggs to make mayonnaise.

"Can he eat mayonnaise?"

"He can eat everything," said my aunt in an oddly detached voice.

I chose brown eggs, and asked the shopkeeper to remove the white one because I didn't like them. Then I helped to make the mayonnaise. The kitchen had checkered curtains and matching cushions on the chairs. There was a big window where the sun shined in and you could see people walking by on the street, not far off.

"Where is he?" I asked.

"He's fixing the chicken coop."

"Can I go then?"

"Let's finish this first, hmm?"

"Okay."

We finished, and on my way out of the kitchen I noticed there were some flies. *At home sometimes there are, too*, I thought. *It's just because someone left the door open.* And the grass wasn't long, it was cut evenly. *Even nicer than at home*, I thought on my way to the chicken coop. My uncle was sitting down, resting on a tree trunk.

"You're tired," I said.

"A little."

"Anyway," I said reassuringly, "you worked all morning."

"Not really," he said. "It's only eleven o'clock."

"But you're retired," I insisted. "You worked your whole life."

He didn't say anything back, he just gestured like he was going to start working again and then he did something I've never seen before: he walked around the chicken coop, running his hand over the wood, as if he were about to get down to work, and then—who knows why—he just inspected everything and sat down again to look at some seedlings.

I thought for sure that his first impulse had been to work. I almost asked him if he wanted some help, but then it seemed inappropriate. Instead I said:

"Would you like to play checkers with me?"

"Bring out the board," he said.

And I couldn't beat him, not even once, but I didn't lose as horrendously as I had the time before.

At night, from my room, I heard them talking. My aunt said:

"You didn't take it."

"So, I didn't take it."

"What do you mean, *so, I didn't take it*? Do you know what this means?"

"Now what was I going to take it for, anyway? ... I'm sorry."

That last part perplexed me. Why had he apologized? Maybe

he'd been rude to her? I couldn't hear so well, but I was sure that he hadn't been rude and it left me wondering. Then I heard her insisting, but I still couldn't believe the part before. I thought I would be embarrassed the next morning because they didn't know that I knew about "it"… Just what was "it"? I went back over the dialogue. *In the end,* I told myself, *it was something that he was supposed to take and didn't. It seems like he didn't want to take it, and then he said he was sorry but I don't know why. What's all the fuss about?* The next morning after breakfast my aunt told me:

"There's a boy next door, he used to come over a lot. Take the checkerboard over to play with him."

"But I don't even know him. I don't know who he is."

"Tell him you came to stay with us a few days and that you want to play. Better yet, I'll tell him."

And my aunt stopped doing something important to go tell the lady next door that I had come to visit for a few days. The neighbors welcomed me with smiles. Meanwhile, I still hadn't seen my uncle and my aunt told me that he hadn't gotten up yet. The neighbor asked how my uncle was doing and my aunt didn't answer. *She could have said 'so-so,'* I thought. *I would have said so-so.* Right away I decided that the boy next door had a fish face, or depending on how you looked at him, a grapefruit for a face.

"Your uncle's sick," he told me.

"I know."

"And he's gonna die."

"That's a lie," I said. "Why did you say he's gonna die?"

"It's not because *I* say so," and now his face looked like a grapefruit, "it's because the doctor says so."

"That's a lie," I said.

"Whatever," said the boy and he took out the checkerboard.

I thought he might let me win on purpose; I decided I was going to let him think I was a complete idiot so he would leave me alone. In the middle of the game he said,

"Last time an ambulance came."

I wanted to say that was a lie, but I stopped myself when I realized the boy, with that fish face of his, knew more than I did, simply because he lived next to my uncle. He wasn't even a relative or anything, and I was his niece, so I said:

"I already knew that."

"Do you know how many times it's come?"

"What does it matter how many times it's come? I know the ambulance comes, and that's that!"

"Seven times," he said.

And then he beat me. *He's skinny*, I thought. *He's skinny and spiteful, too.* And it was twelve o'clock and nobody came over to get me; then it was twelve-thirty and still nobody came. That's when I said:

"I'm going back to eat lunch."

And the neighbor lady said:

"No, stay here and eat with us, with Leopoldo."

"Does my aunt know?"

"Yes, of course."

And I don't remember what I ate, only that it was something mushy. At two o'clock my aunt came to get me. She was wearing a different blouse and she'd put on heels. Her hair had been styled, as if she'd had guests over, and the neighbor squeezed her hand.

"Where's my uncle?" I asked.

"They took him," she said. "They took him to get better."

And Leopoldo raised an eyebrow, sitting in the corner. I noticed that the neighbor took my aunt by the arm and said something to console her. *That lady looks like a bunny rabbit,* I thought, and to my aunt timidly I said:

"Can we go?"

"Yes," she said, "we should."

We walked into the kitchen, with its checkered curtains. It was a splendid, sunny day. And I started to walk around the house as if I were missing something. There were clothes strewn around and the wardrobe had been moved. *I know what I forgot,* I told myself almost enthusiastically. *I forgot the checkerboard at Leopoldo's. I'll go get it.*

"Leopoldo, will you give me the checkerboard?"

"It's mine. I let your uncle borrow it."

"Oh, I didn't know," I said.

That's what it was, I thought. *It was the checkerboard that was missing.* I considered asking my aunt if Leopoldo was lying. *What for?* I thought, *Leopoldo wouldn't lie.* In the afternoon, after a lot of thinking, I said:

"Auntie, I'm leaving."

"Don't you want to stay until tomorrow?"

"Alright," I said, "but I'll just get my suitcase packed."

For a moment I considered asking her if she had any perfume, but then it seemed inappropriate. *I don't have any perfume*, I said to myself, *and not only that: I don't have socks, or a scarf, or a cape either. And what's more, I'm going to leave a coat here, and I'm going to throw something out on the street, too, when no one's looking, because I don't want to carry around such a heavy suitcase.* That thought made me smile all afternoon. And the next morning (I left the ball and the coat at my aunt's house), when I threw a skirt out on the street, I trembled and my heart skipped a beat.

The Piano Recital

"SHE'S going to play Chopin's Mazurka No. 2," said Hebe's mother to the woman who lived next door, looking at the program.

"How nice!" the woman said sweetly, almost as if to butter her up, as if it were Hebe's mother who would be playing the piano.

"And she should be at the piano practicing right now, otherwise she'll never learn in time. I'm not saying that she's not *capable*, she's just so careless!"

Hebe knew her mother spoke the truth, but it left her with the dull sensation that something wasn't right.

Actually, she knew what her mother meant by calling her careless: leaving her clothes strewn on the floor, not bathing often enough, putting her feet up on the sofa. When it came to ability, she didn't quite know how to apply herself. And if her mother said she wouldn't learn in time, she wouldn't. Her mother predicted everything: not long ago she had prophesized that the old man next door would die in two or three days, and no sooner said than done, he died.

So, she was going to practice the piano now. She walked over to it silently, without saying a word. She couldn't say:

"Mama, I'm not going to play the piano."

Because her mother would say:

"As far as I know there are no trombones in this house."

Her mother had bought the piano at an auction. She'd bought it because it was an old piano with yellowish keys, like the one Uncle Abel had.

Uncle Abel played the piano too, although several times he'd been chased by the police from rooftop to rooftop. At the auction her mother had haggled so much that Hebe thought she was acting like a gypsy, which embarrassed her.

Sometimes Hebe imagined that her mother was an overweight gypsy who had stolen her as a baby, but she wasn't quite sure why. Up until a few years ago, Hebe imagined her real mother had actually been someone else. Still, for a gypsy, the one she'd ended up with wasn't so bad.

Sometimes the gypsy cried and Hebe felt a little sorry for her, not that she could comfort or say something sweet to her: whenever that gypsy cried she would end up blurting out something entirely out of character to reveal that she was really thinking about something else. For example, she would sniffle and then ask:

"Did you feed the cat?"

Then her mother was no longer a gypsy. She was weak and almighty at the same time. Hebe thought about how a Roman emperor can have moments of weakness. As a Roman emperor her mother was imposing. That massive body in a chair—her very own chair—sitting by the lamp to read the newspaper. She held the newspaper up high, from afar, as if examining something absolutely repugnant. She scrutinized the news with a critical, selective spirit and turned the pages quickly to read whatever piqued her interest. She was always right on the money.

Whenever her mother read the newspaper, Hebe would go out of her way to make a big circle around the chair, as if the surrounding area were prickly.

But she was also a lady with great presence of mind.

Presence of mind meant being up to any task: whether it was buying a pair of shoes or dealing with sickness, any task should be accomplished with grace.

Perhaps it was the lady with great presence of mind who intimidated Hebe the most—more than the gypsy or the Roman emperor. The gypsy was a stranger, Hebe could relax with her to some extent. The Roman emperor was ruthless, but it was just a matter of getting out of her way. The lady with presence of mind absolutely baffled Hebe. How did she always know exactly what to say to rub salt into the wound?

The lady with great presence of mind was mysterious because she seemed to have a plan of action, a strategy for each and every person. What did she have in mind for Hebe? It remained unclear.

Now, Hebe needed a new dress for the recital. She could make do with one of the dresses she already owned, but they didn't shine or stand out. And everyone else was going to have a dress made so they could really shine. When Hebe told her mother that she needed a dress, she was in the middle of recalling her childhood in the countryside. Everything used to be more intense, it seems. Winters were harsh, the way they should be, and the sun scorched the earth in summer, which was logical. Beasts were more ferocious back then, and no one has ever seen frost like that. Back then, she had even more presence of mind than now—if such a thing were possible—because it was an era when people were tough. They struggled; there was no time for funny business. Likewise, people never used to get new dresses all the time. In the countryside you could pick someone out from afar by their clothes, and that was a good thing: you never made a mistake. That's why, at her mother's house, no one talked about clothes—they discussed the Second World War, which had ended by then, and the Maginot Line.

When Hebe reminded her mother that she needed a dress, her mother said:

"Yes, I already spoke to Carmen."

Carmen was Hebe's cousin. She always got Carmen's dresses as hand-me-downs. They were big on her shoulders and small on her hips. Hebe didn't say anything. She knew there would be no new dress and she thought, *you'll see.*

Her, *you'll see*, wasn't referring to anyone in particular—it was everyone. Immediately after she said it she envisioned her own wake. It was an enormous threat, albeit an empty one, but she felt like doing something rash. She didn't quite know what it was they were all going to see, but her wake was something concrete. There she was in the coffin, dead, her mother by her side, and sometimes the neighbor lady too. Her mother was saying how much she regretted having been so cruel to her. How could she have mistreated such a good girl like Hebe? How wrong she had been! And she asked for Hebe's forgiveness. Dead Hebe forgave her mother, filling the real Hebe with a sense of peace. She was going to have to wear her cousin's dress, of course.

She laughed to herself, feeling refreshed by a new, bitter joy. She felt a deep sense of purpose. She was enshrouded by the darkest of shadows; there was no place for her in the sun, but she felt fiercely determined.

There was nothing refreshing or pleasant about the way Carmen's dress felt against her skin. It was made of an expensive fabric, but it had balled up into tiny pills. It was a thick silk covered in small shiny sequins, as if designed to cover a large surface area. It was meant for a wiser, more mature lady to wear— someone who knew how to mask the faint scent emanating from that cloth by adding a touch of perfume, as if to say: *Here I am, poised, a bit chubby, and somewhat morose, so what?*

But Hebe was just a girl and the gleam of those little beads made her look hasty and angry.

Her mother wore the brooch to the piano recital. The brooch was a little rectangle no bigger than a razorblade covered in faux rhinestones, which she wore on her bosom. The brooch was too small for that enormous bosom, but still, it caught the eye because she wore it like a shield, as if to say: Wearing this shield is uncomfortable, it's hot, but at least they know I've got a shield; they know who calls the shots.

Hebe imagined that when she walked out on stage she would briefly nod her head, as a formal greeting; but right beforehand, before they saw her, she tripped on a beam backstage and this discouraged her from following through with the greeting.

She walked over to the piano and sat down. Even though she couldn't see them, she knew that her mother, her cousin Carmen, and the lady from next door were there.

Unlike when she played the piano at home, she couldn't keep her composure now, tentatively sounding out each key. She started to play in a full-on frenzy, as if she were two different people: one was shocked by watching the other—an obedient but unpredictable animal playing of its own free will.

After the first piece there was—absurdly, Hebe thought—applause. They don't notice anything, she realized. She could relax as she played. So, feeling more relaxed, she pretended to connect with Chopin, like she did for real at home, and then there was more applause. That applause gave her a moment to glance up at the audience, out of the corner of her eye. The first thing she saw, in the front row, was the shimmer of the brooch; it was those rhinestones that shone.

She hated that brooch, she had never liked it; that shine aroused her anger and she thought, *you'll see.*

She started to play with all the precision and malice she could muster. And when she knew she had played well, at the end of the piece, she whacked the piano two or three times with open palms, making a racket. Then she got up and walked offstage without taking a bow. They didn't give her any prizes, but Hebe was satisfied thinking about the idea of her wake. It was what comforted her most, what made her felt wholly reconciled with the human race.

Just Another Day

I WAKE up at five o'clock and at six I turn on the radio for the weather report. Once a lady I know said in disgust: "People have to be told the temperature just to know whether they're hot or cold." I didn't say anything back, but I'm extremely sensitive to judgments that correspond to the aesthetics of the soul. Besides, I can't help myself: I need to know the temperature and the time. It annoys me when CNN, after each program (every half hour), lists the temperature of all the cities in the world; in Istanbul it's always cold and they always claim it's ten degrees hotter in Buenos Aires than it really is. What a sham.

I want to know what time it is too, and something too strong to resist compels me to look at the clock on the wall. I used to have some idea of what time it was—not anymore. I look at the clock and if it's two o'clock, I say: "Time to sleep again." But if you'd asked me, it might as well have been seven o'clock. To fall asleep I repeat lists of names from A to Z: Abraham, Abdel, Abenámar, Abdocia, Abdullah. And they're all real names. But when I'm happy about something and I feel accepted by the world, I make up a name. When I'm feeling down or really tired I do it too. (Only one.) If you repeat the same list of names in the same order at siesta, you fall asleep. And then I start to think:

"How interesting the brain is!" That's why it's better not to give it a second thought, because then the sleepiness vanishes. I didn't always list names. I used to use a list of insults and slights from an old boyfriend. I used that list for several years; the idea was to make it to twenty insults. It went more or less like this:

1) He walked out on me.
2) He lost his shit because I told him how a lady had used the term "rest area."
3) He disappeared for two weeks.
4) He told me to go smoke in the other room.

And so on. Trying to think up twenty reasons bored me and I never could so I switched to names; there are so many more of them.

Anyway, every day except Saturdays I turn on Radio Continente at six o'clock and my whole gang of friends are there. They always get there at the same time. The host is Pérez, who's sometimes a bit basic when it comes to his taste in literature—I think he's religious, I'm fond of him in general. Later Antonio Terranova comes on. He's an editorialist who's entitled to reflect on what happens or doesn't happen. Sometimes he's right on, but sometimes he flounders because he thinks he's got the right to make all types of observations about the way things are going in our country and around the world. He asks himself questions like: *As a country, are we perhaps going to hell in a hand basket?* That puts me off because if there's one thing I don't like it's prophecies: doesn't matter if they're ecological or they're from the Bible. On Saturdays I leave the radio off because Fernando Cuenca has a three-hour agribusiness program. He says things like, "Pregnant cow in disuse," "Remaining balance," "Keeping old cows." He also talks about cattle diarrhea. He interviews people who talk about soybean caterpillars. When he starts the program he asks for the blessing of Our Lady of Luján and it conjures up the sad sight of inland Argentina where dingy offices that operate out of old houses have an image of Our Lady of Luján on the wall, and outside the cows are pregnant or in disuse. And I don't want the countryside to make me sad. I don't say "cow in disuse." But sometimes I listen to him anyway on Saturdays because he interviews an agricultural engineer—I don't remember his name but it doesn't matter: his voice is what matters. He's an old man and his voice is deliberate, like someone who has gently taken control of his life. He speaks very clearly, as if everyone else were a little childish, and he manages to calm down Fernando Cuenca, who always sounds somewhat rushed, and who ends by saying: "The voice of the Argentine countryside" in a grandiose tone. Who is he to think he represents the countryside? Even if he did live there, he probably got kicked by a horse. And if he was sent to be reeducated in the countryside, I'll bet he got mixed up in all the wrong places. His job was probably to chase the chickens. The agricultural engineer, on the other hand, I could marry him. Well, I don't know if I would get married at this point in life, but I would like to spend a long time with him in a house in the countryside (if he has one) or in a village, so he could explain to me what a lightweight steer is, what "wintering cattle and breeding cows" mean, and stuff like that. Ten minutes afterwards I'll surely have forgotten it all, but just to hear that voice. But there's more to life than staying by the radio all day. So I tell myself: "C'mon Catriel, it's polka" (they used to say that to Chief Catriel so he would dance faster), and I pick up the pace. I have to go get a little glass I left on the night table to take a pill at night. My little glasses are beautiful, they're like tiny bells, but they have two flaws: they fall and break immediately, and they have a seam. And I didn't see that. It's as if they were made with the remnants of some sort of material and that reminds me again of the lady who says people need to be told the temperature to know whether they're hot or cold. Once she even argued with me about some little cups or glasses. I said that if I liked the shape of a cup or a glass, it didn't matter to me whether it was ordinary or refined. Then she said: "You don't appreciate human craft, or the culture that produces porcelain, etcetera." I'm going to appreciate human craft; I'm going to put on some socks that are a little bit nicer. Dear Lord, how do I even go out on the street in these socks? Today they looked alright to me, but now I realize they're impossible. One day something shifts, and then you see something you've always considered to be acceptable in a bad light. But I'm so fickle that I see it in a bad light and maybe within a couple of hours, I'll see the same thing as good again. So I leave them in a special spot in the closet, which is like a limbo for socks, sweaters, and other trifles. One day I'm going to organize that limbo—I will, but not today. After all, it's nice to hide things, forget that you have them and then discover them all over again as if they were something new. Could this be a trace of old age? I'm always reminded of the myth of Tithonus the sorcerer and the Cumaean Sibyl, who babbled to herself in a bubble. I'm like the sorcerer: I go from the kitchen to the bedroom carrying things back and forth; I forget something and go back to the bedroom. What will old age hold for me? Will I walk pointlessly in circles with no visible objective, or will I search for a potato or a towel with a gesture of heroic determination? Who knows. This must be forestalled: I'm going to go out for a walk, walking renews one's thoughts and strengthens the legs.

Okay, it's time to walk. First I have to decide which direction to take. There's only a few: north, center-north on Córdoba Street until Plaza Serrano, and, if I'm really happy, a few blocks until the strip of bars in Palermo Viejo. By the time I reach "El Taller" or any other bar, I'm happy: people bask in the sun on the sidewalks, their dogs tied up here and there and a street fair in the square. The happiness doesn't last; even early in the day idle people are about, and that entire neighborhood makes me think of a life of permanent idleness: reading the newspaper in the sun, then taking the dog for a walk in the park, the street fair... Besides, the route from my place to Córdoba Street is dark, not even the sun can lighten those eyesores that look like old camels. I can go directly north and end up in Palermo, but I've walked that way so many times and, besides, crossing from Almagro into Palermo is difficult: it's an area where they sell bolts, nuts, and screws, like a no man's land. And, anyway, my sense of justice tells me that I can't always take the same path. I'm going to give the west a chance. My sense of justice is like that: a little bit in each neighborhood, a little bit for each shop-keeper, when I haven't been to a shop for a while I remember and I tell myself: *I should go there.* I'm going to give the west a chance, I'm going to walk down Rivadavia Avenue until Primera Junta—although I'm also reminded of a shop called "Designs for the Soul," which is near the Abasto shopping mall, but I don't want to risk disillusionment if I change direction, because it's always closed and the storefront is dark and dirty. I'm going to Rivadavia Avenue, which keeps getting wider as I walk, remind-ing me of the pampas; way out west is the countryside. Rivadavia is flanked by eyesores, but they're a lighter shade than the ones in Serrano: reddish, yellowish and light brown. The avenue is so wide that you can see the number 26 bus from afar. Out here the buses don't hurtle around the corner; they glide along with a certain somberness, almost a gracefulness. The 26 turns onto various side streets, as if to say: "Live around here? I'll drop you off." If I had been born in the neighborhood of Caballito and stayed there my whole life, I would have married a construction foreman who had wanted to be an engineer but never made it, because he had to contribute around the house. But, at a certain point, we would have moved from a one-story house to an apartment with reddish walls and a bit of gold on the door (gold adds luster to dreams), and I would be like that woman over there who is heading out now, all dressed up with her dark blonde hair. She's well dressed but proud of being working-class; in fact, she likes people to notice her worn hands. They're worn because she worked so hard polishing the brass on the door and took great, great care of her husband, like I would have taken care of the construction foreman until he was a little old man—and the dog too, sewing winter coats for it. Tartan coats, because tartan is refined. And now the dogs are out, the furry little one with legs that go *tiki tiki* as it struts along, and another one with a rectangular face, the one I call "ugly mug"; that face astonishes me. I talk with the owner of one of those dogs and ask her:

"Have you gotten used to it? To your dog's face?"

"Whatever do you mean, he's a saint!"

Virtue surpasses the most improbable appearances. In my neighborhood there's one teeny-tiny dog, the owner puts a clip in its hair, it must weigh less than two pounds. Once I spoke with the owner and she said:

"She's a girl and she can't breathe with her hair in her face."

Of course she can't breathe, she's got more hair than she does body. In Almagro people give their dogs outlandish names, like Madonna and Beethoven; in Caballito they're more traditional, they're called Batuque and Colita. In Caballito the graffiti is politically correct. It says:

CHURCH = CENSORSHIP

FIGHT THE POWER

PSYCHEDELIC ROCK

SON OF A GUN

In Almagro, illegible hieroglyphs are used to write graffiti, the names of rock bands are scrawled in red and black paint, and then written very clearly: LUCAS IS A FAGGOT.

I get nowhere in my conversations with dog owners and it's because I'm too quick with my compliments: "What a cute dog, all bundled up!" Etcetera. Just what are people going to say back to me? "What a nice purse?" They limit themselves to a single response. The other day I told a lady about what the dogs on the eighth floor had done. They took everything out on the balcony, as if they'd had a premeditated objective: one day there were pieces of a Harry Potter book, the telephone bill, toilet paper; that day it was all paper products. The following afternoon they took out footwear: boots, flip-flops and tennis shoes. And the last time they ripped up everything on the balcony, bags of charcoal and flower pots; it was a thematic destruction. All the lady can say back to me is: "It's true, they tend to break things." Nothing else. And I started saying: "You shouldn't have big dogs cooped up like that in an apartment." And I don't even really think that way. I'd actually be amused if there was an elephant in our building. I just said it to have something to say. "You shouldn't" is my specialty, but I've noticed that speeches about obligations don't really go anywhere. And there I stood, half embarrassed, without knowing what else to say because she was walking in the same direction as I was. "Well, see you later," I said. She was right behind me and there I was, a few feet in front, dying to turn around.

But luckily it's a different time of day now. There's horrendous traffic, the time when the only light hailing from the bakeries has come and gone. The light from the bakeries is diffuse and dim, as if radiating from a central oven, the light and the smell of bread drift out together. Now it's time for the school kids, with their oversized backpacks. It's time for a coffee. I'm so thankful that the hours go by and the action on the street changes. First you think there's only going to be bakeries open, then the school kids are out, and by the time I leave the café there's frenetic movement. Since I've been reading, I've lost track of time; it's time for the workers dressed to the nines on their way downtown. At the café I read about Argentine history and also about the lives of animals. Depending on the café, I take along one book on each subject. When I go to the cafés by my house, where the waiters know me, I don't take books about animals because they have large illustrations. I've got one book with a monkey feeding breakfast to a baby with a little spoon. I'm worried the waiters will see it and think I'm nuts. The ones I like best are books about chimpanzees: I remember exactly when I bought *Our Cousins the Monkeys*. And I haven't lent out that book, nor will I. If I could live all over again I would go to Africa to research the lives of chimpanzees, recording all their developments every day in a notebook. It seems that after two years you can get a chimpanzee to shake your hand. It's the same with dolphins; one man trained a dolphin and five years later it called him "Papa." The man abandoned the dolphin, saying abruptly: "I'm not your papa." I don't want to disappoint anyone or for anyone to be disappointed by me; nor do I want to make a bad impression. That's why sometimes I go to those enormous cafés where the waiters don't look at anyone, and I constantly change places because otherwise they'll think: "Who is that lady who spends her life reading and writing things down?" Sometimes I want the waiter or the man at the newspaper stand to see me with someone, so they don't think my life is reduced to studying, always alone. The rare times that I have someone with me, in the morning, I walk by the newspaper stand and the waiter with an air of triumph.

I wouldn't dare stay on the street until twelve o'clock because the cars accumulate into one big gridlock, one behind the other, and they make a squeaking sound that indicates morning has ended. By that time I start to mix up the signs: where it says "Resfriol," I read "refrain." What is that all about? Capriciously changing names around, as if they should be called whatever I think? I do the same thing with people's names: if someone's called Liliana but she looks like a Gabriela to me, I think of her as Gabriela. Luckily, I have to go back to see if I've gotten any messages. Surely someone has called me. I play the answering machine and a voice tells me:

"You have no messages."

And I feel like the voice sounds glad I haven't received any messages and that someone, somewhere, knows how I mix up names and I read books about monkeys; someone thinks I don't deserve them. But then I get a call offering me broadband, and someone else calls from the Garden of Peace, and members of the Children of God sect press my buzzer. I tell them all "no" in a rude voice. I don't want anything—no cemetery allotments, no cards, no messages from God. They can all go to hell. But every once in a while a man or woman calls and asks in a playful voice: "Do you know who this is?" I don't want to give the impression that I don't know, so I chat with them a bit—but I have a hard time with voices and I only recognize the ones I hear all the time. I don't give up, I continue chit-chatting a while longer, but eventually it becomes unsustainable; I want to know without them telling me. On the other end of the line they say readily:

"You don't know who this is."

"No," I answer like a fool caught red-handed. It's almost always someone I couldn't care less about: an old classmate who wants to do God knows what and the like.

"No, I can't go."

I can't, I don't want to, I shouldn't. Do I really say no to everything?

I'm going to hang the clothes out to dry on hangers in memory of Arturo, the great launderer. He would hole up in the bathroom and wash his clothes in the tub making loud banging noises that sounded like he was smacking something. I never did find out why he made so much noise because he locked himself in when he washed. Then he went quickly out to the balcony and

I snuck a glimpse of him from the side. I'm going to cook using as few pots as possible in memory of my mother, who used to say: "The less you take out, the better." And I'll make the bed, too, because she also used to say that a house with the beds made and the dishes washed is something worthwhile. I also turn the bread back over, in memory of my father, who used to say that the bread shouldn't be left upright on the table and that tomato jam goes well with walnuts.

I'm going to cook and I'm amazed at my competence because I only became this way recently. How it came to be, I'm not sure, but one day I realized that I could do three things at the same time, for example put the water on to boil, fill the bathtub, and talk on the telephone. And with this new skill my gestures have become minimal. I toss in some salt while I think about something else, tossing in the salt requires minimal movement—not like before, when it felt like tossing in the salt was an event or I would watch the water from the basin until it had drained completely, as if it were a mystery, or I would wait until the water boiled. I don't know what I was thinking—that it wasn't going to boil unless I watched it? I'm filled with a sense of pride, I've become so accomplished, but it's spoiled when I go to my room: I've got socks heaped under the pillow, for when it's warmer or colder. There's a nest there. I don't like how the whole house has become a hen's nest. There's another nest in the closest, with clothes that aren't dirty or clean. Where do those clothes go? Into limbo. Those clothes are just in case—who knows what they're for, in case of… Limbo is where God sent people when he couldn't decide whether to send them to heaven or hell. He must have thought: *Who knows, later on when there's more room, but for now…* But something I really do enjoy is sending things to hell, that is, throwing them into the garbage. I blissfully fill the trashcan almost as if my things were begging: *Throw me out!* It's as if I run smack into them, I'm frightened by what comes next. What will be next? Will objects jump directly into my hands? It's cloudy. I'm going to water the plants in memory of myself.

Now I draw the curtains to take a nap; I'm going to keep them drawn for a long time so the neighbors think I'm involved in some sort of important activity outside my home, as if I had real obligations. I'm going to take a nap and I start with "E"; I'm content when I discover new names (this happens rarely) and I settle for not forgetting the names I already know. I'm running out of letters, I'm getting bored! What will I do? Bah, I've still got countries and rivers, although I don't know much about rivers; rivers conjure up something melancholy and depressing. I dream and I never remember my dreams from my naps, as if it were an absurd slumber. I don't make much effort to remember either; there's still a lot of the day left. To do what? To do what?

At four o'clock in the afternoon I can't think of anything. My mind gets stuck and even if I were to say: "C'mon Catriel, it's polka," it's useless; I think my brain is corroding. There are a few minor things to do: organize the bills, go to a phone booth to talk to a friend from the South to... When I used to organize the bills it felt like I was taking care of a necessary evil. Now I realize nobody's actually going to steal them if they're just sitting there. I think I should be doing something else, but what? Going to the phone booth is an excuse to stretch my legs and if I don't get a hold of my friend it doesn't matter. I used to think it was absolutely imperative to make the call; now I think I go there just to stretch my legs, nothing else. It's no good to discover what's behind one's actions, because once you know it, it's as if there's no way around it. In the past, when Saturday came around, I used to think I should go out or do something fitting with a day like Saturday, honor Saturday's mere presence. It was as if I wasn't sure whether Saturday would ever arrive. Now I know that Saturday comes, and Sunday, and the rest of the calendar; I do any old thing on any old day. What am I going to do? I could go out for a walk in the afternoon, but I should put a stop to "anything goes" because it seems like walking in the afternoon is ludicrous. What is the point of the afternoon? To wait for the evening; I want to see how the sun sets. It's incorrect to say "night falls" because it doesn't happen suddenly. In the morning it does, the sun rises all of a sudden; it lights everything up. In the evening nighttime comes gradually. Time now seems paradoxically shorter and longer to me at the same time. I don't suspend time according to some central event where I used to place all my fantasies. Now it's as if everything were important and irrelevant at the same time. And if time has become my master, it seems as if I have likewise become a greater master of time. I hope it lasts.

Nothing but Shadows

IT'S curious what happens to me with people. When I meet them, I have an overall impression of who they are, but as I get to know them, that idea disintegrates and I no longer know what the other person is like. I let myself get carried away by different perspectives. I give someone points, then take them away. Everything about them I see through one light, and then through another. I'm thrown off course. That's what happened with Miguel, who I met at a party. We were together at that party, but on our own—we both danced with all the other people there. Every once in a while I'd ask myself absentmindedly, how do I know that we're together? Then I'd forget and feel reassured. When it started getting late, he asked me:

"Wanna go?"

And we left.

That night he got leg cramps and kept crying out sporadically whenever they flared up. In between, he would talk about interesting things. But then, in the middle of a story, the cramps would come back. I didn't understand, nor did I search for an explanation. I was very polite, like a guest trying to help while keeping a distance. I gave him some random advice which he rejected as counterproductive. The following day, I returned to his house with some food only to be informed about other counterproductive things: he didn't eat chard because it made his belly swell up as if he were pregnant. The doctor had prescribed him a diet of pizza, sardines, and wine. That was the best combination for his constitution. I was surprised by the diet, but I chalked it up to the variety of possible diets and individual idiosyncrasies. Once I saw him admiring a teddy bear at a toy store and guessed that he liked small objects, whether they were plants or toys. Then he told me that he'd been to Amsterdam, which was like a toy city where the driver of the tiny streetcar announces every street, which all end with *dam* Budesdam, Kudasdam, Osterdam. The way he pronounced the *dams* so perfectly, just like the drivers in Holland, I made believe I was there.

He liked Ireland because of the ponies and the low wagons.

I also had a hunch about which colors he liked and the styles I could wear based on those colors and textures: light pink, blue, wool that didn't itch or scratch. I'd always owned lots of clothing like that: clothes that made me feel suited to life, to the weather, clothes I found comfortable and made others feel comfortable…but sometimes I wanted to wear defiant black: I felt it lent an intensity to my facial expressions.

My first big confrontation with him happened while I was wearing black. It was over politics. I considered myself to be a Peronist, while he was a Radical. The more radical he proved himself to be, the more I flaunted my Peronism. He associated Peronism with the power of annihilation, like a dark and terrible force to be reckoned with. Although that particular debate seemed irrelevant to me—there was nothing good or new about either of our arguments—we ending up quarreling in the street. A light rain began to fall and yet we both clung to our ideas, they were all we had to defend our poor, damp bodies. For a moment I took pleasure in that frailty, but then it slipped away. When we finally broke up it was on good terms, but as if we were two opposing forces to be reckoned with. There was something about that relationship that clicked and something that didn't. The part that didn't almost compelled me to break up that very night. After all, political differences can be smoothed over, so why on earth was I getting myself all worked up? Because when it really came down to it…I…I didn't believe much in anything. But he did, he did. The day his party won he bought a little flag to celebrate. He didn't go to a rally or celebrate with a group: he did it alone, at home; it was a solitary demonstration. He put on a great show in front of me, as if I were a crowd. His joy was so great that it was impossible to bring him down. It was also impossible to discourage him when he played the harmonica, even though he didn't know how to do it. He'd bought one for himself, and resolutely blew out a series of strange sounds. He was so concentrated on what he was doing that I didn't have the heart to tell him what I really thought: *It sounded nothing like music.*

I had already begun to see him through more than one light. I was glad he was happy, but I didn't want him to celebrate at my expense. And I wouldn't have played the harmonica without knowing how. But after all, a democracy is a democracy.

Still, these were just thoughts I kept to myself. At that point, we went everywhere hand in hand, like children four or five years old.

The second big fight didn't stem from political or cultural debates. It was about a can of sardines (the ones his doctor had recommended as part of his diet). I'd never learned how to use a can opener the right way: they always slip on the surface of the can, springing upward and making a fool out of me. Instead, I opened cans by piercing them with a knife. When he heard the scraping sound and came to see the gash I'd made in the can, he screamed *sardine murderer* at me—or something like that. He said they'd end up all broken and stabbed; they'd lose their noble symmetry and their metallic sheen; by no means would he eat a sardine that had gone through such an ordeal. I'd never thought about it that way, so I continued to open cans as always when I was by myself, but with a certain degree of perplexity. I asked myself: *Could I be doing something wrong without realizing, because I'm so clumsy? Or because of some primal and deep-rooted flaw?* And that thought was followed by: *Could the sardines be a reason for us to end things for good?* But that wasn't the case: the next day he came over as if nothing had happened, talking about the rivers of the Buenos Aires province, the floods, and the different ethnicities living in Argentina.

Miguel said that the Italians were a disaster when it came to making payments, but they were great company when it came to emotional matters, for example when you lose someone you hold very dear. Jews were obsessed with New York, but they always made their payments on time. Paraguayans were the worst, but when one of them turned out to be alright, he was the best. I thought: *Now. Now's the time to ask him: Why did you get so upset yesterday?* But the conversation just followed its course and I couldn't get a word in edgewise. By then he was analyzing all the unions: the worst one was the plumbers' union. On the one hand, his sociological considerations gave me a sense of belonging—a place, a country. On the other, it was pathetic how little I could bring to the table: at most, some anecdote about a plumber, which did nothing more than confirm his stereotypes. When Miguel recalled an important historical or political event, he spoke in the slow, deliberate tone a real teacher uses to instill facts in the mind of his student (who was me).

When he told me how he was a victim of circumstances, his words got muddled, but I understood what he was really trying to say: so many cruel and sordid individuals, so many con artists had materialized in his life to exploit him. Since one of my passions was level-headedness, I tried sympathizing with all the people he had mentioned. This I did only once and never again, as it was a sore spot.

Sometimes he apologized, but quickly and in a low voice, as if to erase the apology. He didn't write letters or notes, either. He left no traces and was blind to the impact of his sermons. When he was nasty he reminded me of those characters from *Wuthering Heights*: rural landowners who unleashed their dogs on visitors. The visitor froze, unable to believe his eyes, and waited to make a move until someone came to lock up the dogs, but you never knew when things would calm down. Miguel's didactic side was very sweet and witty: he imitated Brazilians, artfully exaggerating that judgmental cadence; his arguments culminated in hilarious nonsense. I already felt his disapproval because of the sardine incident and also because of my yellow raincoat, which was ill-fitting. He thought it was hideous—as if I were someone else when I wore it, a strange apparition. And every time I waited for him at a café I played the role of a specimen. I arrived beforehand so I could get used to the space. I checked my hair and face in the bathroom to make sure I looked good, and then I would read a book so he would think I was just sitting there, as natural as can be. Plus, that way, in case there was any sort of conflict,

I would simply be doing what I had always done: reading a book in a café.

I was tempted to reveal my true self—even if it was just once, out of the blue, unveiling my ugliest features. For example, by brushing my hair into my eyes and wearing colors that clashed in every way. But I was afraid of conflict. My plan ended up coming to fruition, but not in the way I had expected. I kept getting uglier without even trying, but not like a strange apparition. I was ugly in a humble way. I've never done anything out of the ordinary, but one sweltering afternoon, dressed in an old shirt and underwear, I invited him into my house. I told him:

"I'm sorry I didn't put on anything nicer, it's really hot."

He said:

"At home, one should feel free to do as one likes."

So he *could* be easygoing and free. On another occasion, after long and complicated deliberations, I asked his advice on how to give some things away, and to whom. He said:

"Oh, one should give whatever one wants to whomever one chooses."

I felt like he enjoyed a mysterious sense of freedom, and I wasn't about to inquire any further. But, now that I knew him better, how could a person contemplate the facts with such noble indifference (no doubt resulting from an honorable upbringing), and at the same time drown himself in a glass of water, tormenting the both of us for an hour about a can of sardines? How could he be such a generous, happy teacher, filled with such a vast range of knowledge, and, at the same time, a gruff man with all that fucking angst that hardened his face and got the best of him? The more I got to know him, the more clueless I became as to who he really was, as if he had shattered into a million little pieces. I only had a vague notion, like an animal instinct, on how to keep things from going sour.

Once I tried walking like him, just to see what it was like. His stride was slow but steady, seemingly relaxed but very constrained. It was much like his attitude toward paying the bills. When it came to the bills we got along just fine. I did have a bourgeois streak—I had well-defined limits which he went along with. My bourgeois streak had already led to a break-up with a previous boyfriend, who'd said: "One must have strength of character and common sense. He who resists, wins."

When I ran into Miguel again after one of our break-ups I decided to share my new ideas about possible business ventures; but on that particular day all he wanted to do was teach me the Russian alphabet. I was annoyed by his notion that this was a productive use of our time. What was the point of learning Russian for just one day if we were never going to use it again? I agreed because he was so enthusiastic, as if in a previous life he had been Russian; I accepted. It was as if he were a heavy drinker coaxing me, a teetotaler, into having a drink. That's when the non-drinker ends up drinking with complete abandon, partaking in something entirely meaningless in her life. And that's how we ended up eating pizza and sardines and drinking wine again. I got used to him coming over every night for long stretches of time; then he would disappear. When he came back, it was like he'd never left.

I missed out on the perfect opportunity to express myself when he asked me one New Year's Eve: "Are you happy?"

I hesitated: happiness is something so generic and diffuse, you can't really know if you're happy or not. Besides, the notion of happiness is outdated. I wanted to tell him some of the things that upset me, mostly because I'd remembered an old boyfriend asking me one day: "Don't you set down any ground rules for a man?" I had answered no. Because the truth is that rules seem made to get broken—even when it comes to dogs. An owner tells their dog, "Sit down, Stay here, Stay…" and within two minutes the dog is jumping up and down, happy as a clam. Imposing rules is easy; what's difficult is getting people to abide by them. Thinking all this over, I told him:

"Yes. I'm happy."

And I missed my chance again when—not having laid down any ground rules—I'd gotten used to telling him irrelevant bits of gossip, the kind that make life more bearable and make time stand still, because nothing changes after a bit of small talk. One day, when I was rambling on about nothing in particular, he shut one eye and looked at me with the other. It was an eye that wanted to know more. It was powerful. It made such an impression on me that I didn't ask him why he was doing it. I wanted that test—or whatever it was—to be over with. I wanted to pretend he had never looked at me with just one eye.

We kept holding hands, but it was different now, always in the midst of fighting or making up. When we got back together he would become overly passionate, and I was confused by the way he played it up. I thought: *It's gotten too intense, this can't last forever.* I wanted something more lighthearted, but also more stable. Then, after talking so much about plumbers, boyars, social classes, advantage, and disadvantage, he started to show a little interest in learning something about me. Somewhat distractedly, as he uncorked a bottle or opened a can (he was always in charge of opening the cans), he'd casually say, "So, how did you end up living in…"

And I'd answer quickly, saying any old thing, because by now our conversations had become almost scripted and it was hard to switch things up. Besides, I didn't want to answer those types of questions anymore—he should have asked me earlier. I also felt that personal questions should be asked using a special tone of voice, and he treated me as if I were a coworker, or just some incidental traveling companion that fate had set in his path.

I took pleasure in working myself into an animal rage. As I waited for him at a café—and sometimes he didn't show up—I would say to myself, "It's for the best." Or, if he announced that he had to leave early, I'd think, thank goodness. I had become as jaded as a little orphan girl, and although he didn't notice it, I had become grouchier than he gets when he's nasty and obnoxious. I was like an orphan girl who's been trained to follow very strict rules. For example, one must be polite to guests—but the guest could be anyone. Besides, I couldn't spend my whole life without any guests because then I would end up alone in the world.

Eventually we started seeing less of each other, and we avoided entering into any type of confrontation. Without these bursts of anger we became grateful, like people who are happy just because the sun comes out: that's all they need. We started to walk a lot; when we were on a walk we didn't fight. One night in January we were walking in a neighborhood with jasmine plants. I asked him timidly: "What's your favorite tango?"

And he sang:

Íbamos tomados de la mano
bajo un cielo de verano.

We were walking hand in hand
under summer skies.

It was truly beautiful, but I had a premonition. We were under summer skies and I wanted to tell him, "Don't leave me." But he was already pointing to a pink house, giving me explanations, and I missed my chance to say it. Once the moment to say something slips by, I can no longer get it out. I would have had to ask him to stop walking and that request would have seemed melodramatic: all those old houses around us, gaping at me in surprise.

Not long ago, I dreamed of Miguel. I was blocking out his shadow with my own—his was a civilized, discreet, and proper shadow. Mine got bigger the longer I looked at it. He was right, but I didn't want to let him twist my arm. I told him: "It's not my fault that I've got this shadow."

For a moment he looked mortified, in pain. I wanted to make up. He said something complicated, as if he were talking about a legal protocol, and held up one finger: "Should we end this once and for all?"

Emboldened, I said: "Yes. Alright. Let's."

I knew that anything definitive, anything that was once and for all, would cost me dearly. Then the dream faded.

Dear Mama

DEAR Mama,
Here goes the third time I've written this letter to you. I didn't like the first one and I lost the second. These days when I don't like something, I don't throw it out, I misplace it—then later, when I regain interest, I know it will make its way back to me. These days I always try to do two things at once. For example, when I dust the shelves, I end up finding something I've been looking for, and when I sweep, I listen to the radio. If I'm out enjoying the sunshine I tend to the plants. I used to get so upset when you told me, "As long as you're at it, why don't you do this or that." I didn't want to do anything else while I was engaged in one task; I wanted to focus on the main activity. Now I don't know whether the main activity is sweeping or listening to the radio. And now I understand what you meant when you used to say to yourself, "*Sí, sí, sí…,*" as if something were taking shape, like how life has its own momentum regardless of one's intentions.

I know you won't believe this, but I try to get rid of everything I don't need now too. I've amassed so many papers and exams from the students, because ever since democracy returned, I've been working at the university. But you left before the democracy. Let me fill you in: the military junta went to war with England; they occupied the Malvinas, and then the entire British fleet came at us. We lost the war, the military junta lost its prestige, and they had to relinquish power. Then Alfonsín became president, but he was forced to step down before his term was up because of the economic situation: the price of things kept skyrocketing over the course of a single day. Now Menem is president, in case you didn't know. It's like we've been pissed on by elephant seals. Money is tight, but I get by. I don't live in the apartment on Calle Gascón anymore. I moved to a place with a big balcony, I filled it with plants, and I have an arbor I call the grapevine. That's what I wanted to tell you. Once I forgot to sweep the leaves off the balcony, the drain clogged, and my whole apartment was flooded. I used a bunch of old student papers and cardboard boxes to soak up the water, but water is so evasive and uncontainable—it seeped out all the way to the elevator. That kind of thing doesn't happen to me anymore. And there's not a single cockroach because I've become a real neat freak. Sometimes I do the laundry to avoid smoking so much or I grade papers to keep myself from spending money. At the end of the month I automatically start to look for some money I hid in a book once and have never found. But that only goes on for two or three days. Times were worse during the military dictatorship. Once there were seven of us for dinner, and when we pooled our money we only had enough to buy flour and a can of tomato sauce. Luis, Lea's husband, the artisan, rolled out tagliatelle for the first time in his life. He set us up cutting noodles, we worked all in a line, and ended up eating the most delicious meal. Mama, I have a cat whose name is Andrés, Marabú, Misho, and Catito. He's adorable; his coat is white, gray, and tawny. I feed him fish to make his coat shiny. He sinks his claws into a rug you never saw, into my jeans, and every so often he goes after me, when he's really frustrated. He sleeps at my feet—and don't say "Santa Madonna," because he doesn't have fleas, and even if he did he wouldn't pass them on to me, and even if I've got them they don't bite. He eats off the china dishes you left me, the ones you always saved for special occasions. But it feels right to me. It only seems a little strange when someone points it out, and just so they don't think I'm out of my mind, I promise myself I'm going to buy a cat bowl, but then I forget. I still have some of the wine glasses, but they keep breaking one by one at different parties or just because. As for the tea sets, there's nothing left. I had to sell almost all the china one summer to pay the bills. Once I even sold a china plate to a gypsy. The linen tablecloths I gave to my cousins. You were right—linen tablecloths are not for me, and anyway now they make cheap washable ones out of synthetic fabric, in different colors. You just throw them out when you want to change things up a bit.

You were right about so many things I've only realized now. For example, when I used to go lie out in the summer sun right after lunch and you would say to me, "How can you bear this heat!" Now I, too, wonder how I used to do that, because now I take a nap after lunch whenever I can. You were right that naps are a beautiful thing. And you were also right that time when I asked you to fire the cleaning lady, the one who made the house dirtier instead of cleaner, and you didn't want to. You said, "Let her stay, the beating she'll get if she loses her job!" Now I've got this Bolivian woman who comes, she's new to the city. I had to teach her how to use the elevator—I don't know how she does this, but every now and then she still gets stuck in it. If she finds the bottle cap from a container that's been thrown away, she stacks it on top of another container like a little hat, inventing a pointless decoration. Sometimes she annoys me, but I also like seeing someone else's hand at work in the house, innovations, different ways of tidying up. Oh Mama, how I wish you could come sit under the grapevine with your cane! I wouldn't pick any fights with you, like when you'd get paid and buy yourself a bottle of port and a bag of candy. Do you remember how I used to go along with you, impatient and upset, and ask, "Why do you want all that candy if you don't even eat it?" And you'd say to me hesitantly, "Just because, just in case someone comes over." Mama, all the fights we had, all the love—after you were gone,

I thought: *How is it possible that everything we once shared is gone, and now she's unaware of everything that's happening to me?* Black or white, it makes no difference. I think this letter is so hard for me to write because I don't want to cry. I don't know why I don't want to cry, it's been so long since I cried and it would be good for me. Maybe if I watched a sappy movie. Mama, I cried my eyes out when you left; and then over that boyfriend, the one you only ever spoke to on the telephone. One morning I wept thinking about you, and then a little later in the day, thinking about him. Since I live alone now I don't think I want a boyfriend, or maybe what we want is just what we're used to, like anything else. And speaking of what I want—because I try to do too many things at once, I put them off or let them slip away—I wanted to ask you a favor. I sense I might be deserving of some small sort of grace, a gift. But the fact that I've got a lot of memories weighing me down could make things difficult. Since you were a believer, I'd like to ask you to entrust God with your memories. That way I'll only have to look after my own. And once I feel lighter, I'll be able to receive my grace.

From your daughter, who has given you so much work, but who also loved you so much.

archipelago books

is a not-for-profit literary press devoted to
promoting cross-cultural exchange through innovative
classic and contemporary international literature
www.archipelagobooks.org